THE COMPLETE VOLUME ONE FIRST VOLUME

# LADY MECHANIKA™

## Volume 1: The Mystery of the Mechanical Corpse

Special Thanks to:

M. M. Chen *for Writing Assists*
Martin Montiel *for Pencil Assists, Chapter 5*
Mike Garcia *for Color Assists, Chapters 4 & 5*

Cover Illustration and Cover Gallery Art by:

Joe Benitez & Peter Steigerwald
*(except where noted otherwise)*

Editor: Marcia Chen
Production: Michael Heisler
Original Edition Letters by: Josh Reed
Book Design: Mark Roslan, Peter Steigerwald
Lady Mechanika Logo by: Peter Steigerwald

Contains material originally published in single magazine form as Lady Mechanika #0-5 by Aspen MLT, Inc. and Benitez Productions, Inc.



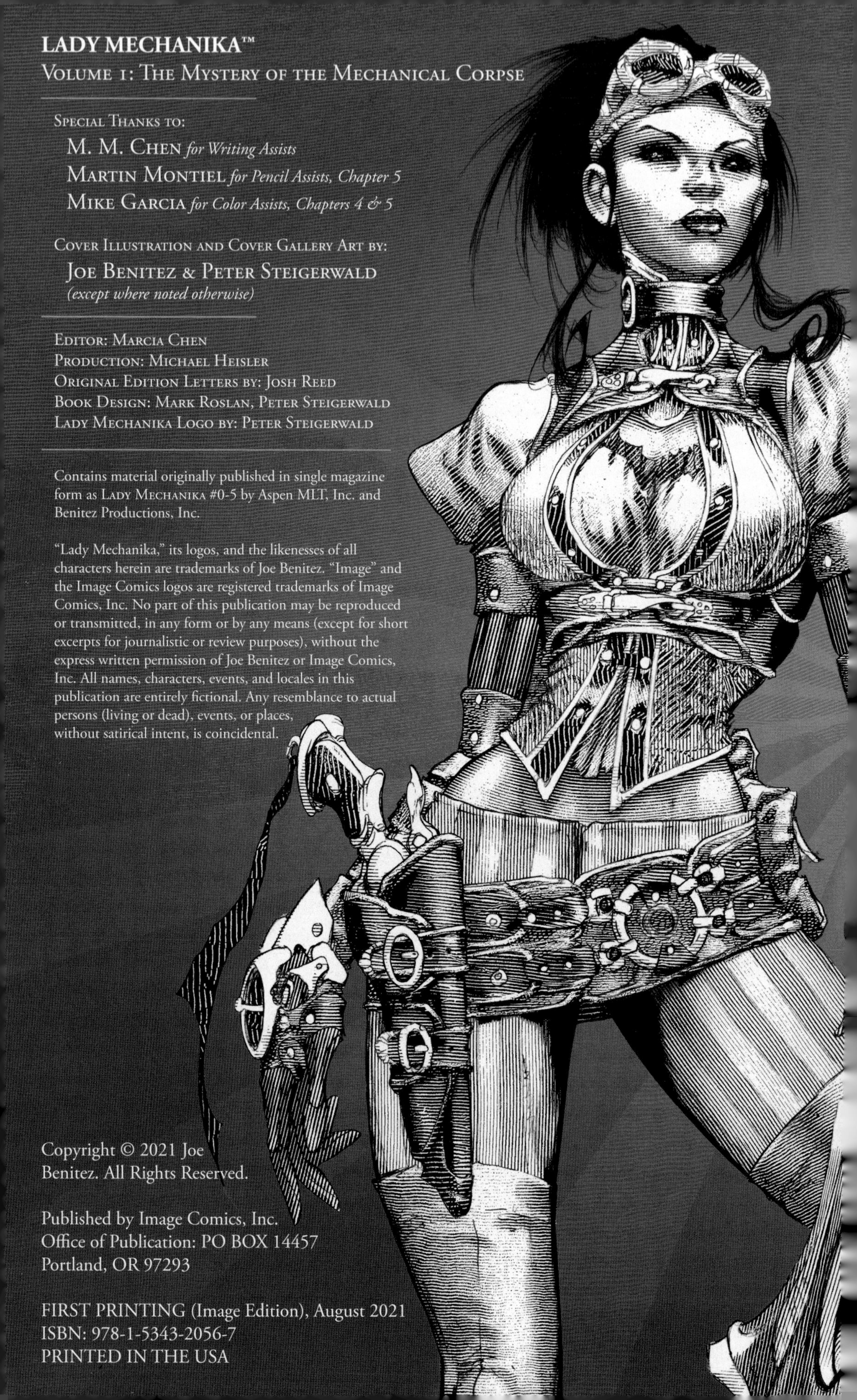



Published by Image Comics, Inc.
Office of Publication: PO BOX 14457
Portland, OR 97293

FIRST PRINTING (Image Edition), August 2021
ISBN: 978-1-5343-2056-7
PRINTED IN THE USA

Created, Written & Drawn
by JOE
BENITEZ

Colors
by PETER
STEIGERWALD

Letters
by MICHAEL
HEISLER

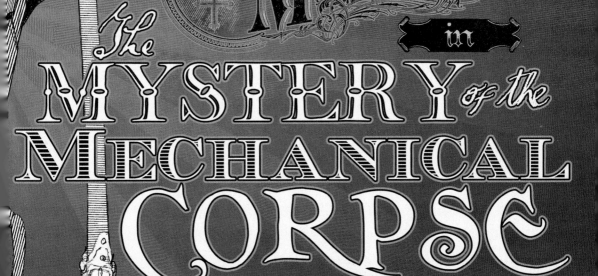

JOE BENITEZ'S

Lady Mechanika

in

The
MYSTERY of the
MECHANICAL
CORPSE

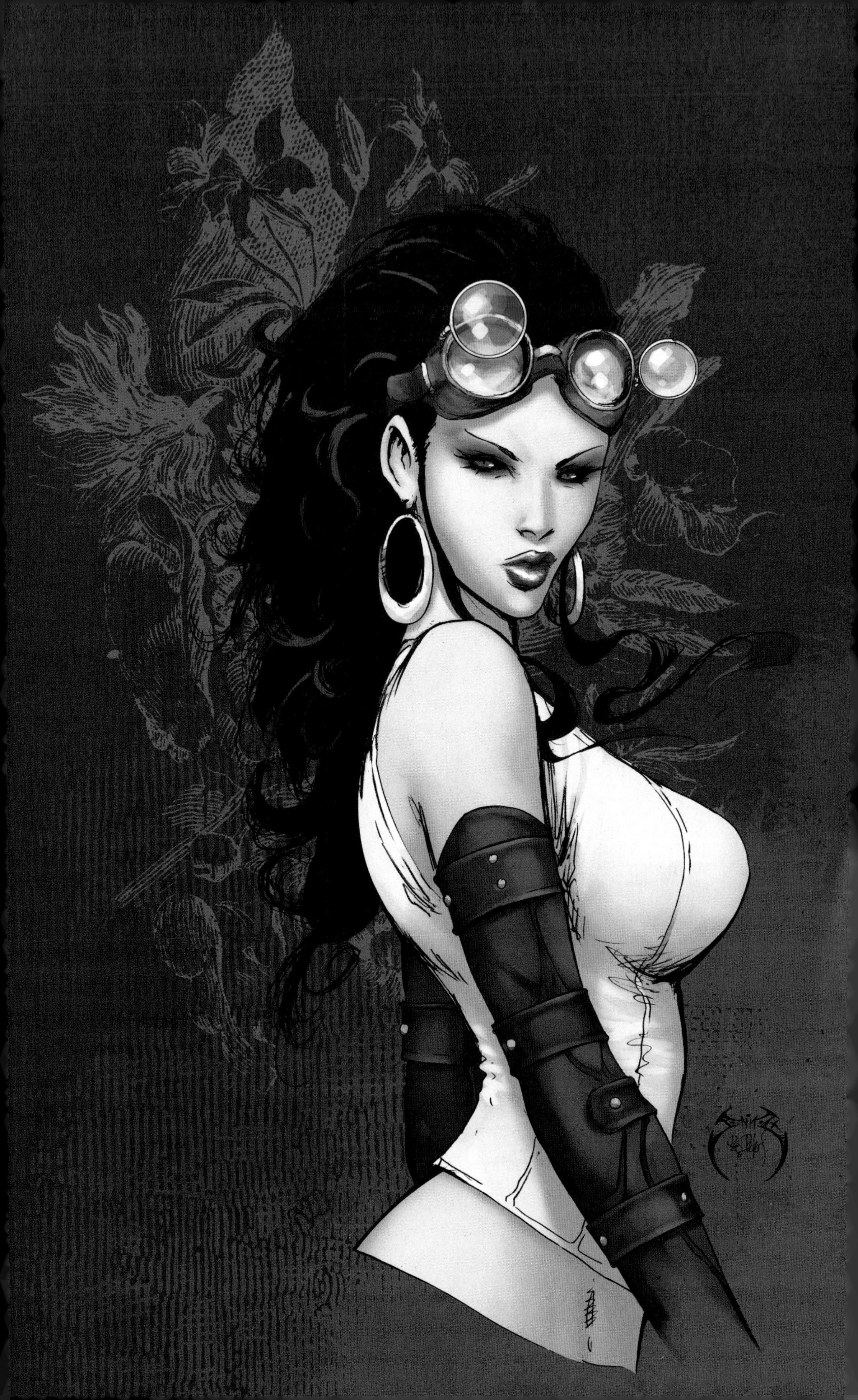

# Chapter Zero

## The Demon of Satan's Alley

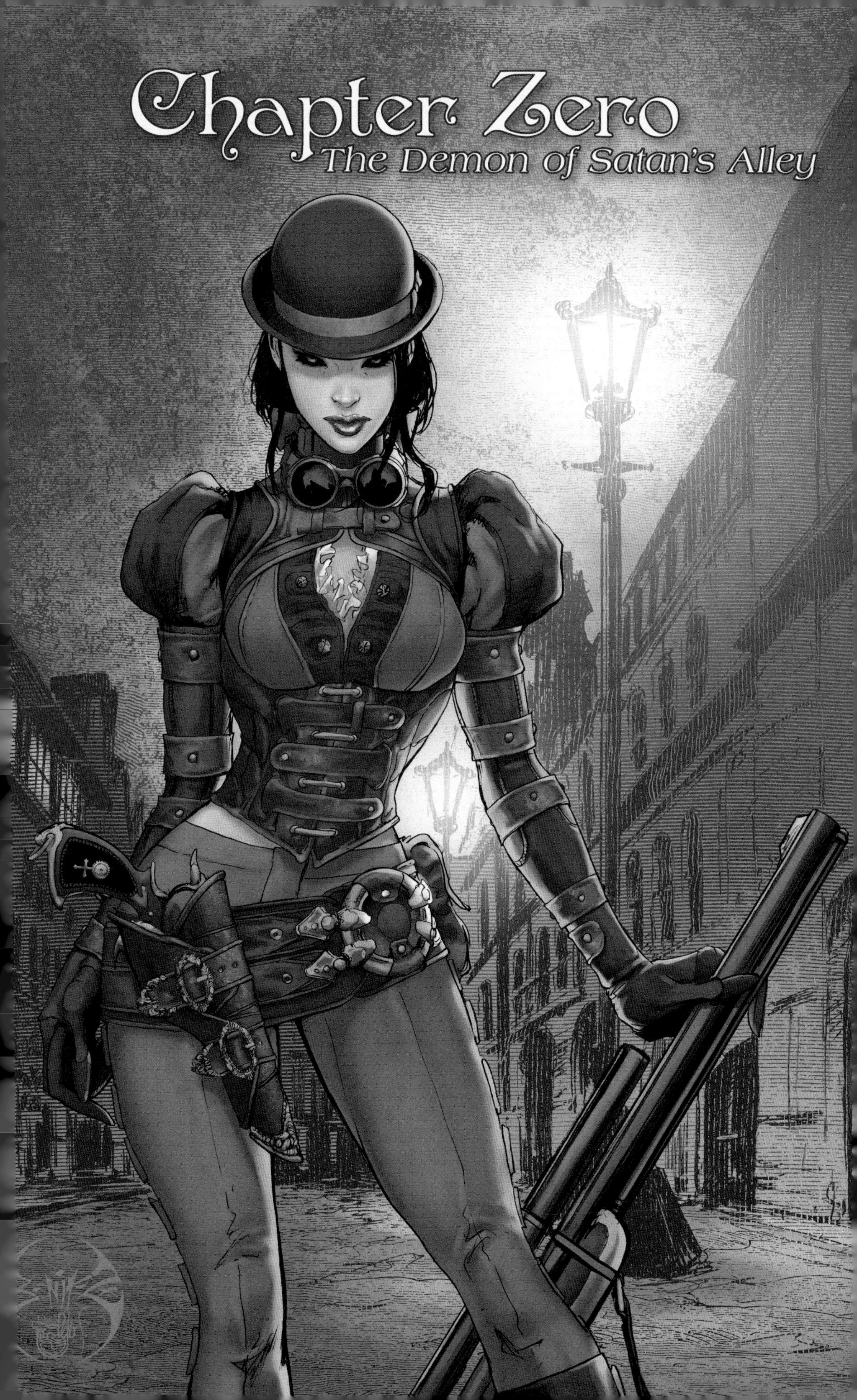

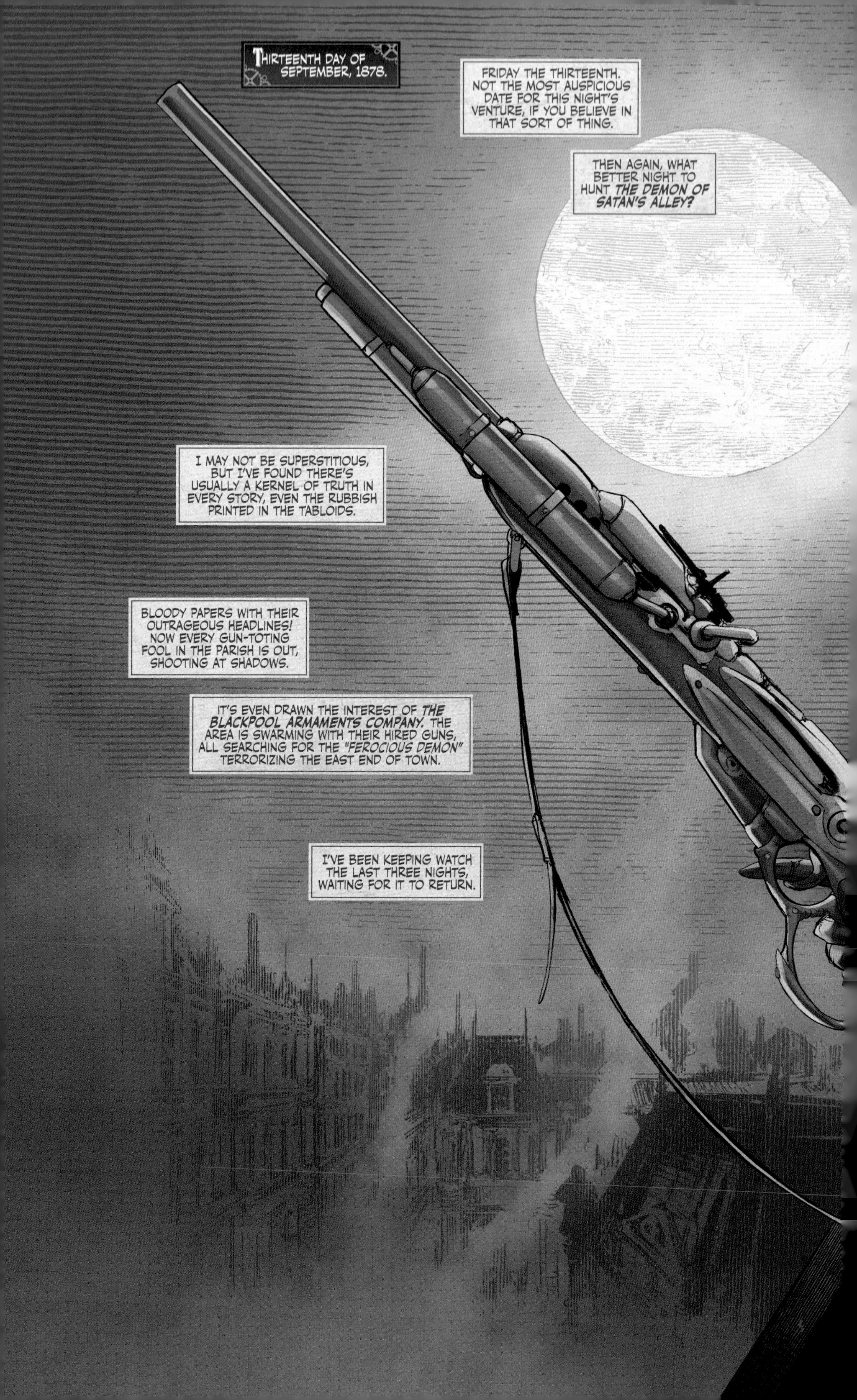
THIRTEENTH DAY OF SEPTEMBER, 1878.
FRIDAY THE THIRTEENTH. NOT THE MOST AUSPICIOUS DATE FOR THIS NIGHT'S VENTURE, IF YOU BELIEVE IN THAT SORT OF THING.
THEN AGAIN, WHAT BETTER NIGHT TO HUNT *THE DEMON OF SATAN'S ALLEY?*
I MAY NOT BE SUPERSTITIOUS, BUT I'VE FOUND THERE'S USUALLY A KERNEL OF TRUTH IN EVERY STORY, EVEN THE RUBBISH PRINTED IN THE TABLOIDS.
BLOODY PAPERS WITH THEIR OUTRAGEOUS HEADLINES! NOW EVERY GUN-TOTING FOOL IN THE PARISH IS OUT, SHOOTING AT SHADOWS.
IT'S EVEN DRAWN THE INTEREST OF *THE BLACKPOOL ARMAMENTS COMPANY.* THE AREA IS SWARMING WITH THEIR HIRED GUNS, ALL SEARCHING FOR THE *"FEROCIOUS DEMON"* TERRORIZING THE EAST END OF TOWN.
I'VE BEEN KEEPING WATCH THE LAST THREE NIGHTS, WAITING FOR IT TO RETURN.

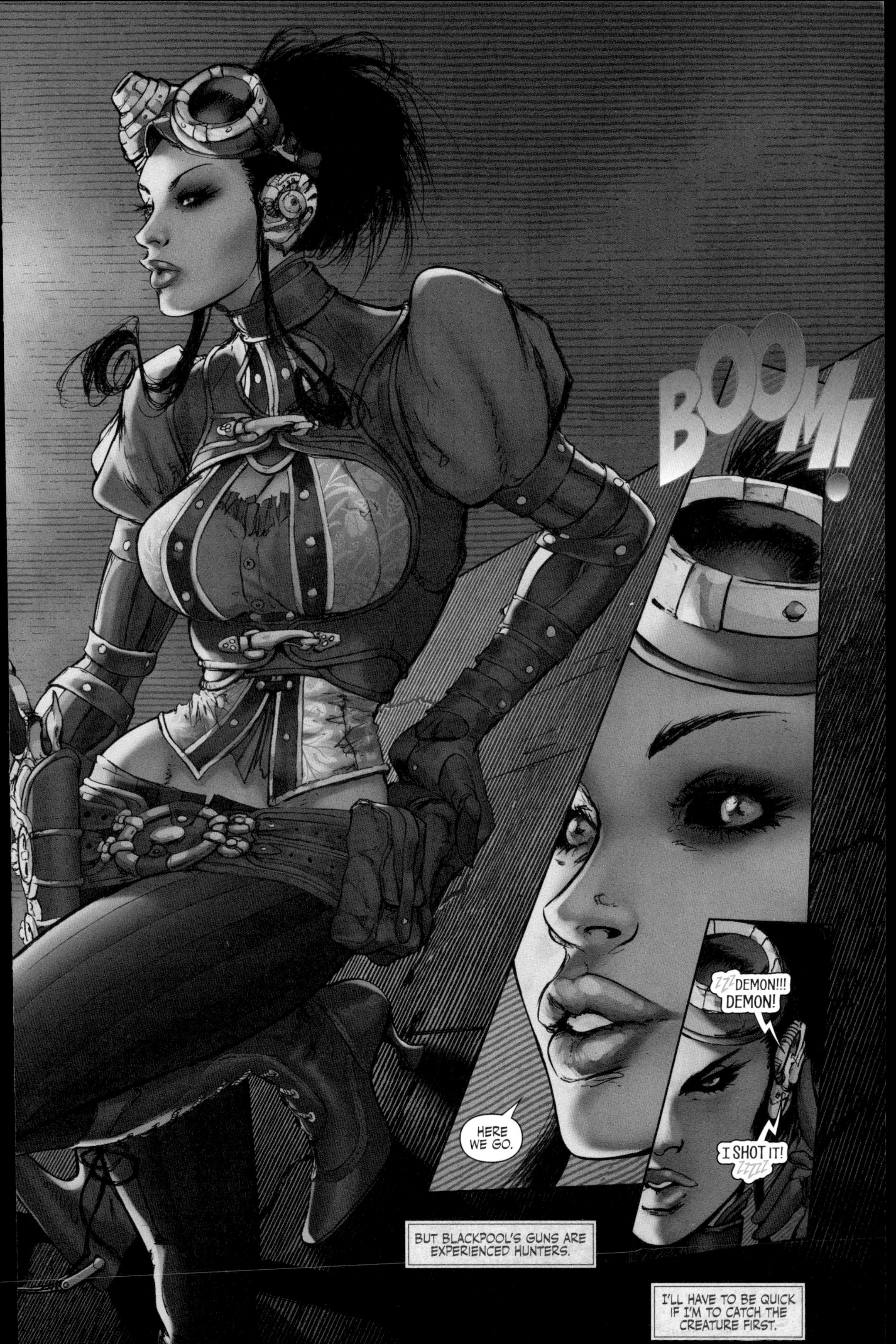
BOOM!
HERE WE GO.
DEMON!!! DEMON!
I SHOT IT!
BUT BLACKPOOL'S GUNS ARE EXPERIENCED HUNTERS.
I'LL HAVE TO BE QUICK IF I'M TO CATCH THE CREATURE FIRST.

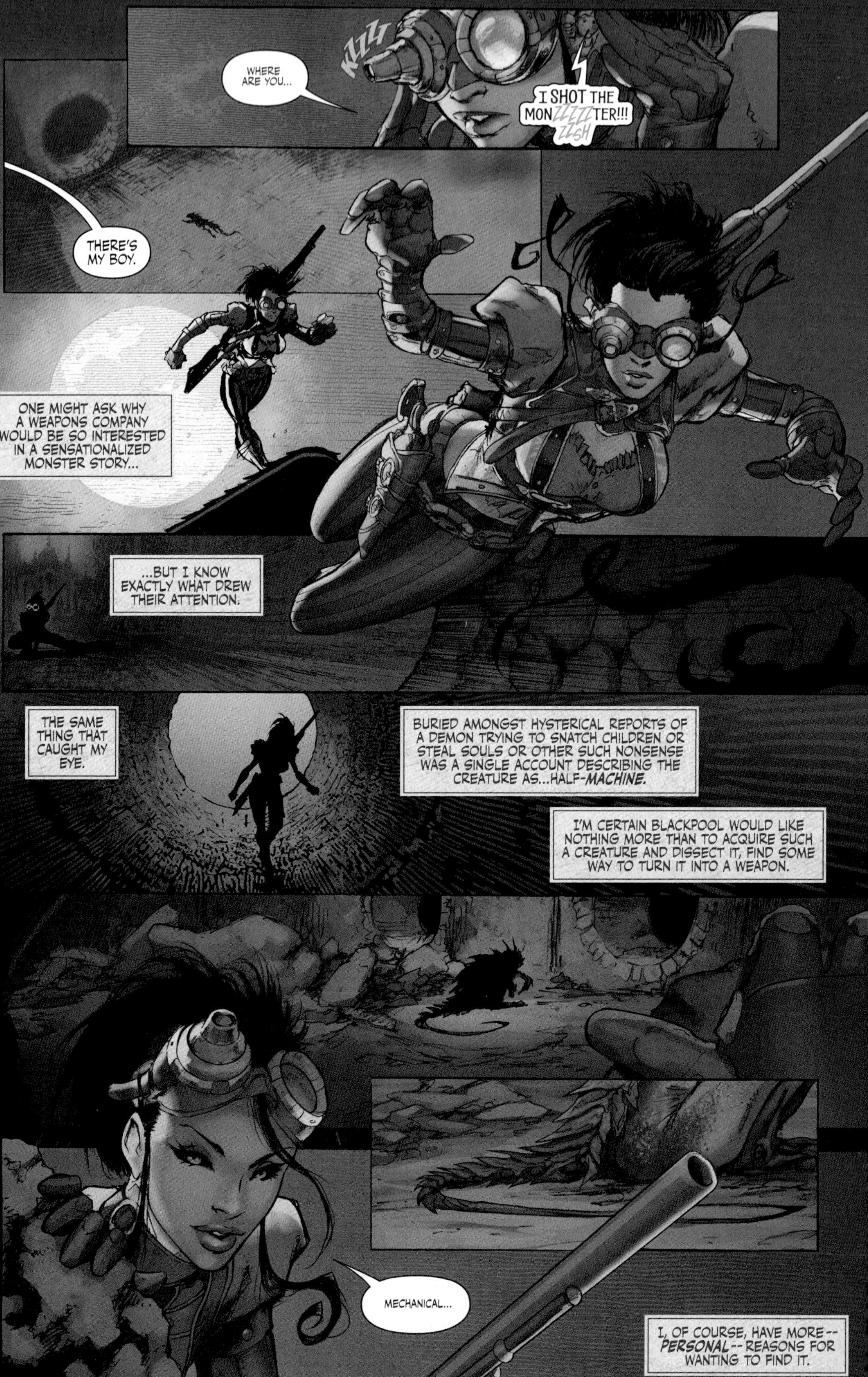
KZZZ
WHERE ARE YOU...
I SHOT THE MONZZZZZTER!!! ZZSH
THERE'S MY BOY.
ONE MIGHT ASK WHY A WEAPONS COMPANY WOULD BE SO INTERESTED IN A SENSATIONALIZED MONSTER STORY...
...BUT I KNOW EXACTLY WHAT DREW THEIR ATTENTION.
THE SAME THING THAT CAUGHT MY EYE.
BURIED AMONGST HYSTERICAL REPORTS OF A DEMON TRYING TO SNATCH CHILDREN OR STEAL SOULS OR OTHER SUCH NONSENSE WAS A SINGLE ACCOUNT DESCRIBING THE CREATURE AS...HALF-*MACHINE.*
I'M CERTAIN BLACKPOOL WOULD LIKE NOTHING MORE THAN TO ACQUIRE SUCH A CREATURE AND DISSECT IT, FIND SOME WAY TO TURN IT INTO A WEAPON.
MECHANICAL...
I, OF COURSE, HAVE MORE-- *PERSONAL*-- REASONS FOR WANTING TO FIND IT.

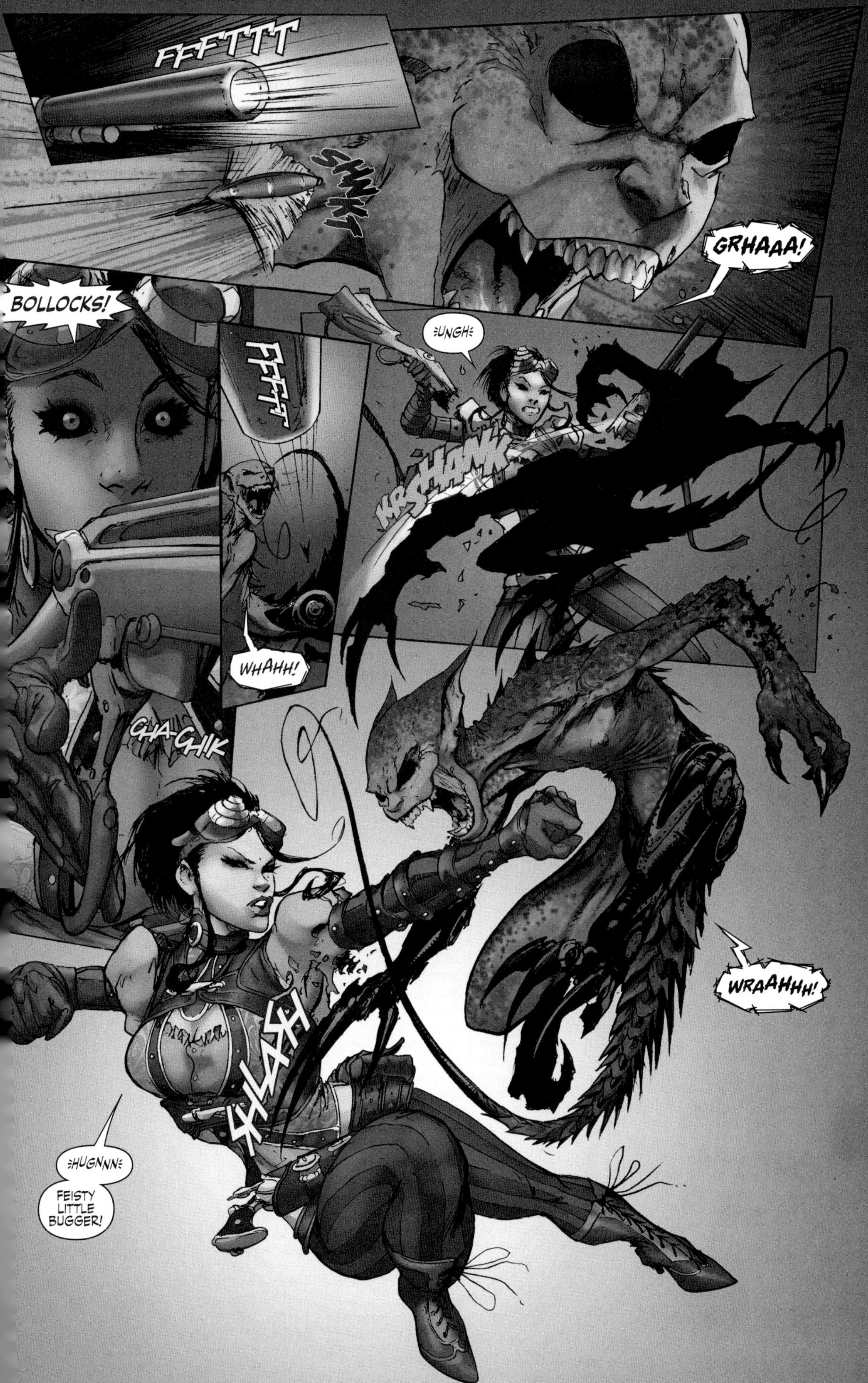
FFFTTT
SHWKT
GRHAAA!
BOLLOCKS!
UNGH
FFFT
KRSHANK
WHAHH!
CHA-CHIK
WRAAHHH!
KHLASH
HUGNNN
FEISTY LITTLE BUGGER!

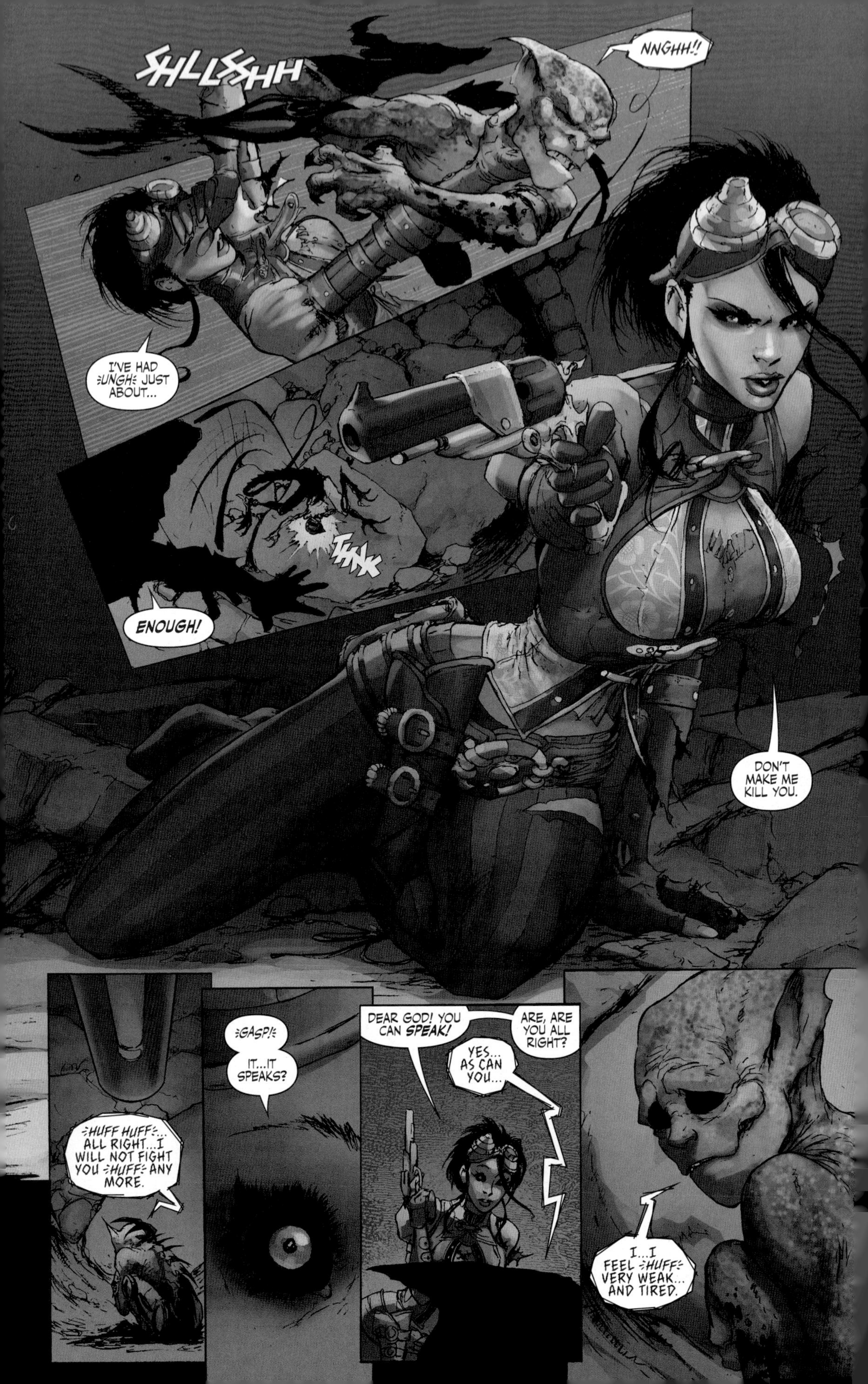
SHLLSSHH
NNGHH!!
I'VE HAD =UNGH= JUST ABOUT...
THNK
ENOUGH!
DON'T MAKE ME KILL YOU.
=HUFF HUFF=... ALL RIGHT... I WILL NOT FIGHT YOU =HUFF= ANY MORE.
=GASP!=
IT... IT SPEAKS?
DEAR GOD! YOU CAN SPEAK!
ARE, ARE YOU ALL RIGHT?
YES... AS CAN YOU...
I... I FEEL =HUFF= VERY WEAK... AND TIRED.

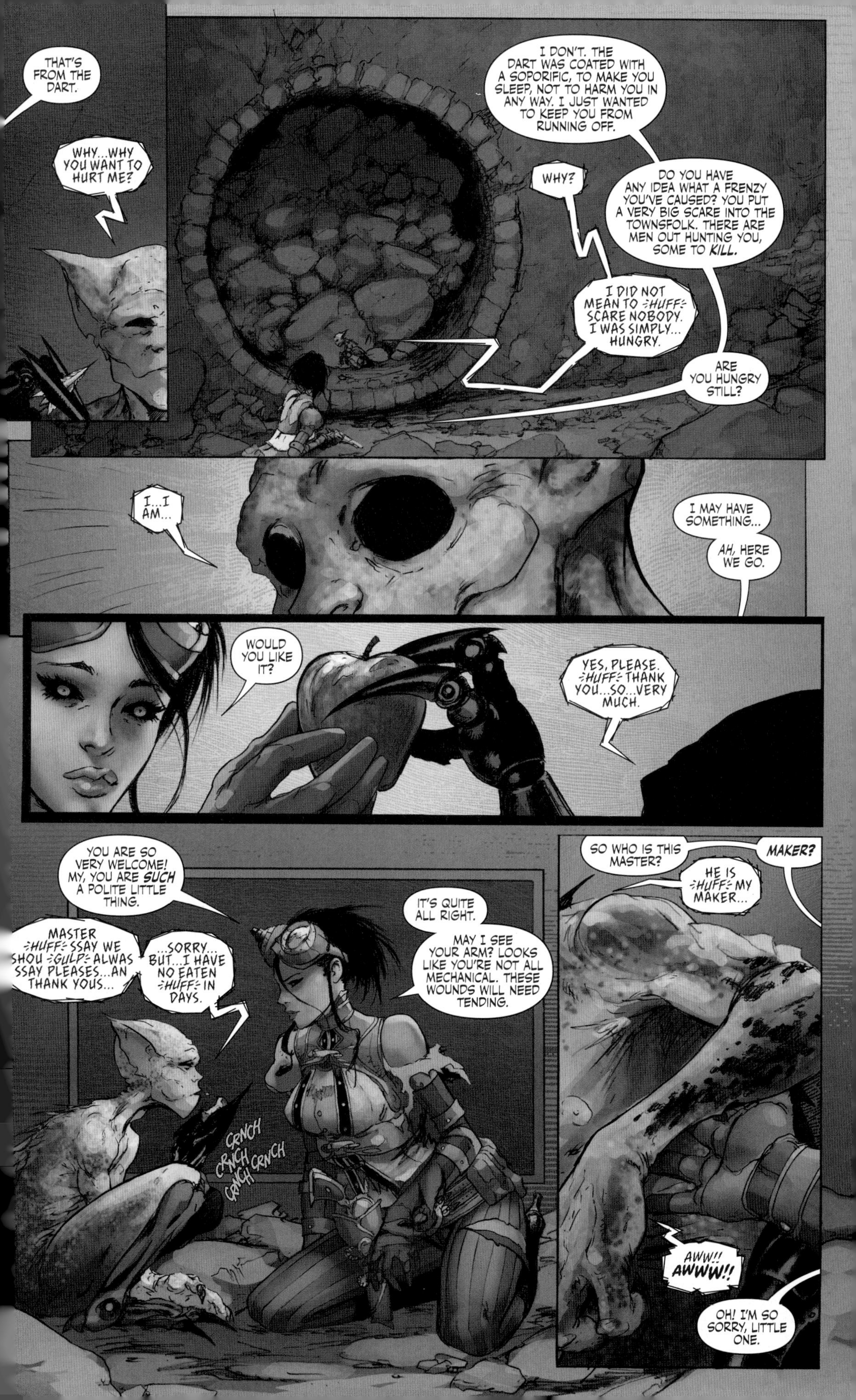
THAT'S FROM THE DART.
WHY...WHY YOU WANT TO HURT ME?
I DON'T. THE DART WAS COATED WITH A SOPORIFIC, TO MAKE YOU SLEEP, NOT TO HARM YOU IN ANY WAY. I JUST WANTED TO KEEP YOU FROM RUNNING OFF.
WHY?
DO YOU HAVE ANY IDEA WHAT A FRENZY YOU'VE CAUSED? YOU PUT A VERY BIG SCARE INTO THE TOWNSFOLK. THERE ARE MEN OUT HUNTING YOU, SOME TO KILL.
I DID NOT MEAN TO HUFF SCARE NOBODY. I WAS SIMPLY... HUNGRY.
ARE YOU HUNGRY STILL?
I...I AM...
I MAY HAVE SOMETHING...
AH, HERE WE GO.
WOULD YOU LIKE IT?
YES, PLEASE. HUFF THANK YOU...SO...VERY MUCH.
YOU ARE SO VERY WELCOME! MY, YOU ARE SUCH A POLITE LITTLE THING.
MASTER HUFF SSAY WE SHOU GULP ALWAS SSAY PLEASES...AN THANK YOUS...
...SORRY... BUT...I HAVE NO EATEN HUFF IN DAYS.
IT'S QUITE ALL RIGHT.
MAY I SEE YOUR ARM? LOOKS LIKE YOU'RE NOT ALL MECHANICAL. THESE WOUNDS WILL NEED TENDING.
CRNCH CRNCH CRNCH CRNCH
SO WHO IS THIS MASTER?
MAKER?
HE IS HUFF MY MAKER...
AWW!! AWWW!!
OH! I'M SO SORRY, LITTLE ONE.

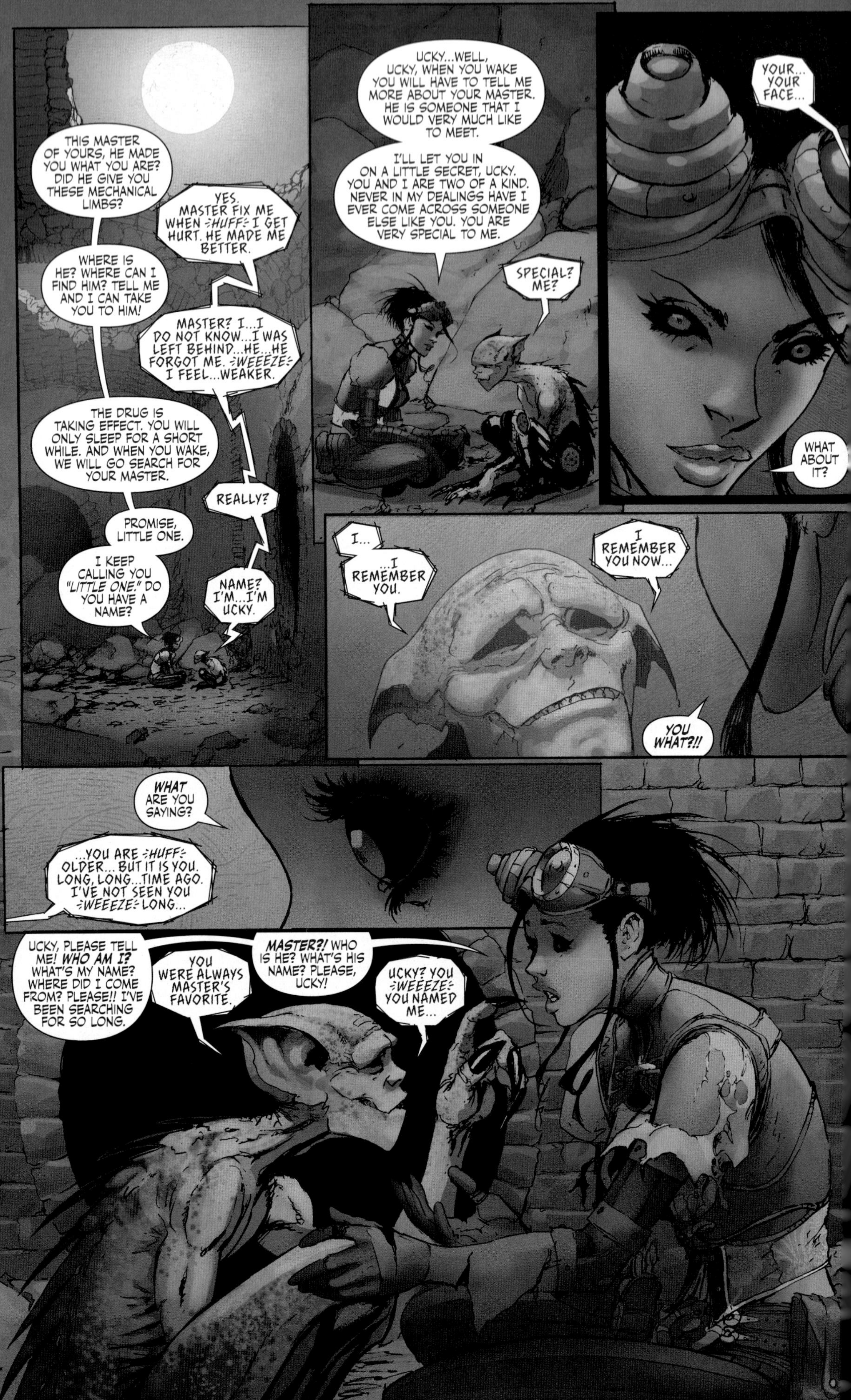
THIS MASTER OF YOURS, HE MADE YOU WHAT YOU ARE? DID HE GIVE YOU THESE MECHANICAL LIMBS?
YES. MASTER FIX ME WHEN =HUFF= I GET HURT. HE MADE ME BETTER.
WHERE IS HE? WHERE CAN I FIND HIM? TELL ME AND I CAN TAKE YOU TO HIM!
MASTER? I...I DO NOT KNOW...I WAS LEFT BEHIND...HE...HE FORGOT ME. =WEEEZE= I FEEL...WEAKER.
THE DRUG IS TAKING EFFECT. YOU WILL ONLY SLEEP FOR A SHORT WHILE. AND WHEN YOU WAKE, WE WILL GO SEARCH FOR YOUR MASTER.
REALLY?
PROMISE, LITTLE ONE.
I KEEP CALLING YOU "LITTLE ONE." DO YOU HAVE A NAME?
NAME? I'M...I'M UCKY.
UCKY...WELL, UCKY, WHEN YOU WAKE YOU WILL HAVE TO TELL ME MORE ABOUT YOUR MASTER. HE IS SOMEONE THAT I WOULD VERY MUCH LIKE TO MEET.
I'LL LET YOU IN ON A LITTLE SECRET, UCKY. YOU AND I ARE TWO OF A KIND. NEVER IN MY DEALINGS HAVE I EVER COME ACROSS SOMEONE ELSE LIKE YOU. YOU ARE VERY SPECIAL TO ME.
SPECIAL? ME?
YOUR... YOUR FACE...
WHAT ABOUT IT?
I...
...I REMEMBER YOU.
I REMEMBER YOU NOW...
YOU WHAT?!!
WHAT ARE YOU SAYING?
...YOU ARE =HUFF= OLDER... BUT IT IS YOU. LONG, LONG...TIME AGO. I'VE NOT SEEN YOU =WEEEZE= LONG...
UCKY, PLEASE TELL ME! WHO AM I? WHAT'S MY NAME? WHERE DID I COME FROM? PLEASE!! I'VE BEEN SEARCHING FOR SO LONG.
YOU WERE ALWAYS MASTER'S FAVORITE.
MASTER?! WHO IS HE? WHAT'S HIS NAME? PLEASE, UCKY!
UCKY? YOU =WEEEZE= YOU NAMED ME...

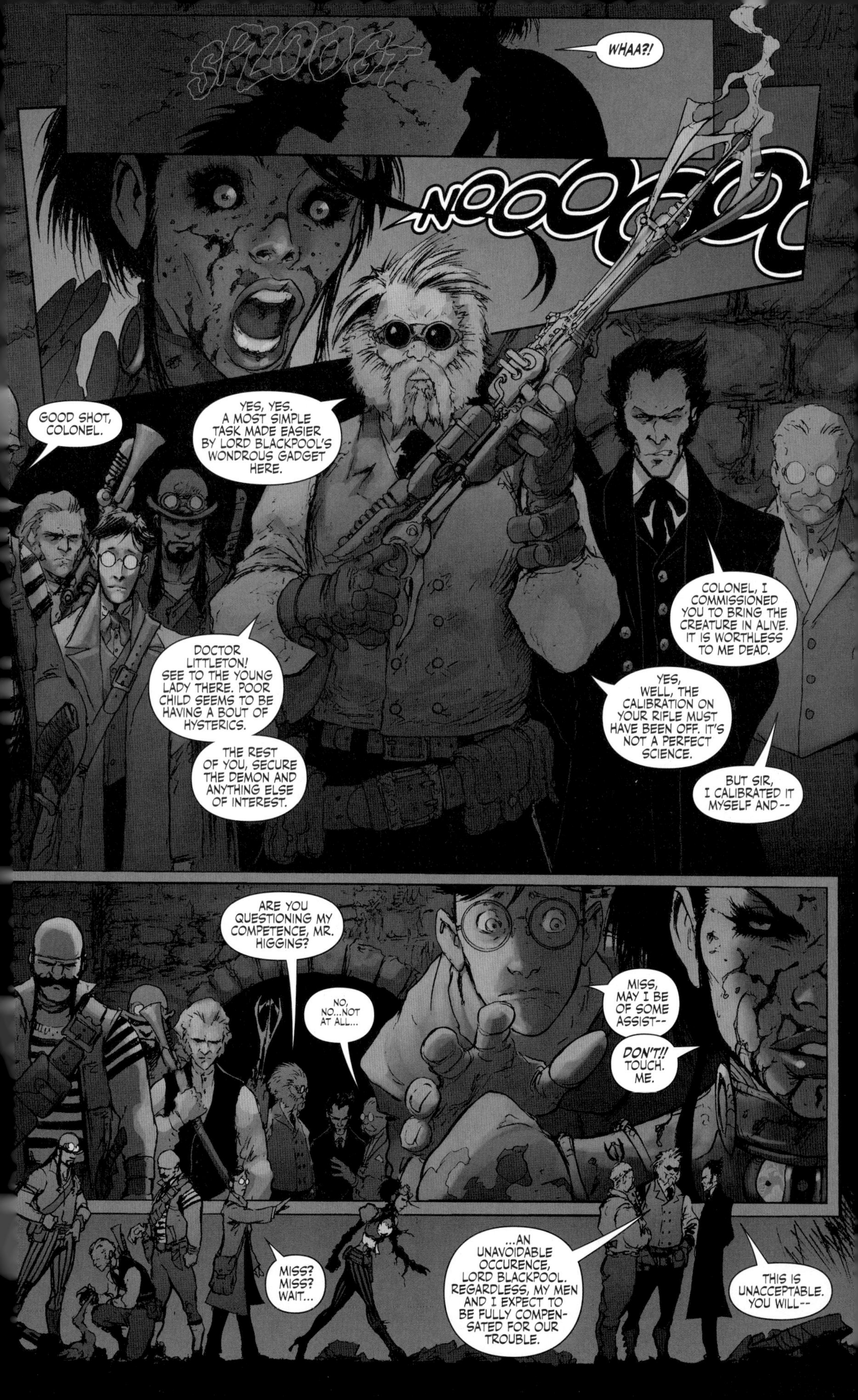
SPLOOSH
WHAA?!
NOOOOOOO
GOOD SHOT, COLONEL.
YES, YES. A MOST SIMPLE TASK MADE EASIER BY LORD BLACKPOOL'S WONDROUS GADGET HERE.
COLONEL, I COMMISSIONED YOU TO BRING THE CREATURE IN ALIVE. IT IS WORTHLESS TO ME DEAD.
DOCTOR LITTLETON! SEE TO THE YOUNG LADY THERE. POOR CHILD SEEMS TO BE HAVING A BOUT OF HYSTERICS.
THE REST OF YOU, SECURE THE DEMON AND ANYTHING ELSE OF INTEREST.
YES, WELL, THE CALIBRATION ON YOUR RIFLE MUST HAVE BEEN OFF. IT'S NOT A PERFECT SCIENCE.
BUT SIR, I CALIBRATED IT MYSELF AND--
ARE YOU QUESTIONING MY COMPETENCE, MR. HIGGINS?
NO, NO...NOT AT ALL...
MISS, MAY I BE OF SOME ASSIST--
DON'T!! TOUCH. ME.
MISS? MISS? WAIT...
...AN UNAVOIDABLE OCCURENCE, LORD BLACKPOOL. REGARDLESS, MY MEN AND I EXPECT TO BE FULLY COMPENSATED FOR OUR TROUBLE.
THIS IS UNACCEPTABLE. YOU WILL--

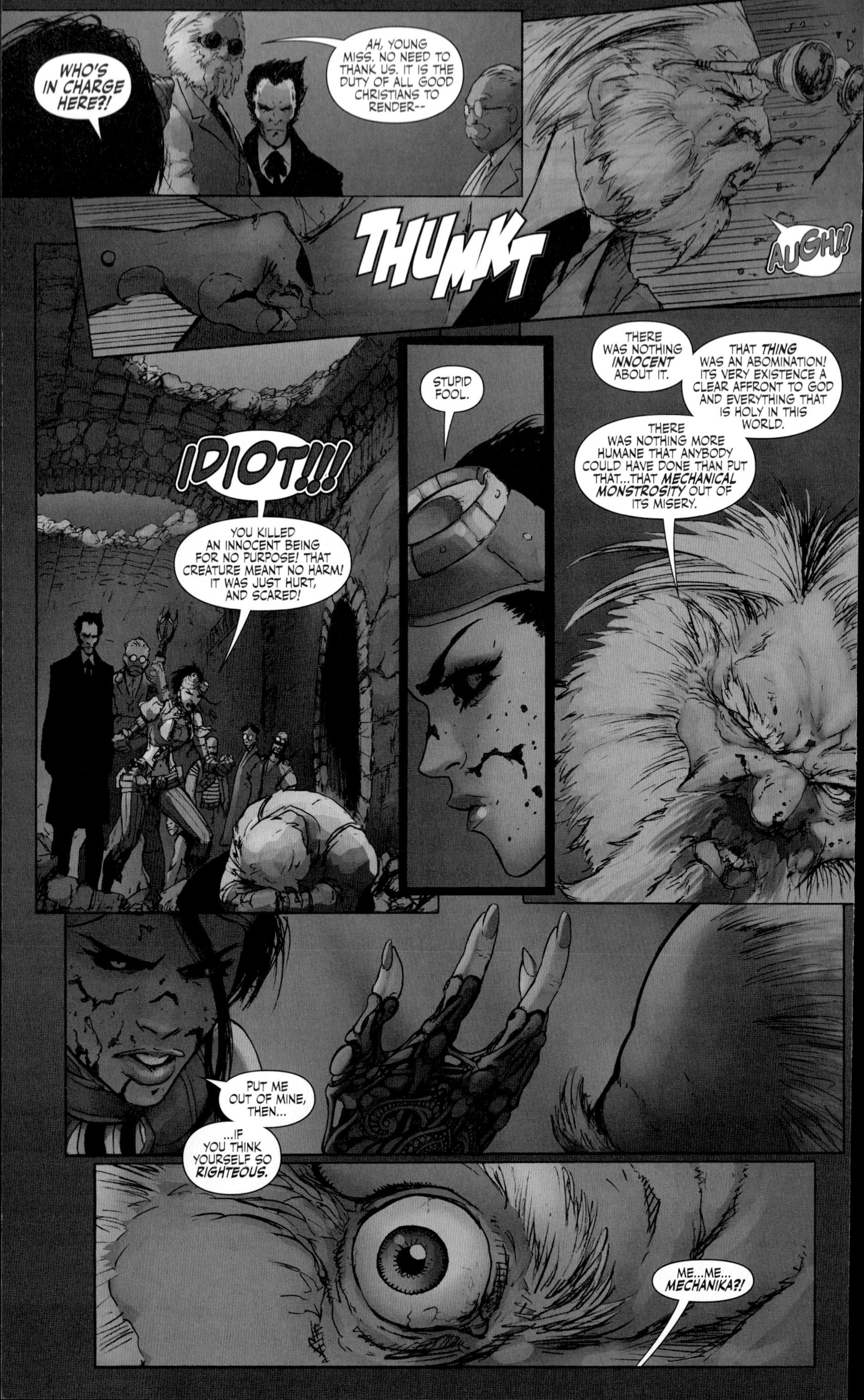
WHO'S IN CHARGE HERE?!
AH, YOUNG MISS. NO NEED TO THANK US. IT IS THE DUTY OF ALL GOOD CHRISTIANS TO RENDER--
THUMKT
AUGH!!
IDIOT!!!
YOU KILLED AN INNOCENT BEING FOR NO PURPOSE! THAT CREATURE MEANT NO HARM! IT WAS JUST HURT, AND SCARED!
STUPID FOOL.
THERE WAS NOTHING INNOCENT ABOUT IT.
THAT THING WAS AN ABOMINATION! ITS VERY EXISTENCE A CLEAR AFFRONT TO GOD AND EVERYTHING THAT IS HOLY IN THIS WORLD.
THERE WAS NOTHING MORE HUMANE THAT ANYBODY COULD HAVE DONE THAN PUT THAT...THAT MECHANICAL MONSTROSITY OUT OF ITS MISERY.
PUT ME OUT OF MINE, THEN...
...IF YOU THINK YOURSELF SO RIGHTEOUS.
ME...ME... MECHANIKA?!

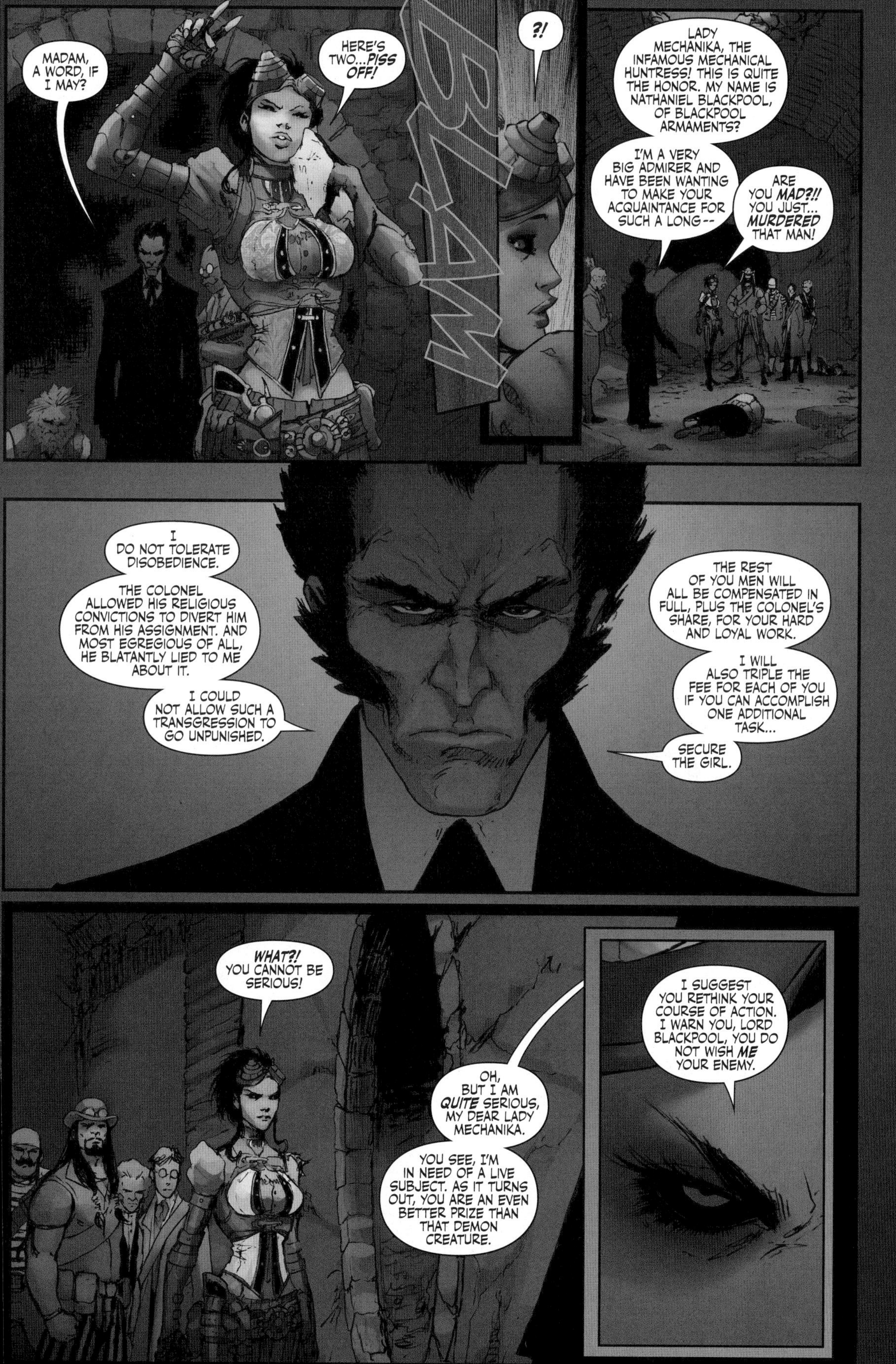
MADAM, A WORD, IF I MAY?
HERE'S TWO...PISS OFF!
BLAM!
?!
LADY MECHANIKA, THE INFAMOUS MECHANICAL HUNTRESS! THIS IS QUITE THE HONOR. MY NAME IS NATHANIEL BLACKPOOL, OF BLACKPOOL ARMAMENTS?
I'M A VERY BIG ADMIRER AND HAVE BEEN WANTING TO MAKE YOUR ACQUAINTANCE FOR SUCH A LONG--
ARE YOU MAD?!! YOU JUST... MURDERED THAT MAN!
I DO NOT TOLERATE DISOBEDIENCE.
THE COLONEL ALLOWED HIS RELIGIOUS CONVICTIONS TO DIVERT HIM FROM HIS ASSIGNMENT. AND MOST EGREGIOUS OF ALL, HE BLATANTLY LIED TO ME ABOUT IT.
I COULD NOT ALLOW SUCH A TRANSGRESSION TO GO UNPUNISHED.
THE REST OF YOU MEN WILL ALL BE COMPENSATED IN FULL, PLUS THE COLONEL'S SHARE, FOR YOUR HARD AND LOYAL WORK.
I WILL ALSO TRIPLE THE FEE FOR EACH OF YOU IF YOU CAN ACCOMPLISH ONE ADDITIONAL TASK...
SECURE THE GIRL.
WHAT?! YOU CANNOT BE SERIOUS!
OH, BUT I AM QUITE SERIOUS, MY DEAR LADY MECHANIKA.
YOU SEE, I'M IN NEED OF A LIVE SUBJECT. AS IT TURNS OUT, YOU ARE AN EVEN BETTER PRIZE THAN THAT DEMON CREATURE.
I SUGGEST YOU RETHINK YOUR COURSE OF ACTION. I WARN YOU, LORD BLACKPOOL, YOU DO NOT WISH ME YOUR ENEMY.

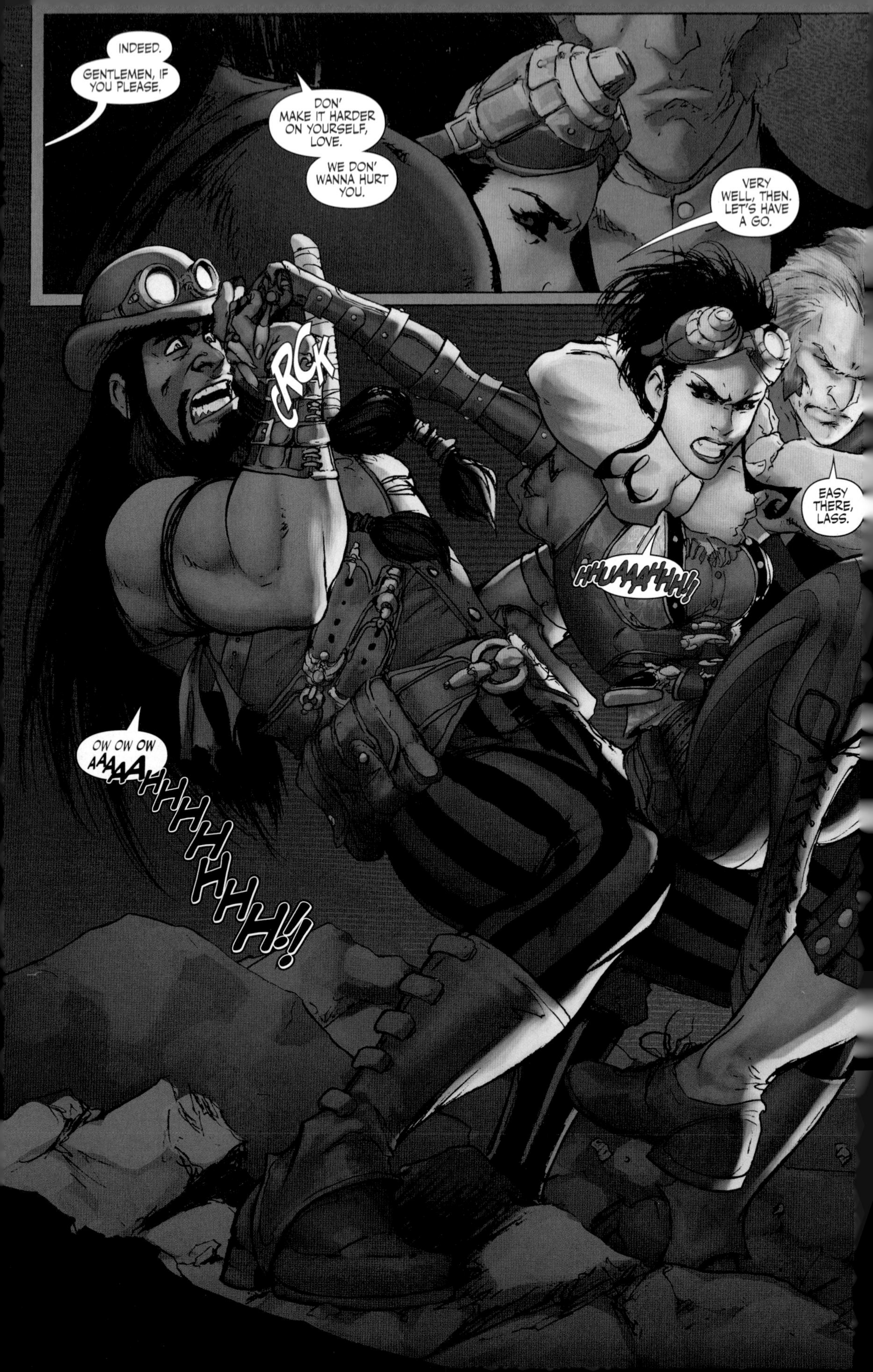
INDEED.
GENTLEMEN, IF YOU PLEASE.
DON' MAKE IT HARDER ON YOURSELF, LOVE.
WE DON' WANNA HURT YOU.
VERY WELL, THEN. LET'S HAVE A GO.
CRCK
EASY THERE, LASS.
HHUAAAHHH!!
OW OW OW AAAAAHHHHHHHHHHH!!

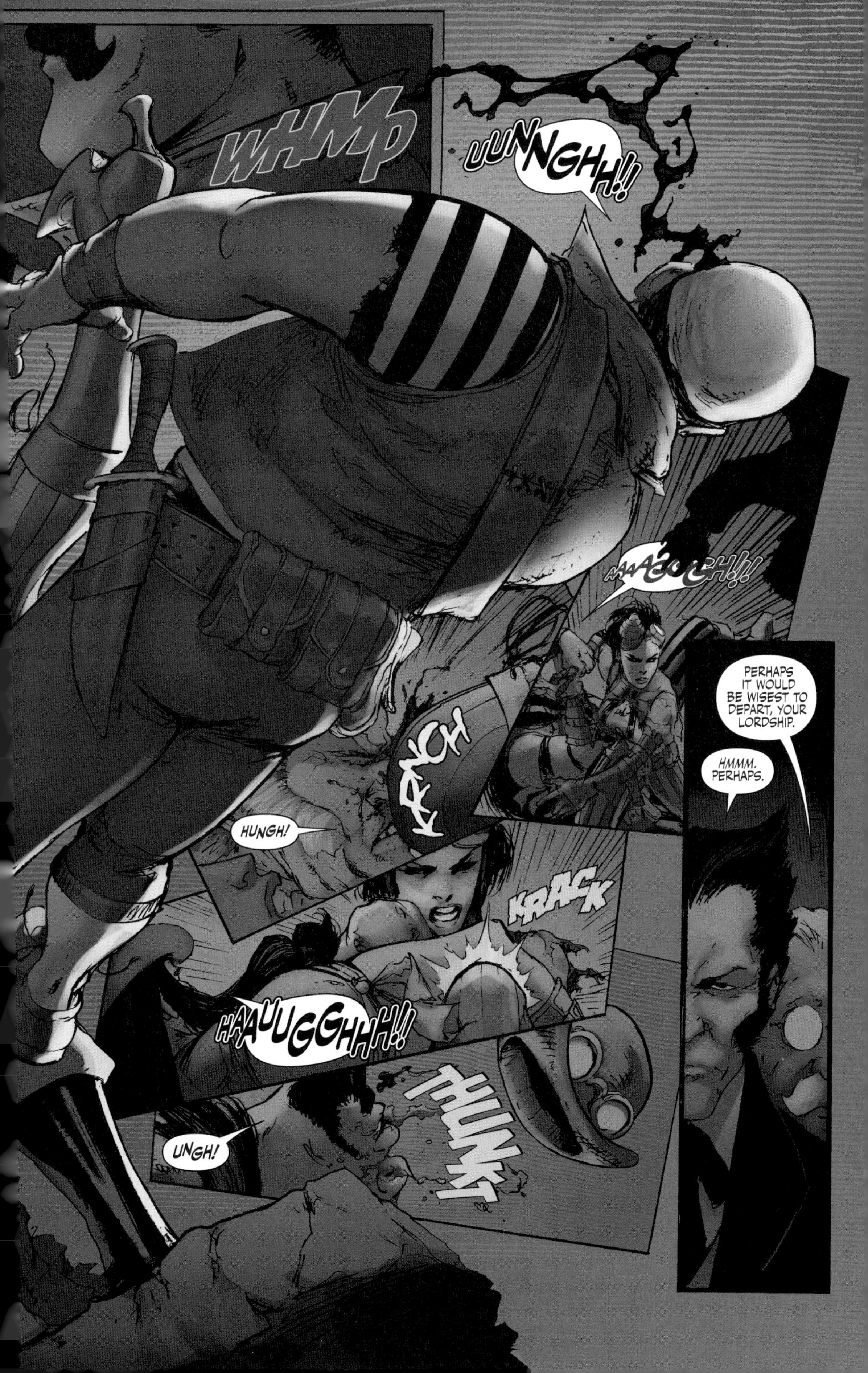
WHUMP
UUNNGHH!!
AAAAGGGGH!!!
KRNCH
HUNGH!
KRACK
PERHAPS IT WOULD BE WISEST TO DEPART, YOUR LORDSHIP.
HMMM. PERHAPS.
HAAUUGGHHH!!
THUNKT
UNGH!

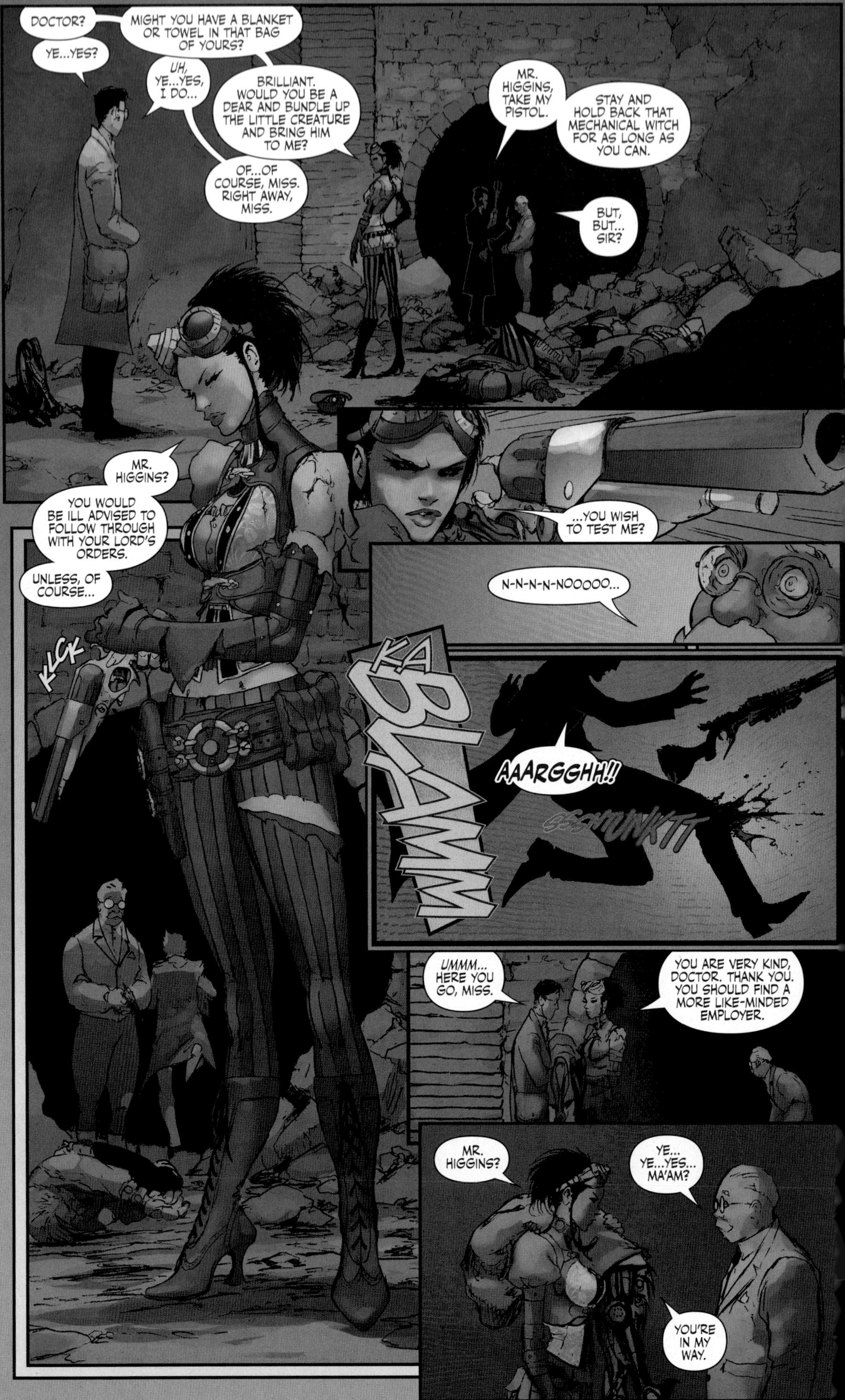
DOCTOR?
MIGHT YOU HAVE A BLANKET OR TOWEL IN THAT BAG OF YOURS?
YE...YES?
UH, YE...YES, I DO...
BRILLIANT. WOULD YOU BE A DEAR AND BUNDLE UP THE LITTLE CREATURE AND BRING HIM TO ME?
OF...OF COURSE, MISS. RIGHT AWAY, MISS.
MR. HIGGINS, TAKE MY PISTOL.
STAY AND HOLD BACK THAT MECHANICAL WITCH FOR AS LONG AS YOU CAN.
BUT, BUT... SIR?
MR. HIGGINS?
YOU WOULD BE ILL ADVISED TO FOLLOW THROUGH WITH YOUR LORD'S ORDERS.
UNLESS, OF COURSE...
KLCK
...YOU WISH TO TEST ME?
N-N-N-N-NOOOOO...
KA BLAMM
AAARGGHH!!
SSSCHUNKTT
UMMM... HERE YOU GO, MISS.
YOU ARE VERY KIND, DOCTOR. THANK YOU. YOU SHOULD FIND A MORE LIKE-MINDED EMPLOYER.
MR. HIGGINS?
YE... YE...YES... MA'AM?
YOU'RE IN MY WAY.

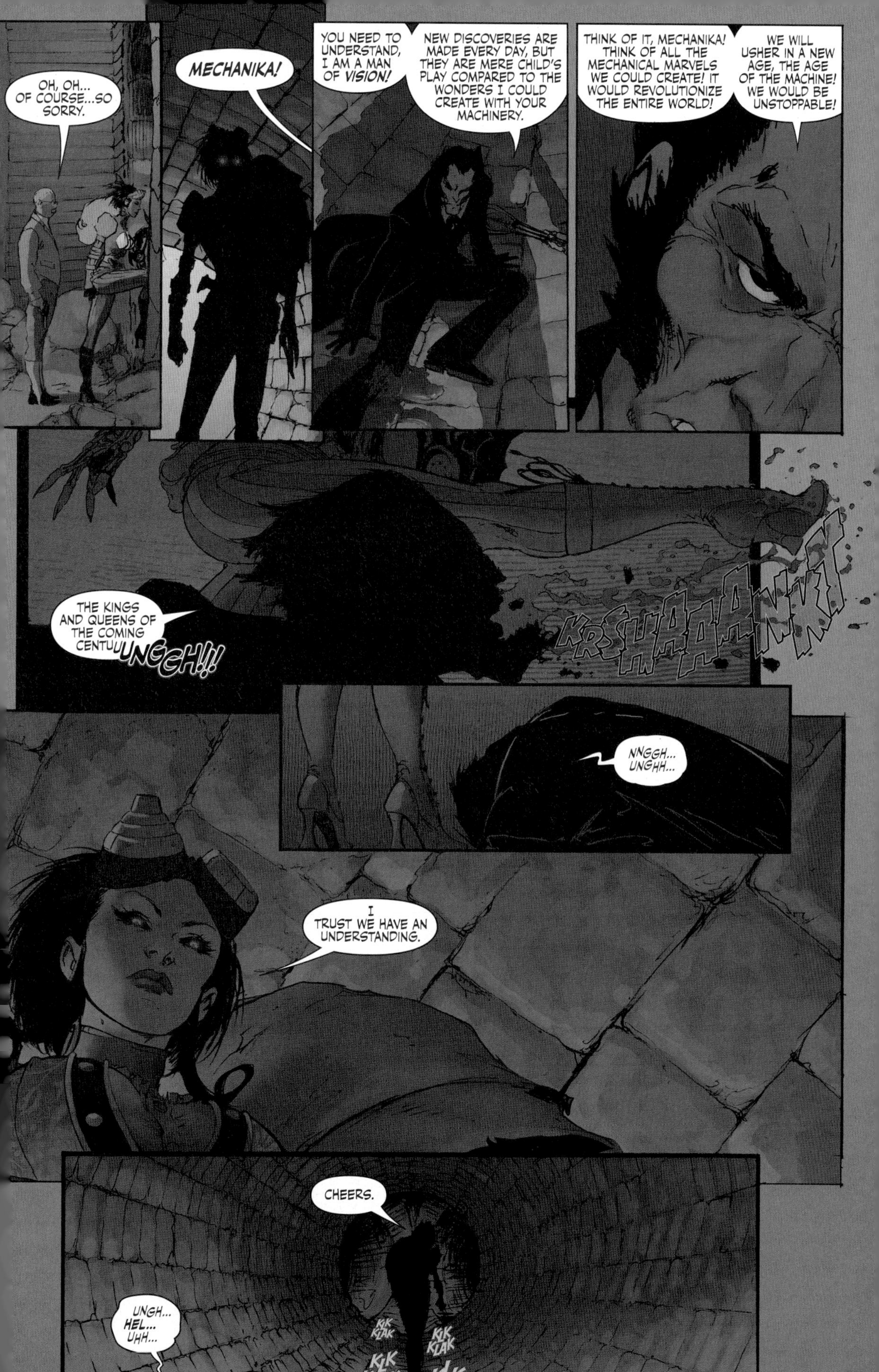
OH, OH... OF COURSE...SO SORRY.
MECHANIKA!
YOU NEED TO UNDERSTAND, I AM A MAN OF VISION!
NEW DISCOVERIES ARE MADE EVERY DAY, BUT THEY ARE MERE CHILD'S PLAY COMPARED TO THE WONDERS I COULD CREATE WITH YOUR MACHINERY.
THINK OF IT, MECHANIKA! THINK OF ALL THE MECHANICAL MARVELS WE COULD CREATE! IT WOULD REVOLUTIONIZE THE ENTIRE WORLD!
WE WILL USHER IN A NEW AGE, THE AGE OF THE MACHINE! WE WOULD BE UNSTOPPABLE!
THE KINGS AND QUEENS OF THE COMING CENTUUUNGGH!!!
KRSHWAAANK!
NNGGH... UNGHH...
I TRUST WE HAVE AN UNDERSTANDING.
CHEERS.
UNGH... HEL... UHH...
KLK KLAK
KLK KLAK
KLK KLAK
KLK KLAK

# Chapter One

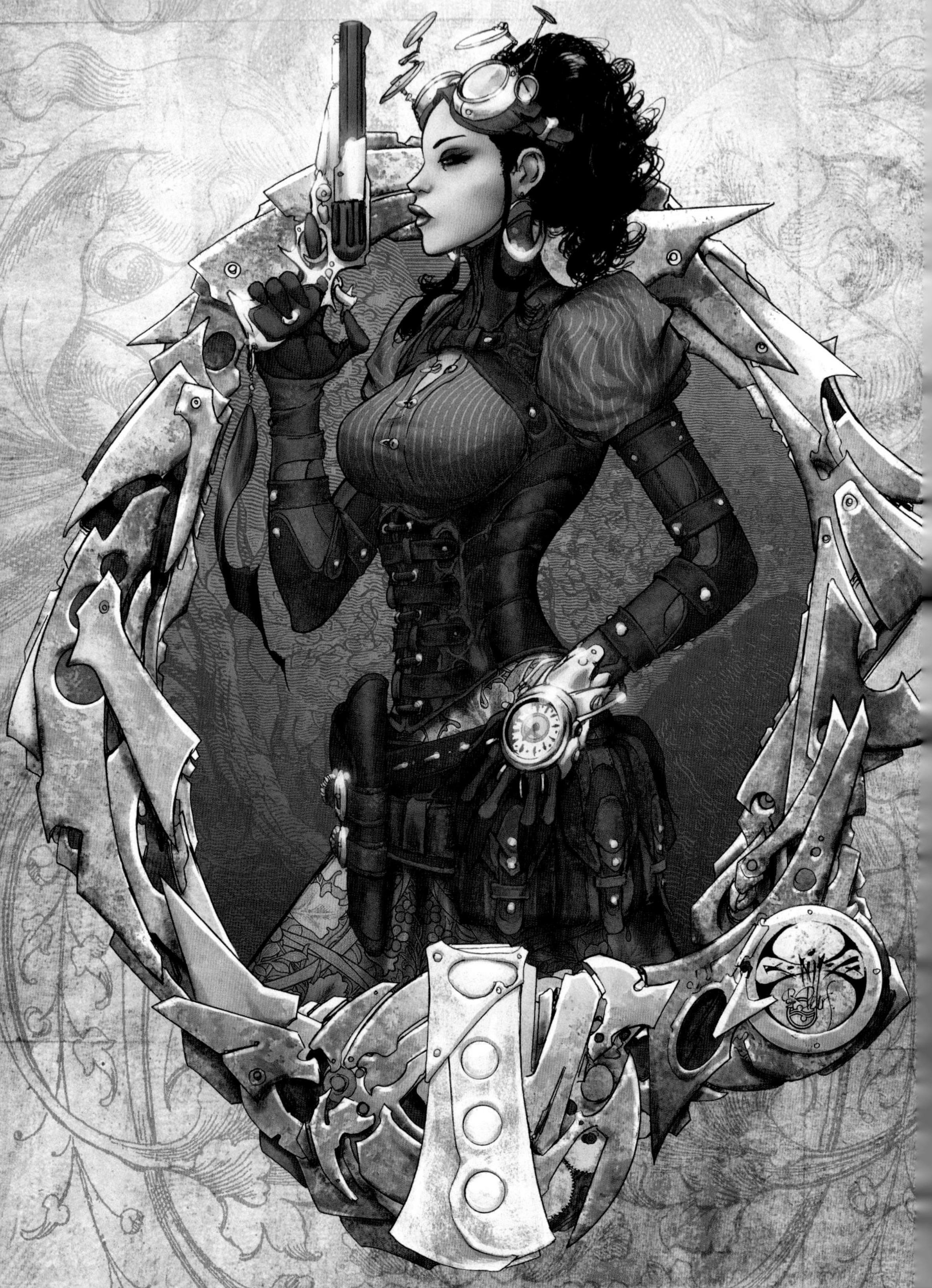

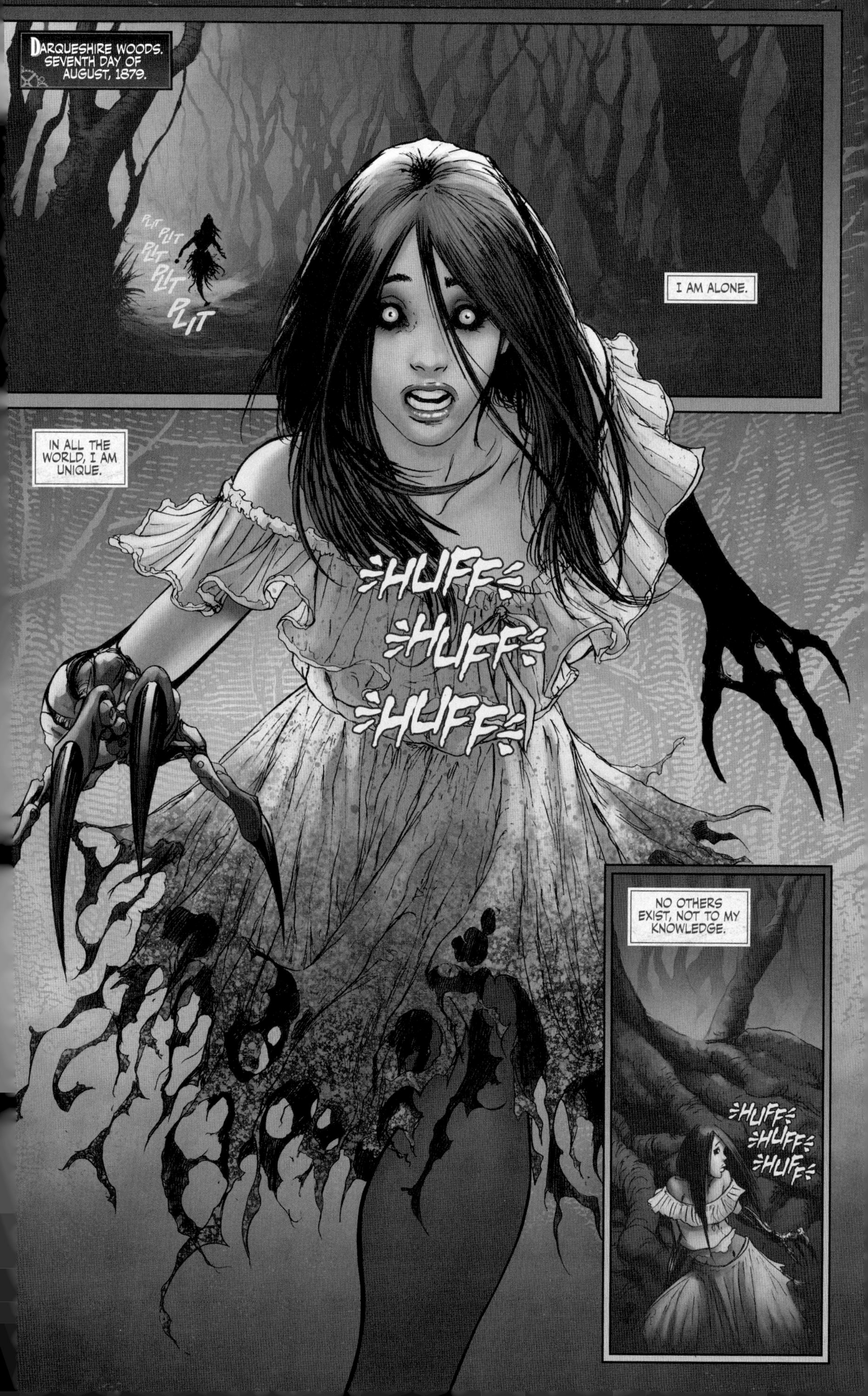

DARQUESHIRE WOODS. SEVENTH DAY OF AUGUST, 1879.
PLIT PLIT PLIT PLIT PLIT PLIT
I AM ALONE.
IN ALL THE WORLD, I AM UNIQUE.
HUFF HUFF HUFF
NO OTHERS EXIST, NOT TO MY KNOWLEDGE.
HUFF HUFF HUFF

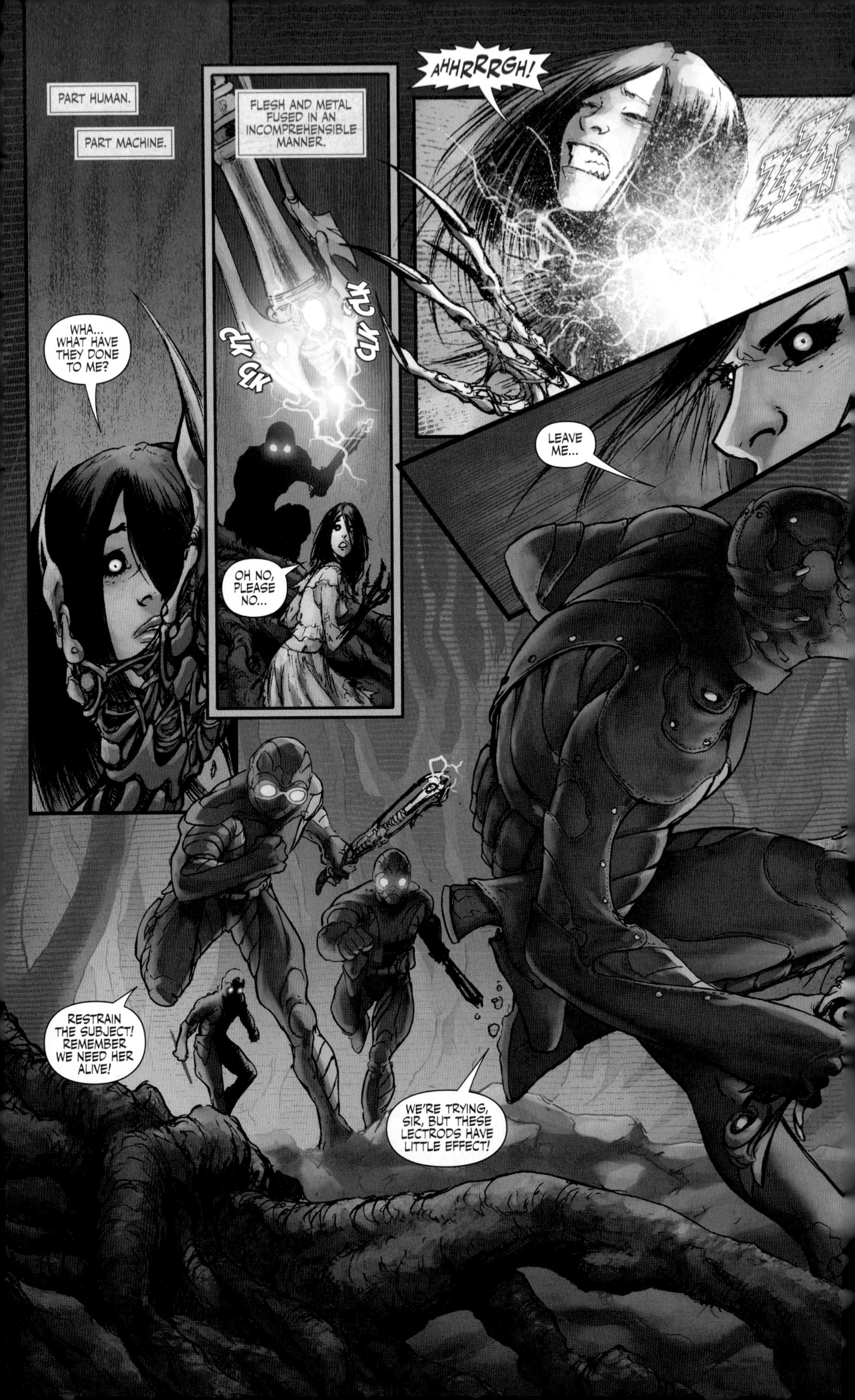
PART HUMAN.
PART MACHINE.
FLESH AND METAL FUSED IN AN INCOMPREHENSIBLE MANNER.
CLK CLK
CLK CLK
OH NO, PLEASE NO...
AHHRRRGH!
WHA... WHAT HAVE THEY DONE TO ME?
LEAVE ME...
RESTRAIN THE SUBJECT! REMEMBER WE NEED HER ALIVE!
WE'RE TRYING, SIR, BUT THESE LECTRODS HAVE LITTLE EFFECT!

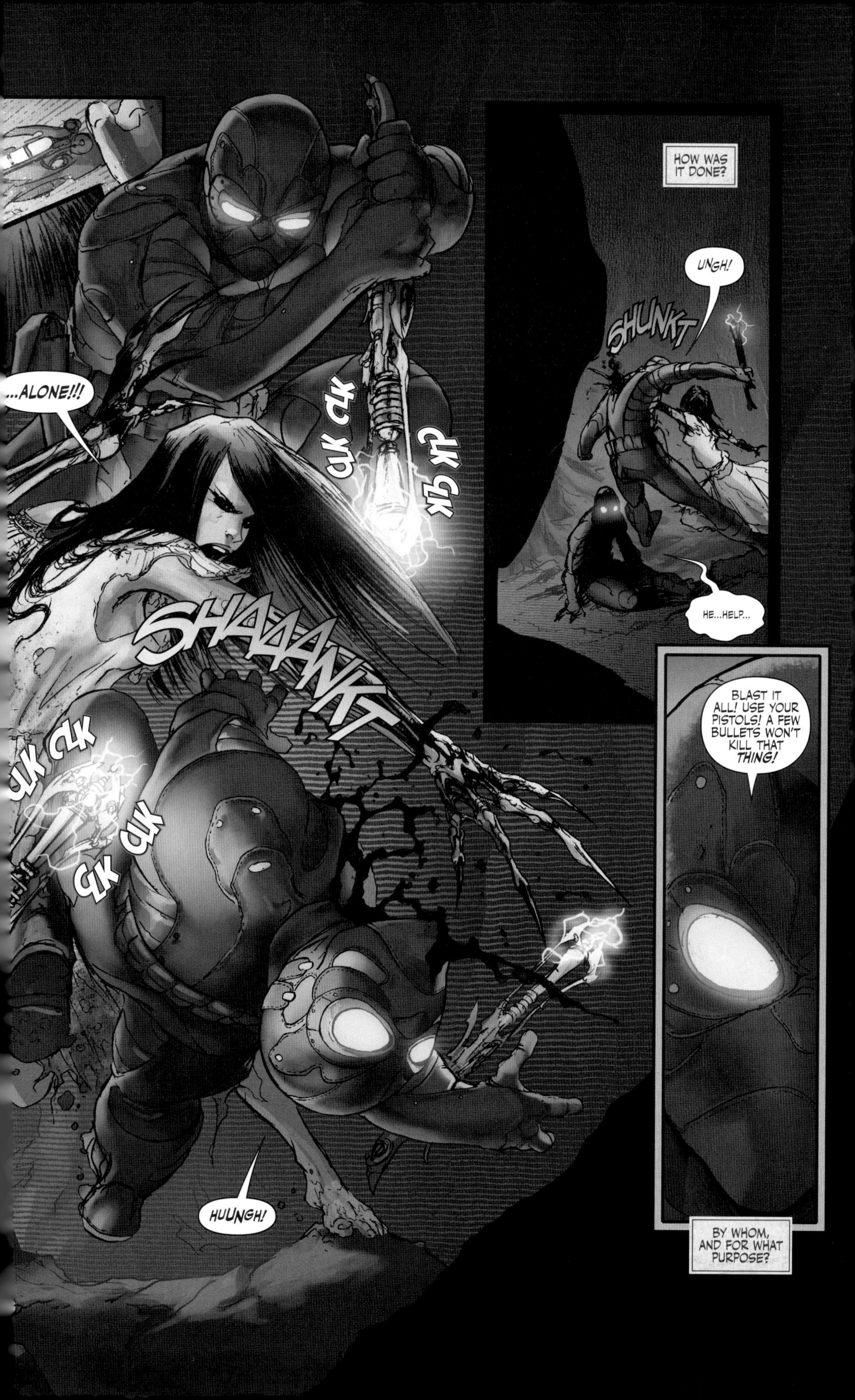
...ALONE!!!
CLK CLK
CLK CLK
SHAAANKT
CLK CLK
CLK CLK
HUUNGH!
HOW WAS IT DONE?
UNGH!
SHUNKT
HE...HELP...
BLAST IT ALL! USE YOUR PISTOLS! A FEW BULLETS WON'T KILL THAT THING!
BY WHOM, AND FOR WHAT PURPOSE?

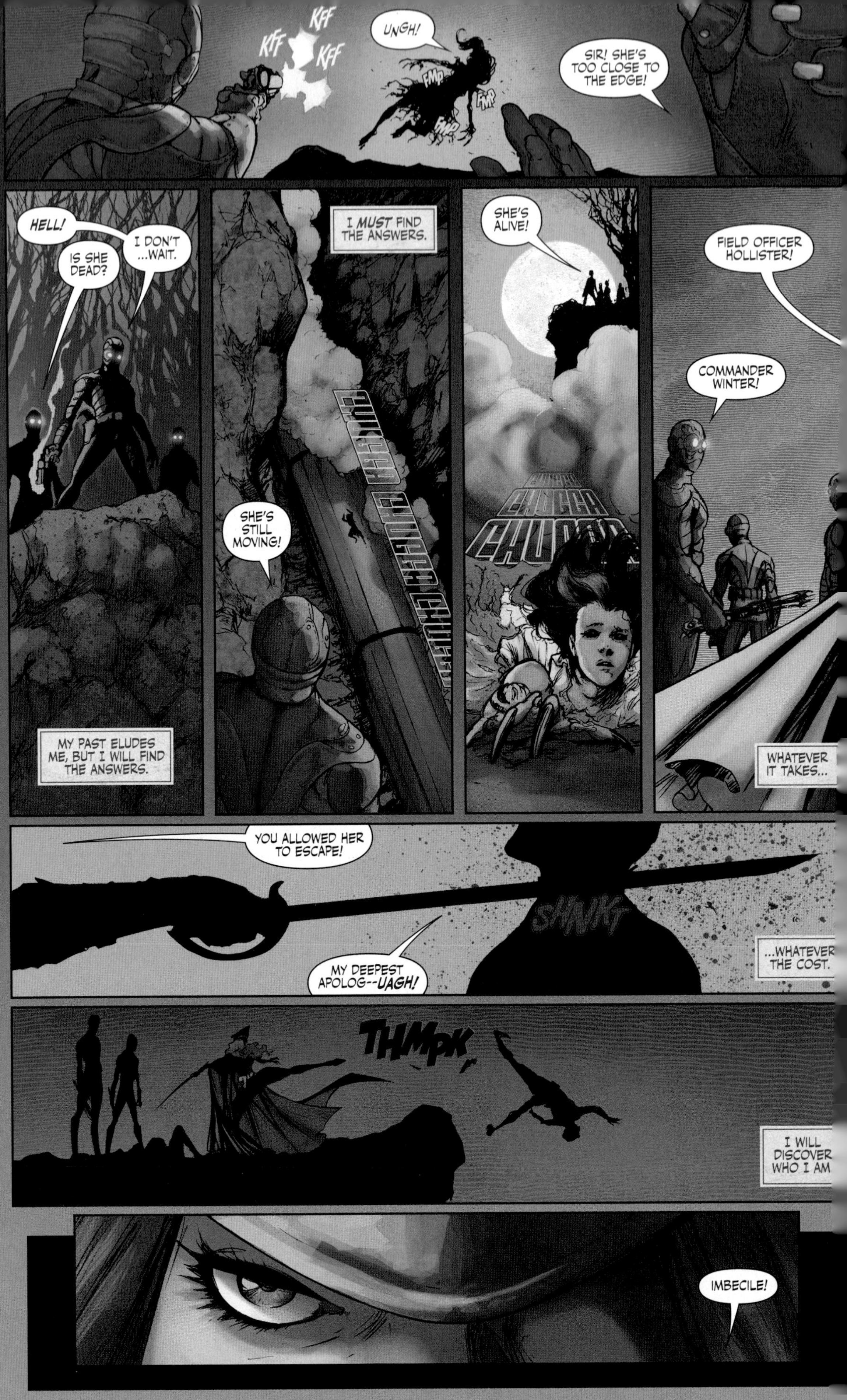
KFF KFF KFF
UNGH!
FMP FMP FMP
SIR! SHE'S TOO CLOSE TO THE EDGE!
HELL!
IS SHE DEAD?
I DON'T ...WAIT.
MY PAST ELUDES ME, BUT I WILL FIND THE ANSWERS.
I MUST FIND THE ANSWERS.
SHE'S STILL MOVING!
SHE'S ALIVE!
CHUGGA CHUGGA CHUGGA
FIELD OFFICER HOLLISTER!
COMMANDER WINTER!
WHATEVER IT TAKES...
YOU ALLOWED HER TO ESCAPE!
SHNKT
MY DEEPEST APOLOG--UAGH!
...WHATEVER THE COST.
THMPK
I WILL DISCOVER WHO I AM
IMBECILE!

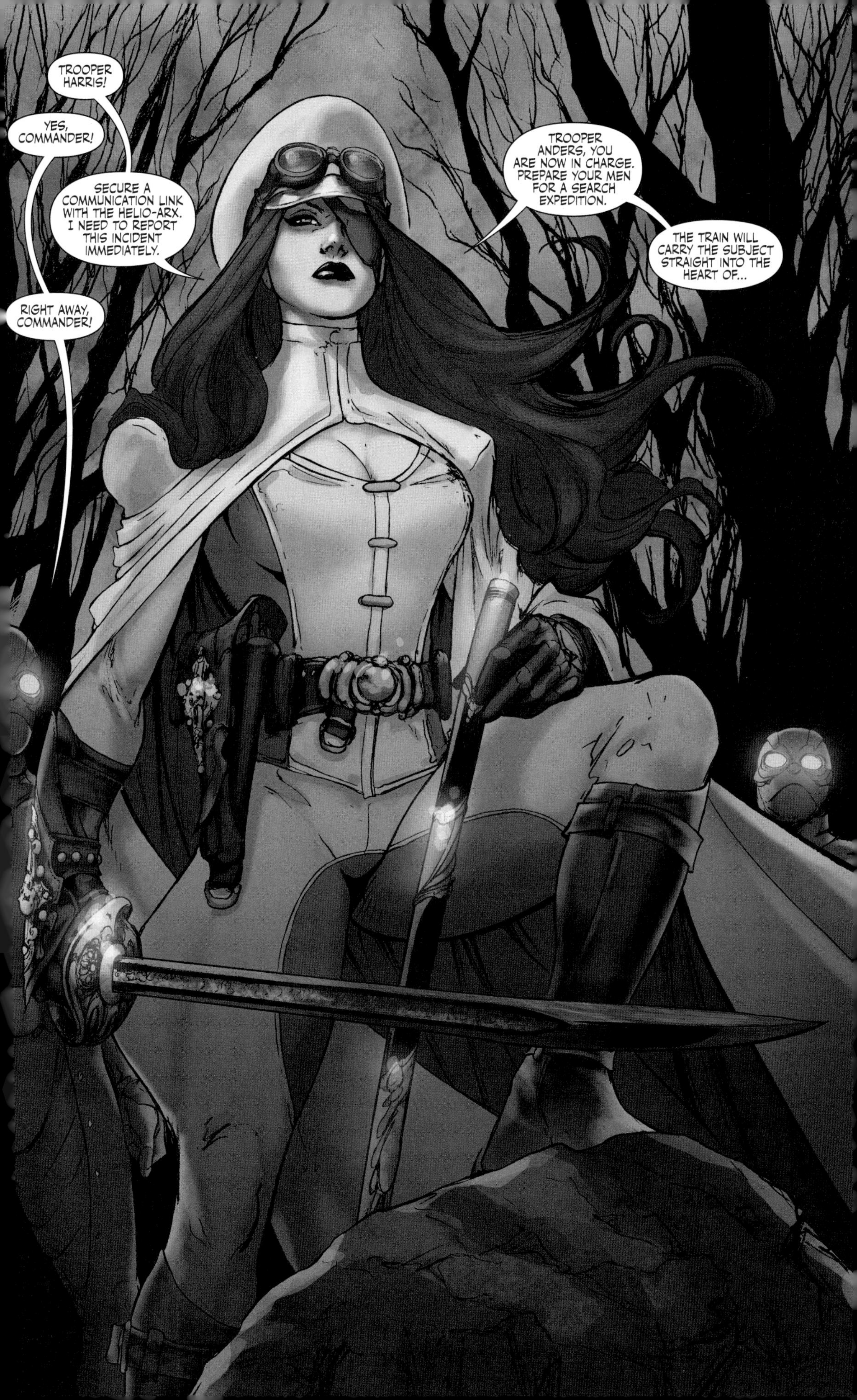
TROOPER HARRIS!
YES, COMMANDER!
SECURE A COMMUNICATION LINK WITH THE HELIO-ARX. I NEED TO REPORT THIS INCIDENT IMMEDIATELY.
RIGHT AWAY, COMMANDER!
TROOPER ANDERS, YOU ARE NOW IN CHARGE. PREPARE YOUR MEN FOR A SEARCH EXPEDITION.
THE TRAIN WILL CARRY THE SUBJECT STRAIGHT INTO THE HEART OF...

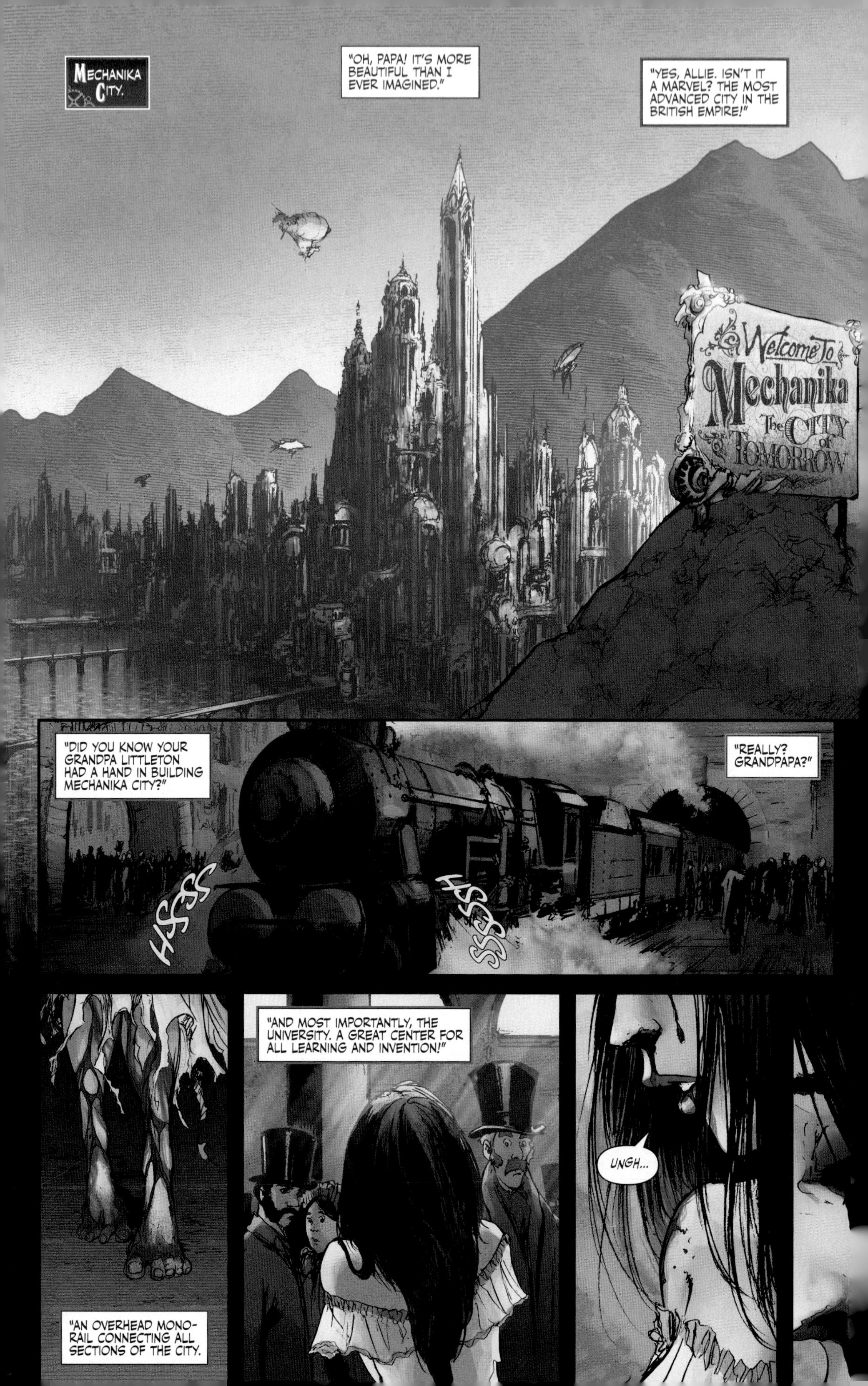
MECHANIKA CITY.
"OH, PAPA! IT'S MORE BEAUTIFUL THAN I EVER IMAGINED."
"YES, ALLIE. ISN'T IT A MARVEL? THE MOST ADVANCED CITY IN THE BRITISH EMPIRE!"
Welcome To Mechanika The CITY of TOMORROW
"DID YOU KNOW YOUR GRANDPA LITTLETON HAD A HAND IN BUILDING MECHANIKA CITY?"
"REALLY? GRANDPAPA?"
HSSSH
HSSSS
"AN OVERHEAD MONO-RAIL CONNECTING ALL SECTIONS OF THE CITY.
"AND MOST IMPORTANTLY, THE UNIVERSITY. A GREAT CENTER FOR ALL LEARNING AND INVENTION!"
UNGH...

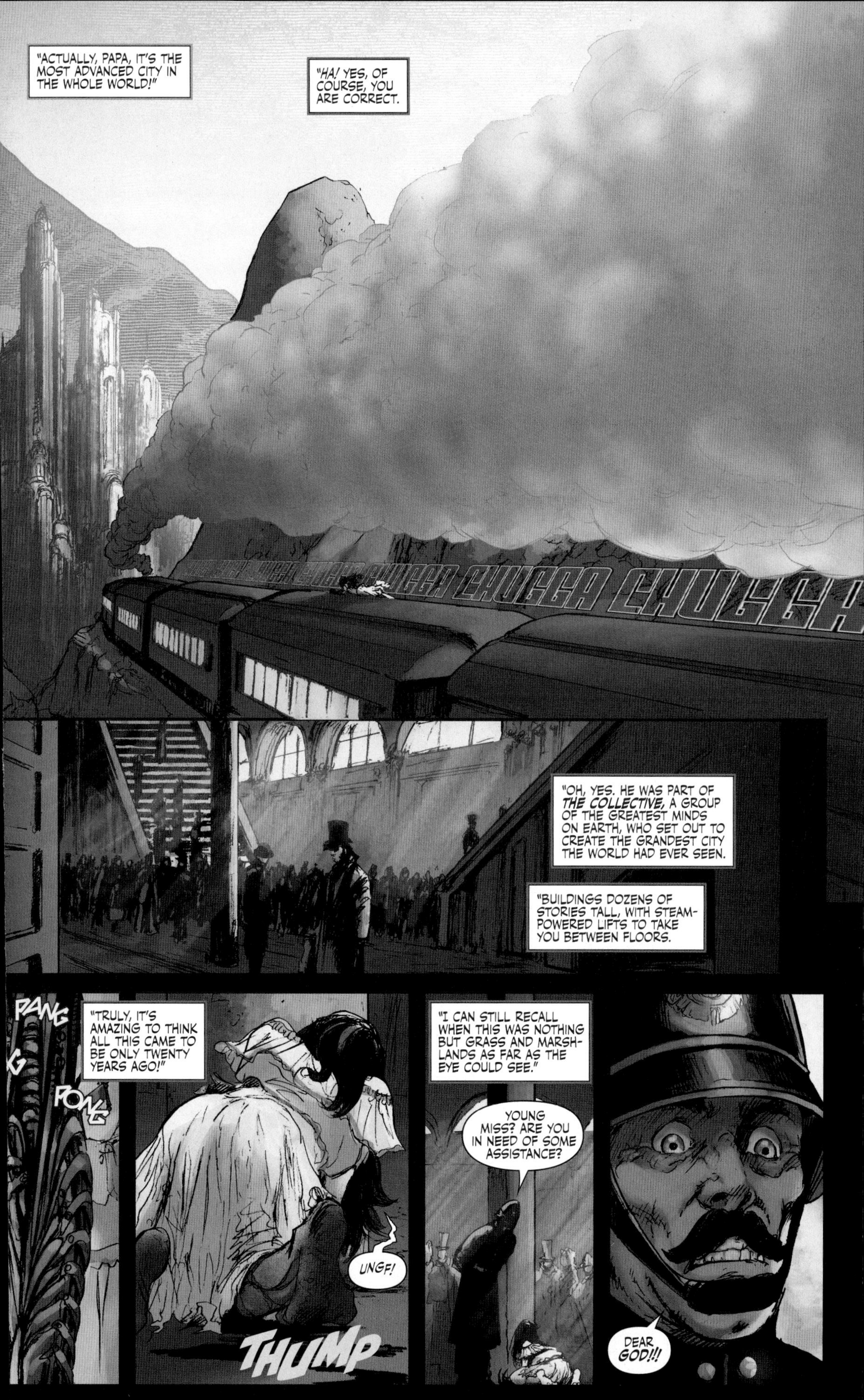
"ACTUALLY, PAPA, IT'S THE MOST ADVANCED CITY IN THE WHOLE WORLD!"
"HA! YES, OF COURSE, YOU ARE CORRECT.
CHUGGA CHUGGA
"OH, YES. HE WAS PART OF THE COLLECTIVE, A GROUP OF THE GREATEST MINDS ON EARTH, WHO SET OUT TO CREATE THE GRANDEST CITY THE WORLD HAD EVER SEEN.
"BUILDINGS DOZENS OF STORIES TALL, WITH STEAM-POWERED LIFTS TO TAKE YOU BETWEEN FLOORS.
PANG
PONG
"TRULY, IT'S AMAZING TO THINK ALL THIS CAME TO BE ONLY TWENTY YEARS AGO!"
UNGF!
THUMP
"I CAN STILL RECALL WHEN THIS WAS NOTHING BUT GRASS AND MARSH-LANDS AS FAR AS THE EYE COULD SEE."
YOUNG MISS? ARE YOU IN NEED OF SOME ASSISTANCE?
DEAR GOD!!!

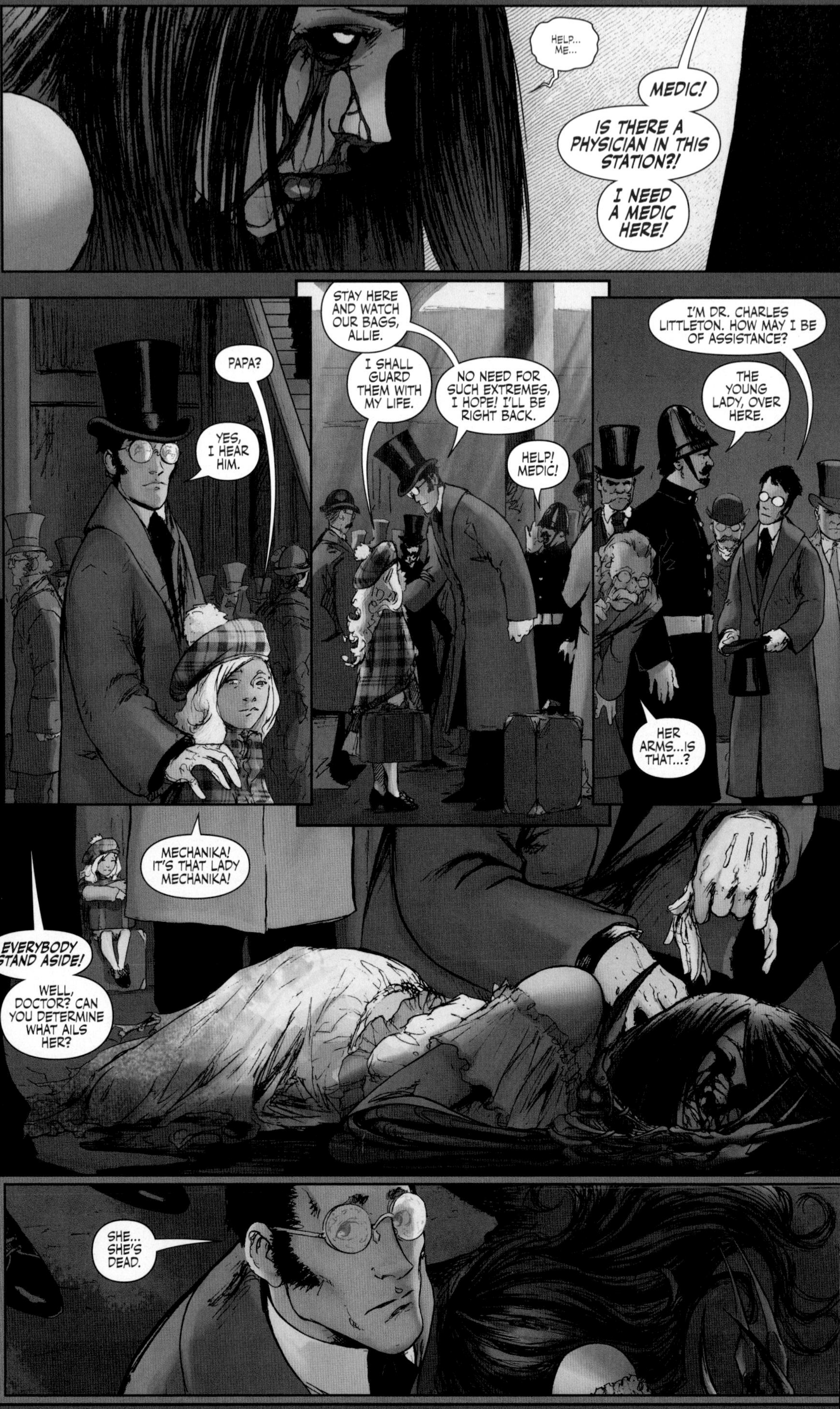
HELP... ME...
MEDIC!
IS THERE A PHYSICIAN IN THIS STATION?!
I NEED A MEDIC HERE!
PAPA?
YES, I HEAR HIM.
STAY HERE AND WATCH OUR BAGS, ALLIE.
I SHALL GUARD THEM WITH MY LIFE.
NO NEED FOR SUCH EXTREMES, I HOPE! I'LL BE RIGHT BACK.
HELP! MEDIC!
I'M DR. CHARLES LITTLETON. HOW MAY I BE OF ASSISTANCE?
THE YOUNG LADY, OVER HERE.
HER ARMS...IS THAT...?
MECHANIKA! IT'S THAT LADY MECHANIKA!
EVERYBODY STAND ASIDE!
WELL, DOCTOR? CAN YOU DETERMINE WHAT AILS HER?
SHE... SHE'S DEAD.

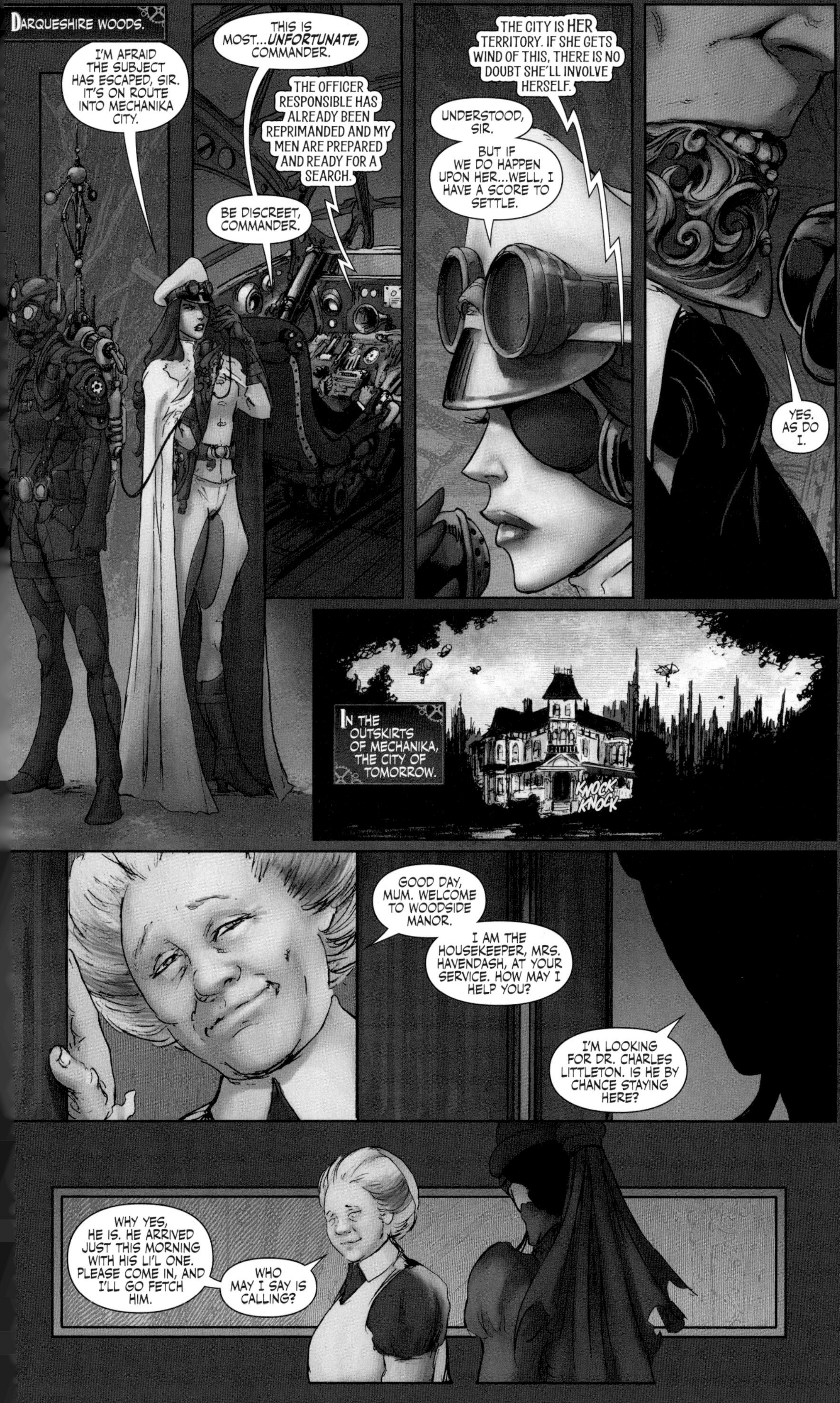
DARQUESHIRE WOODS.
I'M AFRAID THE SUBJECT HAS ESCAPED, SIR. IT'S ON ROUTE INTO MECHANIKA CITY.
THIS IS MOST...UNFORTUNATE, COMMANDER.
THE OFFICER RESPONSIBLE HAS ALREADY BEEN REPRIMANDED AND MY MEN ARE PREPARED AND READY FOR A SEARCH.
BE DISCREET, COMMANDER.
THE CITY IS HER TERRITORY. IF SHE GETS WIND OF THIS, THERE IS NO DOUBT SHE'LL INVOLVE HERSELF.
UNDERSTOOD, SIR.
BUT IF WE DO HAPPEN UPON HER...WELL, I HAVE A SCORE TO SETTLE.
YES. AS DO I.
IN THE OUTSKIRTS OF MECHANIKA, THE CITY OF TOMORROW.
KNOCK KNOCK
GOOD DAY, MUM. WELCOME TO WOODSIDE MANOR.
I AM THE HOUSEKEEPER, MRS. HAVENDASH, AT YOUR SERVICE. HOW MAY I HELP YOU?
I'M LOOKING FOR DR. CHARLES LITTLETON. IS HE BY CHANCE STAYING HERE?
WHY YES, HE IS. HE ARRIVED JUST THIS MORNING WITH HIS LI'L ONE. PLEASE COME IN, AND I'LL GO FETCH HIM.
WHO MAY I SAY IS CALLING?

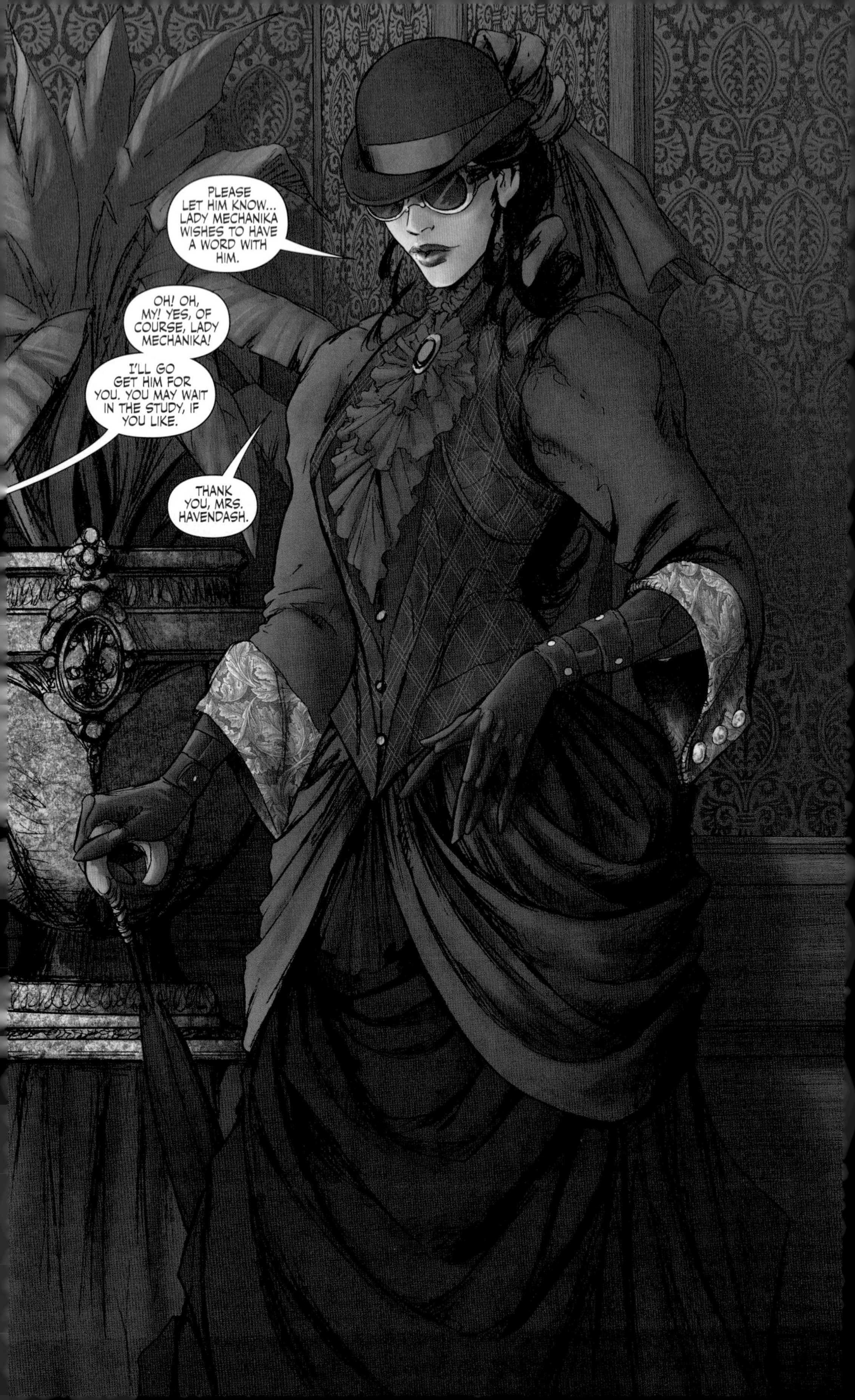
PLEASE LET HIM KNOW... LADY MECHANIKA WISHES TO HAVE A WORD WITH HIM.
OH! OH, MY! YES, OF COURSE, LADY MECHANIKA!
I'LL GO GET HIM FOR YOU. YOU MAY WAIT IN THE STUDY, IF YOU LIKE.
THANK YOU, MRS. HAVENDASH.

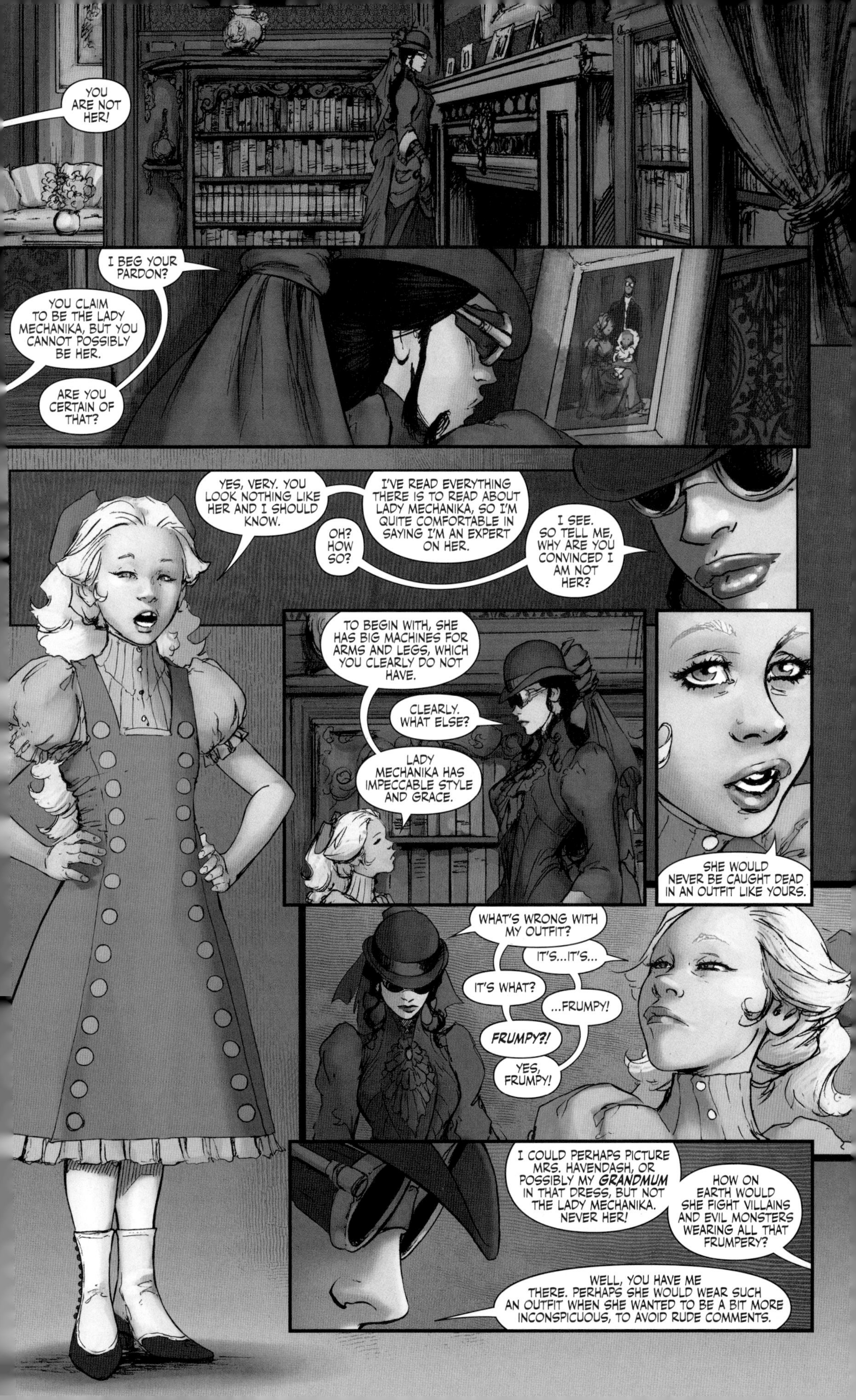
YOU ARE NOT HER!
I BEG YOUR PARDON?
YOU CLAIM TO BE THE LADY MECHANIKA, BUT YOU CANNOT POSSIBLY BE HER.
ARE YOU CERTAIN OF THAT?
YES, VERY. YOU LOOK NOTHING LIKE HER AND I SHOULD KNOW.
OH? HOW SO?
I'VE READ EVERYTHING THERE IS TO READ ABOUT LADY MECHANIKA, SO I'M QUITE COMFORTABLE IN SAYING I'M AN EXPERT ON HER.
I SEE. SO TELL ME, WHY ARE YOU CONVINCED I AM NOT HER?
TO BEGIN WITH, SHE HAS BIG MACHINES FOR ARMS AND LEGS, WHICH YOU CLEARLY DO NOT HAVE.
CLEARLY. WHAT ELSE?
LADY MECHANIKA HAS IMPECCABLE STYLE AND GRACE.
SHE WOULD NEVER BE CAUGHT DEAD IN AN OUTFIT LIKE YOURS.
WHAT'S WRONG WITH MY OUTFIT?
IT'S...IT'S...
IT'S WHAT?
...FRUMPY!
FRUMPY?!
YES, FRUMPY!
I COULD PERHAPS PICTURE MRS. HAVENDASH, OR POSSIBLY MY GRANDMUM IN THAT DRESS, BUT NOT THE LADY MECHANIKA. NEVER HER!
HOW ON EARTH WOULD SHE FIGHT VILLAINS AND EVIL MONSTERS WEARING ALL THAT FRUMPERY?
WELL, YOU HAVE ME THERE. PERHAPS SHE WOULD WEAR SUCH AN OUTFIT WHEN SHE WANTED TO BE A BIT MORE INCONSPICUOUS, TO AVOID RUDE COMMENTS.

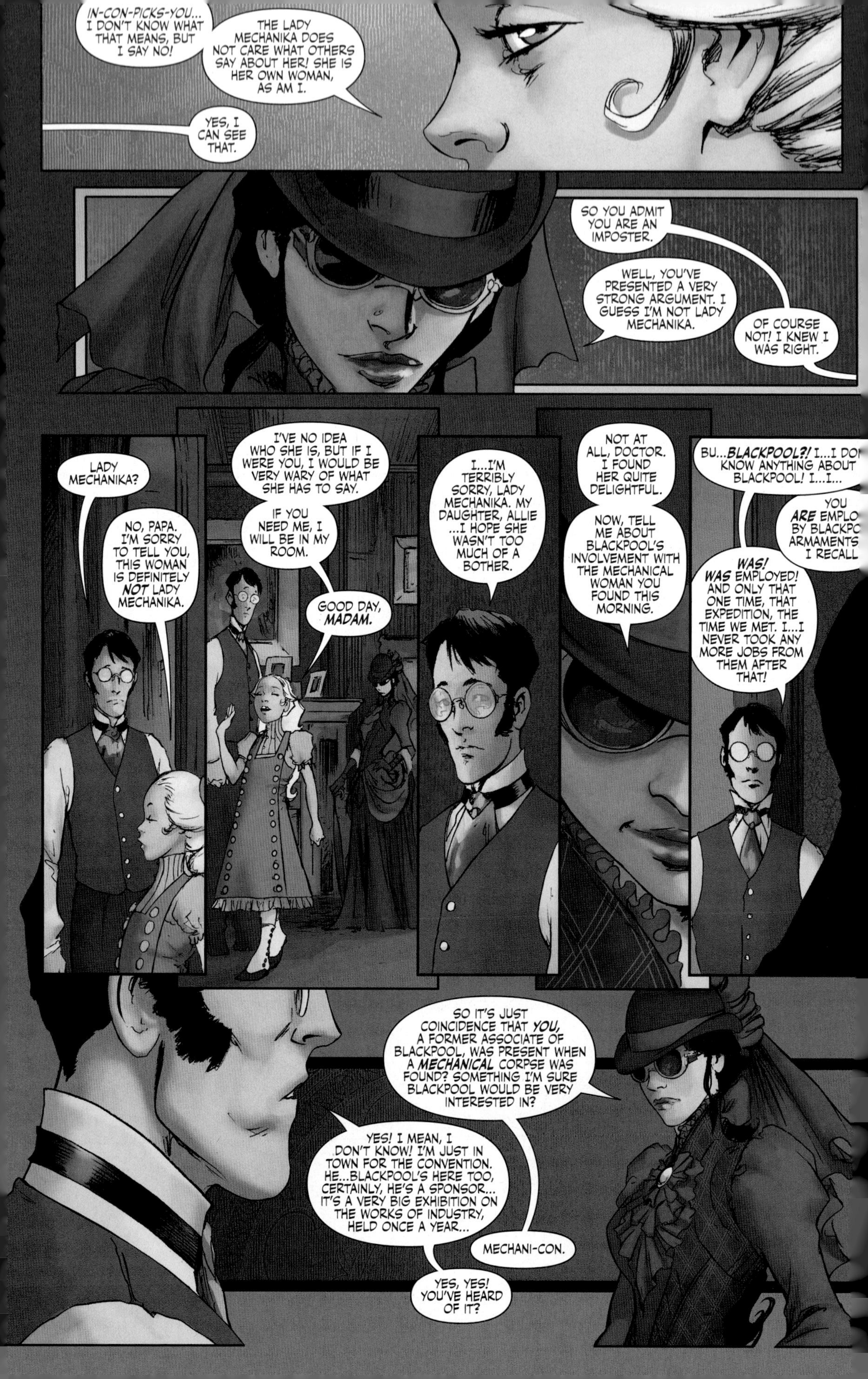
IN-CON-PICKS-YOU... I DON'T KNOW WHAT THAT MEANS, BUT I SAY NO!
THE LADY MECHANIKA DOES NOT CARE WHAT OTHERS SAY ABOUT HER! SHE IS HER OWN WOMAN, AS AM I.
YES, I CAN SEE THAT.
SO YOU ADMIT YOU ARE AN IMPOSTER.
WELL, YOU'VE PRESENTED A VERY STRONG ARGUMENT. I GUESS I'M NOT LADY MECHANIKA.
OF COURSE NOT! I KNEW I WAS RIGHT.
LADY MECHANIKA?
NO, PAPA. I'M SORRY TO TELL YOU, THIS WOMAN IS DEFINITELY NOT LADY MECHANIKA.
I'VE NO IDEA WHO SHE IS, BUT IF I WERE YOU, I WOULD BE VERY WARY OF WHAT SHE HAS TO SAY.
IF YOU NEED ME, I WILL BE IN MY ROOM.
GOOD DAY, MADAM.
I...I'M TERRIBLY SORRY, LADY MECHANIKA. MY DAUGHTER, ALLIE ...I HOPE SHE WASN'T TOO MUCH OF A BOTHER.
NOT AT ALL, DOCTOR. I FOUND HER QUITE DELIGHTFUL.
NOW, TELL ME ABOUT BLACKPOOL'S INVOLVEMENT WITH THE MECHANICAL WOMAN YOU FOUND THIS MORNING.
WAS! WAS EMPLOYED! AND ONLY THAT ONE TIME, THAT EXPEDITION, THE TIME WE MET. I...I NEVER TOOK ANY MORE JOBS FROM THEM AFTER THAT!
SO IT'S JUST COINCIDENCE THAT YOU, A FORMER ASSOCIATE OF BLACKPOOL, WAS PRESENT WHEN A MECHANICAL CORPSE WAS FOUND? SOMETHING I'M SURE BLACKPOOL WOULD BE VERY INTERESTED IN?
YES! I MEAN, I DON'T KNOW! I'M JUST IN TOWN FOR THE CONVENTION. HE...BLACKPOOL'S HERE TOO, CERTAINLY, HE'S A SPONSOR... IT'S A VERY BIG EXHIBITION ON THE WORKS OF INDUSTRY, HELD ONCE A YEAR...
MECHANI-CON.
YES, YES! YOU'VE HEARD OF IT?

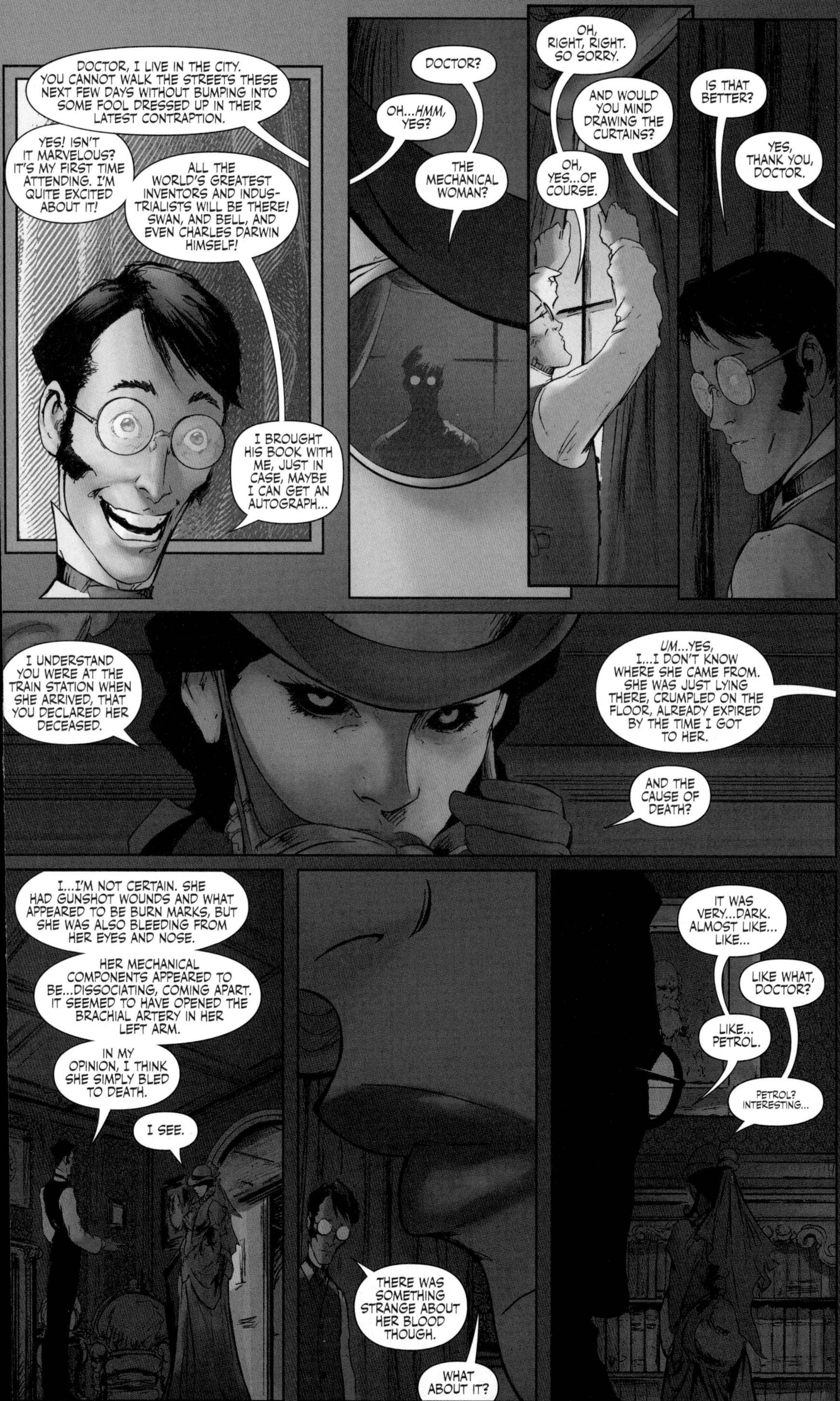
DOCTOR, I LIVE IN THE CITY. YOU CANNOT WALK THE STREETS THESE NEXT FEW DAYS WITHOUT BUMPING INTO SOME FOOL DRESSED UP IN THEIR LATEST CONTRAPTION.
YES! ISN'T IT MARVELOUS? IT'S MY FIRST TIME ATTENDING. I'M QUITE EXCITED ABOUT IT!
ALL THE WORLD'S GREATEST INVENTORS AND INDUSTRIALISTS WILL BE THERE! SWAN, AND BELL, AND EVEN CHARLES DARWIN HIMSELF!
I BROUGHT HIS BOOK WITH ME, JUST IN CASE, MAYBE I CAN GET AN AUTOGRAPH...
DOCTOR?
OH...*HMM*, YES?
THE MECHANICAL WOMAN?
OH, RIGHT, RIGHT. SO SORRY.
AND WOULD YOU MIND DRAWING THE CURTAINS?
OH, YES...OF COURSE.
IS THAT BETTER?
YES, THANK YOU, DOCTOR.
I UNDERSTAND YOU WERE AT THE TRAIN STATION WHEN SHE ARRIVED, THAT YOU DECLARED HER DECEASED.
*UM*...YES, I...I DON'T KNOW WHERE SHE CAME FROM. SHE WAS JUST LYING THERE, CRUMPLED ON THE FLOOR, ALREADY EXPIRED BY THE TIME I GOT TO HER.
AND THE CAUSE OF DEATH?
I...I'M NOT CERTAIN. SHE HAD GUNSHOT WOUNDS AND WHAT APPEARED TO BE BURN MARKS, BUT SHE WAS ALSO BLEEDING FROM HER EYES AND NOSE.
HER MECHANICAL COMPONENTS APPEARED TO BE...DISSOCIATING, COMING APART. IT SEEMED TO HAVE OPENED THE BRACHIAL ARTERY IN HER LEFT ARM.
IN MY OPINION, I THINK SHE SIMPLY BLED TO DEATH.
I SEE.
THERE WAS SOMETHING STRANGE ABOUT HER BLOOD THOUGH.
WHAT ABOUT IT?
IT WAS VERY...DARK. ALMOST LIKE... LIKE...
LIKE WHAT, DOCTOR?
LIKE... PETROL.
PETROL? INTERESTING...

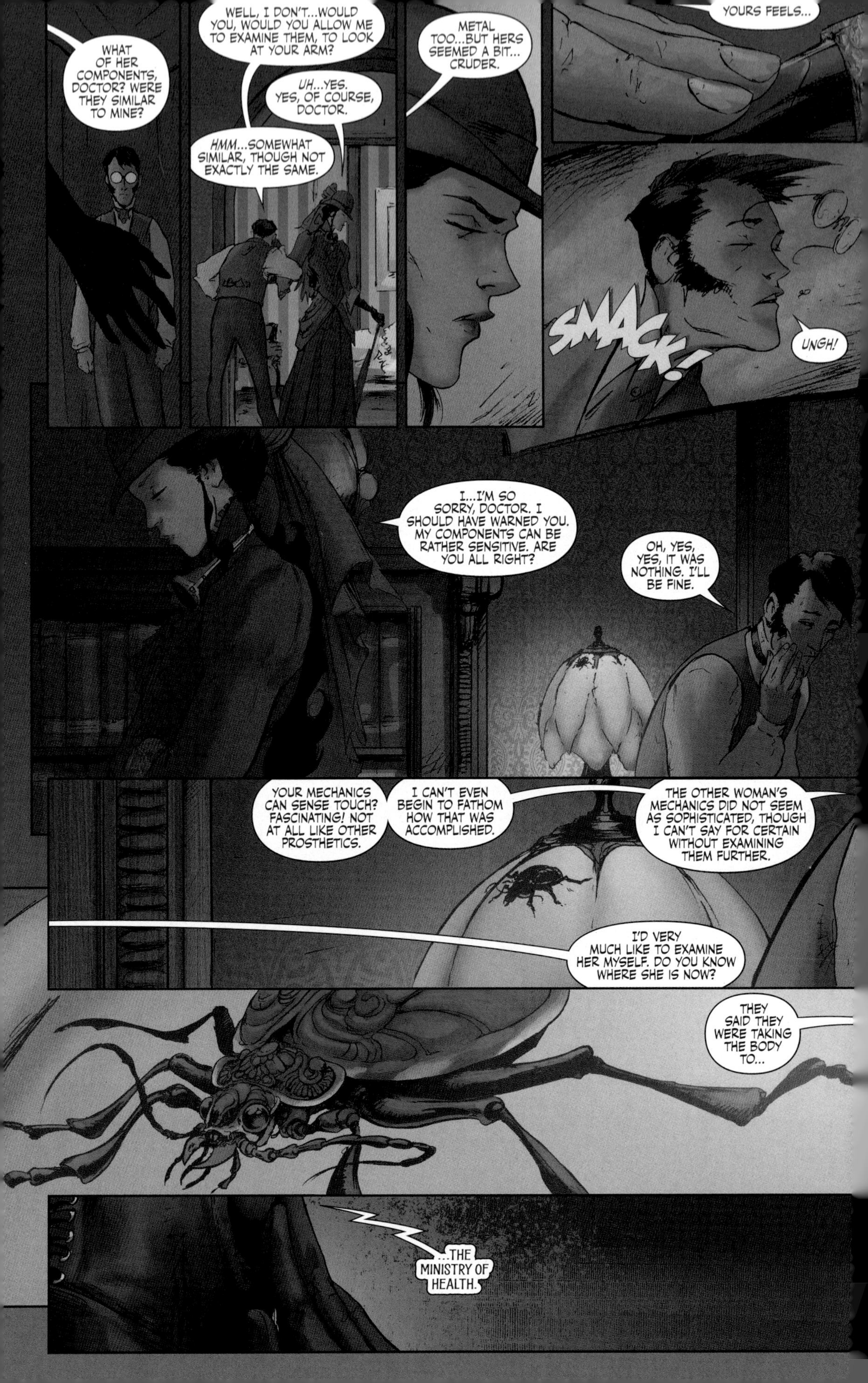
WHAT OF HER COMPONENTS, DOCTOR? WERE THEY SIMILAR TO MINE?
WELL, I DON'T...WOULD YOU, WOULD YOU ALLOW ME TO EXAMINE THEM, TO LOOK AT YOUR ARM?
HMM...SOMEWHAT SIMILAR, THOUGH NOT EXACTLY THE SAME.
UH...YES. YES, OF COURSE, DOCTOR.
METAL TOO...BUT HERS SEEMED A BIT... CRUDER.
YOURS FEELS...
SMACK!
UNGH!
I...I'M SO SORRY, DOCTOR. I SHOULD HAVE WARNED YOU. MY COMPONENTS CAN BE RATHER SENSITIVE. ARE YOU ALL RIGHT?
OH, YES, YES, IT WAS NOTHING. I'LL BE FINE.
YOUR MECHANICS CAN SENSE TOUCH? FASCINATING! NOT AT ALL LIKE OTHER PROSTHETICS.
I CAN'T EVEN BEGIN TO FATHOM HOW THAT WAS ACCOMPLISHED.
THE OTHER WOMAN'S MECHANICS DID NOT SEEM AS SOPHISTICATED, THOUGH I CAN'T SAY FOR CERTAIN WITHOUT EXAMINING THEM FURTHER.
I'D VERY MUCH LIKE TO EXAMINE HER MYSELF. DO YOU KNOW WHERE SHE IS NOW?
THEY SAID THEY WERE TAKING THE BODY TO...
...THE MINISTRY OF HEALTH.

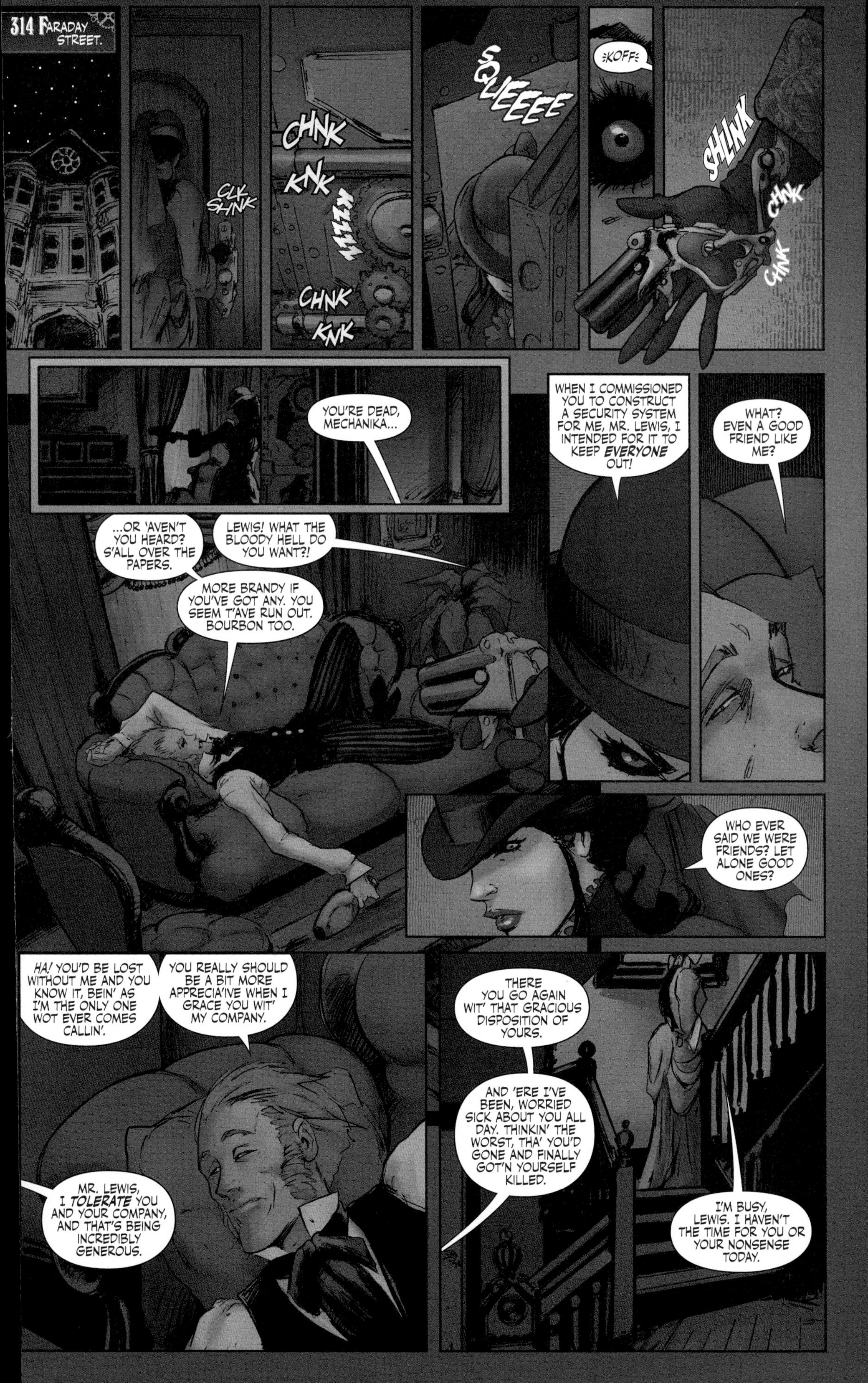

314 FARADAY STREET.
CLK SHNK
CHNK
KNK
KZZZZ
CHNK
KNK
SQUEEEEE
KOFF
SHLNK
CHNK
CHNK
YOU'RE DEAD, MECHANIKA...
...OR 'AVEN'T YOU HEARD? S'ALL OVER THE PAPERS.
LEWIS! WHAT THE BLOODY HELL DO YOU WANT?!
MORE BRANDY IF YOU'VE GOT ANY. YOU SEEM T'AVE RUN OUT. BOURBON TOO.
WHEN I COMMISSIONED YOU TO CONSTRUCT A SECURITY SYSTEM FOR ME, MR. LEWIS, I INTENDED FOR IT TO KEEP EVERYONE OUT!
WHAT? EVEN A GOOD FRIEND LIKE ME?
WHO EVER SAID WE WERE FRIENDS? LET ALONE GOOD ONES?
HA! YOU'D BE LOST WITHOUT ME AND YOU KNOW IT, BEIN' AS I'M THE ONLY ONE WOT EVER COMES CALLIN'.
YOU REALLY SHOULD BE A BIT MORE APPRECIA'IVE WHEN I GRACE YOU WIT' MY COMPANY.
MR. LEWIS, I TOLERATE YOU AND YOUR COMPANY, AND THAT'S BEING INCREDIBLY GENEROUS.
THERE YOU GO AGAIN WIT' THAT GRACIOUS DISPOSITION OF YOURS.
AND 'ERE I'VE BEEN, WORRIED SICK ABOUT YOU ALL DAY. THINKIN' THE WORST, THA' YOU'D GONE AND FINALLY GOT'N YOURSELF KILLED.
I'M BUSY, LEWIS. I HAVEN'T THE TIME FOR YOU OR YOUR NONSENSE TODAY.

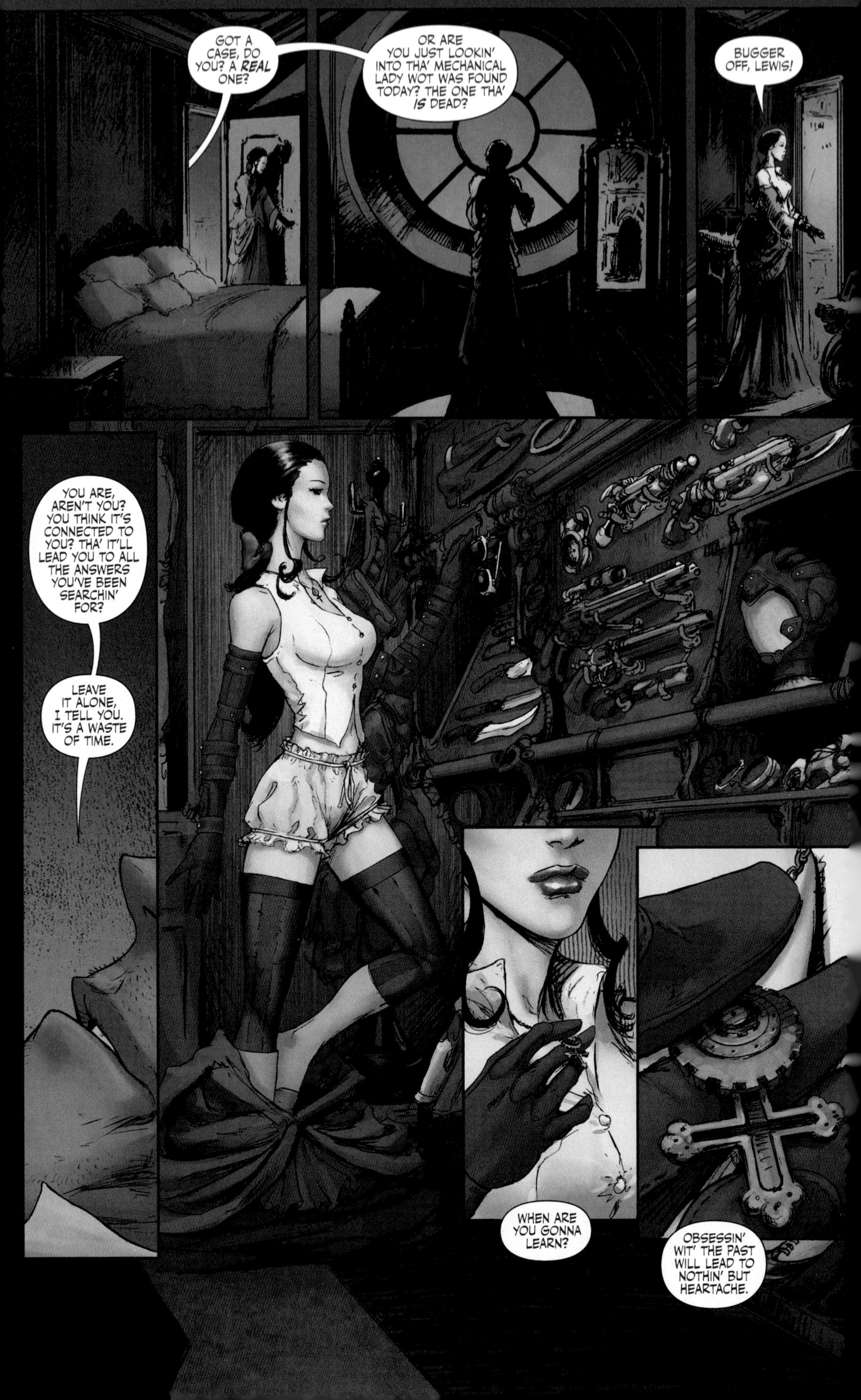
GOT A CASE, DO YOU? A REAL ONE?
OR ARE YOU JUST LOOKIN' INTO THA' MECHANICAL LADY WOT WAS FOUND TODAY? THE ONE THA' IS DEAD?
BUGGER OFF, LEWIS!
YOU ARE, AREN'T YOU? YOU THINK IT'S CONNECTED TO YOU? THA' IT'LL LEAD YOU TO ALL THE ANSWERS YOU'VE BEEN SEARCHIN' FOR?
LEAVE IT ALONE, I TELL YOU. IT'S A WASTE OF TIME.
WHEN ARE YOU GONNA LEARN?
OBSESSIN' WIT' THE PAST WILL LEAD TO NOTHIN' BUT HEARTACHE.

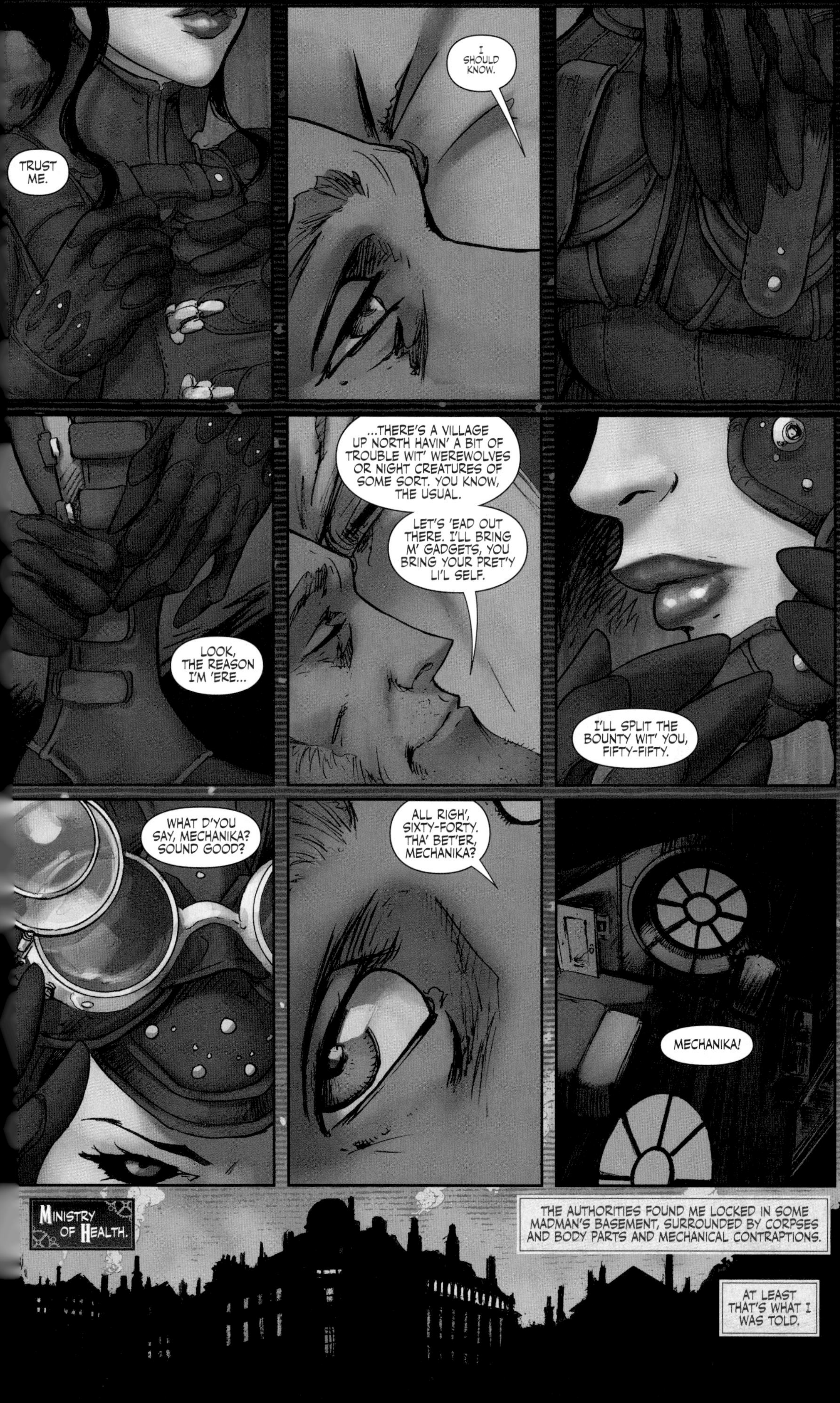
TRUST ME.
I SHOULD KNOW.
LOOK, THE REASON I'M 'ERE...
...THERE'S A VILLAGE UP NORTH HAVIN' A BIT OF TROUBLE WIT' WEREWOLVES OR NIGHT CREATURES OF SOME SORT. YOU KNOW, THE USUAL.
LET'S 'EAD OUT THERE. I'LL BRING M' GADGETS, YOU BRING YOUR PRET'Y LI'L SELF.
I'LL SPLIT THE BOUNTY WIT' YOU, FIFTY-FIFTY.
WHAT D'YOU SAY, MECHANIKA? SOUND GOOD?
ALL RIGH', SIXTY-FORTY. THA' BET'ER, MECHANIKA?
MECHANIKA!
MINISTRY OF HEALTH.
THE AUTHORITIES FOUND ME LOCKED IN SOME MADMAN'S BASEMENT, SURROUNDED BY CORPSES AND BODY PARTS AND MECHANICAL CONTRAPTIONS.
AT LEAST THAT'S WHAT I WAS TOLD.

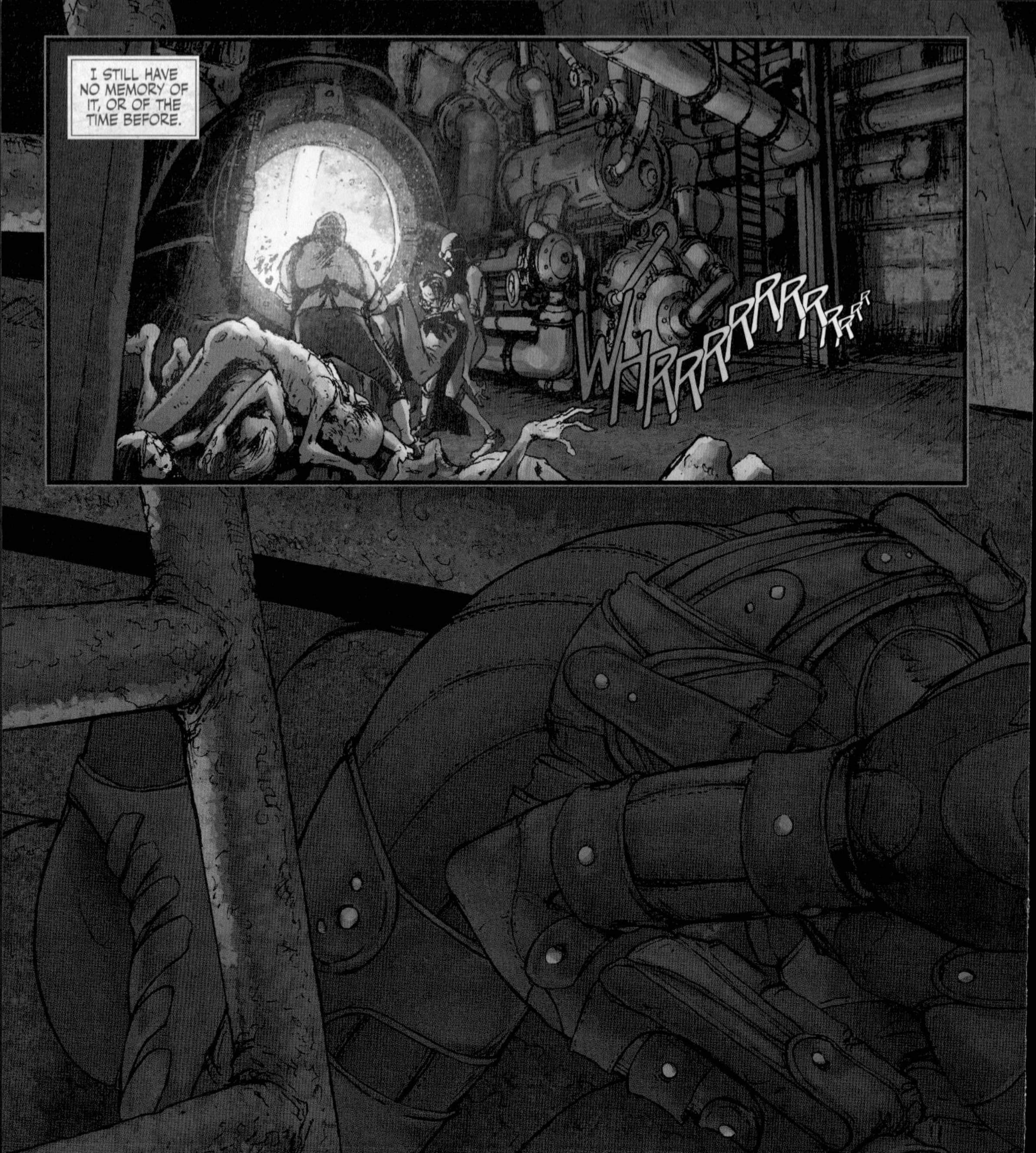
I STILL HAVE NO MEMORY OF IT, OR OF THE TIME BEFORE.
WHRRRRRRRRRRRRR

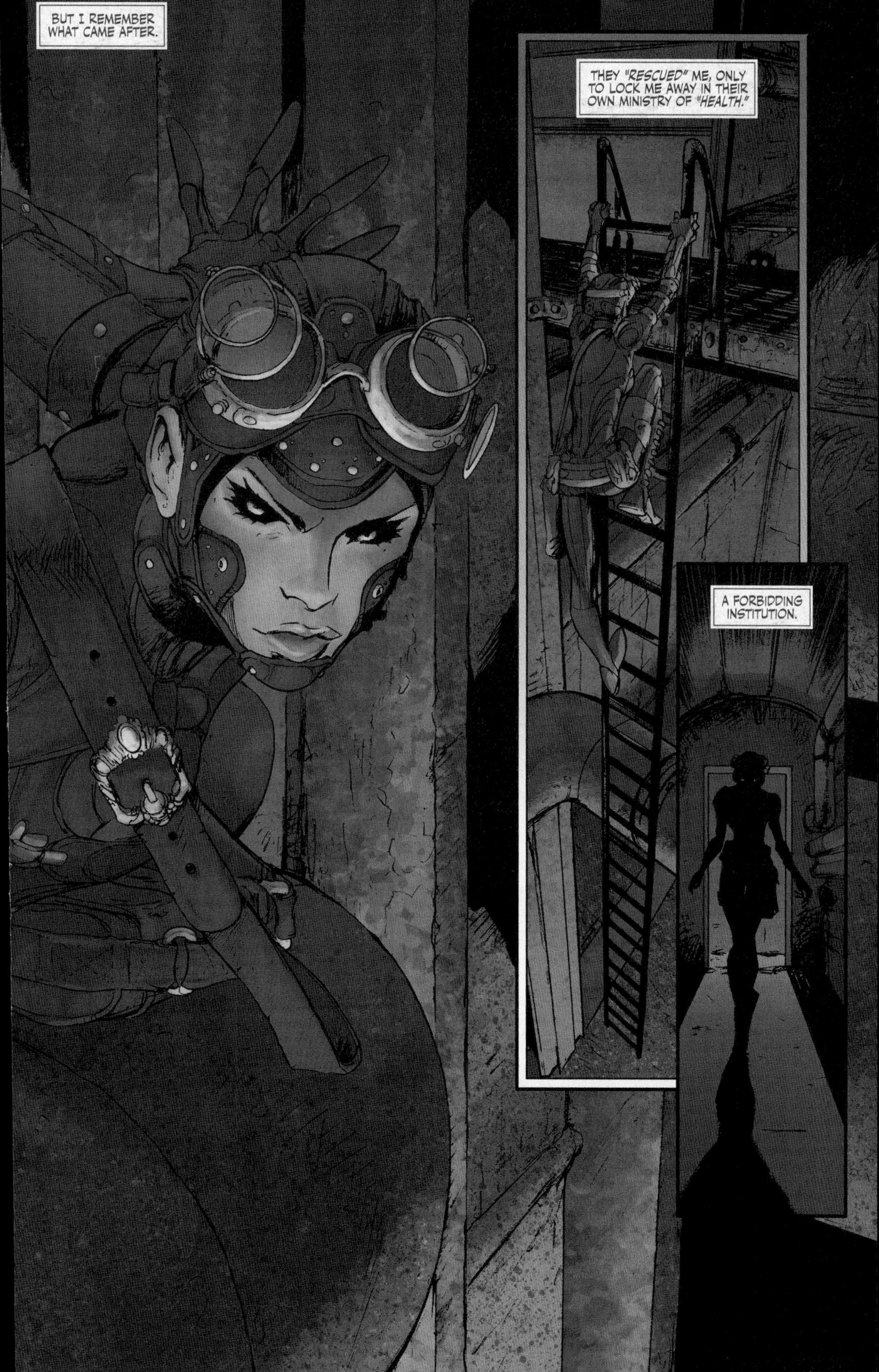
BUT I REMEMBER WHAT CAME AFTER.
THEY "RESCUED" ME, ONLY TO LOCK ME AWAY IN THEIR OWN MINISTRY OF "HEALTH."
A FORBIDDING INSTITUTION.

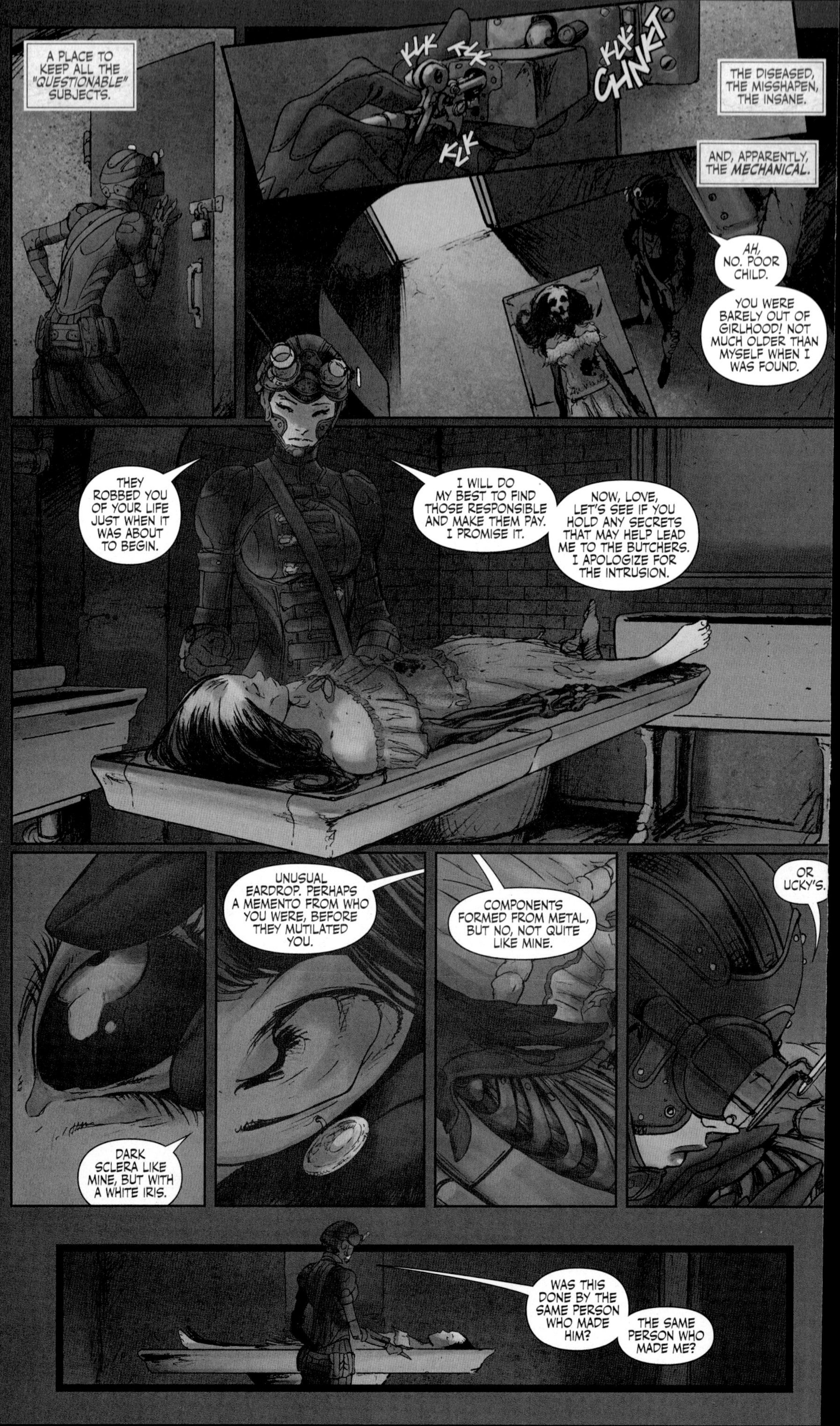
A PLACE TO KEEP ALL THE "QUESTIONABLE" SUBJECTS.
KLK KLK
KLK CHNKT
KLK
THE DISEASED, THE MISSHAPEN, THE INSANE.
AND, APPARENTLY, THE MECHANICAL.
AH, NO. POOR CHILD.
YOU WERE BARELY OUT OF GIRLHOOD! NOT MUCH OLDER THAN MYSELF WHEN I WAS FOUND.
THEY ROBBED YOU OF YOUR LIFE JUST WHEN IT WAS ABOUT TO BEGIN.
I WILL DO MY BEST TO FIND THOSE RESPONSIBLE AND MAKE THEM PAY. I PROMISE IT.
NOW, LOVE, LET'S SEE IF YOU HOLD ANY SECRETS THAT MAY HELP LEAD ME TO THE BUTCHERS. I APOLOGIZE FOR THE INTRUSION.
DARK SCLERA LIKE MINE, BUT WITH A WHITE IRIS.
UNUSUAL EARDROP. PERHAPS A MEMENTO FROM WHO YOU WERE, BEFORE THEY MUTILATED YOU.
COMPONENTS FORMED FROM METAL, BUT NO, NOT QUITE LIKE MINE.
OR UCKY'S.
WAS THIS DONE BY THE SAME PERSON WHO MADE HIM?
THE SAME PERSON WHO MADE ME?

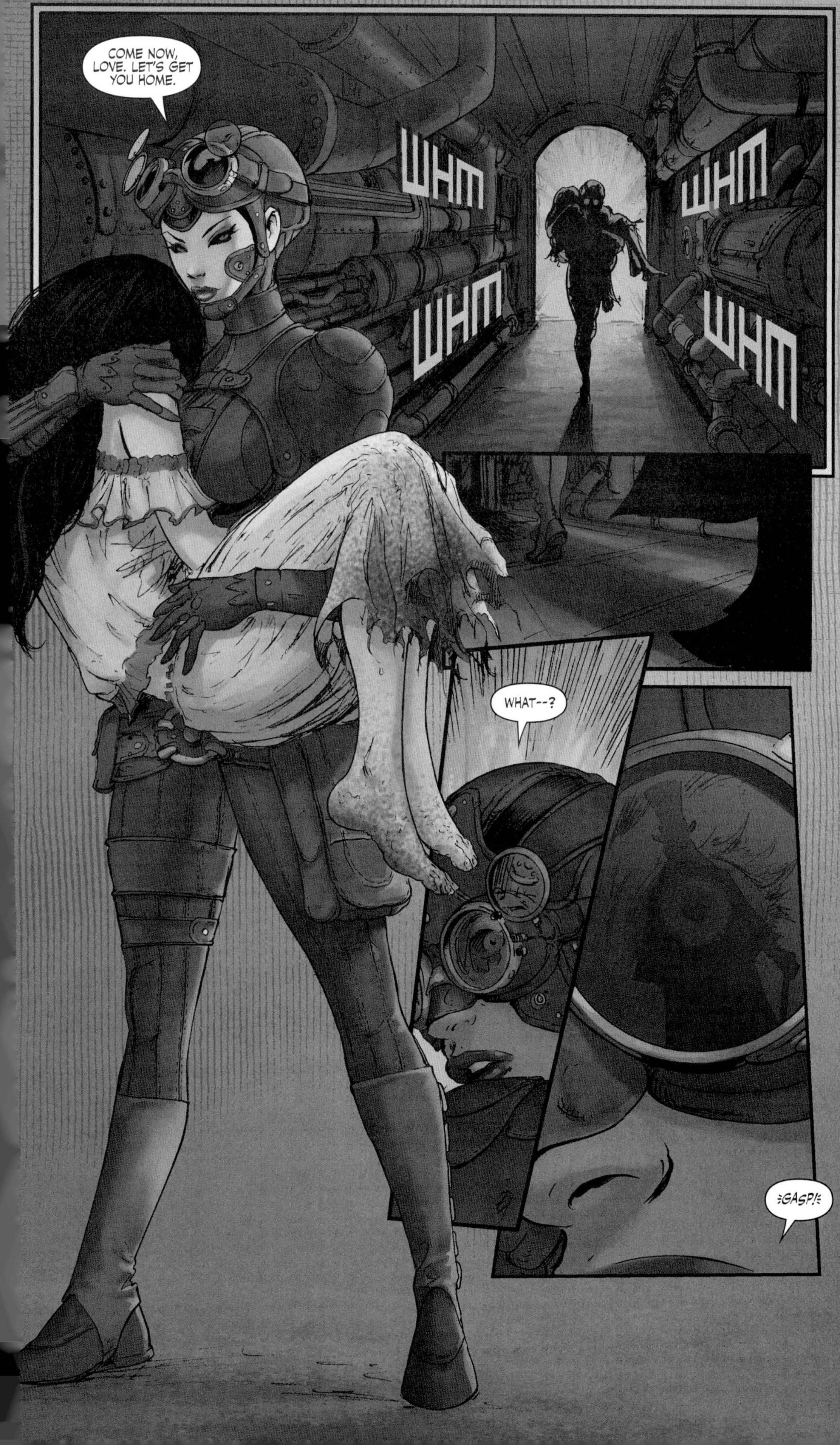
COME NOW, LOVE. LET'S GET YOU HOME.
WHM
WHM
WHM
WHM
WHAT--?
!GASP!

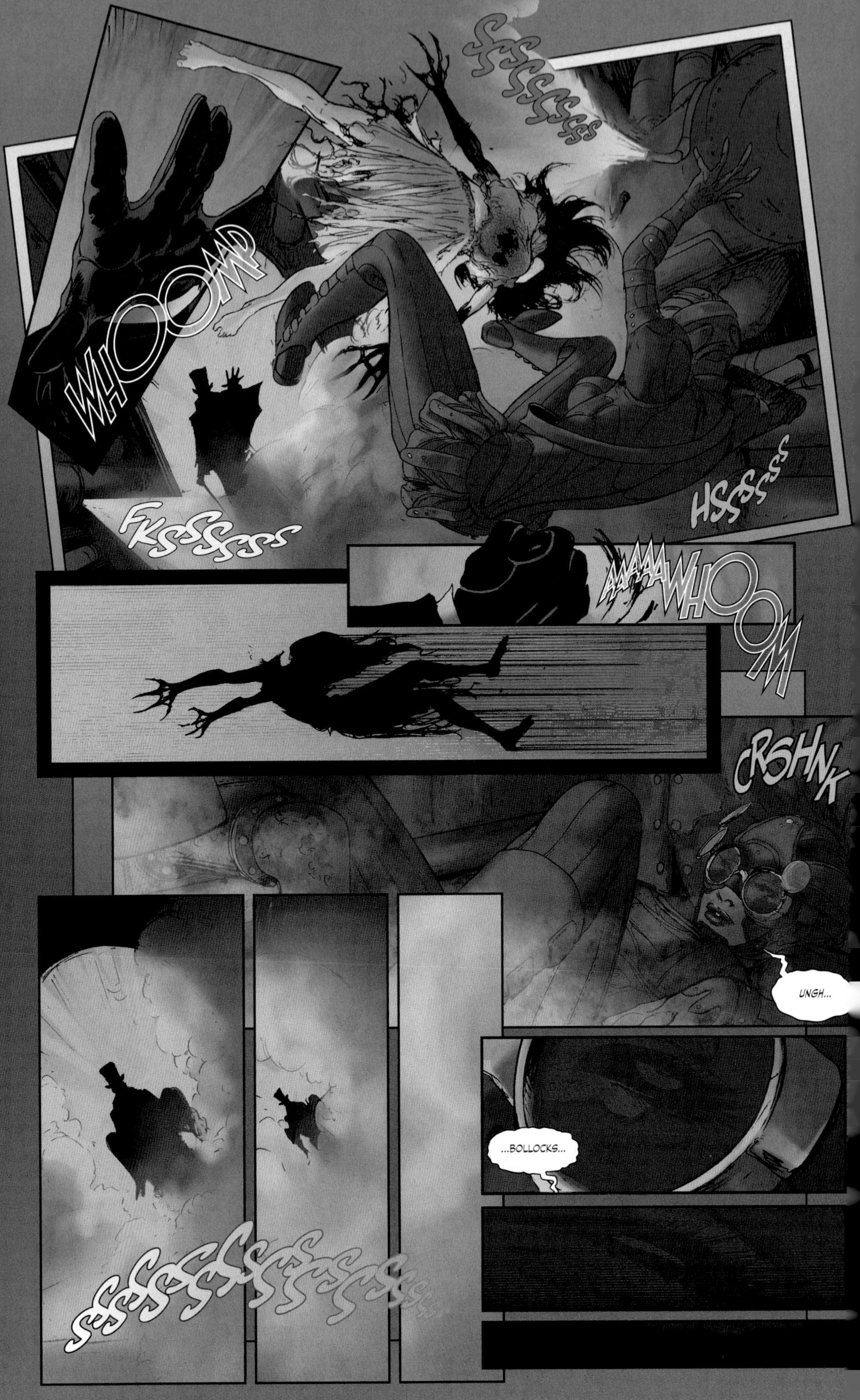
SSSSSSSSS
WHOOMP
FKSSSSSSS
HSSSSSSSH
AAAAWHOOM
CRSHNK
UNGH...
...BOLLOCKS...
SSSSSSSSSSSSSSSSSSS

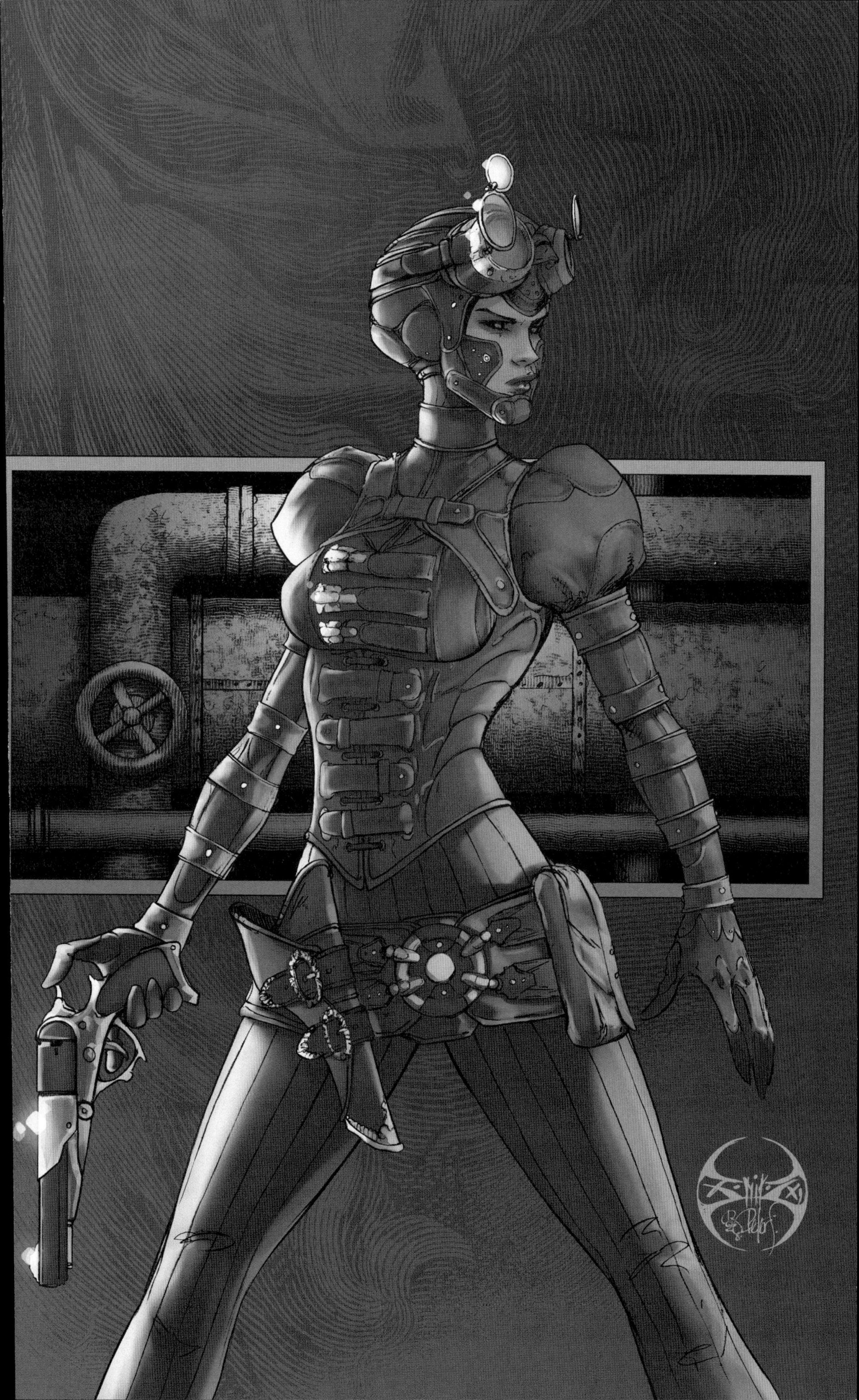

# Chapter Two

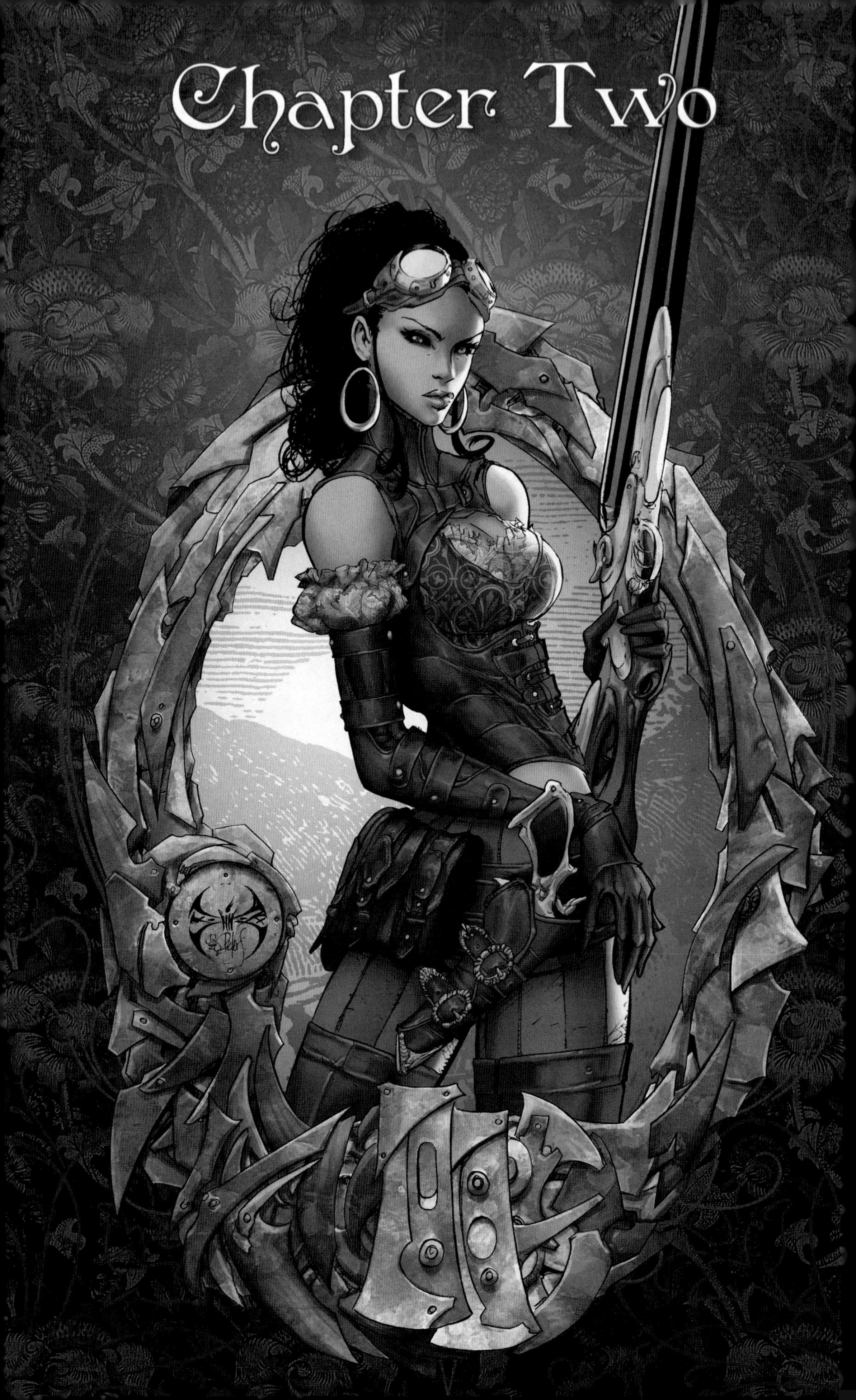

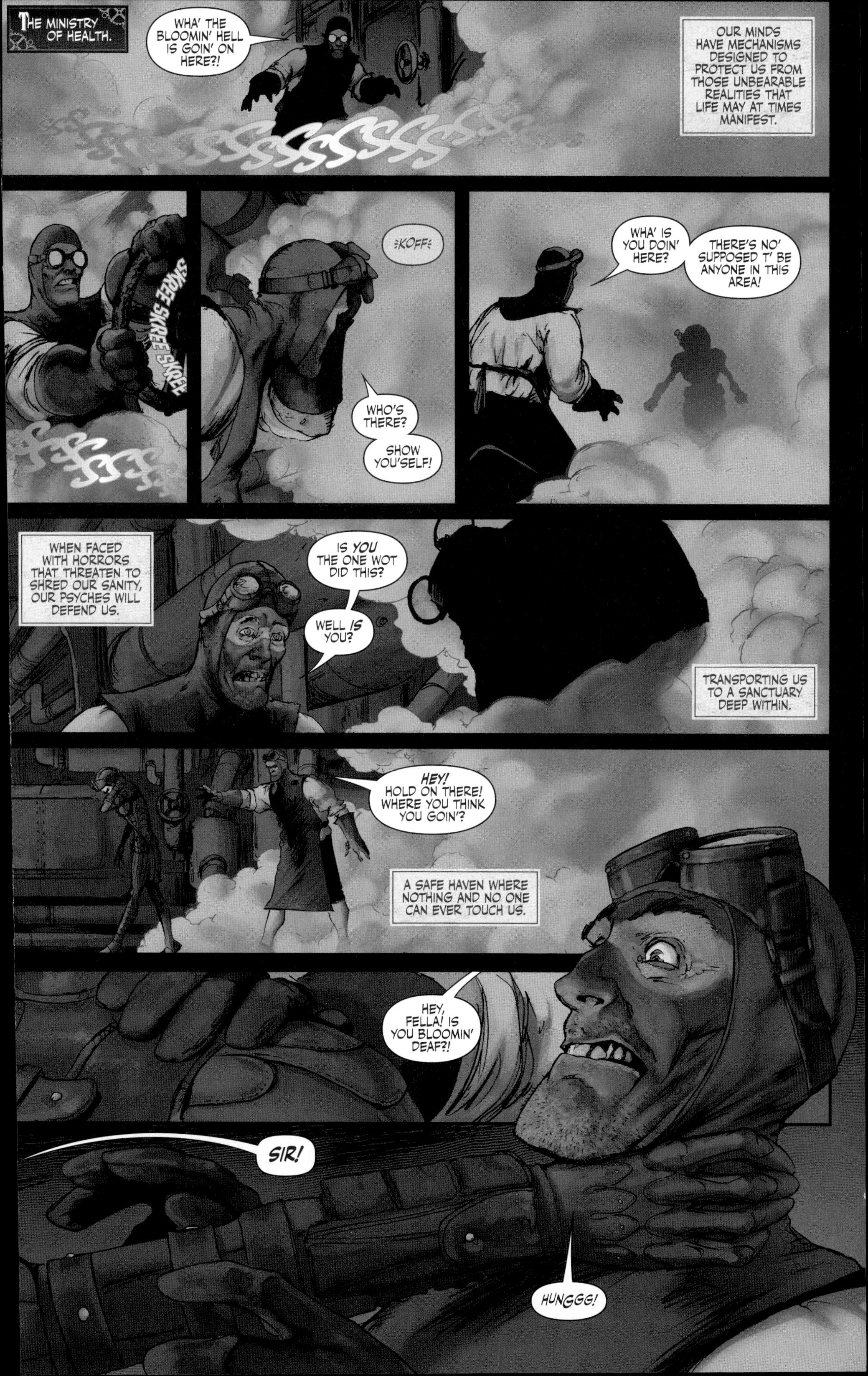
THE MINISTRY OF HEALTH.
WHA' THE BLOOMIN' HELL IS GOIN' ON HERE?!
OUR MINDS HAVE MECHANISMS DESIGNED TO PROTECT US FROM THOSE UNBEARABLE REALITIES THAT LIFE MAY AT TIMES MANIFEST.
SSSSSSSSSSSSSS
SKREE SKREE SKREE
SSSSS
KOFF
WHO'S THERE?
SHOW YOU'SELF!
WHA' IS YOU DOIN' HERE?
THERE'S NO' SUPPOSED T' BE ANYONE IN THIS AREA!
WHEN FACED WITH HORRORS THAT THREATEN TO SHRED OUR SANITY, OUR PSYCHES WILL DEFEND US.
IS YOU THE ONE WOT DID THIS?
WELL IS YOU?
TRANSPORTING US TO A SANCTUARY DEEP WITHIN.
HEY! HOLD ON THERE! WHERE YOU THINK YOU GOIN'?
A SAFE HAVEN WHERE NOTHING AND NO ONE CAN EVER TOUCH US.
HEY, FELLA! IS YOU BLOOMIN' DEAF?!
SIR!
HUNGGG!

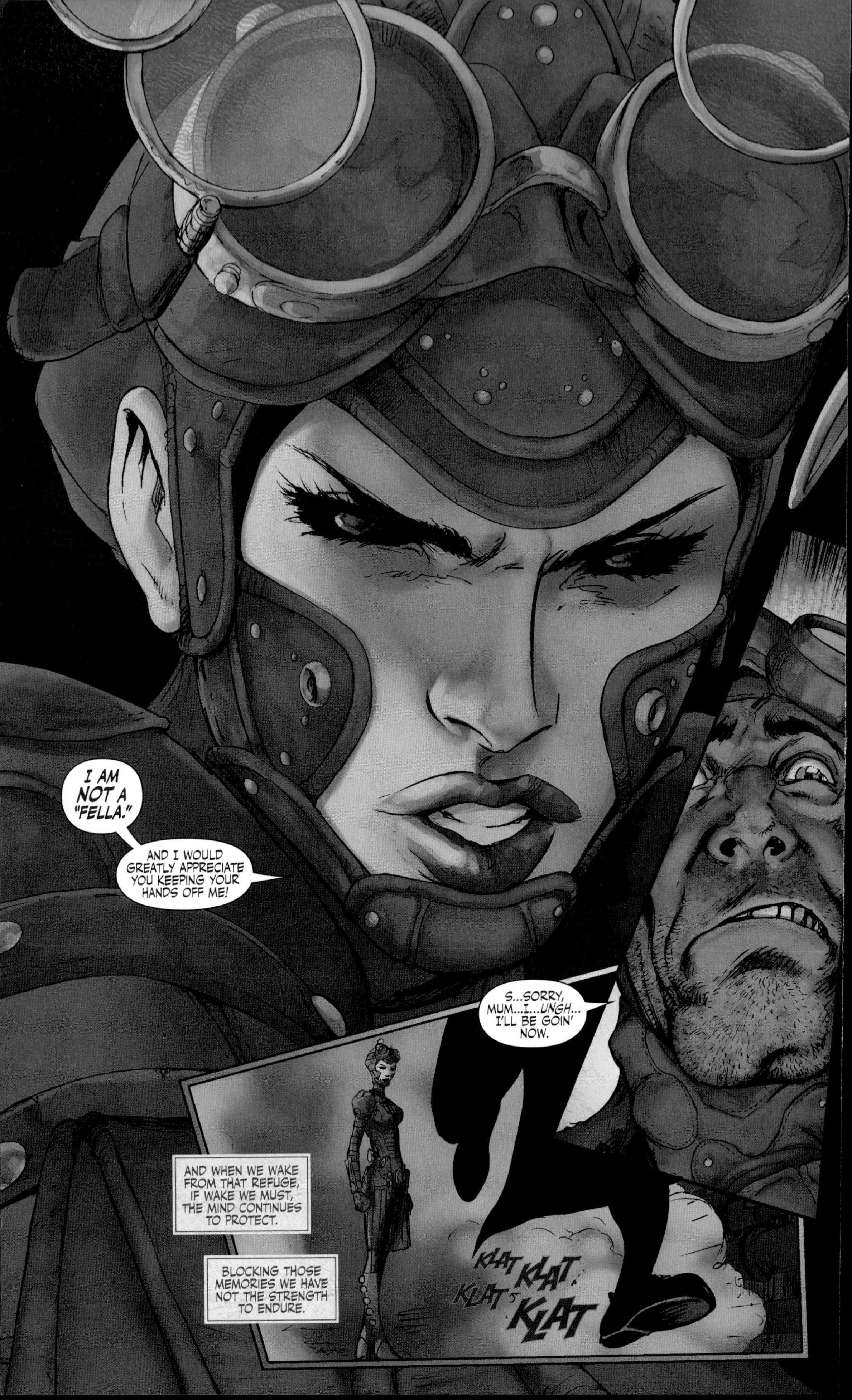
I AM NOT A "FELLA."
AND I WOULD GREATLY APPRECIATE YOU KEEPING YOUR HANDS OFF ME!
S...SORRY, MUM...I...UNGH... I'LL BE GOIN' NOW.
AND WHEN WE WAKE FROM THAT REFUGE, IF WAKE WE MUST, THE MIND CONTINUES TO PROTECT.
BLOCKING THOSE MEMORIES WE HAVE NOT THE STRENGTH TO ENDURE.
KLAT KLAT KLAT KLAT

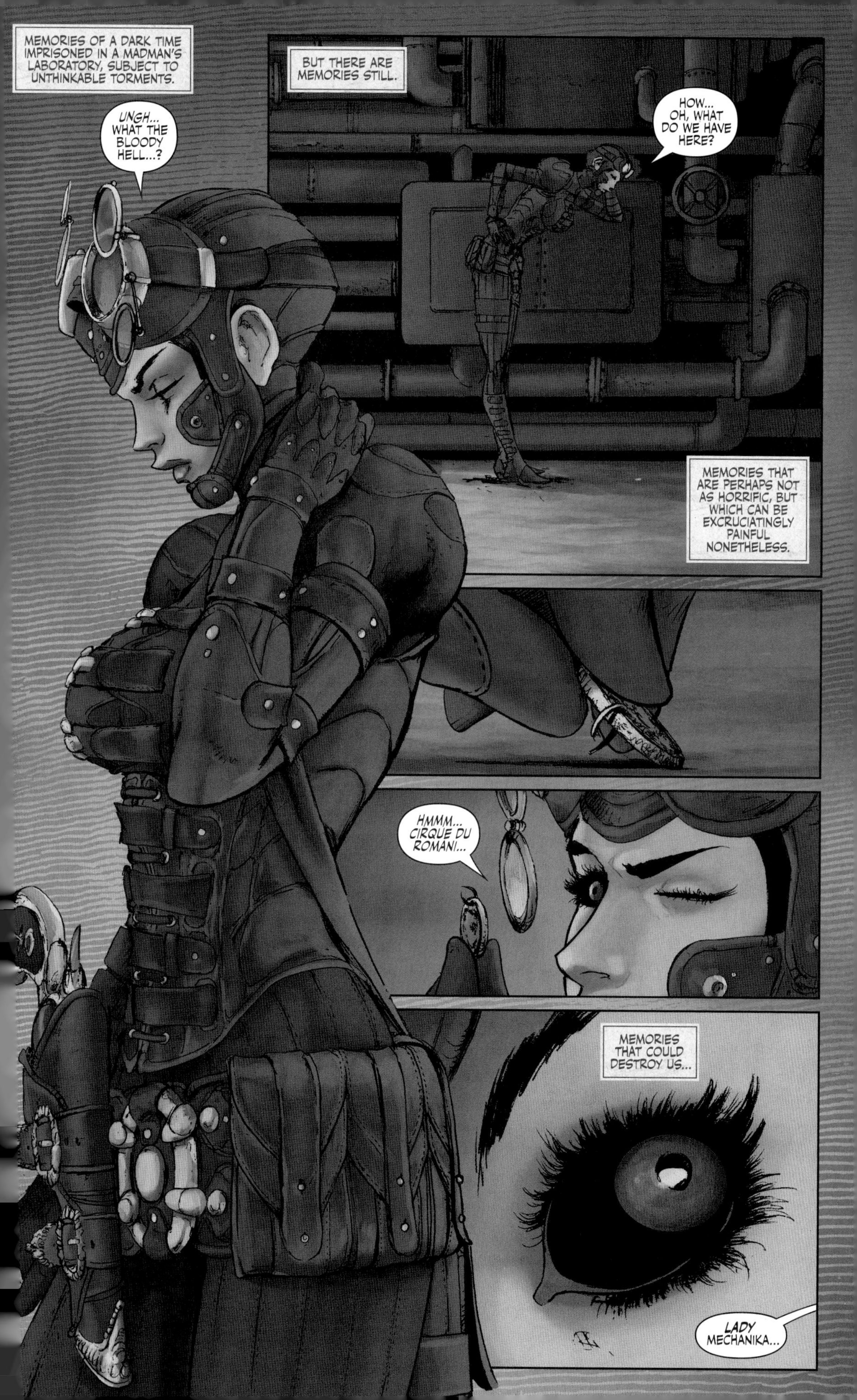
MEMORIES OF A DARK TIME IMPRISONED IN A MADMAN'S LABORATORY, SUBJECT TO UNTHINKABLE TORMENTS.
UNGH... WHAT THE BLOODY HELL...?
BUT THERE ARE MEMORIES STILL.
HOW... OH, WHAT DO WE HAVE HERE?
MEMORIES THAT ARE PERHAPS NOT AS HORRIFIC, BUT WHICH CAN BE EXCRUCIATINGLY PAINFUL NONETHELESS.
HMMM... CIRQUE DU ROMANI...
MEMORIES THAT COULD DESTROY US...
LADY MECHANIKA...

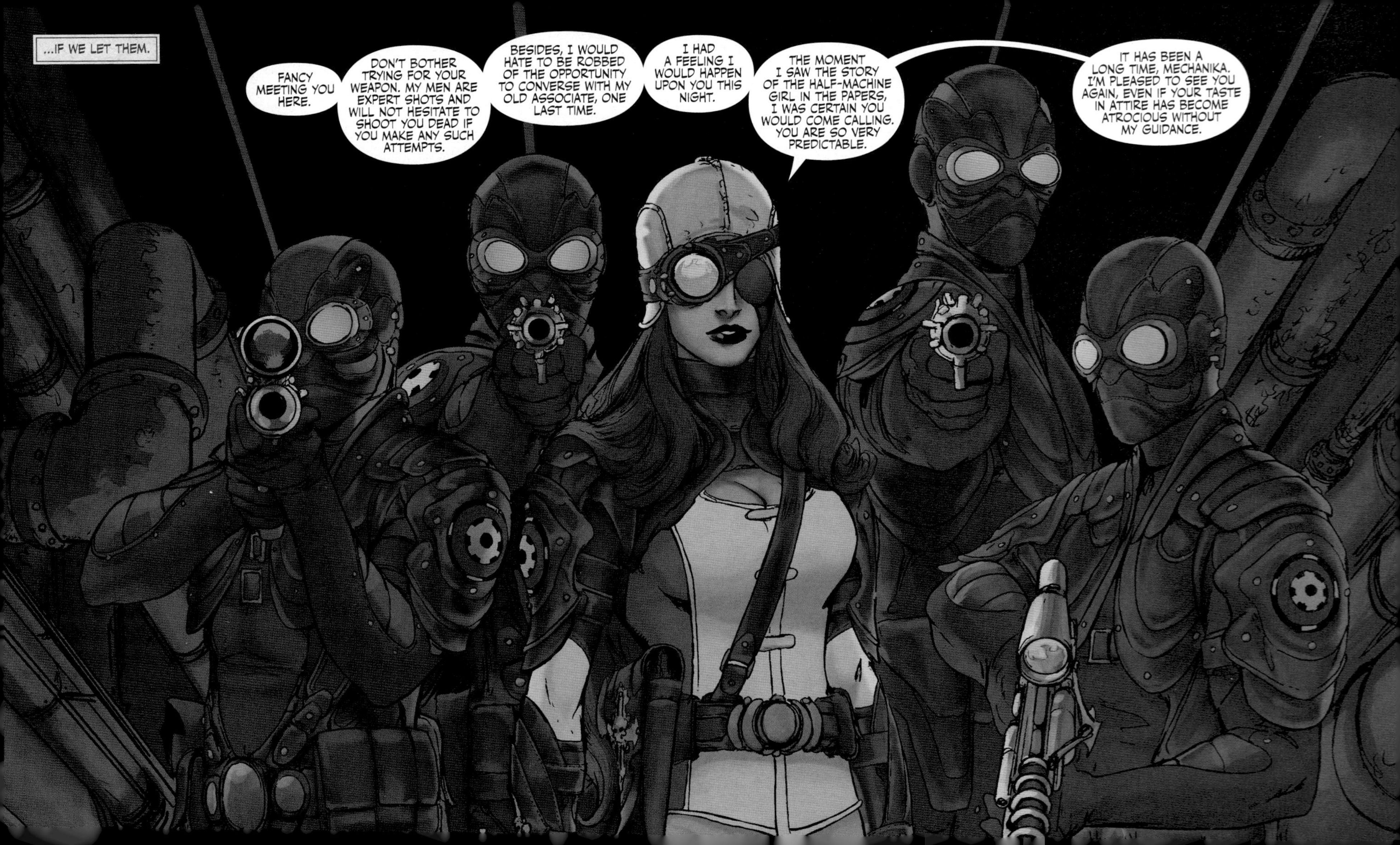
...IF WE LET THEM.
FANCY MEETING YOU HERE.
DON'T BOTHER TRYING FOR YOUR WEAPON. MY MEN ARE EXPERT SHOTS AND WILL NOT HESITATE TO SHOOT YOU DEAD IF YOU MAKE ANY SUCH ATTEMPTS.
BESIDES, I WOULD HATE TO BE ROBBED OF THE OPPORTUNITY TO CONVERSE WITH MY OLD ASSOCIATE, ONE LAST TIME.
I HAD A FEELING I WOULD HAPPEN UPON YOU THIS NIGHT.
THE MOMENT I SAW THE STORY OF THE HALF-MACHINE GIRL IN THE PAPERS, I WAS CERTAIN YOU WOULD COME CALLING. YOU ARE SO VERY PREDICTABLE.
IT HAS BEEN A LONG TIME, MECHANIKA. I'M PLEASED TO SEE YOU AGAIN, EVEN IF YOUR TASTE IN ATTIRE HAS BECOME ATROCIOUS WITHOUT MY GUIDANCE.

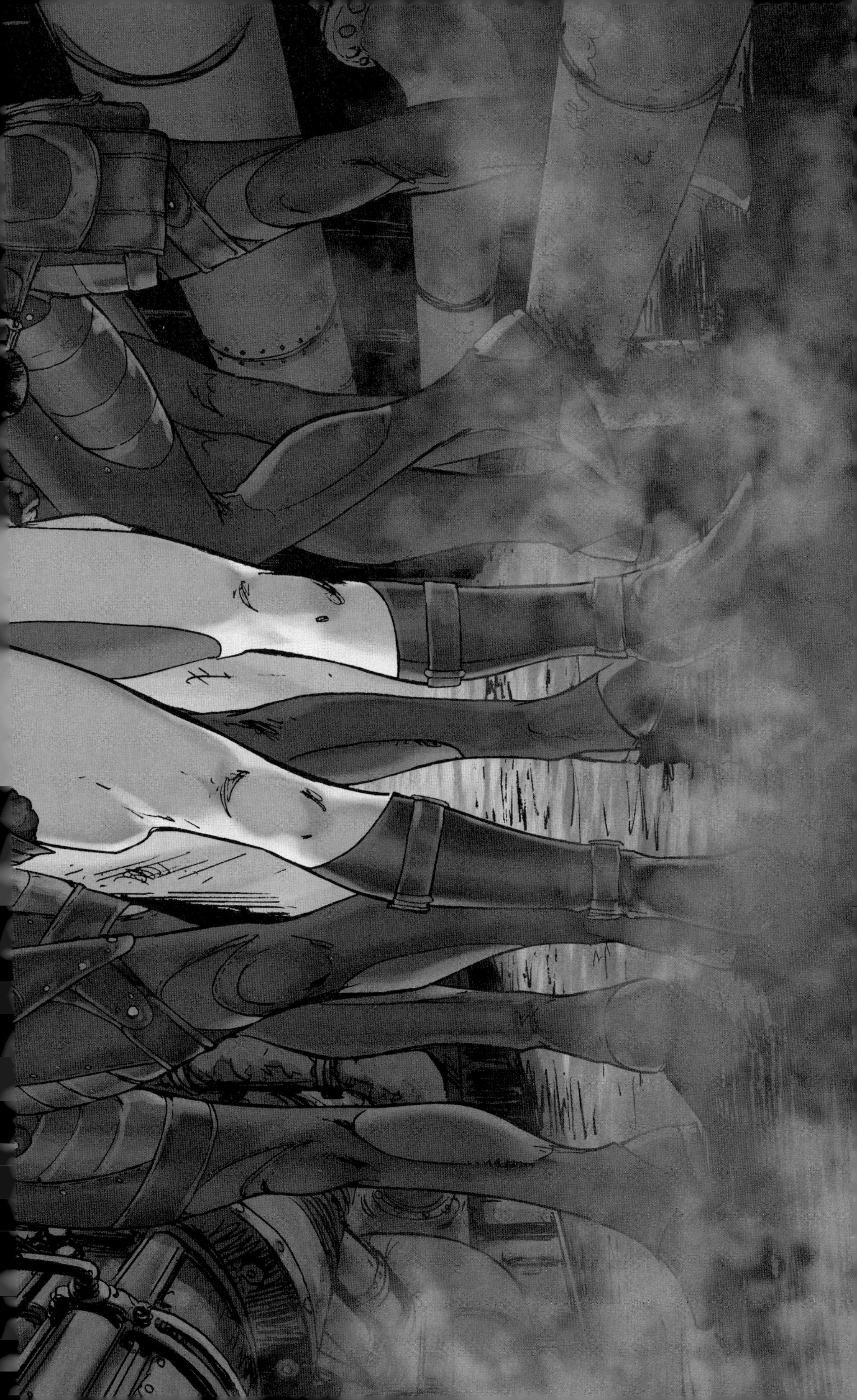

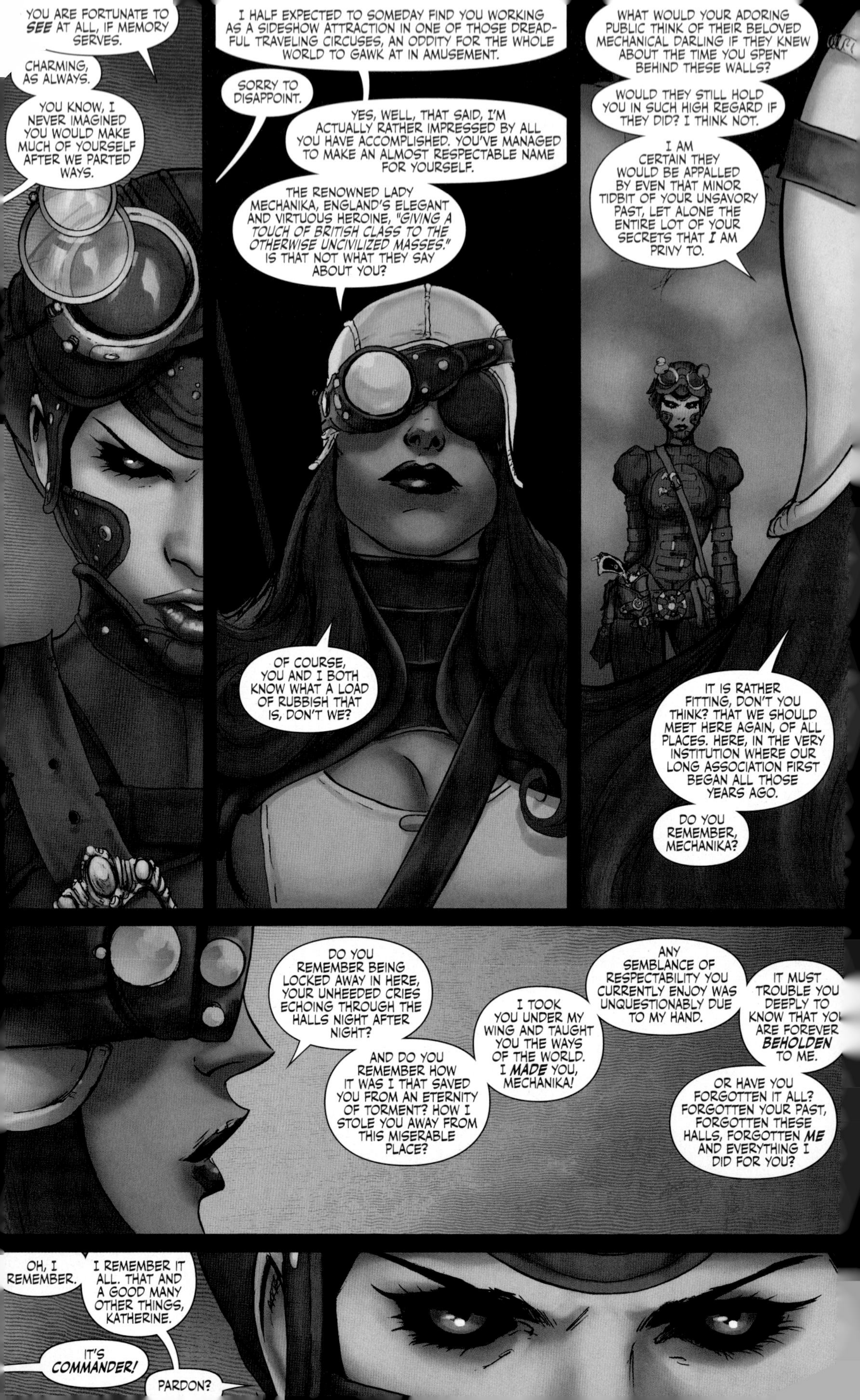
YOU ARE FORTUNATE TO SEE AT ALL, IF MEMORY SERVES.
CHARMING, AS ALWAYS.
YOU KNOW, I NEVER IMAGINED YOU WOULD MAKE MUCH OF YOURSELF AFTER WE PARTED WAYS.
I HALF EXPECTED TO SOMEDAY FIND YOU WORKING AS A SIDESHOW ATTRACTION IN ONE OF THOSE DREADFUL TRAVELING CIRCUSES, AN ODDITY FOR THE WHOLE WORLD TO GAWK AT IN AMUSEMENT.
SORRY TO DISAPPOINT.
YES, WELL, THAT SAID, I'M ACTUALLY RATHER IMPRESSED BY ALL YOU HAVE ACCOMPLISHED. YOU'VE MANAGED TO MAKE AN ALMOST RESPECTABLE NAME FOR YOURSELF.
THE RENOWNED LADY MECHANIKA, ENGLAND'S ELEGANT AND VIRTUOUS HEROINE, "GIVING A TOUCH OF BRITISH CLASS TO THE OTHERWISE UNCIVILIZED MASSES." IS THAT NOT WHAT THEY SAY ABOUT YOU?
OF COURSE, YOU AND I BOTH KNOW WHAT A LOAD OF RUBBISH THAT IS, DON'T WE?
WHAT WOULD YOUR ADORING PUBLIC THINK OF THEIR BELOVED MECHANICAL DARLING IF THEY KNEW ABOUT THE TIME YOU SPENT BEHIND THESE WALLS?
WOULD THEY STILL HOLD YOU IN SUCH HIGH REGARD IF THEY DID? I THINK NOT.
I AM CERTAIN THEY WOULD BE APPALLED BY EVEN THAT MINOR TIDBIT OF YOUR UNSAVORY PAST, LET ALONE THE ENTIRE LOT OF YOUR SECRETS THAT I AM PRIVY TO.
IT IS RATHER FITTING, DON'T YOU THINK? THAT WE SHOULD MEET HERE AGAIN, OF ALL PLACES. HERE, IN THE VERY INSTITUTION WHERE OUR LONG ASSOCIATION FIRST BEGAN ALL THOSE YEARS AGO.
DO YOU REMEMBER, MECHANIKA?
DO YOU REMEMBER BEING LOCKED AWAY IN HERE, YOUR UNHEEDED CRIES ECHOING THROUGH THE HALLS NIGHT AFTER NIGHT?
AND DO YOU REMEMBER HOW IT WAS I THAT SAVED YOU FROM AN ETERNITY OF TORMENT? HOW I STOLE YOU AWAY FROM THIS MISERABLE PLACE?
I TOOK YOU UNDER MY WING AND TAUGHT YOU THE WAYS OF THE WORLD. I MADE YOU, MECHANIKA!
ANY SEMBLANCE OF RESPECTABILITY YOU CURRENTLY ENJOY WAS UNQUESTIONABLY DUE TO MY HAND.
IT MUST TROUBLE YOU DEEPLY TO KNOW THAT YOU ARE FOREVER BEHOLDEN TO ME.
OR HAVE YOU FORGOTTEN IT ALL? FORGOTTEN YOUR PAST, FORGOTTEN THESE HALLS, FORGOTTEN ME AND EVERYTHING I DID FOR YOU?
OH, I REMEMBER.
I REMEMBER IT ALL. THAT AND A GOOD MANY OTHER THINGS, KATHERINE.
IT'S COMMANDER!
PARDON?

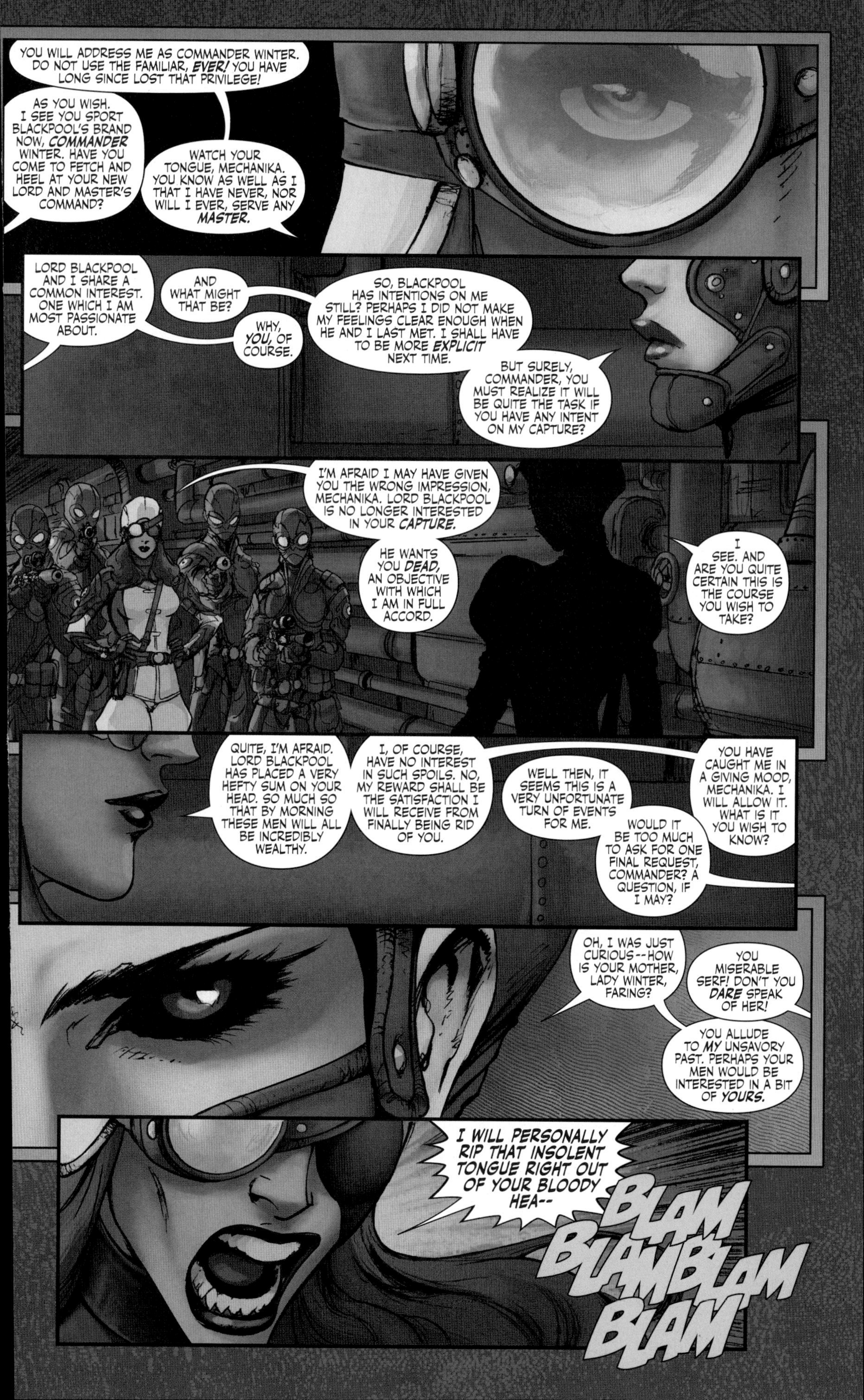
YOU WILL ADDRESS ME AS COMMANDER WINTER. DO NOT USE THE FAMILIAR, EVER! YOU HAVE LONG SINCE LOST THAT PRIVILEGE!
AS YOU WISH. I SEE YOU SPORT BLACKPOOL'S BRAND NOW, COMMANDER WINTER. HAVE YOU COME TO FETCH AND HEEL AT YOUR NEW LORD AND MASTER'S COMMAND?
WATCH YOUR TONGUE, MECHANIKA. YOU KNOW AS WELL AS I THAT I HAVE NEVER, NOR WILL I EVER, SERVE ANY MASTER.
LORD BLACKPOOL AND I SHARE A COMMON INTEREST. ONE WHICH I AM MOST PASSIONATE ABOUT.
AND WHAT MIGHT THAT BE?
WHY, YOU, OF COURSE.
SO, BLACKPOOL HAS INTENTIONS ON ME STILL? PERHAPS I DID NOT MAKE MY FEELINGS CLEAR ENOUGH WHEN HE AND I LAST MET. I SHALL HAVE TO BE MORE EXPLICIT NEXT TIME.
BUT SURELY, COMMANDER, YOU MUST REALIZE IT WILL BE QUITE THE TASK IF YOU HAVE ANY INTENT ON MY CAPTURE?
I'M AFRAID I MAY HAVE GIVEN YOU THE WRONG IMPRESSION, MECHANIKA. LORD BLACKPOOL IS NO LONGER INTERESTED IN YOUR CAPTURE.
HE WANTS YOU DEAD, AN OBJECTIVE WITH WHICH I AM IN FULL ACCORD.
I SEE. AND ARE YOU QUITE CERTAIN THIS IS THE COURSE YOU WISH TO TAKE?
QUITE, I'M AFRAID. LORD BLACKPOOL HAS PLACED A VERY HEFTY SUM ON YOUR HEAD. SO MUCH SO THAT BY MORNING THESE MEN WILL ALL BE INCREDIBLY WEALTHY.
I, OF COURSE, HAVE NO INTEREST IN SUCH SPOILS. NO, MY REWARD SHALL BE THE SATISFACTION I WILL RECEIVE FROM FINALLY BEING RID OF YOU.
WELL THEN, IT SEEMS THIS IS A VERY UNFORTUNATE TURN OF EVENTS FOR ME.
WOULD IT BE TOO MUCH TO ASK FOR ONE FINAL REQUEST, COMMANDER? A QUESTION, IF I MAY?
YOU HAVE CAUGHT ME IN A GIVING MOOD, MECHANIKA. I WILL ALLOW IT. WHAT IS IT YOU WISH TO KNOW?
OH, I WAS JUST CURIOUS--HOW IS YOUR MOTHER, LADY WINTER, FARING?
YOU MISERABLE SERF! DON'T YOU DARE SPEAK OF HER!
YOU ALLUDE TO MY UNSAVORY PAST. PERHAPS YOUR MEN WOULD BE INTERESTED IN A BIT OF YOURS.
I WILL PERSONALLY RIP THAT INSOLENT TONGUE RIGHT OUT OF YOUR BLOODY HEA--
BLAM BLAM BLAM BLAM BLAM

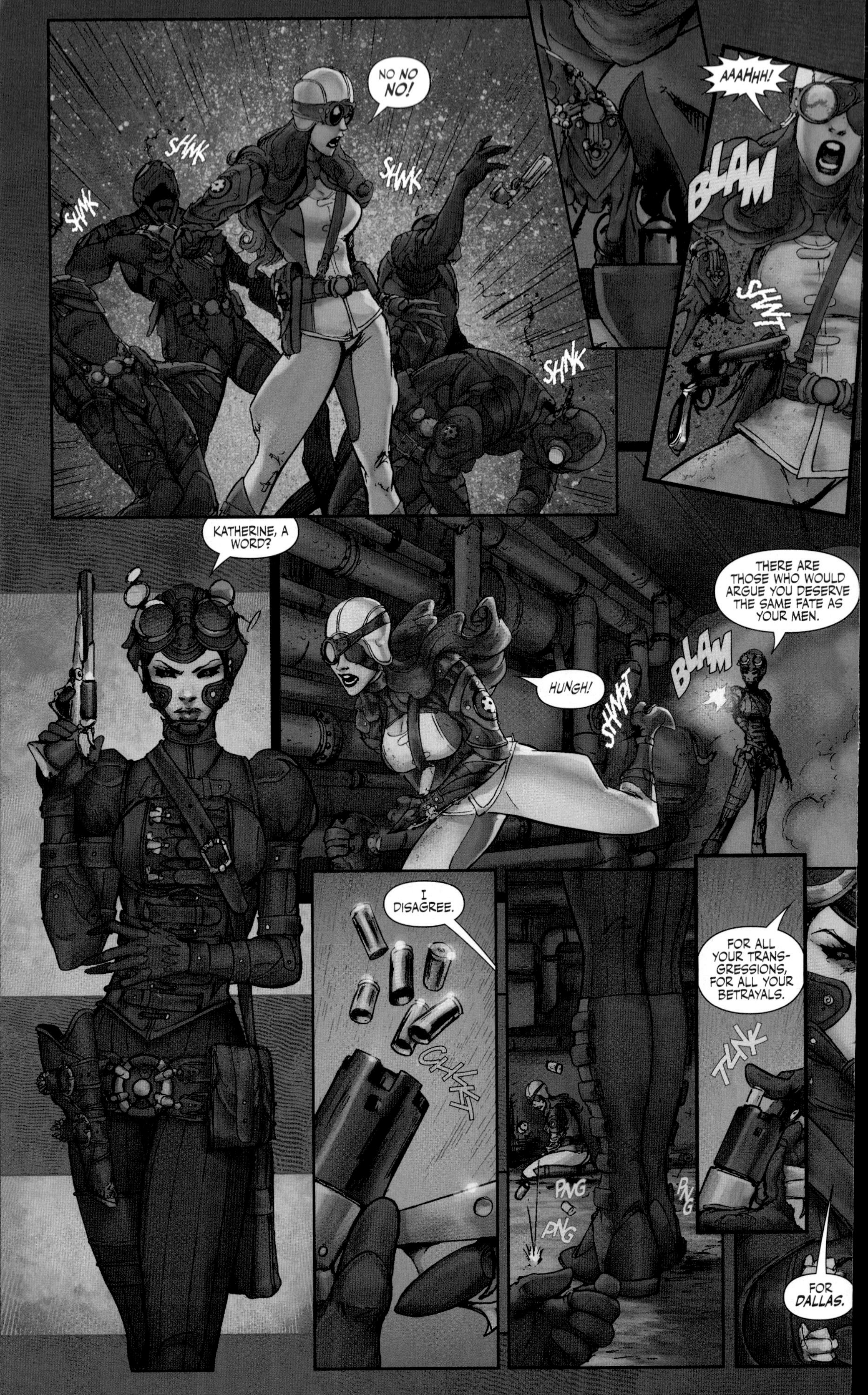
SHNK
SHNK
NO NO NO!
SHNK
SHNK
AAAHHH!
BLAM
SHNT
KATHERINE, A WORD?
HUNGH!
SHNPT
BLAM
THERE ARE THOSE WHO WOULD ARGUE YOU DESERVE THE SAME FATE AS YOUR MEN.
I DISAGREE.
CHKKT
PNG
PNG
PNG
FOR ALL YOUR TRANS-GRESSIONS, FOR ALL YOUR BETRAYALS.
TUNK
FOR DALLAS.

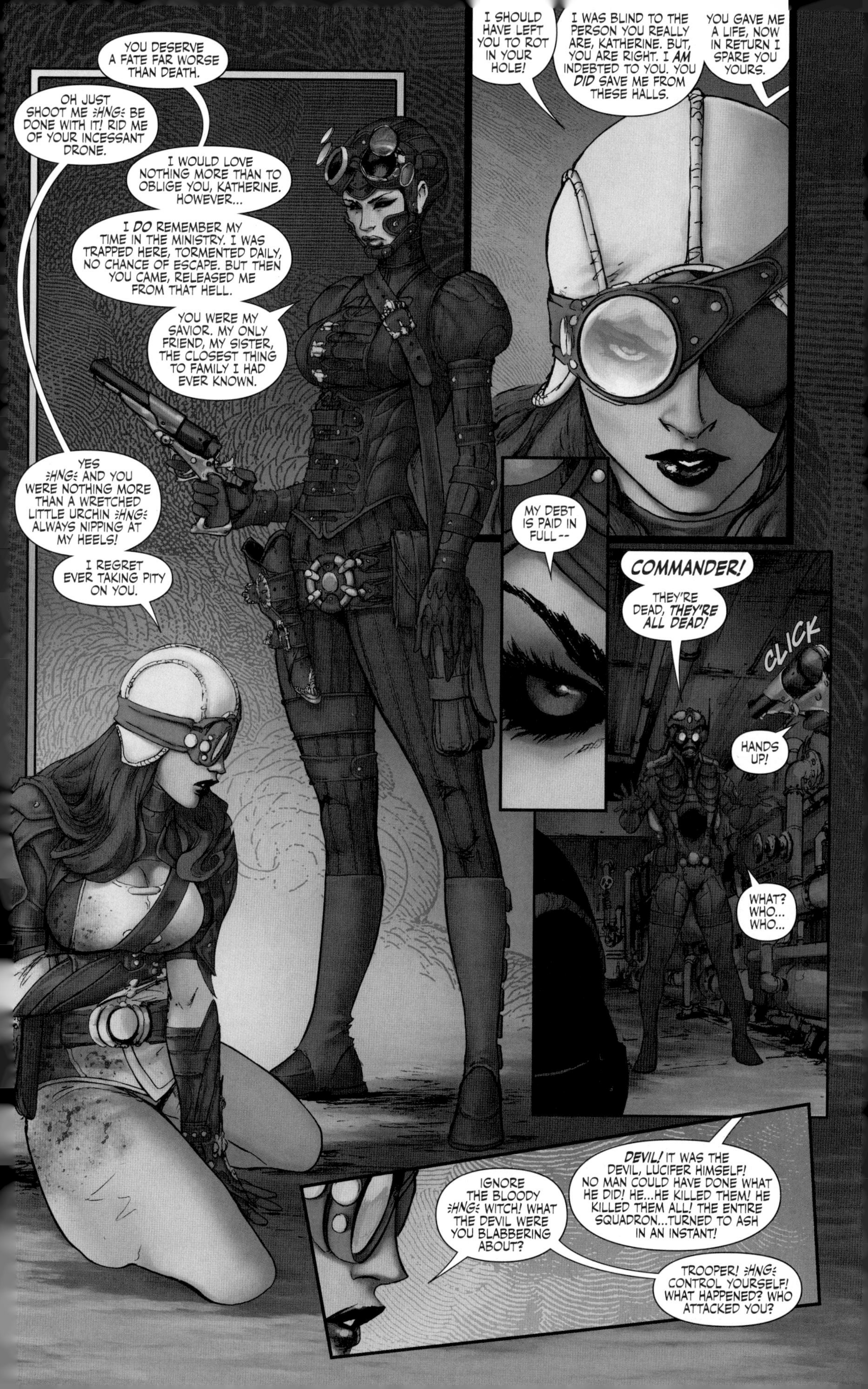

YOU DESERVE A FATE FAR WORSE THAN DEATH.
OH JUST SHOOT ME ≠HNG≠ BE DONE WITH IT! RID ME OF YOUR INCESSANT DRONE.
I WOULD LOVE NOTHING MORE THAN TO OBLIGE YOU, KATHERINE. HOWEVER...
I DO REMEMBER MY TIME IN THE MINISTRY. I WAS TRAPPED HERE, TORMENTED DAILY, NO CHANCE OF ESCAPE. BUT THEN YOU CAME, RELEASED ME FROM THAT HELL.
YOU WERE MY SAVIOR. MY ONLY FRIEND, MY SISTER, THE CLOSEST THING TO FAMILY I HAD EVER KNOWN.
YES ≠HNG≠ AND YOU WERE NOTHING MORE THAN A WRETCHED LITTLE URCHIN ≠HNG≠ ALWAYS NIPPING AT MY HEELS!
I REGRET EVER TAKING PITY ON YOU.
I SHOULD HAVE LEFT YOU TO ROT IN YOUR HOLE!
I WAS BLIND TO THE PERSON YOU REALLY ARE, KATHERINE. BUT, YOU ARE RIGHT. I AM INDEBTED TO YOU. YOU DID SAVE ME FROM THESE HALLS.
YOU GAVE ME A LIFE, NOW IN RETURN I SPARE YOU YOURS.
MY DEBT IS PAID IN FULL--
COMMANDER!
THEY'RE DEAD, THEY'RE ALL DEAD!
CLICK
HANDS UP!
WHAT? WHO... WHO...
DEVIL! IT WAS THE DEVIL, LUCIFER HIMSELF! NO MAN COULD HAVE DONE WHAT HE DID! HE...HE KILLED THEM! HE KILLED THEM ALL! THE ENTIRE SQUADRON...TURNED TO ASH IN AN INSTANT!
IGNORE THE BLOODY ≠HNG≠ WITCH! WHAT THE DEVIL WERE YOU BLABBERING ABOUT?
TROOPER! ≠HNG≠ CONTROL YOURSELF! WHAT HAPPENED? WHO ATTACKED YOU?

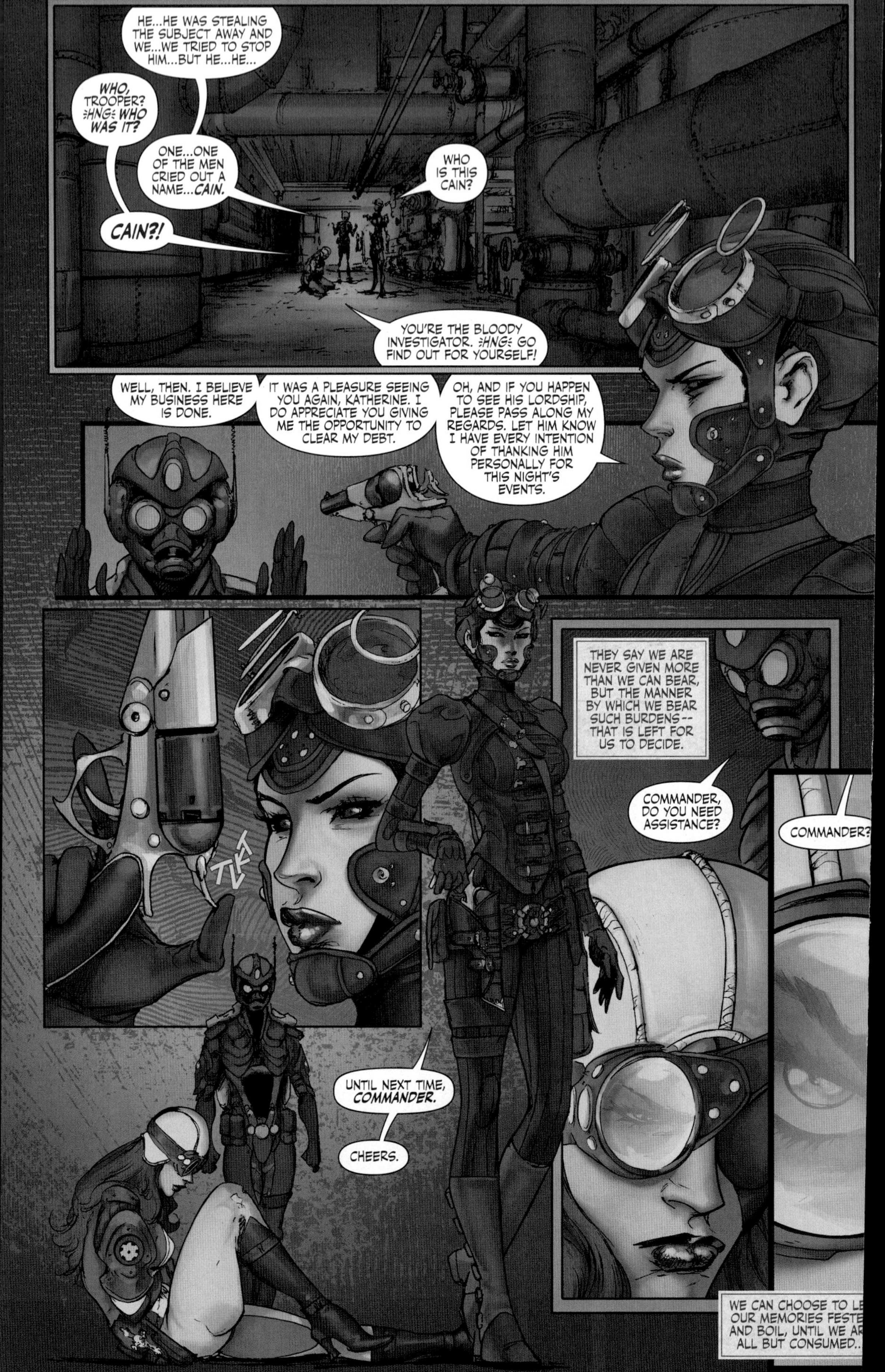
HE...HE WAS STEALING THE SUBJECT AWAY AND WE...WE TRIED TO STOP HIM...BUT HE...HE...
WHO, TROOPER? ≡HNG≡ WHO WAS IT?
ONE...ONE OF THE MEN CRIED OUT A NAME...CAIN.
CAIN?!
WHO IS THIS CAIN?
YOU'RE THE BLOODY INVESTIGATOR. ≡HNG≡ GO FIND OUT FOR YOURSELF!
WELL, THEN. I BELIEVE MY BUSINESS HERE IS DONE.
IT WAS A PLEASURE SEEING YOU AGAIN, KATHERINE. I DO APPRECIATE YOU GIVING ME THE OPPORTUNITY TO CLEAR MY DEBT.
OH, AND IF YOU HAPPEN TO SEE HIS LORDSHIP, PLEASE PASS ALONG MY REGARDS. LET HIM KNOW I HAVE EVERY INTENTION OF THANKING HIM PERSONALLY FOR THIS NIGHT'S EVENTS.
TLKT
THEY SAY WE ARE NEVER GIVEN MORE THAN WE CAN BEAR, BUT THE MANNER BY WHICH WE BEAR SUCH BURDENS-- THAT IS LEFT FOR US TO DECIDE.
COMMANDER, DO YOU NEED ASSISTANCE?
COMMANDER?
UNTIL NEXT TIME, COMMANDER.
CHEERS.
WE CAN CHOOSE TO LE OUR MEMORIES FESTE AND BOIL, UNTIL WE AR ALL BUT CONSUMED..

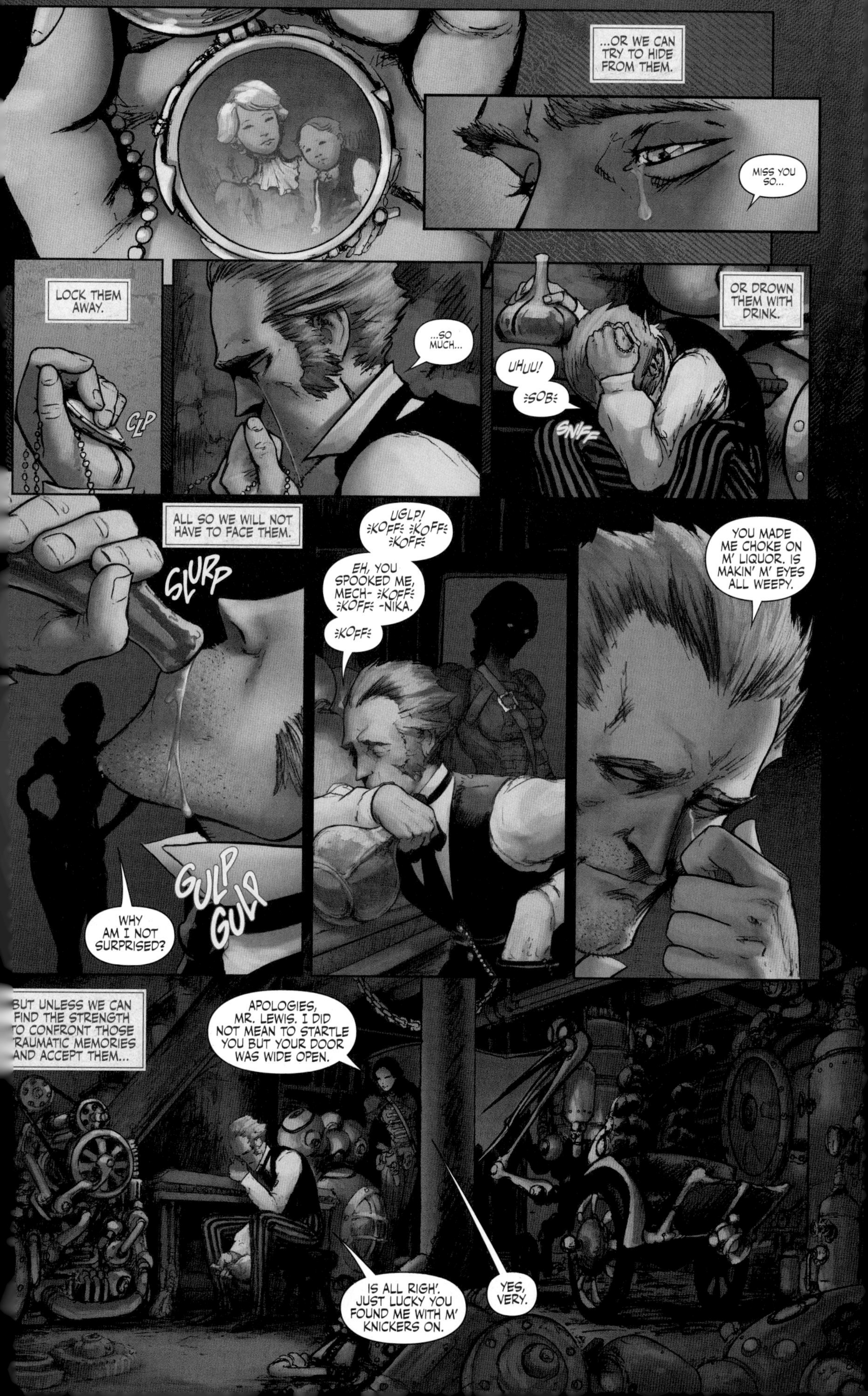
...OR WE CAN TRY TO HIDE FROM THEM.
MISS YOU SO...
LOCK THEM AWAY.
CLP
...SO MUCH...
OR DROWN THEM WITH DRINK.
UHUU!
SOB
SNIFF
ALL SO WE WILL NOT HAVE TO FACE THEM.
SLURP
GULP GULP
WHY AM I NOT SURPRISED?
UGLP! KOFF KOFF KOFF
EH, YOU SPOOKED ME, MECH- KOFF KOFF -NIKA.
KOFF
YOU MADE ME CHOKE ON M' LIQUOR. IS MAKIN' M' EYES ALL WEEPY.
BUT UNLESS WE CAN FIND THE STRENGTH TO CONFRONT THOSE TRAUMATIC MEMORIES AND ACCEPT THEM...
APOLOGIES, MR. LEWIS. I DID NOT MEAN TO STARTLE YOU BUT YOUR DOOR WAS WIDE OPEN.
IS ALL RIGH'. JUST LUCKY YOU FOUND ME WITH M' KNICKERS ON.
YES, VERY.

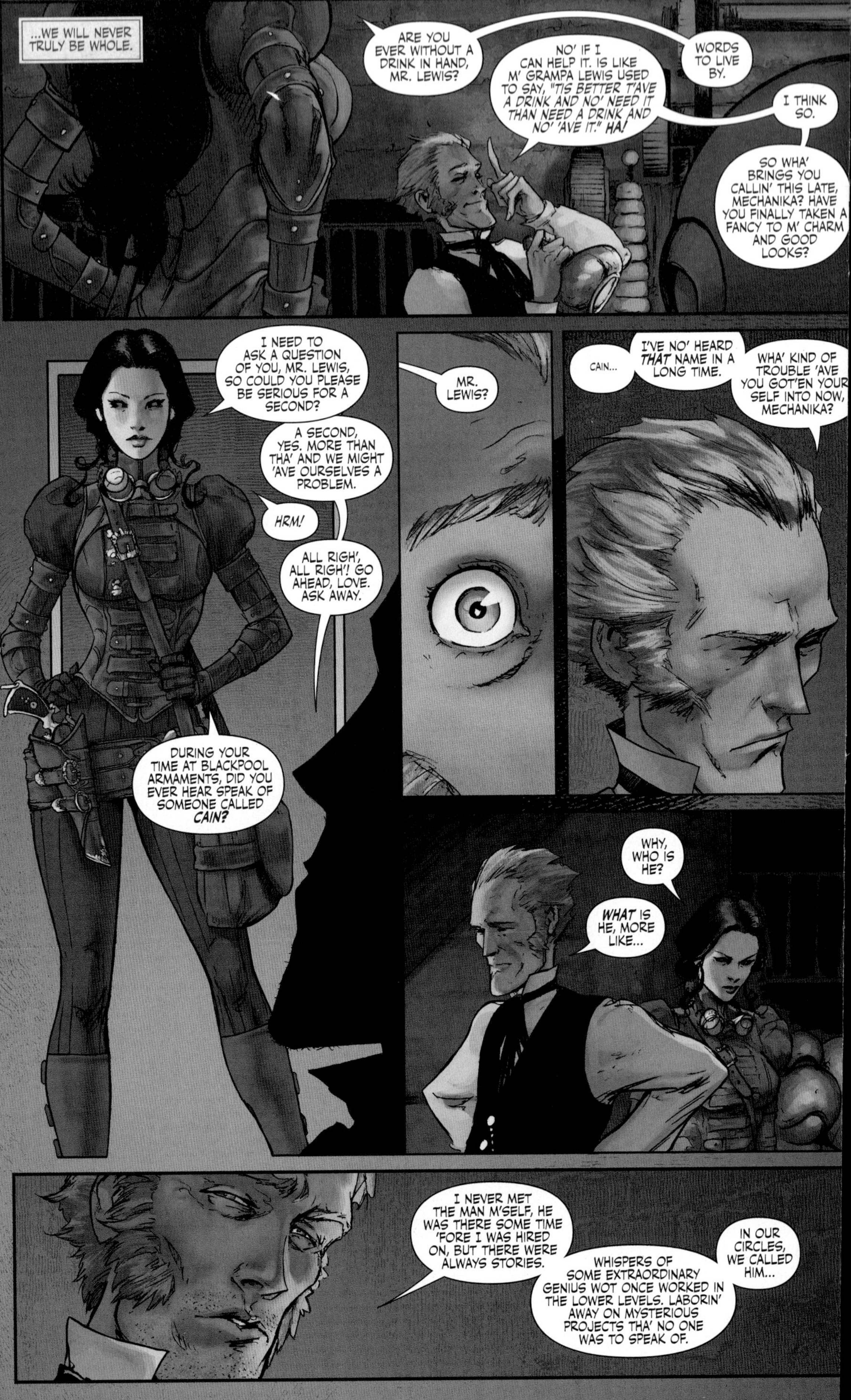
...WE WILL NEVER TRULY BE WHOLE.
ARE YOU EVER WITHOUT A DRINK IN HAND, MR. LEWIS?
NO' IF I CAN HELP IT. IS LIKE M' GRAMPA LEWIS USED TO SAY, "TIS BETTER T'AVE A DRINK AND NO' NEED IT THAN NEED A DRINK AND NO' 'AVE IT." HA!
WORDS TO LIVE BY.
I THINK SO.
SO WHA' BRINGS YOU CALLIN' THIS LATE, MECHANIKA? HAVE YOU FINALLY TAKEN A FANCY TO M' CHARM AND GOOD LOOKS?
I NEED TO ASK A QUESTION OF YOU, MR. LEWIS, SO COULD YOU PLEASE BE SERIOUS FOR A SECOND?
A SECOND, YES. MORE THAN THA' AND WE MIGHT 'AVE OURSELVES A PROBLEM.
HRM!
ALL RIGH', ALL RIGH'! GO AHEAD, LOVE. ASK AWAY.
DURING YOUR TIME AT BLACKPOOL ARMAMENTS, DID YOU EVER HEAR SPEAK OF SOMEONE CALLED CAIN?
MR. LEWIS?
CAIN...
I'VE NO' HEARD THAT NAME IN A LONG TIME.
WHA' KIND OF TROUBLE 'AVE YOU GOT'EN YOUR SELF INTO NOW, MECHANIKA?
WHY, WHO IS HE?
WHAT IS HE, MORE LIKE...
I NEVER MET THE MAN M'SELF, HE WAS THERE SOME TIME 'FORE I WAS HIRED ON, BUT THERE WERE ALWAYS STORIES.
WHISPERS OF SOME EXTRAORDINARY GENIUS WOT ONCE WORKED IN THE LOWER LEVELS. LABORIN' AWAY ON MYSTERIOUS PROJECTS THA' NO ONE WAS TO SPEAK OF.
IN OUR CIRCLES, WE CALLED HIM...

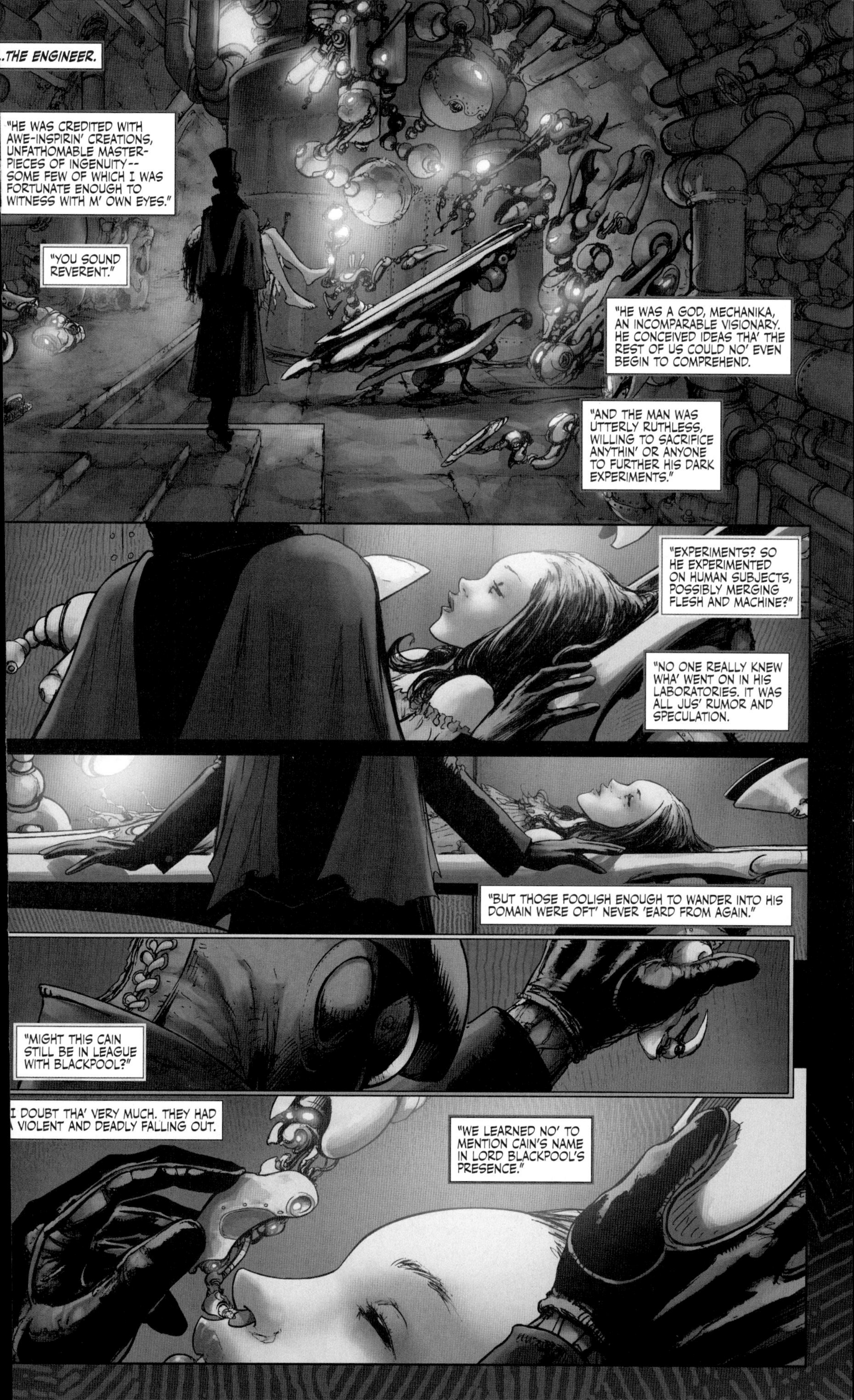
...THE ENGINEER.
"HE WAS CREDITED WITH AWE-INSPIRIN' CREATIONS, UNFATHOMABLE MASTER-PIECES OF INGENUITY-- SOME FEW OF WHICH I WAS FORTUNATE ENOUGH TO WITNESS WITH M' OWN EYES."
"YOU SOUND REVERENT."
"HE WAS A GOD, MECHANIKA, AN INCOMPARABLE VISIONARY. HE CONCEIVED IDEAS THA' THE REST OF US COULD NO' EVEN BEGIN TO COMPREHEND.
"AND THE MAN WAS UTTERLY RUTHLESS, WILLING TO SACRIFICE ANYTHIN' OR ANYONE TO FURTHER HIS DARK EXPERIMENTS."
"EXPERIMENTS? SO HE EXPERIMENTED ON HUMAN SUBJECTS, POSSIBLY MERGING FLESH AND MACHINE?"
"NO ONE REALLY KNEW WHA' WENT ON IN HIS LABORATORIES. IT WAS ALL JUS' RUMOR AND SPECULATION.
"BUT THOSE FOOLISH ENOUGH TO WANDER INTO HIS DOMAIN WERE OFT' NEVER 'EARD FROM AGAIN."
"MIGHT THIS CAIN STILL BE IN LEAGUE WITH BLACKPOOL?"
I DOUBT THA' VERY MUCH. THEY HAD A VIOLENT AND DEADLY FALLING OUT.
"WE LEARNED NO' TO MENTION CAIN'S NAME IN LORD BLACKPOOL'S PRESENCE."

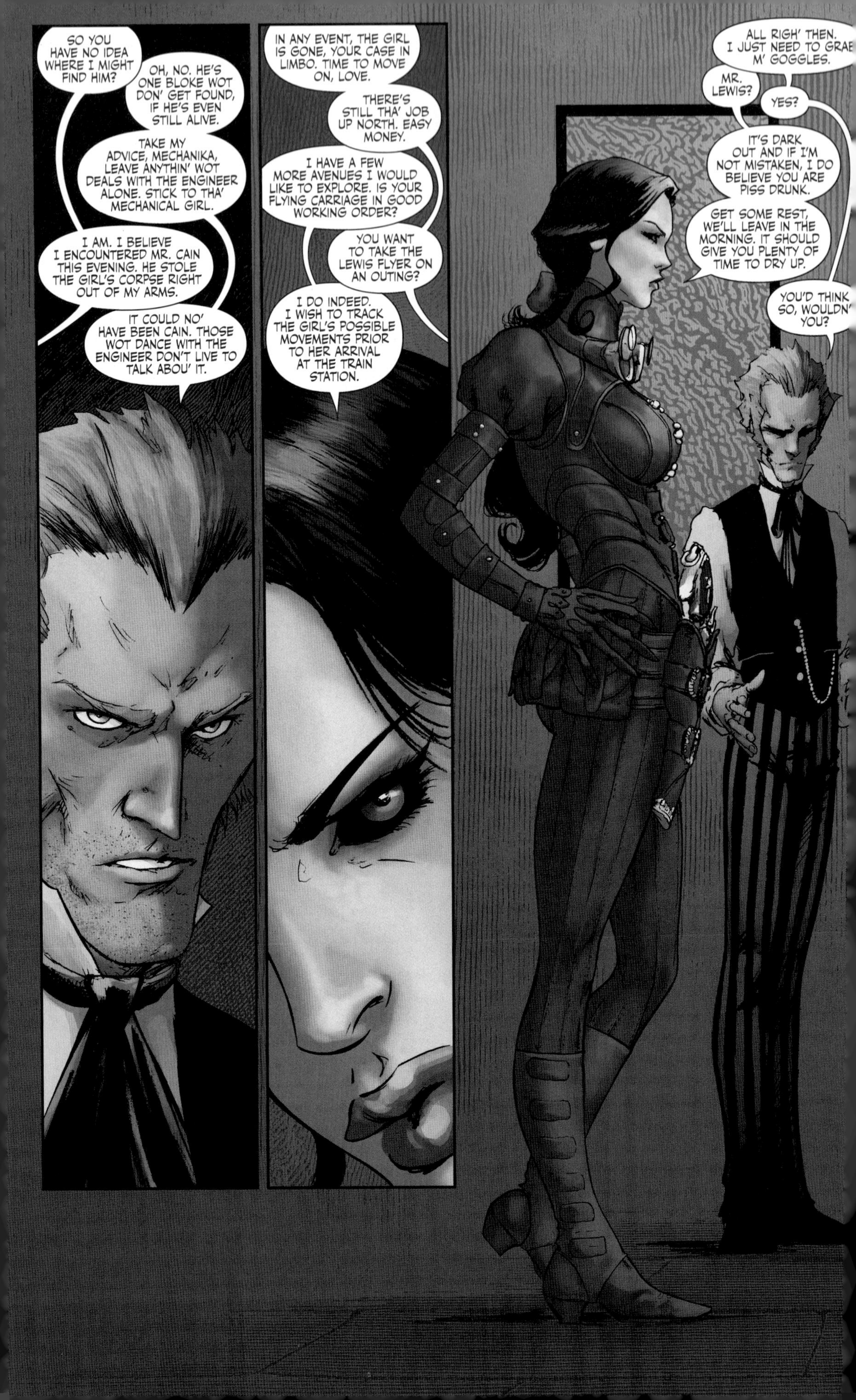
SO YOU HAVE NO IDEA WHERE I MIGHT FIND HIM?
OH, NO. HE'S ONE BLOKE WOT DON' GET FOUND, IF HE'S EVEN STILL ALIVE.
TAKE MY ADVICE, MECHANIKA, LEAVE ANYTHIN' WOT DEALS WITH THE ENGINEER ALONE. STICK TO THA' MECHANICAL GIRL.
I AM. I BELIEVE I ENCOUNTERED MR. CAIN THIS EVENING. HE STOLE THE GIRL'S CORPSE RIGHT OUT OF MY ARMS.
IT COULD NO' HAVE BEEN CAIN. THOSE WOT DANCE WITH THE ENGINEER DON'T LIVE TO TALK ABOU' IT.
IN ANY EVENT, THE GIRL IS GONE, YOUR CASE IN LIMBO. TIME TO MOVE ON, LOVE.
THERE'S STILL THA' JOB UP NORTH. EASY MONEY.
I HAVE A FEW MORE AVENUES I WOULD LIKE TO EXPLORE. IS YOUR FLYING CARRIAGE IN GOOD WORKING ORDER?
YOU WANT TO TAKE THE LEWIS FLYER ON AN OUTING?
I DO INDEED. I WISH TO TRACK THE GIRL'S POSSIBLE MOVEMENTS PRIOR TO HER ARRIVAL AT THE TRAIN STATION.
ALL RIGH' THEN. I JUST NEED TO GRAB M' GOGGLES.
MR. LEWIS?
YES?
IT'S DARK OUT AND IF I'M NOT MISTAKEN, I DO BELIEVE YOU ARE PISS DRUNK.
GET SOME REST, WE'LL LEAVE IN THE MORNING. IT SHOULD GIVE YOU PLENTY OF TIME TO DRY UP.
YOU'D THINK SO, WOULDN' YOU?

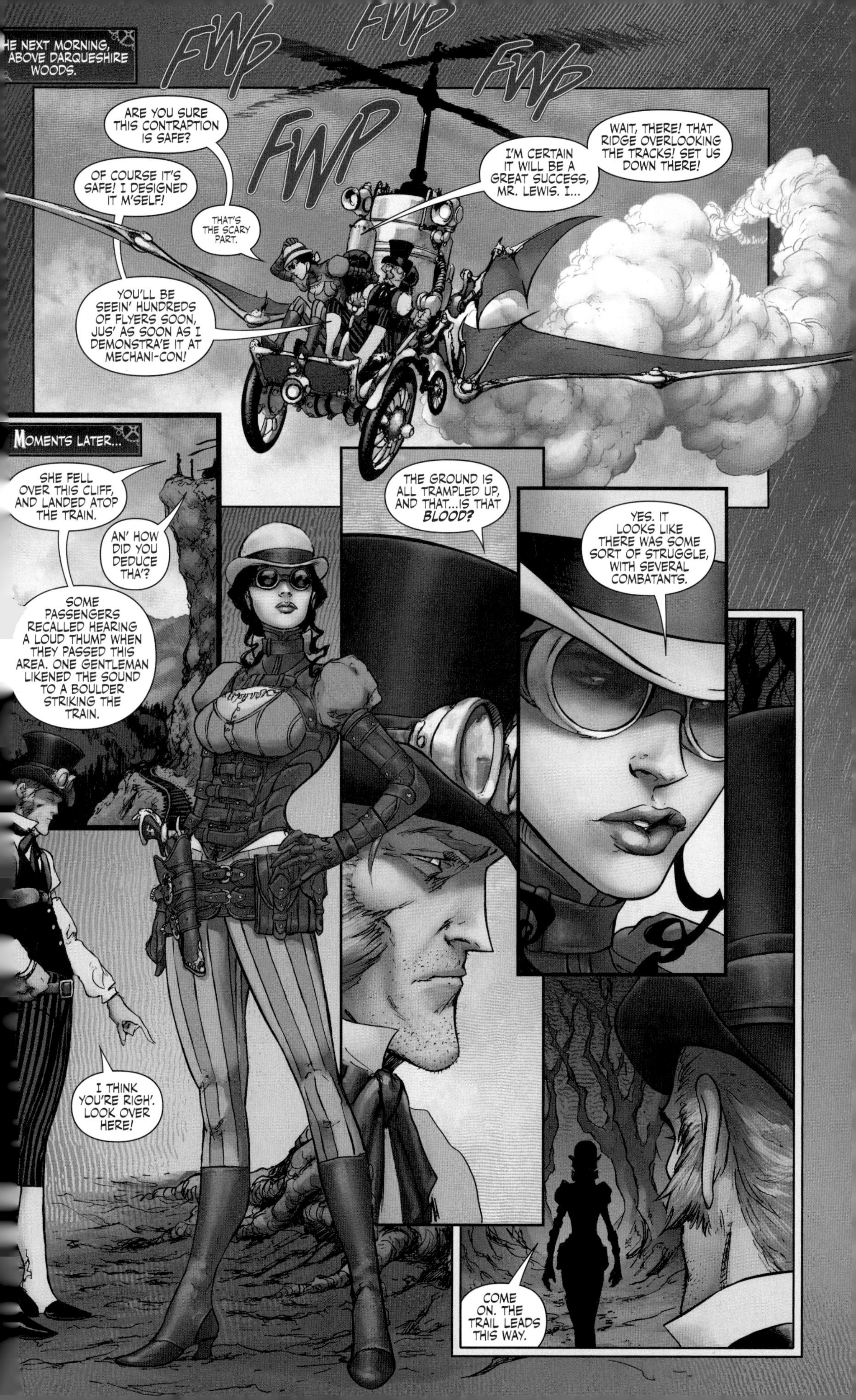

HE NEXT MORNING, ABOVE DARQUESHIRE WOODS.
FWP FWP FWP FWP
ARE YOU SURE THIS CONTRAPTION IS SAFE?
OF COURSE IT'S SAFE! I DESIGNED IT M'SELF!
THAT'S THE SCARY PART.
YOU'LL BE SEEIN' HUNDREDS OF FLYERS SOON, JUS' AS SOON AS I DEMONSTRA'E IT AT MECHANI-CON!
I'M CERTAIN IT WILL BE A GREAT SUCCESS, MR. LEWIS. I...
WAIT, THERE! THAT RIDGE OVERLOOKING THE TRACKS! SET US DOWN THERE!
MOMENTS LATER...
SHE FELL OVER THIS CLIFF, AND LANDED ATOP THE TRAIN.
AN' HOW DID YOU DEDUCE THA'?
SOME PASSENGERS RECALLED HEARING A LOUD THUMP WHEN THEY PASSED THIS AREA. ONE GENTLEMAN LIKENED THE SOUND TO A BOULDER STRIKING THE TRAIN.
I THINK YOU'RE RIGH'. LOOK OVER HERE!
THE GROUND IS ALL TRAMPLED UP, AND THAT...IS THAT BLOOD?
YES. IT LOOKS LIKE THERE WAS SOME SORT OF STRUGGLE, WITH SEVERAL COMBATANTS.
COME ON. THE TRAIL LEADS THIS WAY.

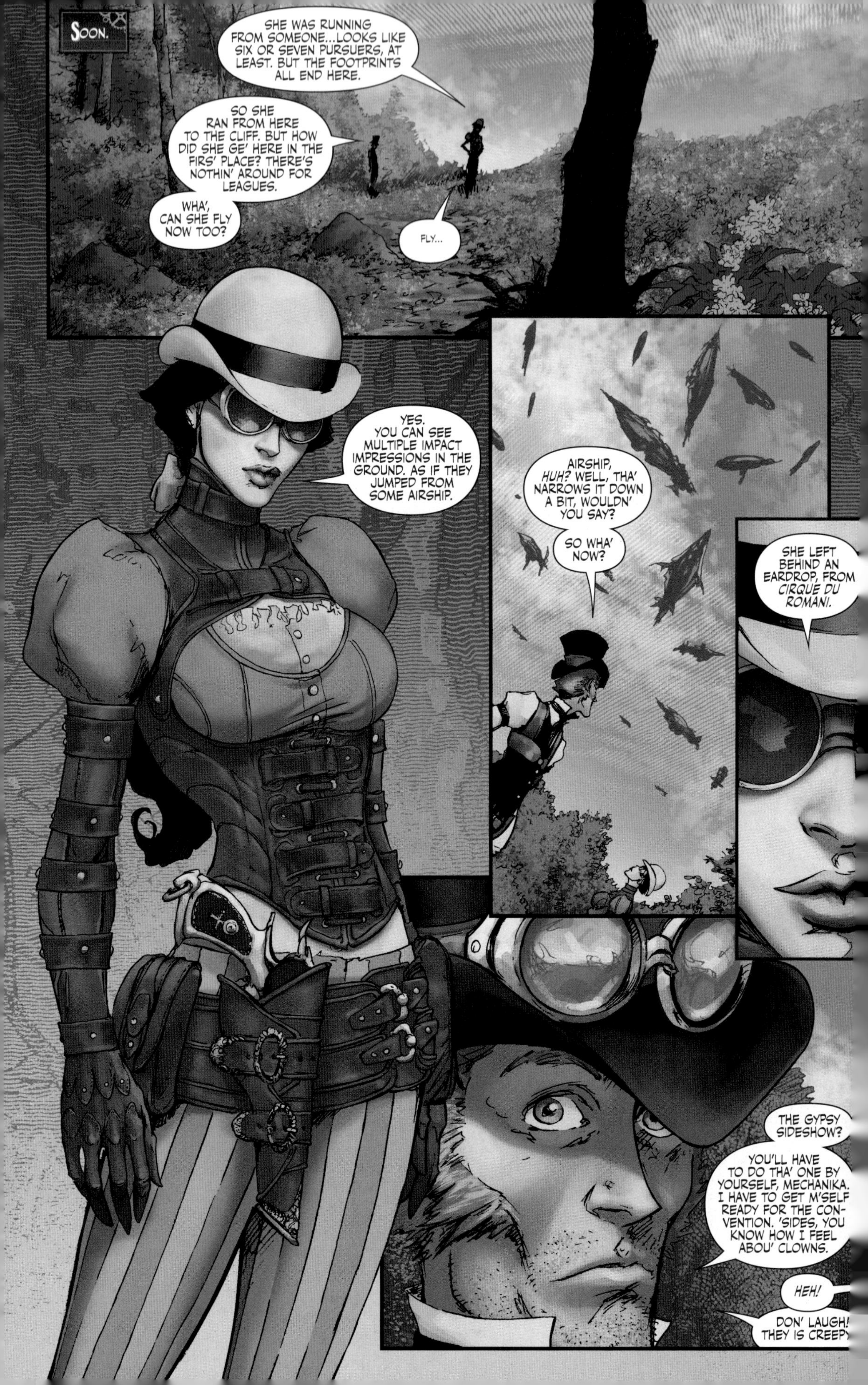
SOON.
SHE WAS RUNNING FROM SOMEONE...LOOKS LIKE SIX OR SEVEN PURSUERS, AT LEAST. BUT THE FOOTPRINTS ALL END HERE.
SO SHE RAN FROM HERE TO THE CLIFF. BUT HOW DID SHE GE' HERE IN THE FIRS' PLACE? THERE'S NOTHIN' AROUND FOR LEAGUES.
WHA', CAN SHE FLY NOW TOO?
FLY...
YES. YOU CAN SEE MULTIPLE IMPACT IMPRESSIONS IN THE GROUND. AS IF THEY JUMPED FROM SOME AIRSHIP.
AIRSHIP, *HUH*? WELL, THA' NARROWS IT DOWN A BIT, WOULDN' YOU SAY?
SO WHA' NOW?
SHE LEFT BEHIND AN EARDROP, FROM *CIRQUE DU ROMANI*.
THE GYPSY SIDESHOW?
YOU'LL HAVE TO DO THA' ONE BY YOURSELF, MECHANIKA. I HAVE TO GET M'SELF READY FOR THE CONVENTION. 'SIDES, YOU KNOW HOW I FEEL ABOU' CLOWNS.
*HEH!*
DON' LAUGH! THEY IS CREEPY

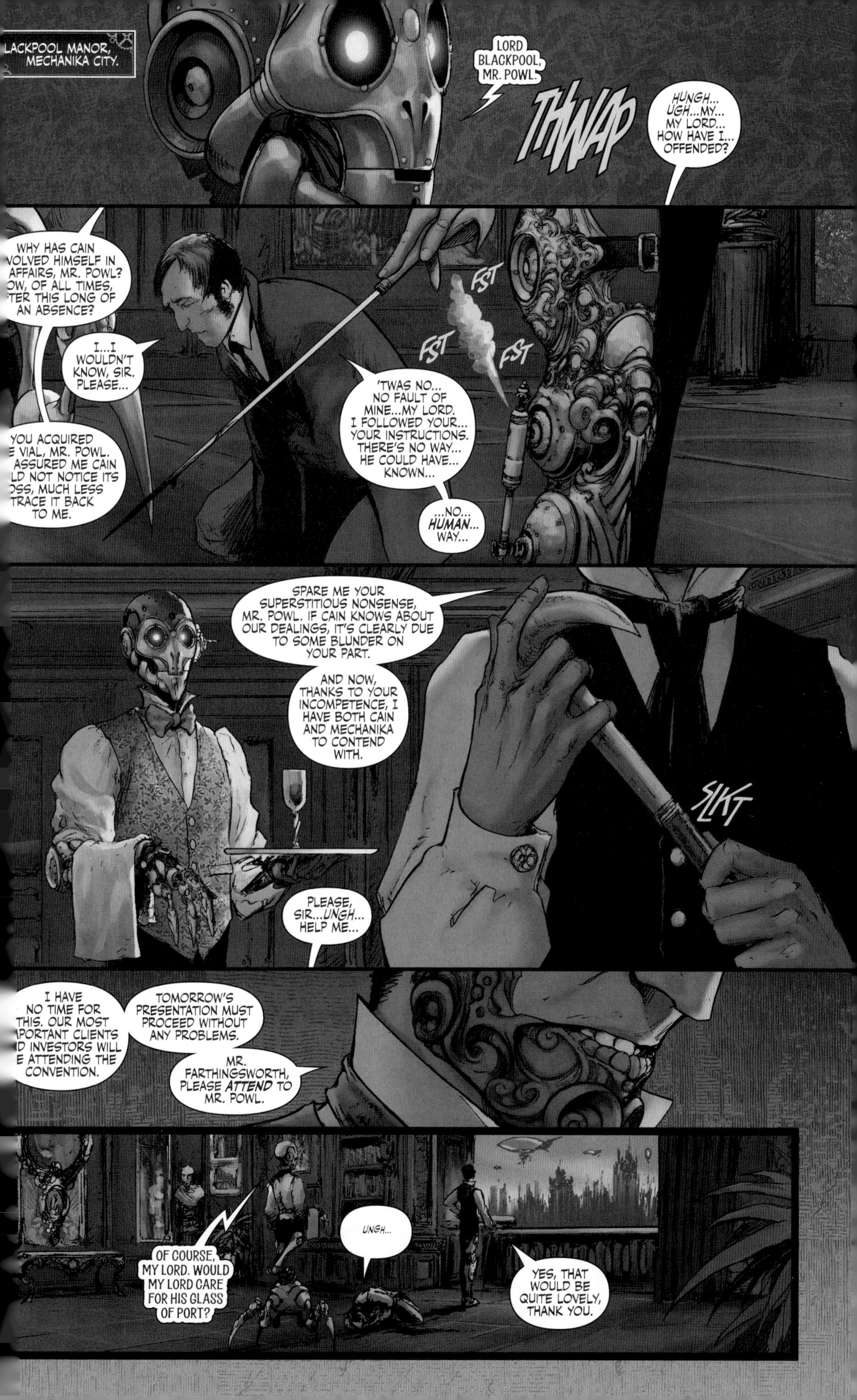
LACKPOOL MANOR, MECHANIKA CITY.
LORD BLACKPOOL, MR. POWL.
THWAP
HUNGH... UGH...MY... MY LORD... HOW HAVE I... OFFENDED?
WHY HAS CAIN VOLVED HIMSELF IN AFFAIRS, MR. POWL? OW, OF ALL TIMES, TER THIS LONG OF AN ABSENCE?
I...I WOULDN'T KNOW, SIR. PLEASE...
FST
FST
FST
YOU ACQUIRED E VIAL, MR. POWL. ASSURED ME CAIN LD NOT NOTICE ITS OSS, MUCH LESS TRACE IT BACK TO ME.
'TWAS NO... NO FAULT OF MINE...MY LORD. I FOLLOWED YOUR... YOUR INSTRUCTIONS. THERE'S NO WAY... HE COULD HAVE... KNOWN...
...NO... HUMAN... WAY...
SPARE ME YOUR SUPERSTITIOUS NONSENSE, MR. POWL. IF CAIN KNOWS ABOUT OUR DEALINGS, IT'S CLEARLY DUE TO SOME BLUNDER ON YOUR PART.
AND NOW, THANKS TO YOUR INCOMPETENCE, I HAVE BOTH CAIN AND MECHANIKA TO CONTEND WITH.
SLKT
PLEASE, SIR...UNGH... HELP ME...
I HAVE NO TIME FOR THIS. OUR MOST PORTANT CLIENTS D INVESTORS WILL E ATTENDING THE CONVENTION.
TOMORROW'S PRESENTATION MUST PROCEED WITHOUT ANY PROBLEMS.
MR. FARTHINGSWORTH, PLEASE ATTEND TO MR. POWL.
OF COURSE, MY LORD. WOULD MY LORD CARE FOR HIS GLASS OF PORT?
UNGH...
YES, THAT WOULD BE QUITE LOVELY, THANK YOU.

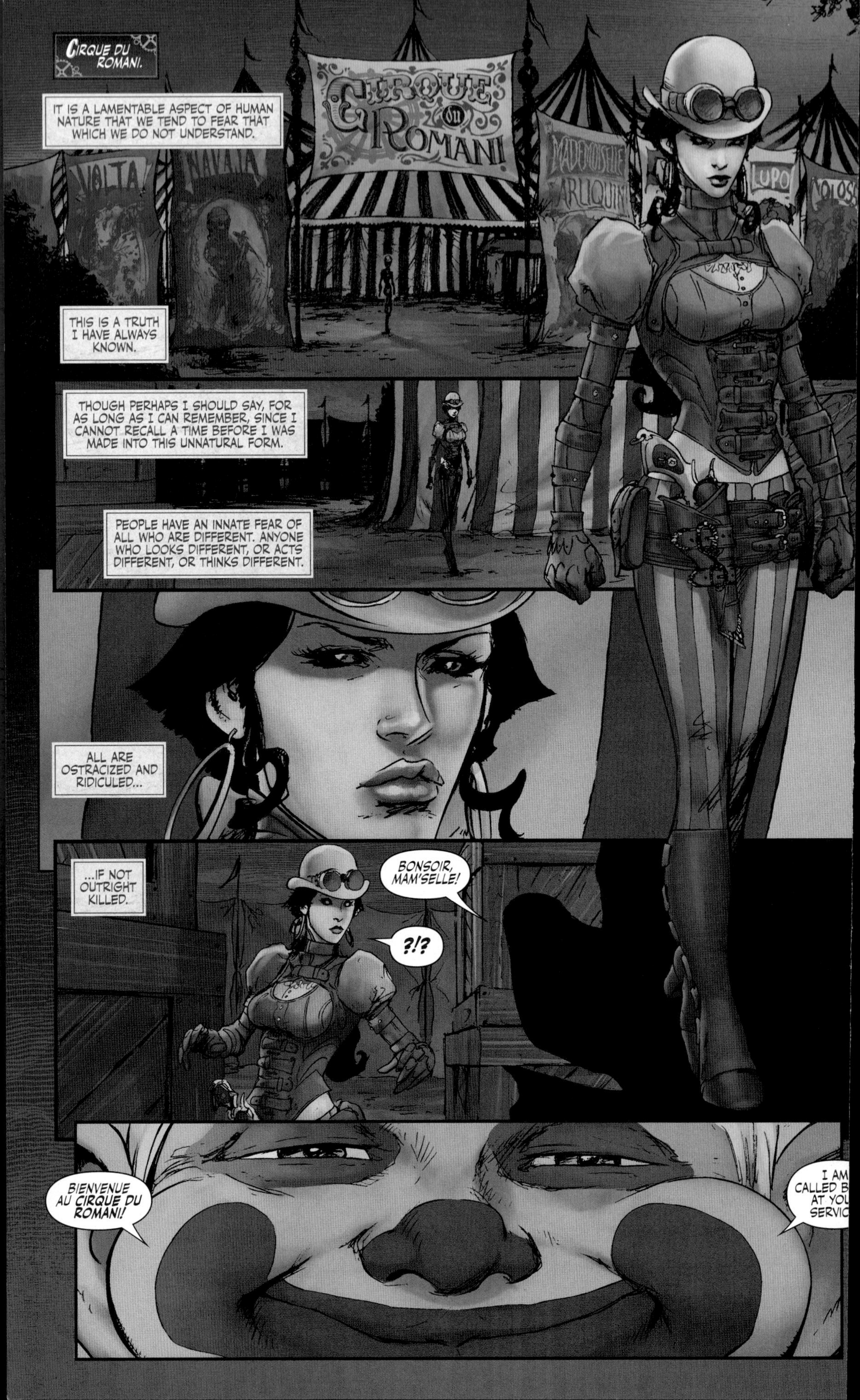
CIRQUE DU ROMANI.
CIRQUE DU ROMANI
VOLTA
NAVAJA
MADEMOISELLE ARLIQUIN
LUPO
IT IS A LAMENTABLE ASPECT OF HUMAN NATURE THAT WE TEND TO FEAR THAT WHICH WE DO NOT UNDERSTAND.
THIS IS A TRUTH I HAVE ALWAYS KNOWN.
THOUGH PERHAPS I SHOULD SAY, FOR AS LONG AS I CAN REMEMBER, SINCE I CANNOT RECALL A TIME BEFORE I WAS MADE INTO THIS UNNATURAL FORM.
PEOPLE HAVE AN INNATE FEAR OF ALL WHO ARE DIFFERENT. ANYONE WHO LOOKS DIFFERENT, OR ACTS DIFFERENT, OR THINKS DIFFERENT.
ALL ARE OSTRACIZED AND RIDICULED...
...IF NOT OUTRIGHT KILLED.
BONSOIR, MAM'SELLE!
?!?
BIENVENUE AU CIRQUE DU ROMANI!
I AM CALLED B AT YOU SERVIC

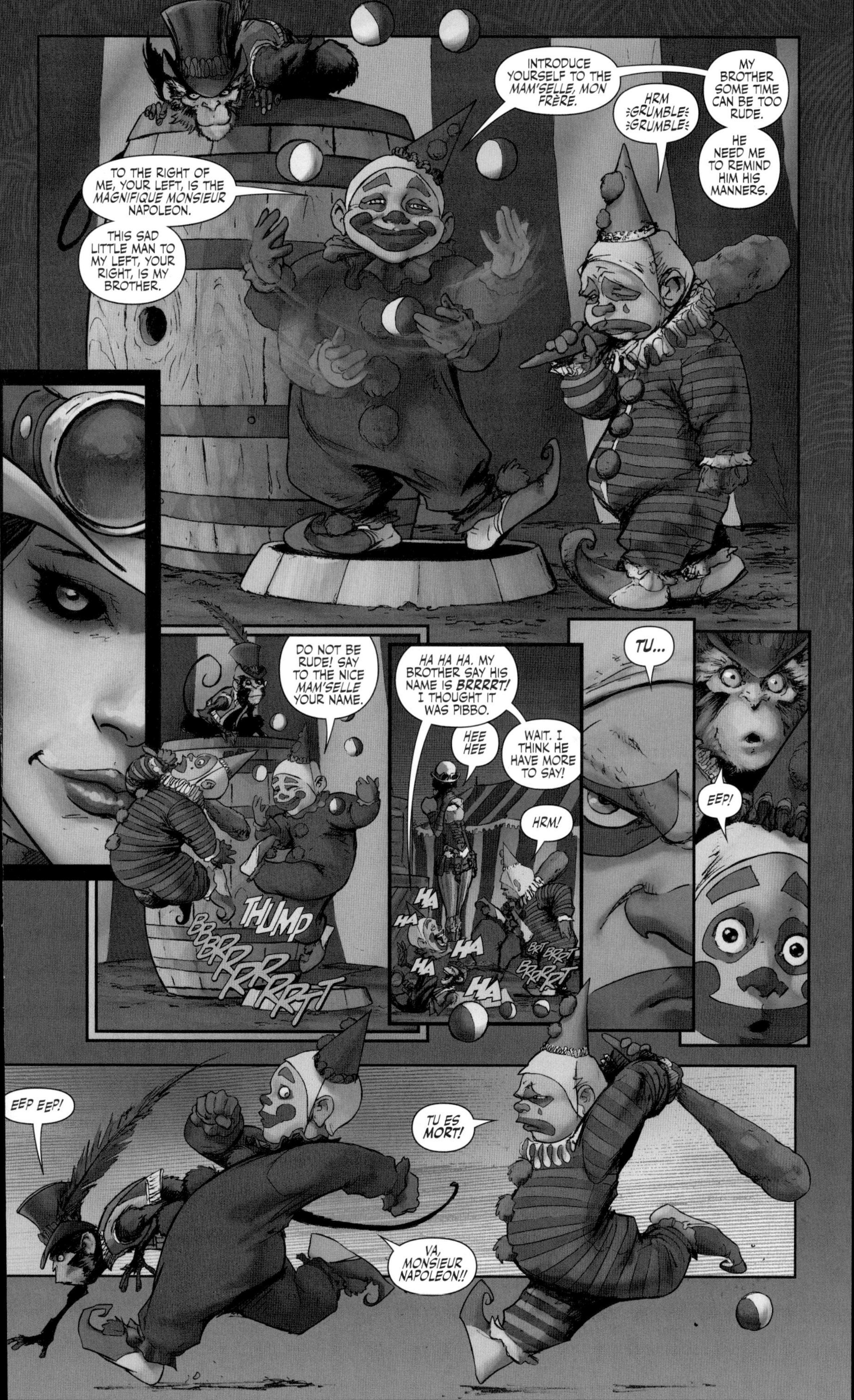

INTRODUCE YOURSELF TO THE MAM'SELLE, MON FRÈRE.
HRM GRUMBLE GRUMBLE
MY BROTHER SOME TIME CAN BE TOO RUDE.
HE NEED ME TO REMIND HIM HIS MANNERS.
TO THE RIGHT OF ME, YOUR LEFT, IS THE MAGNIFIQUE MONSIEUR NAPOLEON.
THIS SAD LITTLE MAN TO MY LEFT, YOUR RIGHT, IS MY BROTHER.
DO NOT BE RUDE! SAY TO THE NICE MAM'SELLE YOUR NAME.
THUMP
BBBRRRRRRRRRTT
HA HA HA. MY BROTHER SAY HIS NAME IS BRRRRT! I THOUGHT IT WAS PIBBO.
HEE HEE
WAIT. I THINK HE HAVE MORE TO SAY!
HRM!
HA HA HA HA HA HA
BRT BRRT BRRRRT
TU...
EEP!
EEP EEP!
TU ES MORT!
VA, MONSIEUR NAPOLEON!!

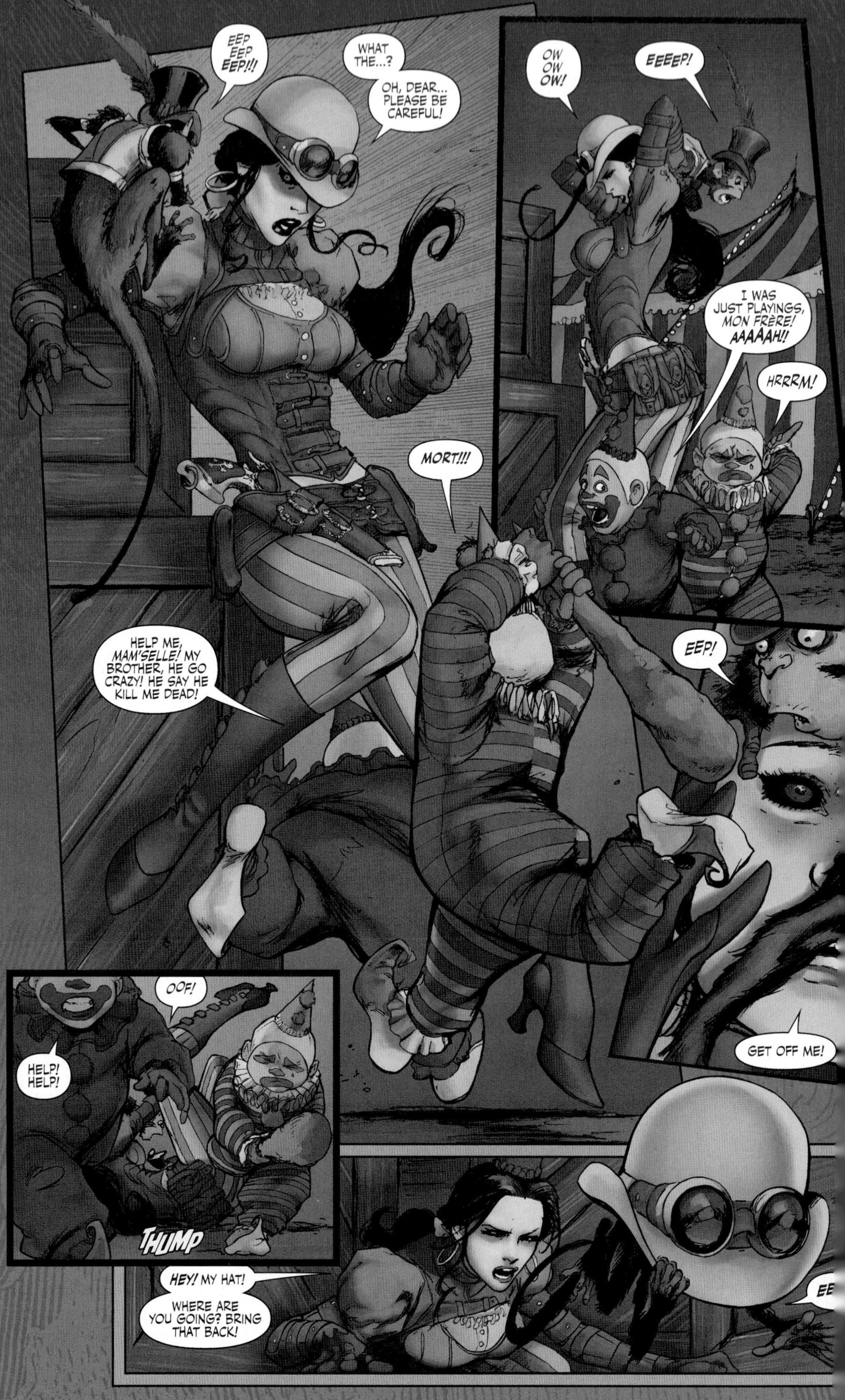
EEP EEP EEP!!!
WHAT THE...?
OH, DEAR... PLEASE BE CAREFUL!
OW OW OW!
EEEEP!
I WAS JUST PLAYINGS, MON FRÈRE! AAAAAH!!
HRRRM!
MORT!!!
HELP ME, MAM'SELLE! MY BROTHER, HE GO CRAZY! HE SAY HE KILL ME DEAD!
EEP!
GET OFF ME!
OOF!
HELP! HELP!
THUMP
HEY! MY HAT!
WHERE ARE YOU GOING? BRING THAT BACK!

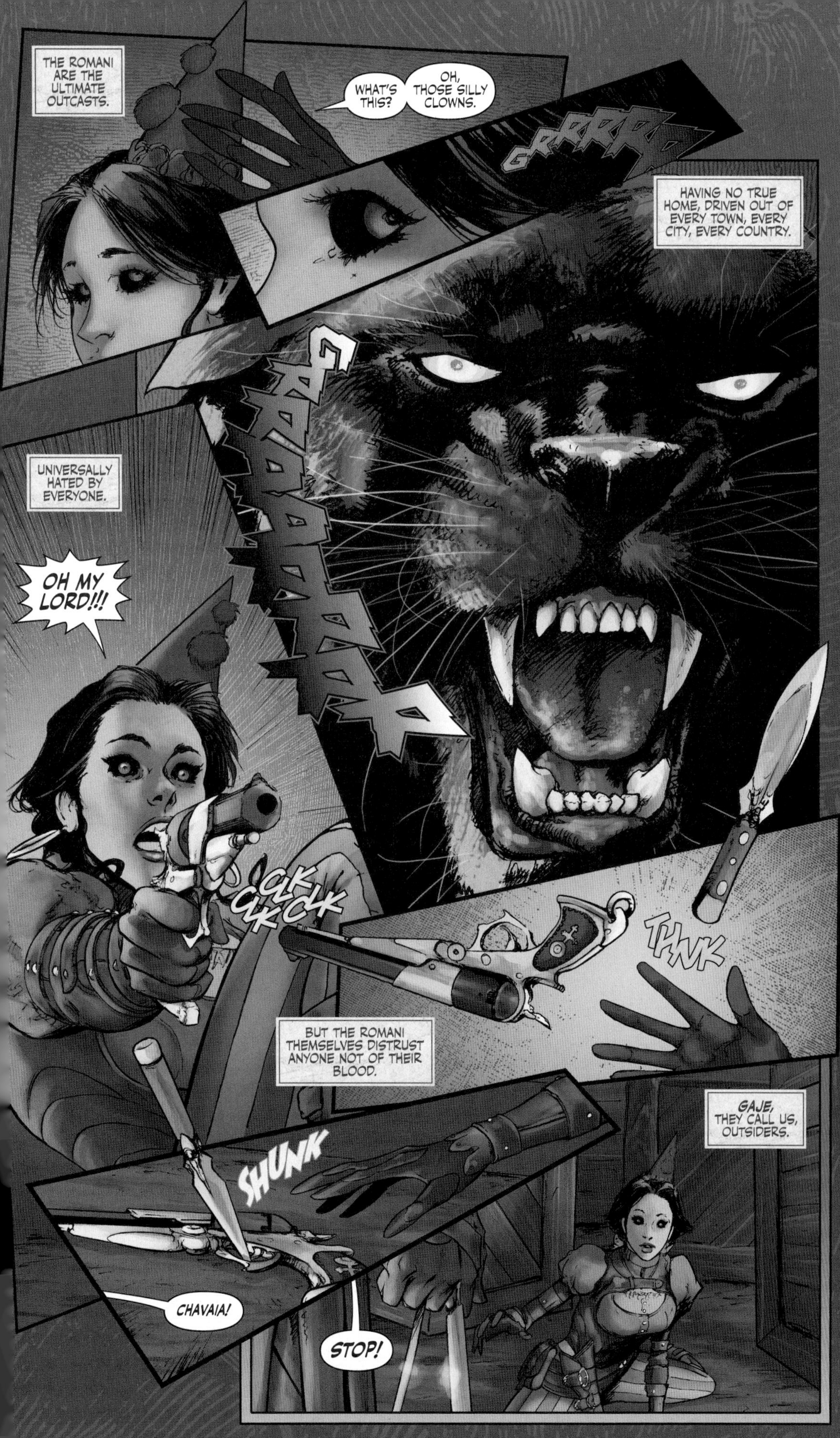
THE ROMANI ARE THE ULTIMATE OUTCASTS.
WHAT'S THIS?
OH, THOSE SILLY CLOWNS.
GRRRRR
HAVING NO TRUE HOME, DRIVEN OUT OF EVERY TOWN, EVERY CITY, EVERY COUNTRY.
UNIVERSALLY HATED BY EVERYONE.
GRRAAARRR
OH MY LORD!!!
CLK CLK CLK CLK
THUNK
BUT THE ROMANI THEMSELVES DISTRUST ANYONE NOT OF THEIR BLOOD.
GAJE, THEY CALL US, OUTSIDERS.
SHUNK
CHAVAIA!
STOP!

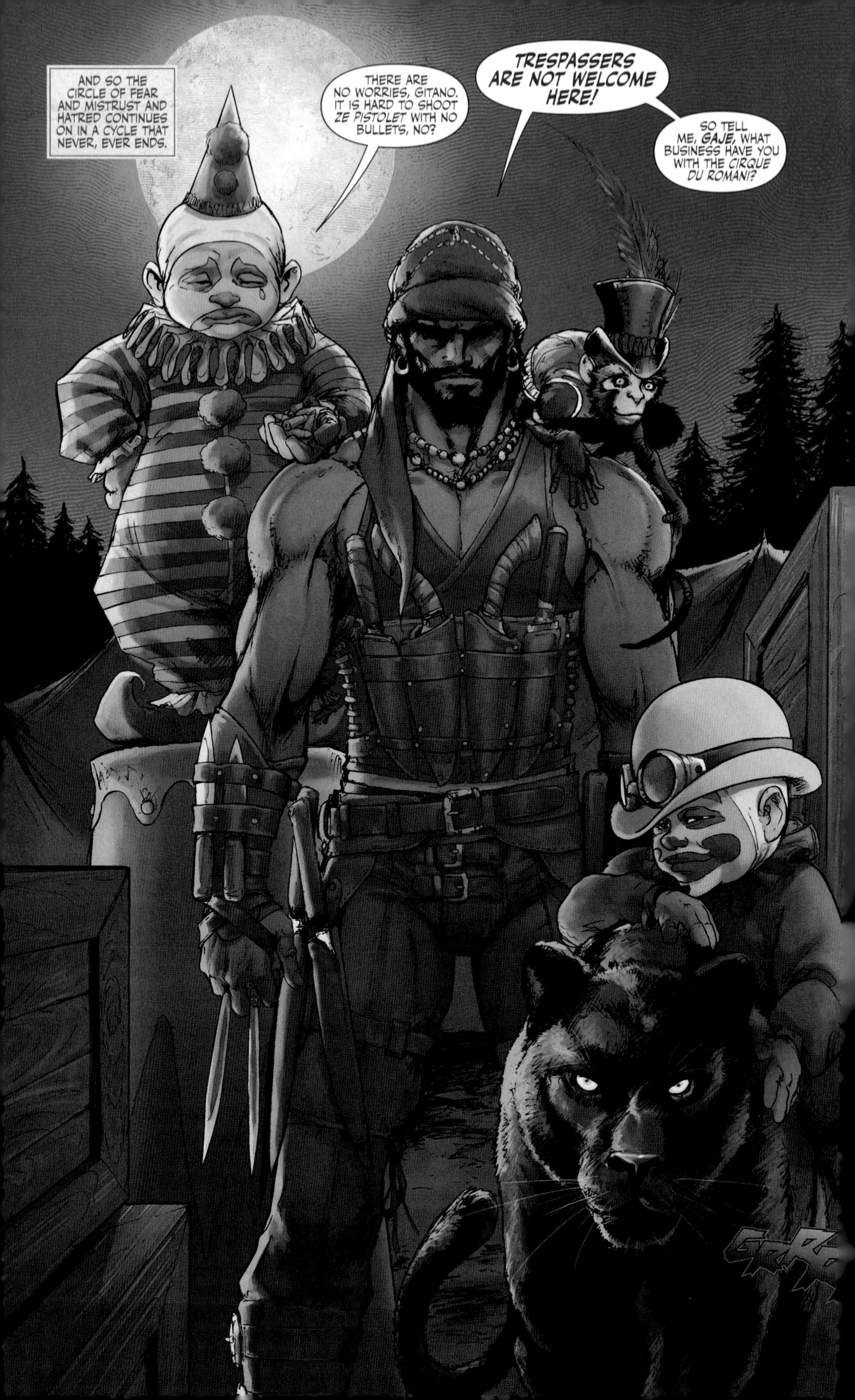
AND SO THE CIRCLE OF FEAR AND MISTRUST AND HATRED CONTINUES ON IN A CYCLE THAT NEVER, EVER ENDS.
THERE ARE NO WORRIES, GITANO. IT IS HARD TO SHOOT ZE PISTOLET WITH NO BULLETS, NO?
TRESPASSERS ARE NOT WELCOME HERE!
SO TELL ME, GAJE, WHAT BUSINESS HAVE YOU WITH THE CIRQUE DU ROMANI?

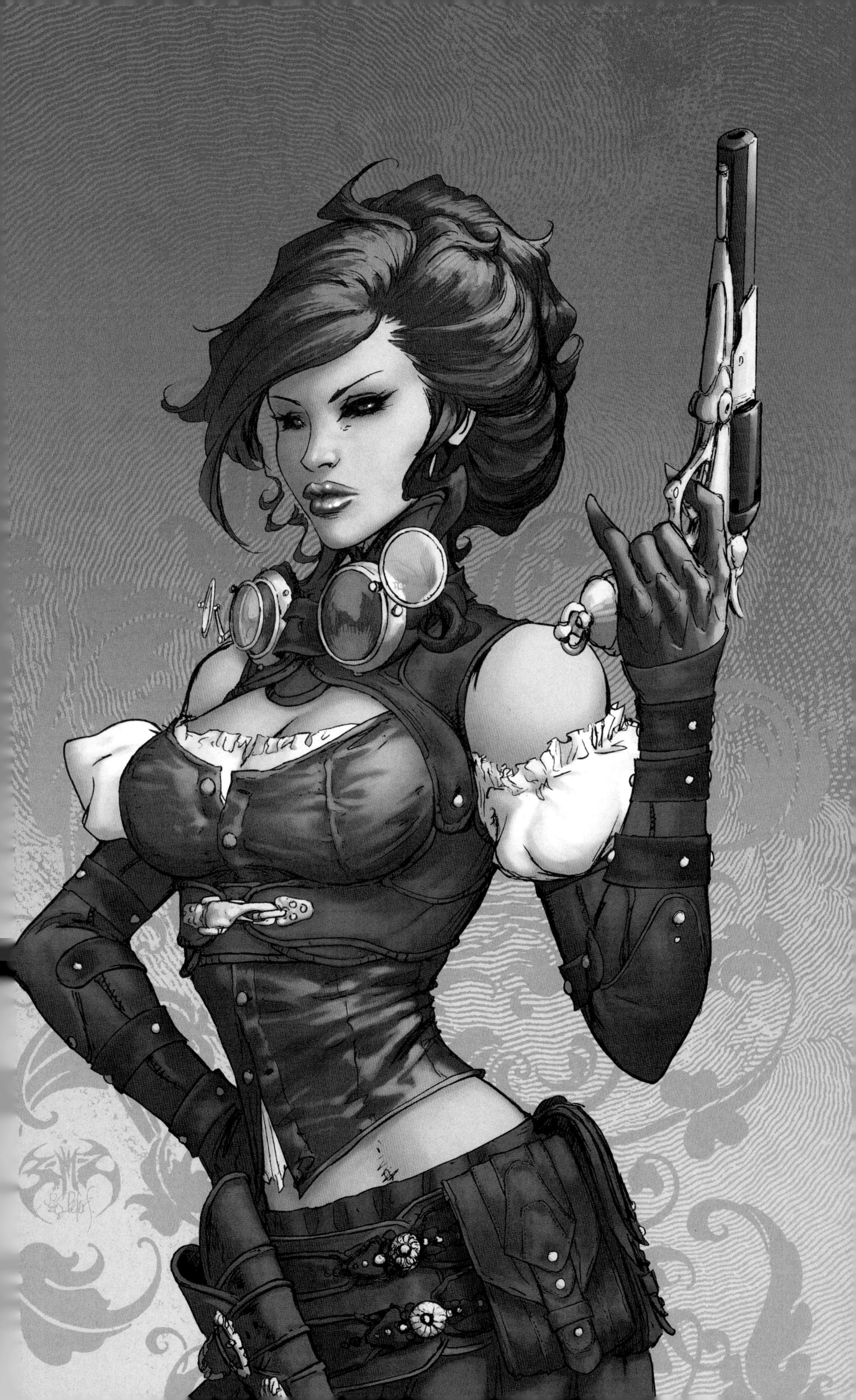

# Chapter Three

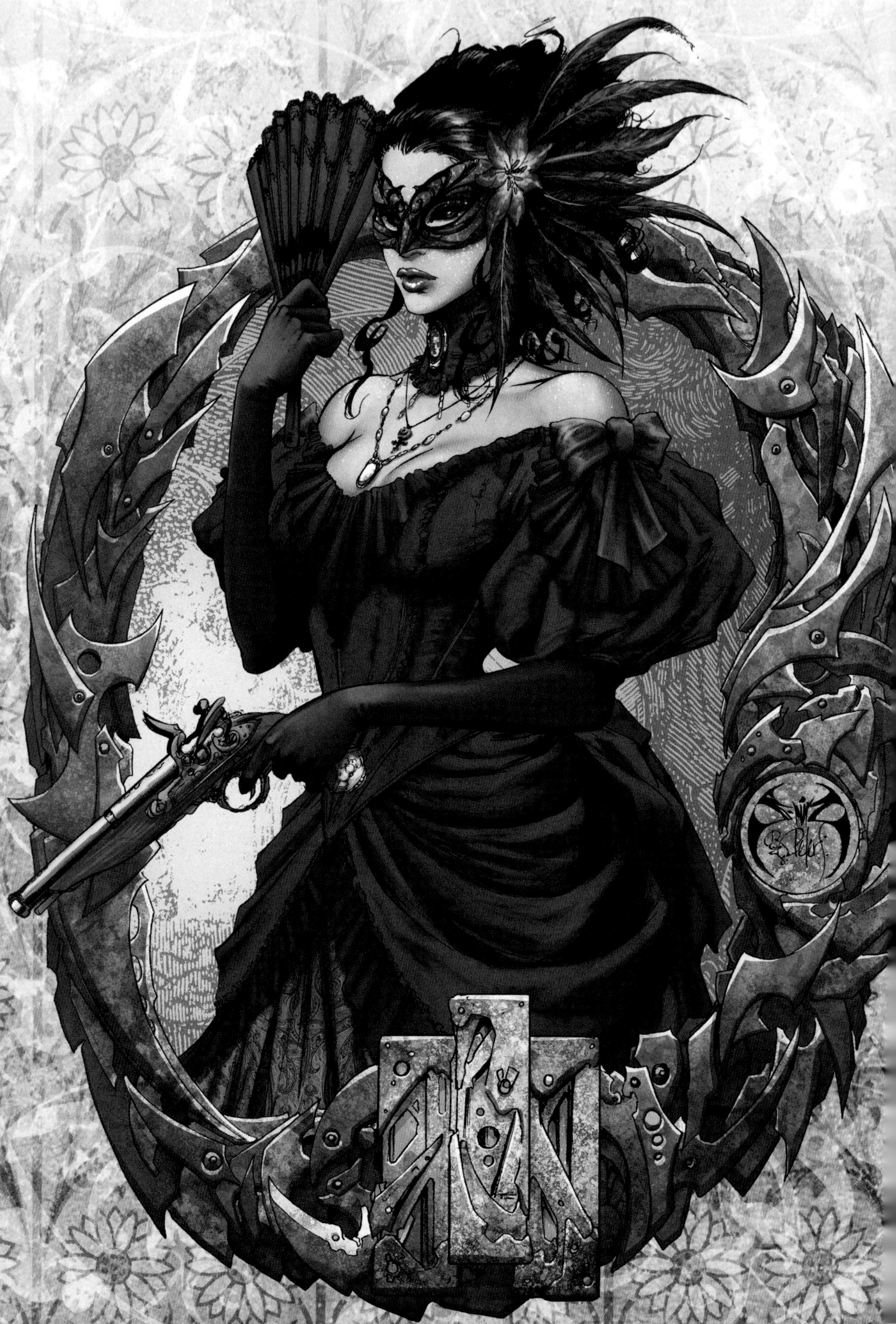

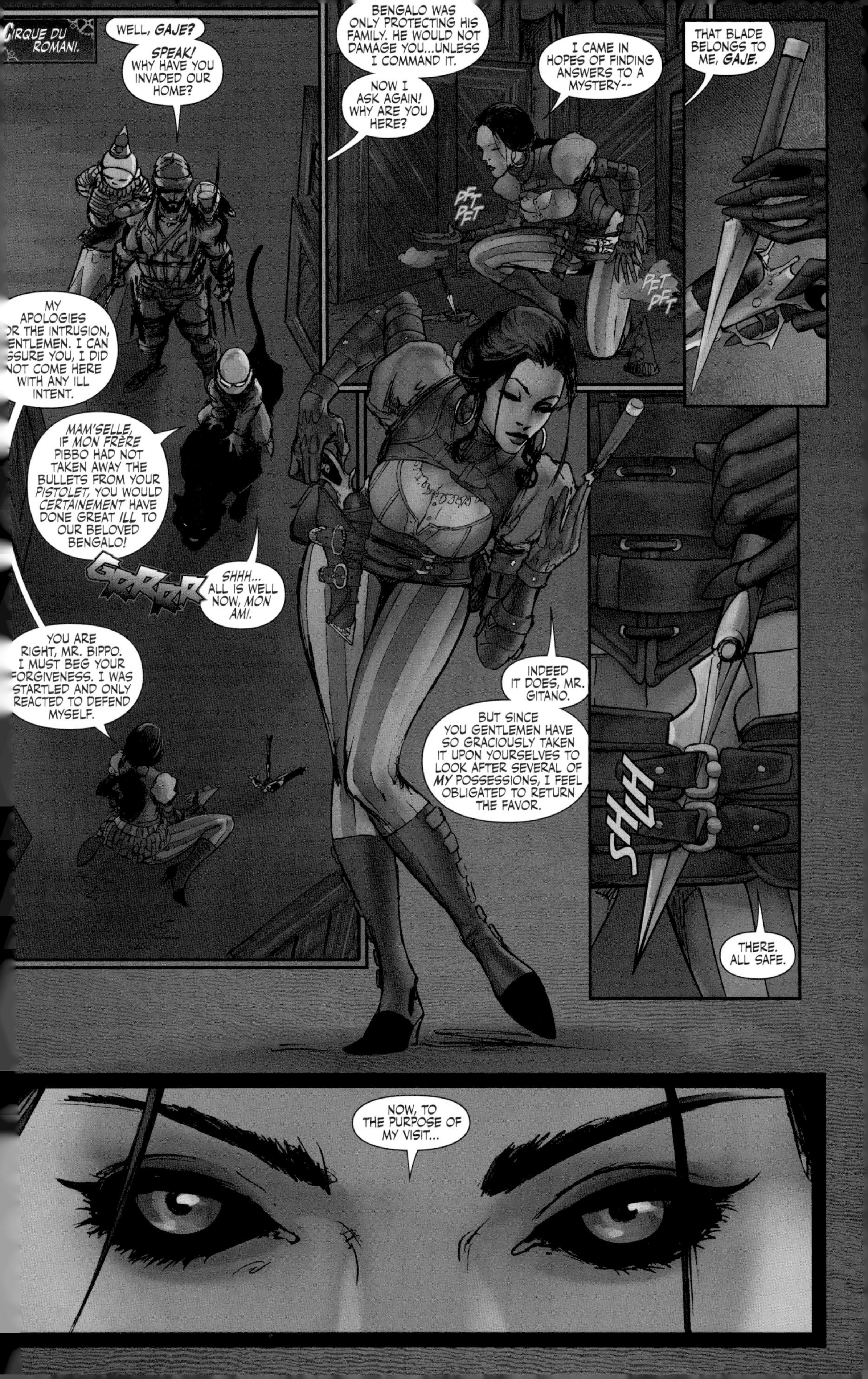
CIRQUE DU ROMANI.
WELL, GAJE? SPEAK! WHY HAVE YOU INVADED OUR HOME?
BENGALO WAS ONLY PROTECTING HIS FAMILY. HE WOULD NOT DAMAGE YOU...UNLESS I COMMAND IT.
NOW I ASK AGAIN! WHY ARE YOU HERE?
I CAME IN HOPES OF FINDING ANSWERS TO A MYSTERY--
PFT PFT
PFT PFT
THAT BLADE BELONGS TO ME, GAJE.
MY APOLOGIES FOR THE INTRUSION, GENTLEMEN. I CAN ASSURE YOU, I DID NOT COME HERE WITH ANY ILL INTENT.
MAM'SELLE, IF MON FRÈRE PIBBO HAD NOT TAKEN AWAY THE BULLETS FROM YOUR PISTOLET, YOU WOULD CERTAINEMENT HAVE DONE GREAT ILL TO OUR BELOVED BENGALO!
GRRRR
SHHH... ALL IS WELL NOW, MON AMI.
YOU ARE RIGHT, MR. BIPPO. I MUST BEG YOUR FORGIVENESS. I WAS STARTLED AND ONLY REACTED TO DEFEND MYSELF.
INDEED IT DOES, MR. GITANO.
BUT SINCE YOU GENTLEMEN HAVE SO GRACIOUSLY TAKEN IT UPON YOURSELVES TO LOOK AFTER SEVERAL OF MY POSSESSIONS, I FEEL OBLIGATED TO RETURN THE FAVOR.
SHIH
THERE. ALL SAFE.
NOW, TO THE PURPOSE OF MY VISIT...

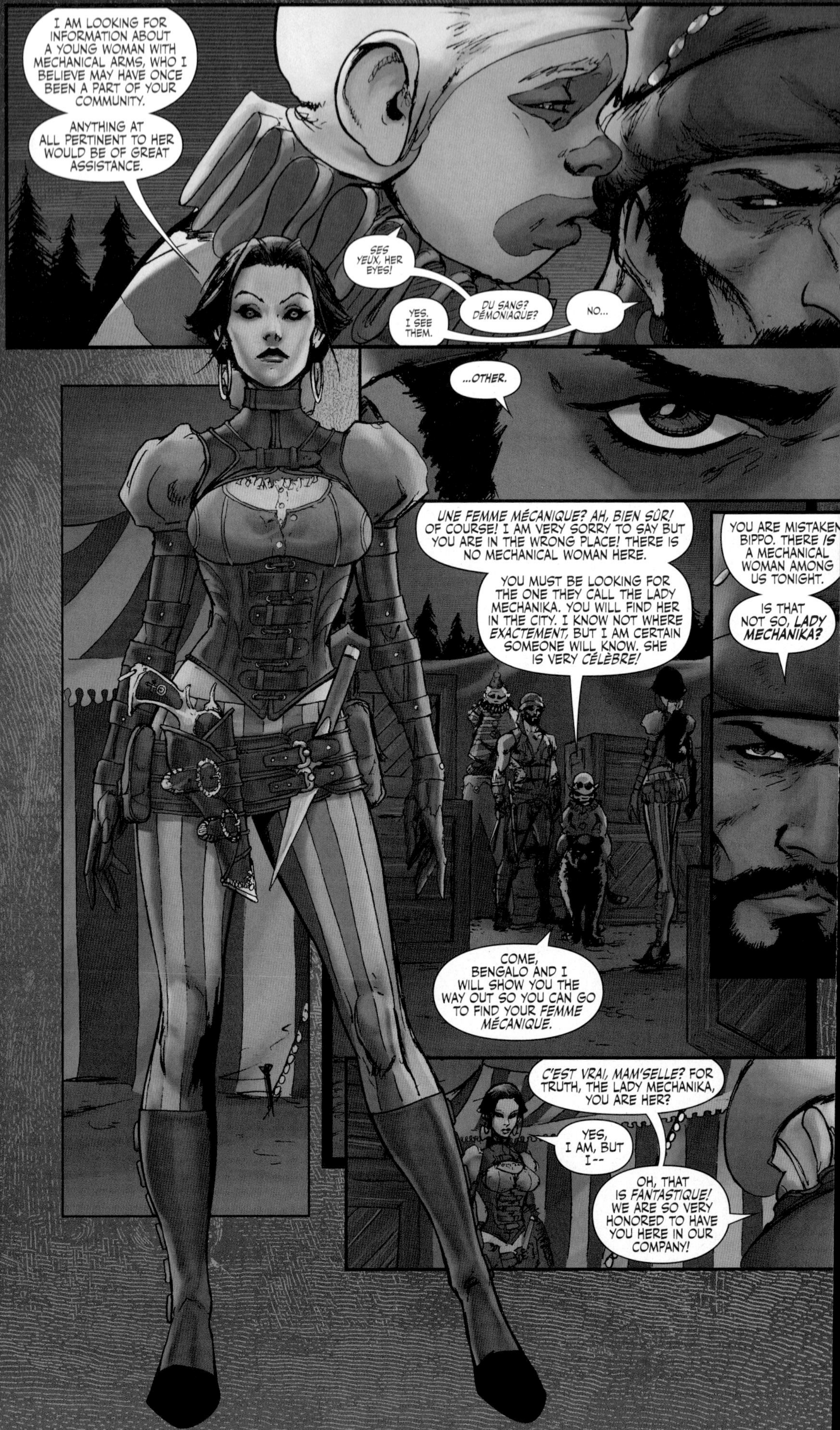
I AM LOOKING FOR INFORMATION ABOUT A YOUNG WOMAN WITH MECHANICAL ARMS, WHO I BELIEVE MAY HAVE ONCE BEEN A PART OF YOUR COMMUNITY.
ANYTHING AT ALL PERTINENT TO HER WOULD BE OF GREAT ASSISTANCE.
SES YEUX, HER EYES!
DU SANG? DÉMONIAQUE?
YES. I SEE THEM.
NO...
...OTHER.
UNE FEMME MÉCANIQUE? AH, BIEN SÛR! OF COURSE! I AM VERY SORRY TO SAY BUT YOU ARE IN THE WRONG PLACE! THERE IS NO MECHANICAL WOMAN HERE.
YOU MUST BE LOOKING FOR THE ONE THEY CALL THE LADY MECHANIKA. YOU WILL FIND HER IN THE CITY. I KNOW NOT WHERE EXACTEMENT, BUT I AM CERTAIN SOMEONE WILL KNOW. SHE IS VERY CÉLÈBRE!
COME, BENGALO AND I WILL SHOW YOU THE WAY OUT SO YOU CAN GO TO FIND YOUR FEMME MÉCANIQUE.
YOU ARE MISTAKEN BIPPO. THERE IS A MECHANICAL WOMAN AMONG US TONIGHT.
IS THAT NOT SO, LADY MECHANIKA?
C'EST VRAI, MAM'SELLE? FOR TRUTH, THE LADY MECHANIKA, YOU ARE HER?
YES, I AM, BUT I--
OH, THAT IS FANTASTIQUE! WE ARE SO VERY HONORED TO HAVE YOU HERE IN OUR COMPANY!

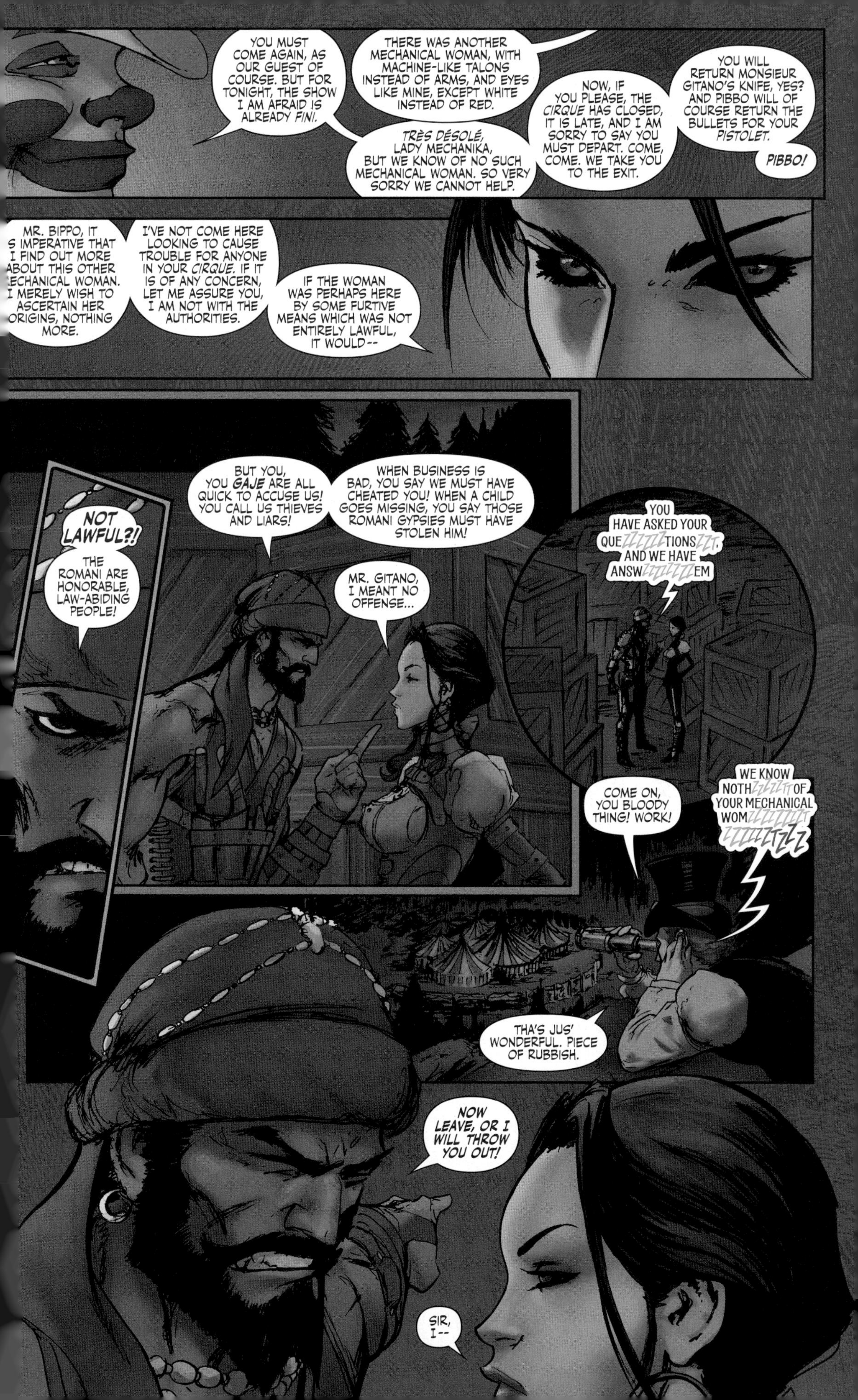
YOU MUST COME AGAIN, AS OUR GUEST OF COURSE. BUT FOR TONIGHT, THE SHOW I AM AFRAID IS ALREADY *FINI*.
THERE WAS ANOTHER MECHANICAL WOMAN, WITH MACHINE-LIKE TALONS INSTEAD OF ARMS, AND EYES LIKE MINE, EXCEPT WHITE INSTEAD OF RED.
*TRÈS DÉSOLÉ*, LADY MECHANIKA, BUT WE KNOW OF NO SUCH MECHANICAL WOMAN. SO VERY SORRY WE CANNOT HELP.
NOW, IF YOU PLEASE, THE *CIRQUE* HAS CLOSED, IT IS LATE, AND I AM SORRY TO SAY YOU MUST DEPART. COME, COME. WE TAKE YOU TO THE EXIT.
YOU WILL RETURN MONSIEUR GITANO'S KNIFE, YES? AND PIBBO WILL OF COURSE RETURN THE BULLETS FOR YOUR *PISTOLET*.
*PIBBO!*
MR. BIPPO, IT S IMPERATIVE THAT I FIND OUT MORE ABOUT THIS OTHER ECHANICAL WOMAN. I MERELY WISH TO ASCERTAIN HER ORIGINS, NOTHING MORE.
I'VE NOT COME HERE LOOKING TO CAUSE TROUBLE FOR ANYONE IN YOUR *CIRQUE*. IF IT IS OF ANY CONCERN, LET ME ASSURE YOU, I AM NOT WITH THE AUTHORITIES.
IF THE WOMAN WAS PERHAPS HERE BY SOME FURTIVE MEANS WHICH WAS NOT ENTIRELY LAWFUL, IT WOULD--
*NOT LAWFUL?!*
THE ROMANI ARE HONORABLE, LAW-ABIDING PEOPLE!
BUT YOU, YOU ***GAJE*** ARE ALL QUICK TO ACCUSE US! YOU CALL US THIEVES AND LIARS!
WHEN BUSINESS IS BAD, YOU SAY WE MUST HAVE CHEATED YOU! WHEN A CHILD GOES MISSING, YOU SAY THOSE ROMANI GYPSIES MUST HAVE STOLEN HIM!
MR. GITANO, I MEANT NO OFFENSE...
YOU HAVE ASKED YOUR QUEZZZZZZTIONSZZT, AND WE HAVE ANSWZZZZZZZZEM
COME ON, YOU BLOODY THING! WORK!
WE KNOW NOTHZZZZTT OF YOUR MECHANICAL WOMZZZZZZZTT ZZZZZZTZZZ
THA'S JUS' WONDERFUL. PIECE OF RUBBISH.
*NOW LEAVE, OR I WILL THROW YOU OUT!*
SIR, I--

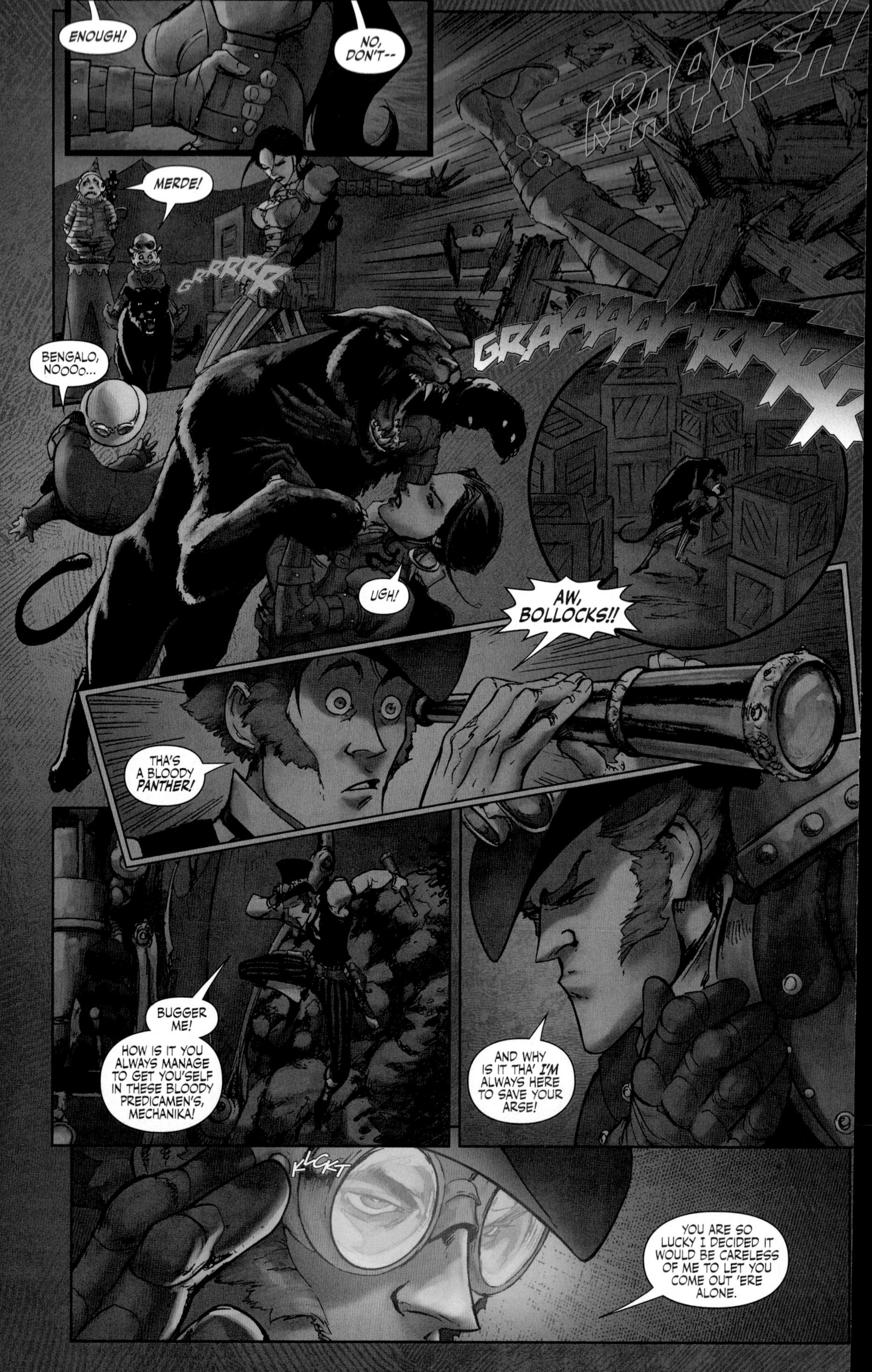
ENOUGH!
NO, DON'T--
KRAAAASH
MERDE!
GRRRRR
BENGALO, NOOOO...
GRAAAARRRR
UGH!
AW, BOLLOCKS!!
THA'S A BLOODY PANTHER!
BUGGER ME!
HOW IS IT YOU ALWAYS MANAGE TO GET YOU'SELF IN THESE BLOODY PREDICAMEN'S, MECHANIKA!
AND WHY IS IT THA' I'M ALWAYS HERE TO SAVE YOUR ARSE!
KLCKT
YOU ARE SO LUCKY I DECIDED IT WOULD BE CARELESS OF ME TO LET YOU COME OUT 'ERE ALONE.

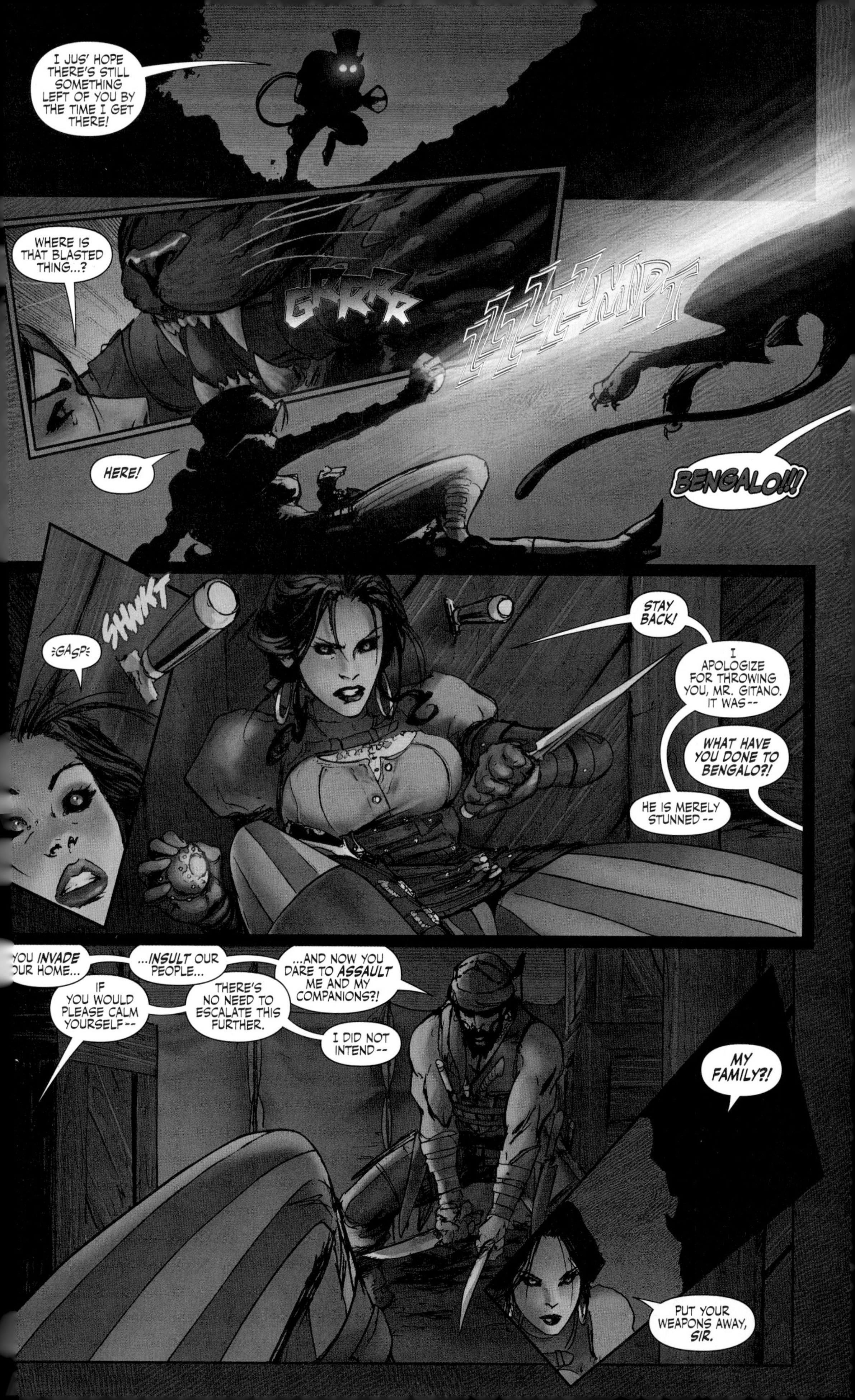
I JUS' HOPE THERE'S STILL SOMETHING LEFT OF YOU BY THE TIME I GET THERE!
WHERE IS THAT BLASTED THING...?
GRRR
ZZZZZMPT
HERE!
BENGALO!!!
SHWKT
GASP
STAY BACK!
I APOLOGIZE FOR THROWING YOU, MR. GITANO. IT WAS--
WHAT HAVE YOU DONE TO BENGALO?!
HE IS MERELY STUNNED --
YOU INVADE OUR HOME...
...INSULT OUR PEOPLE...
...AND NOW YOU DARE TO ASSAULT ME AND MY COMPANIONS?!
IF YOU WOULD PLEASE CALM YOURSELF--
THERE'S NO NEED TO ESCALATE THIS FURTHER.
I DID NOT INTEND--
MY FAMILY?!
PUT YOUR WEAPONS AWAY, SIR.

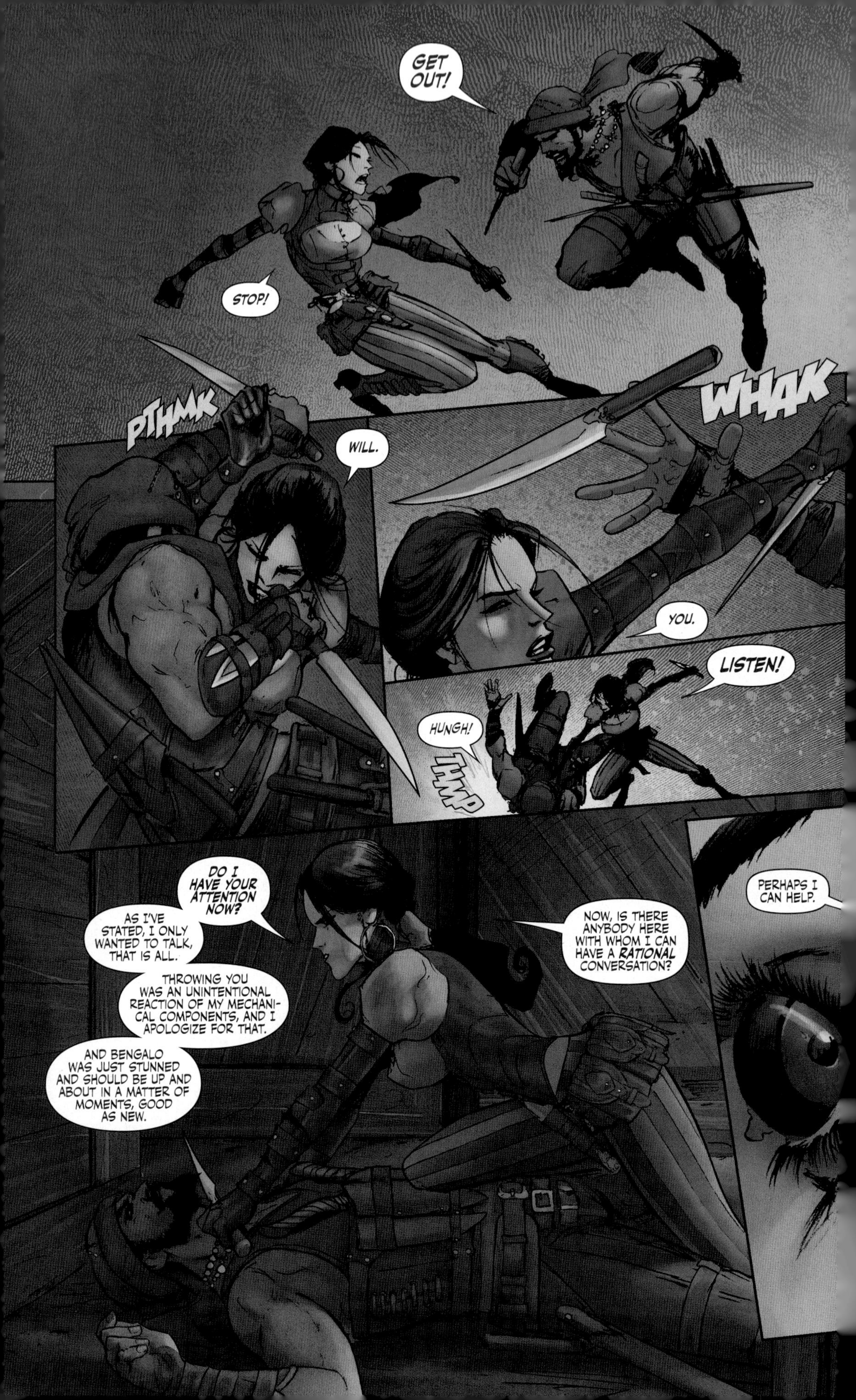
GET OUT!
STOP!
PTHMK
WILL.
WHAK
YOU.
LISTEN!
HUNGH!
THMP
DO I HAVE YOUR ATTENTION NOW?
AS I'VE STATED, I ONLY WANTED TO TALK, THAT IS ALL.
THROWING YOU WAS AN UNINTENTIONAL REACTION OF MY MECHANICAL COMPONENTS, AND I APOLOGIZE FOR THAT.
AND BENGALO WAS JUST STUNNED AND SHOULD BE UP AND ABOUT IN A MATTER OF MOMENTS, GOOD AS NEW.
NOW, IS THERE ANYBODY HERE WITH WHOM I CAN HAVE A RATIONAL CONVERSATION?
PERHAPS I CAN HELP.

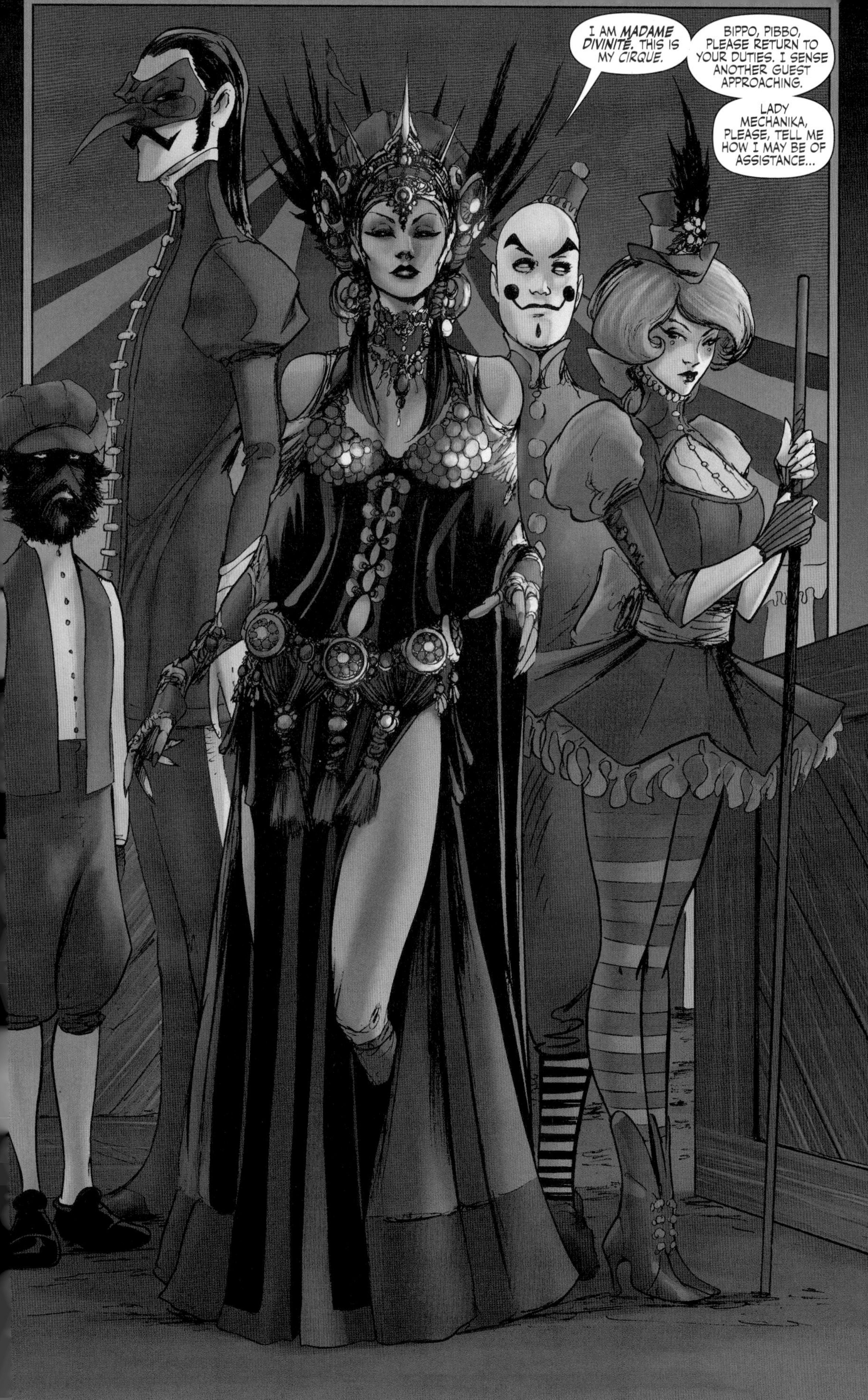
I AM *MADAME DIVINITÉ*. THIS IS MY *CIRQUE*.
BIPPO, PIBBO, PLEASE RETURN TO YOUR DUTIES. I SENSE ANOTHER GUEST APPROACHING.
LADY MECHANIKA, PLEASE, TELL ME HOW I MAY BE OF ASSISTANCE...

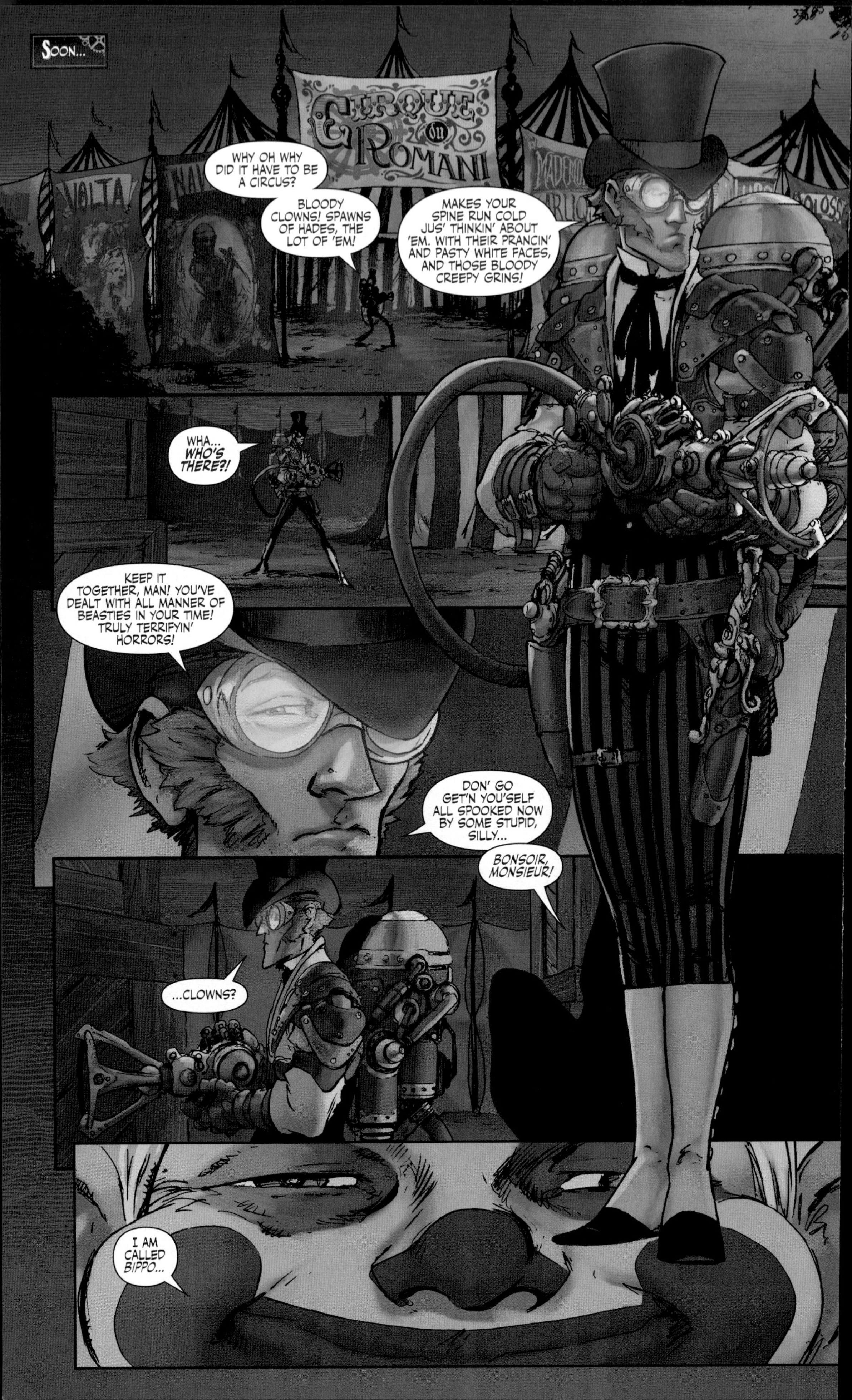
SOON...
CIRQUE DU ROMANI
VOLTA
MADEMO
WHY OH WHY DID IT HAVE TO BE A CIRCUS?
BLOODY CLOWNS! SPAWNS OF HADES, THE LOT OF 'EM!
MAKES YOUR SPINE RUN COLD JUS' THINKIN' ABOUT 'EM. WITH THEIR PRANCIN' AND PASTY WHITE FACES, AND THOSE BLOODY CREEPY GRINS!
WHA... WHO'S THERE?!
KEEP IT TOGETHER, MAN! YOU'VE DEALT WITH ALL MANNER OF BEASTIES IN YOUR TIME! TRULY TERRIFYIN' HORRORS!
DON' GO GET'N YOU'SELF ALL SPOOKED NOW BY SOME STUPID, SILLY...
BONSOIR, MONSIEUR!
...CLOWNS?
I AM CALLED BIPPO...

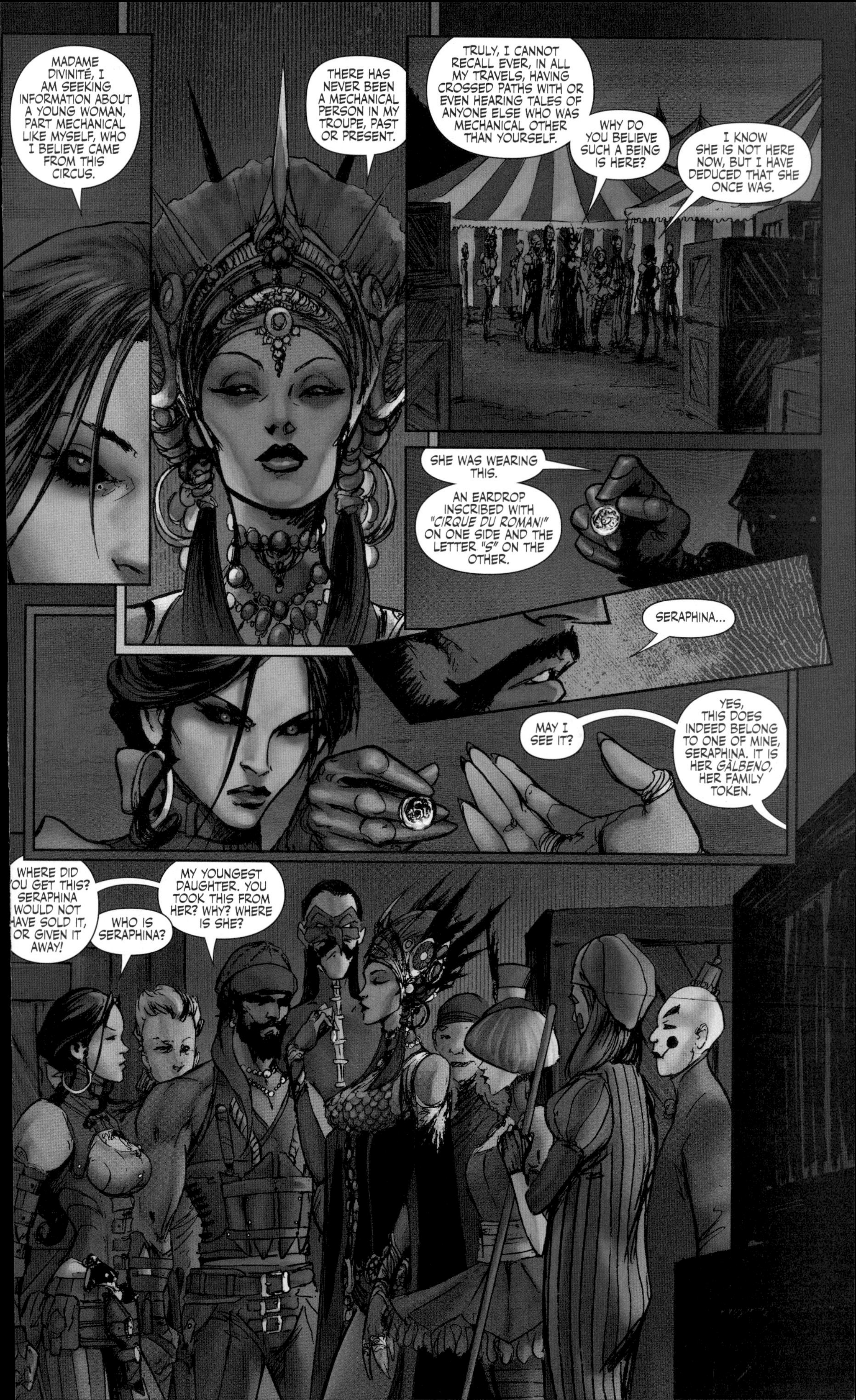
MADAME DIVINITÉ, I AM SEEKING INFORMATION ABOUT A YOUNG WOMAN, PART MECHANICAL LIKE MYSELF, WHO I BELIEVE CAME FROM THIS CIRCUS.
THERE HAS NEVER BEEN A MECHANICAL PERSON IN MY TROUPE, PAST OR PRESENT.
TRULY, I CANNOT RECALL EVER, IN ALL MY TRAVELS, HAVING CROSSED PATHS WITH OR EVEN HEARING TALES OF ANYONE ELSE WHO WAS MECHANICAL OTHER THAN YOURSELF.
WHY DO YOU BELIEVE SUCH A BEING IS HERE?
I KNOW SHE IS NOT HERE NOW, BUT I HAVE DEDUCED THAT SHE ONCE WAS.
SHE WAS WEARING THIS.
AN EARDROP INSCRIBED WITH *"CIRQUE DU ROMANI"* ON ONE SIDE AND THE LETTER "S" ON THE OTHER.
SERAPHINA...
MAY I SEE IT?
YES, THIS DOES INDEED BELONG TO ONE OF MINE, SERAPHINA. IT IS HER *GÄLBENO*, HER FAMILY TOKEN.
WHERE DID YOU GET THIS? SERAPHINA WOULD NOT HAVE SOLD IT, OR GIVEN IT AWAY!
WHO IS SERAPHINA?
MY YOUNGEST DAUGHTER. YOU TOOK THIS FROM HER? WHY? WHERE IS SHE?

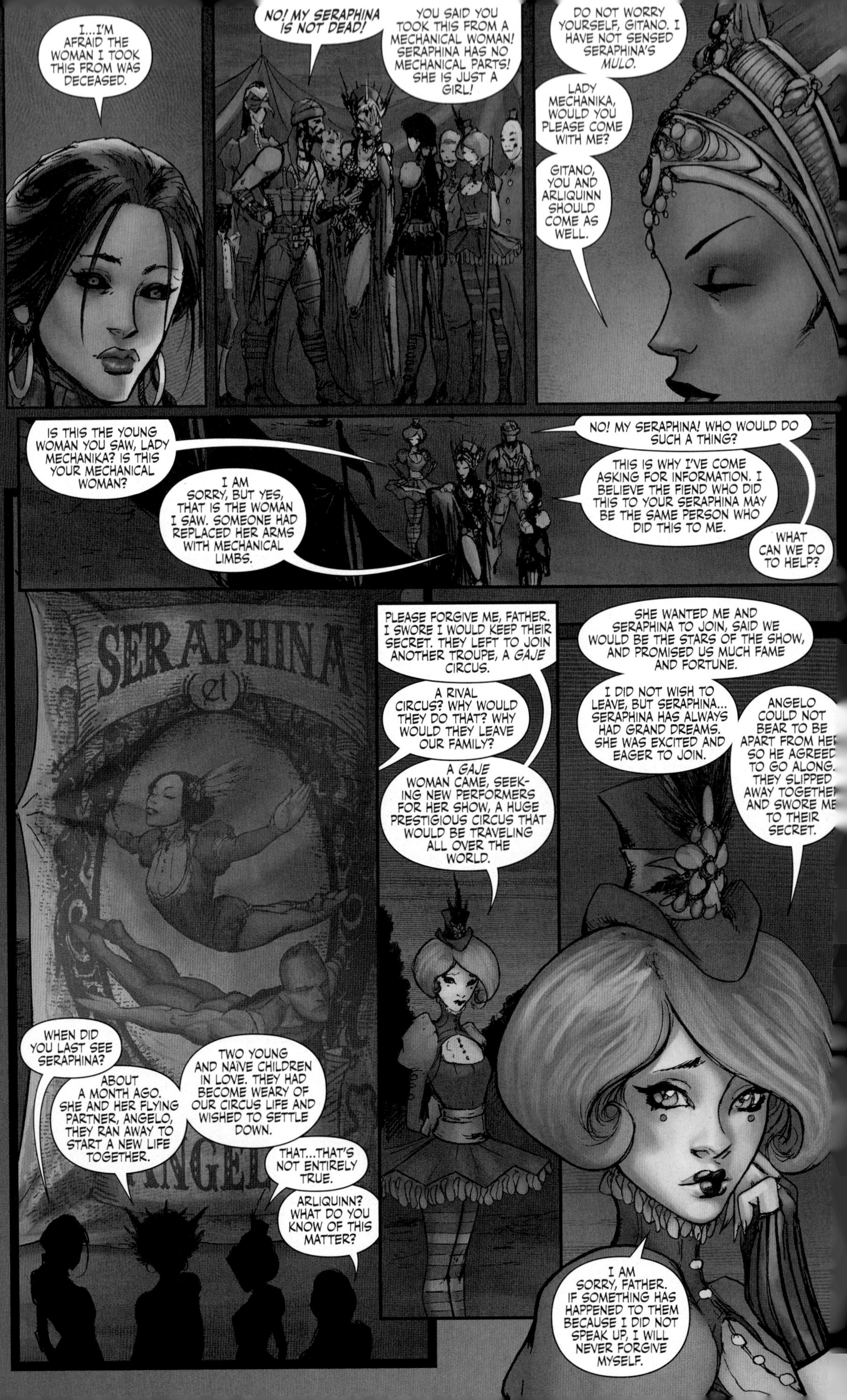
I...I'M AFRAID THE WOMAN I TOOK THIS FROM WAS DECEASED.
NO! MY SERAPHINA IS NOT DEAD!
YOU SAID YOU TOOK THIS FROM A MECHANICAL WOMAN! SERAPHINA HAS NO MECHANICAL PARTS! SHE IS JUST A GIRL!
DO NOT WORRY YOURSELF, GITANO. I HAVE NOT SENSED SERAPHINA'S MULO.
LADY MECHANIKA, WOULD YOU PLEASE COME WITH ME?
GITANO, YOU AND ARLIQUINN SHOULD COME AS WELL.
IS THIS THE YOUNG WOMAN YOU SAW, LADY MECHANIKA? IS THIS YOUR MECHANICAL WOMAN?
I AM SORRY, BUT YES, THAT IS THE WOMAN I SAW. SOMEONE HAD REPLACED HER ARMS WITH MECHANICAL LIMBS.
NO! MY SERAPHINA! WHO WOULD DO SUCH A THING?
THIS IS WHY I'VE COME ASKING FOR INFORMATION. I BELIEVE THE FIEND WHO DID THIS TO YOUR SERAPHINA MAY BE THE SAME PERSON WHO DID THIS TO ME.
WHAT CAN WE DO TO HELP?
SERAPHINA
et
ANGEL
WHEN DID YOU LAST SEE SERAPHINA?
ABOUT A MONTH AGO. SHE AND HER FLYING PARTNER, ANGELO, THEY RAN AWAY TO START A NEW LIFE TOGETHER.
TWO YOUNG AND NAÏVE CHILDREN IN LOVE. THEY HAD BECOME WEARY OF OUR CIRCUS LIFE AND WISHED TO SETTLE DOWN.
THAT...THAT'S NOT ENTIRELY TRUE.
ARLIQUINN? WHAT DO YOU KNOW OF THIS MATTER?
PLEASE FORGIVE ME, FATHER. I SWORE I WOULD KEEP THEIR SECRET. THEY LEFT TO JOIN ANOTHER TROUPE, A GAJE CIRCUS.
A RIVAL CIRCUS? WHY WOULD THEY DO THAT? WHY WOULD THEY LEAVE OUR FAMILY?
A GAJE WOMAN CAME, SEEKING NEW PERFORMERS FOR HER SHOW, A HUGE PRESTIGIOUS CIRCUS THAT WOULD BE TRAVELING ALL OVER THE WORLD.
SHE WANTED ME AND SERAPHINA TO JOIN, SAID WE WOULD BE THE STARS OF THE SHOW, AND PROMISED US MUCH FAME AND FORTUNE.
I DID NOT WISH TO LEAVE, BUT SERAPHINA... SERAPHINA HAS ALWAYS HAD GRAND DREAMS. SHE WAS EXCITED AND EAGER TO JOIN.
ANGELO COULD NOT BEAR TO BE APART FROM HER SO HE AGREED TO GO ALONG. THEY SLIPPED AWAY TOGETHER AND SWORE ME TO THEIR SECRET.
I AM SORRY, FATHER. IF SOMETHING HAS HAPPENED TO THEM BECAUSE I DID NOT SPEAK UP, I WILL NEVER FORGIVE MYSELF.

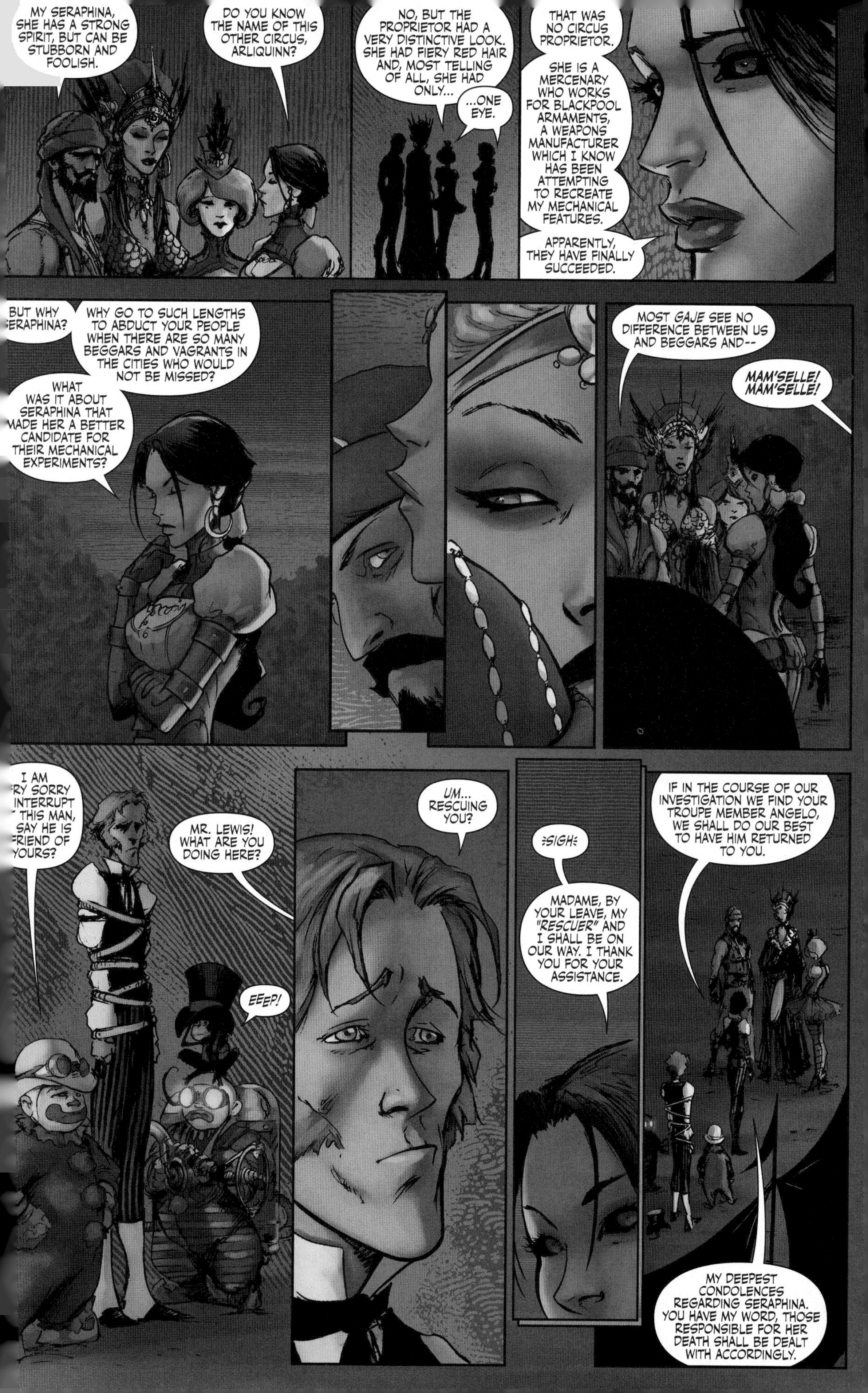
MY SERAPHINA, SHE HAS A STRONG SPIRIT, BUT CAN BE STUBBORN AND FOOLISH.
DO YOU KNOW THE NAME OF THIS OTHER CIRCUS, ARLIQUINN?
NO, BUT THE PROPRIETOR HAD A VERY DISTINCTIVE LOOK. SHE HAD FIERY RED HAIR AND, MOST TELLING OF ALL, SHE HAD ONLY...
...ONE EYE.
THAT WAS NO CIRCUS PROPRIETOR.
SHE IS A MERCENARY WHO WORKS FOR BLACKPOOL ARMAMENTS, A WEAPONS MANUFACTURER WHICH I KNOW HAS BEEN ATTEMPTING TO RECREATE MY MECHANICAL FEATURES.
APPARENTLY, THEY HAVE FINALLY SUCCEEDED.
BUT WHY ERAPHINA?
WHY GO TO SUCH LENGTHS TO ABDUCT YOUR PEOPLE WHEN THERE ARE SO MANY BEGGARS AND VAGRANTS IN THE CITIES WHO WOULD NOT BE MISSED?
WHAT WAS IT ABOUT SERAPHINA THAT MADE HER A BETTER CANDIDATE FOR THEIR MECHANICAL EXPERIMENTS?
MOST GAJE SEE NO DIFFERENCE BETWEEN US AND BEGGARS AND--
MAM'SELLE! MAM'SELLE!
I AM RY SORRY INTERRUPT THIS MAN, SAY HE IS FRIEND OF YOURS?
MR. LEWIS! WHAT ARE YOU DOING HERE?
EEEP!
UM... RESCUING YOU?
SIGH
MADAME, BY YOUR LEAVE, MY "RESCUER" AND I SHALL BE ON OUR WAY. I THANK YOU FOR YOUR ASSISTANCE.
IF IN THE COURSE OF OUR INVESTIGATION WE FIND YOUR TROUPE MEMBER ANGELO, WE SHALL DO OUR BEST TO HAVE HIM RETURNED TO YOU.
MY DEEPEST CONDOLENCES REGARDING SERAPHINA. YOU HAVE MY WORD, THOSE RESPONSIBLE FOR HER DEATH SHALL BE DEALT WITH ACCORDINGLY.

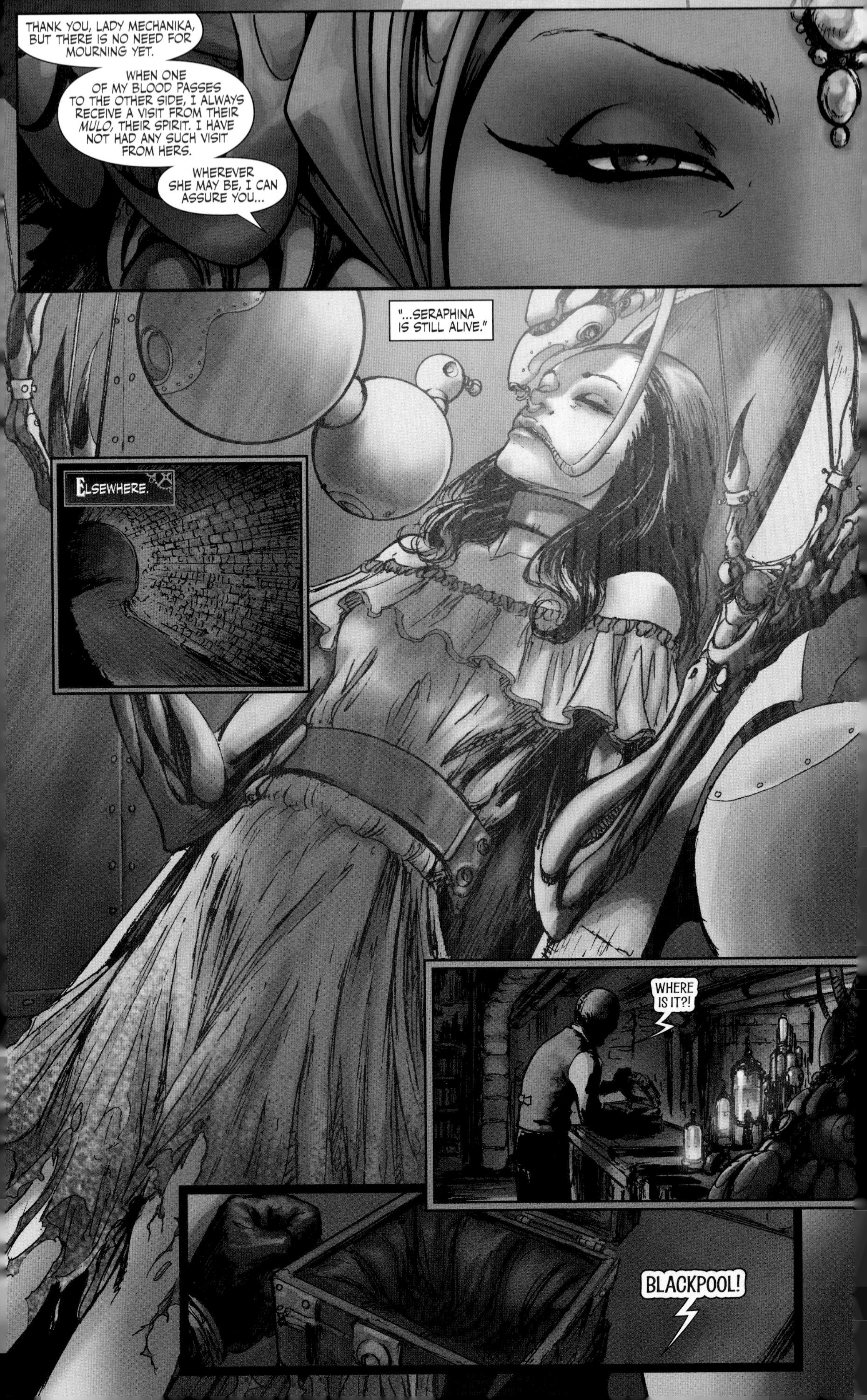

THANK YOU, LADY MECHANIKA, BUT THERE IS NO NEED FOR MOURNING YET.
WHEN ONE OF MY BLOOD PASSES TO THE OTHER SIDE, I ALWAYS RECEIVE A VISIT FROM THEIR *MULO*, THEIR SPIRIT. I HAVE NOT HAD ANY SUCH VISIT FROM HERS.
WHEREVER SHE MAY BE, I CAN ASSURE YOU...
"...SERAPHINA IS STILL ALIVE."
ELSEWHERE.
WHERE IS IT?!
BLACKPOOL!

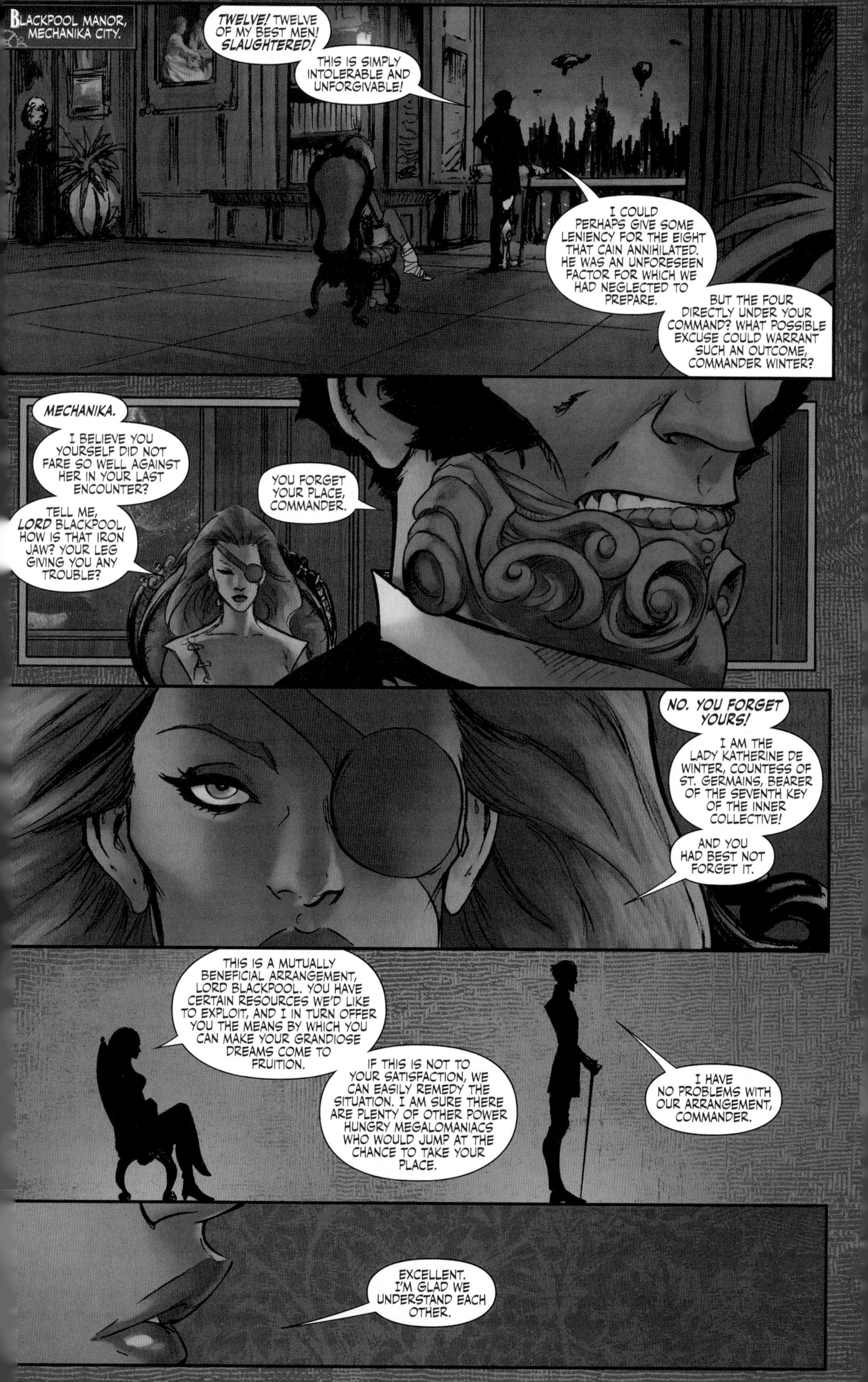

BLACKPOOL MANOR, MECHANIKA CITY.
TWELVE! TWELVE OF MY BEST MEN! SLAUGHTERED!
THIS IS SIMPLY INTOLERABLE AND UNFORGIVABLE!
I COULD PERHAPS GIVE SOME LENIENCY FOR THE EIGHT THAT CAIN ANNIHILATED. HE WAS AN UNFORESEEN FACTOR FOR WHICH WE HAD NEGLECTED TO PREPARE.
BUT THE FOUR DIRECTLY UNDER YOUR COMMAND? WHAT POSSIBLE EXCUSE COULD WARRANT SUCH AN OUTCOME, COMMANDER WINTER?
MECHANIKA.
I BELIEVE YOU YOURSELF DID NOT FARE SO WELL AGAINST HER IN YOUR LAST ENCOUNTER?
TELL ME, LORD BLACKPOOL, HOW IS THAT IRON JAW? YOUR LEG GIVING YOU ANY TROUBLE?
YOU FORGET YOUR PLACE, COMMANDER.
NO. YOU FORGET YOURS!
I AM THE LADY KATHERINE DE WINTER, COUNTESS OF ST. GERMAINS, BEARER OF THE SEVENTH KEY OF THE INNER COLLECTIVE!
AND YOU HAD BEST NOT FORGET IT.
THIS IS A MUTUALLY BENEFICIAL ARRANGEMENT, LORD BLACKPOOL. YOU HAVE CERTAIN RESOURCES WE'D LIKE TO EXPLOIT, AND I IN TURN OFFER YOU THE MEANS BY WHICH YOU CAN MAKE YOUR GRANDIOSE DREAMS COME TO FRUITION.
IF THIS IS NOT TO YOUR SATISFACTION, WE CAN EASILY REMEDY THE SITUATION. I AM SURE THERE ARE PLENTY OF OTHER POWER HUNGRY MEGALOMANIACS WHO WOULD JUMP AT THE CHANCE TO TAKE YOUR PLACE.
I HAVE NO PROBLEMS WITH OUR ARRANGEMENT, COMMANDER.
EXCELLENT. I'M GLAD WE UNDERSTAND EACH OTHER.

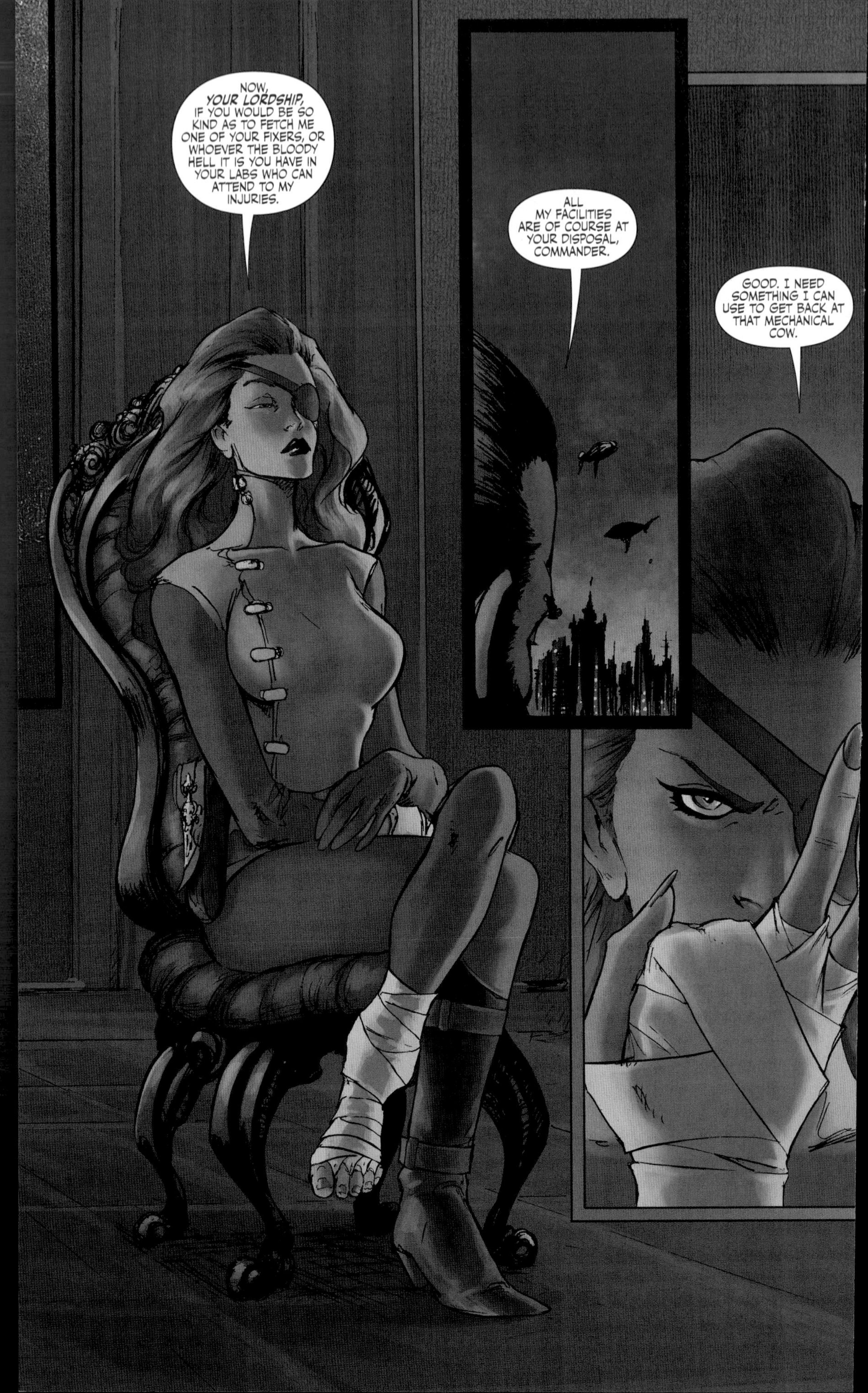
NOW, *YOUR LORDSHIP,* IF YOU WOULD BE SO KIND AS TO FETCH ME ONE OF YOUR FIXERS, OR WHOEVER THE BLOODY HELL IT IS YOU HAVE IN YOUR LABS WHO CAN ATTEND TO MY INJURIES.
ALL MY FACILITIES ARE OF COURSE AT YOUR DISPOSAL, COMMANDER.
GOOD. I NEED SOMETHING I CAN USE TO GET BACK AT THAT MECHANICAL COW.

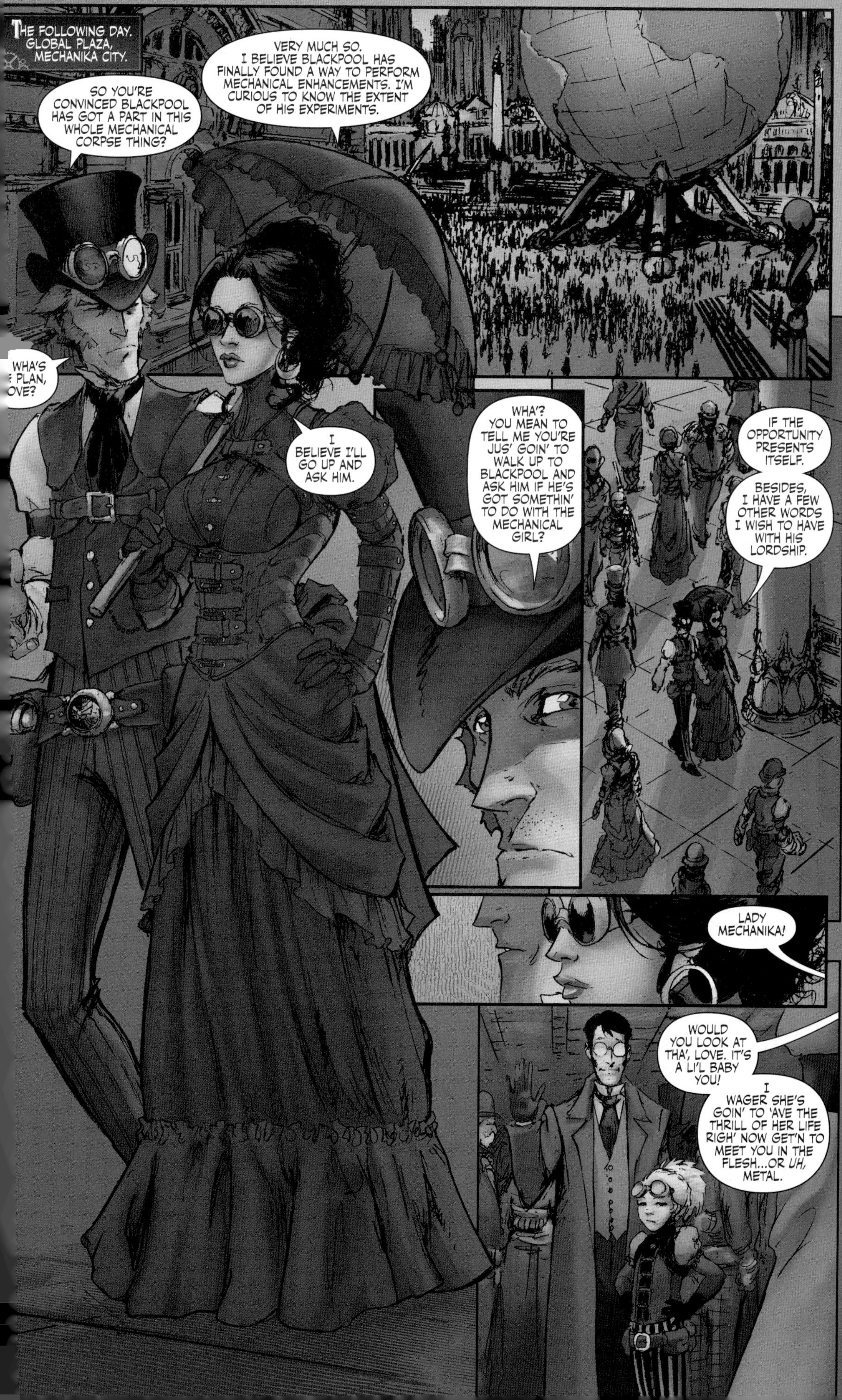
THE FOLLOWING DAY. GLOBAL PLAZA, MECHANIKA CITY.
SO YOU'RE CONVINCED BLACKPOOL HAS GOT A PART IN THIS WHOLE MECHANICAL CORPSE THING?
VERY MUCH SO. I BELIEVE BLACKPOOL HAS FINALLY FOUND A WAY TO PERFORM MECHANICAL ENHANCEMENTS. I'M CURIOUS TO KNOW THE EXTENT OF HIS EXPERIMENTS.
WHA'S E PLAN, OVE?
I BELIEVE I'LL GO UP AND ASK HIM.
WHA'? YOU MEAN TO TELL ME YOU'RE JUS' GOIN' TO WALK UP TO BLACKPOOL AND ASK HIM IF HE'S GOT SOMETHIN' TO DO WITH THE MECHANICAL GIRL?
IF THE OPPORTUNITY PRESENTS ITSELF.
BESIDES, I HAVE A FEW OTHER WORDS I WISH TO HAVE WITH HIS LORDSHIP.
LADY MECHANIKA!
WOULD YOU LOOK AT THA', LOVE. IT'S A LI'L BABY YOU!
I WAGER SHE'S GOIN' TO 'AVE THE THRILL OF HER LIFE RIGH' NOW GET'N TO MEET YOU IN THE FLESH...OR UH, METAL.

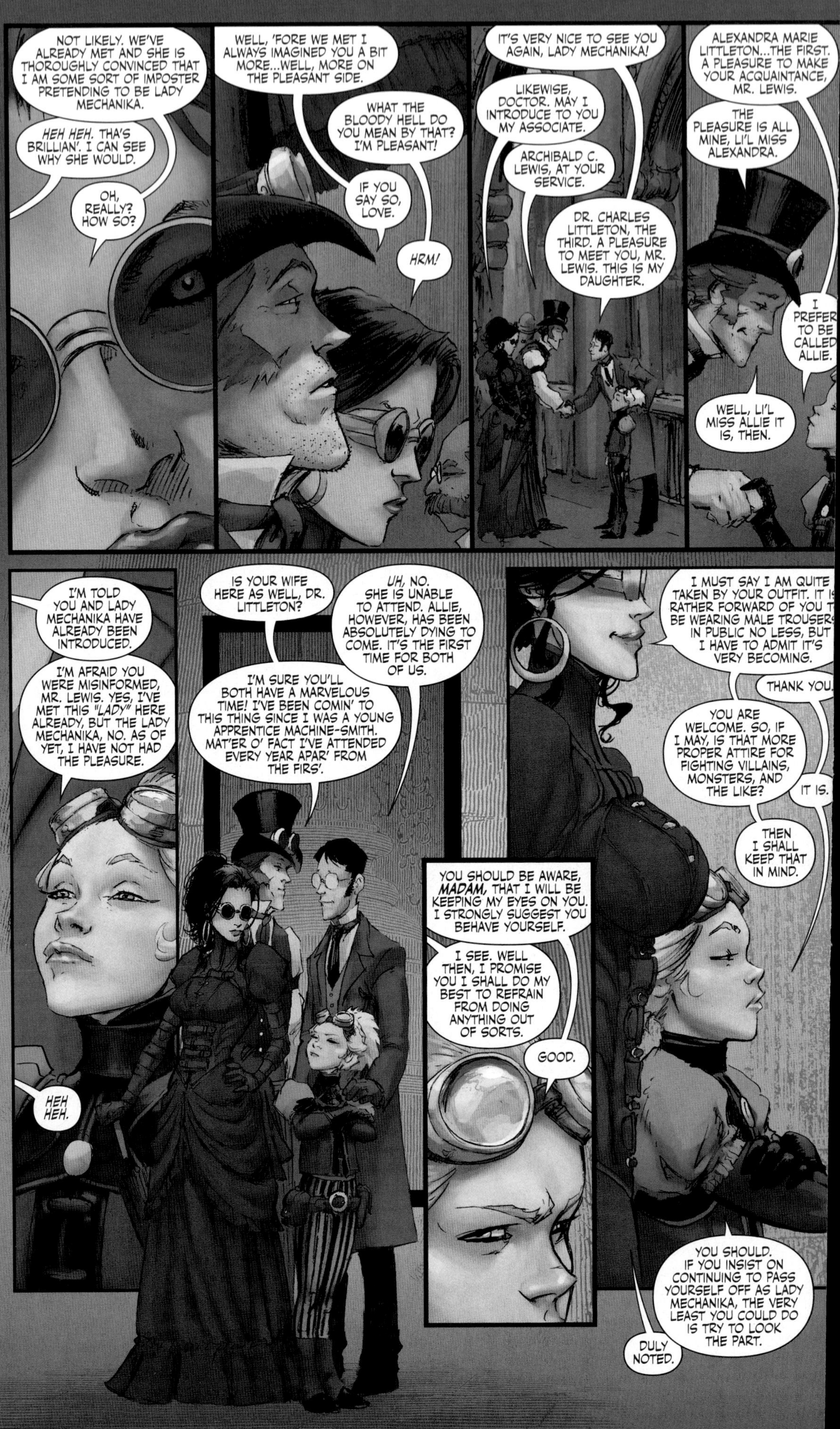
NOT LIKELY. WE'VE ALREADY MET AND SHE IS THOROUGHLY CONVINCED THAT I AM SOME SORT OF IMPOSTER PRETENDING TO BE LADY MECHANIKA.
HEH HEH. THA'S BRILLIAN'. I CAN SEE WHY SHE WOULD.
OH, REALLY? HOW SO?
WELL, 'FORE WE MET I ALWAYS IMAGINED YOU A BIT MORE...WELL, MORE ON THE PLEASANT SIDE.
WHAT THE BLOODY HELL DO YOU MEAN BY THAT? I'M PLEASANT!
IF YOU SAY SO, LOVE.
HRM!
IT'S VERY NICE TO SEE YOU AGAIN, LADY MECHANIKA!
LIKEWISE, DOCTOR. MAY I INTRODUCE TO YOU MY ASSOCIATE.
ARCHIBALD C. LEWIS, AT YOUR SERVICE.
DR. CHARLES LITTLETON, THE THIRD. A PLEASURE TO MEET YOU, MR. LEWIS. THIS IS MY DAUGHTER.
ALEXANDRA MARIE LITTLETON...THE FIRST. A PLEASURE TO MAKE YOUR ACQUAINTANCE, MR. LEWIS.
THE PLEASURE IS ALL MINE, LI'L MISS ALEXANDRA.
I PREFER TO BE CALLED ALLIE.
WELL, LI'L MISS ALLIE IT IS, THEN.
I'M TOLD YOU AND LADY MECHANIKA HAVE ALREADY BEEN INTRODUCED.
I'M AFRAID YOU WERE MISINFORMED, MR. LEWIS. YES, I'VE MET THIS "LADY" HERE ALREADY, BUT THE LADY MECHANIKA, NO. AS OF YET, I HAVE NOT HAD THE PLEASURE.
HEH HEH.
IS YOUR WIFE HERE AS WELL, DR. LITTLETON?
UH, NO. SHE IS UNABLE TO ATTEND. ALLIE, HOWEVER, HAS BEEN ABSOLUTELY DYING TO COME. IT'S THE FIRST TIME FOR BOTH OF US.
I'M SURE YOU'LL BOTH HAVE A MARVELOUS TIME! I'VE BEEN COMIN' TO THIS THING SINCE I WAS A YOUNG APPRENTICE MACHINE-SMITH. MAT'ER O' FACT I'VE ATTENDED EVERY YEAR APAR' FROM THE FIRS'.
YOU SHOULD BE AWARE, MADAM, THAT I WILL BE KEEPING MY EYES ON YOU. I STRONGLY SUGGEST YOU BEHAVE YOURSELF.
I SEE. WELL THEN, I PROMISE YOU I SHALL DO MY BEST TO REFRAIN FROM DOING ANYTHING OUT OF SORTS.
GOOD.
I MUST SAY I AM QUITE TAKEN BY YOUR OUTFIT. IT IS RATHER FORWARD OF YOU TO BE WEARING MALE TROUSERS IN PUBLIC NO LESS, BUT I HAVE TO ADMIT IT'S VERY BECOMING.
THANK YOU.
YOU ARE WELCOME. SO, IF I MAY, IS THAT MORE PROPER ATTIRE FOR FIGHTING VILLAINS, MONSTERS, AND THE LIKE?
IT IS.
THEN I SHALL KEEP THAT IN MIND.
YOU SHOULD. IF YOU INSIST ON CONTINUING TO PASS YOURSELF OFF AS LADY MECHANIKA, THE VERY LEAST YOU COULD DO IS TRY TO LOOK THE PART.
DULY NOTED.

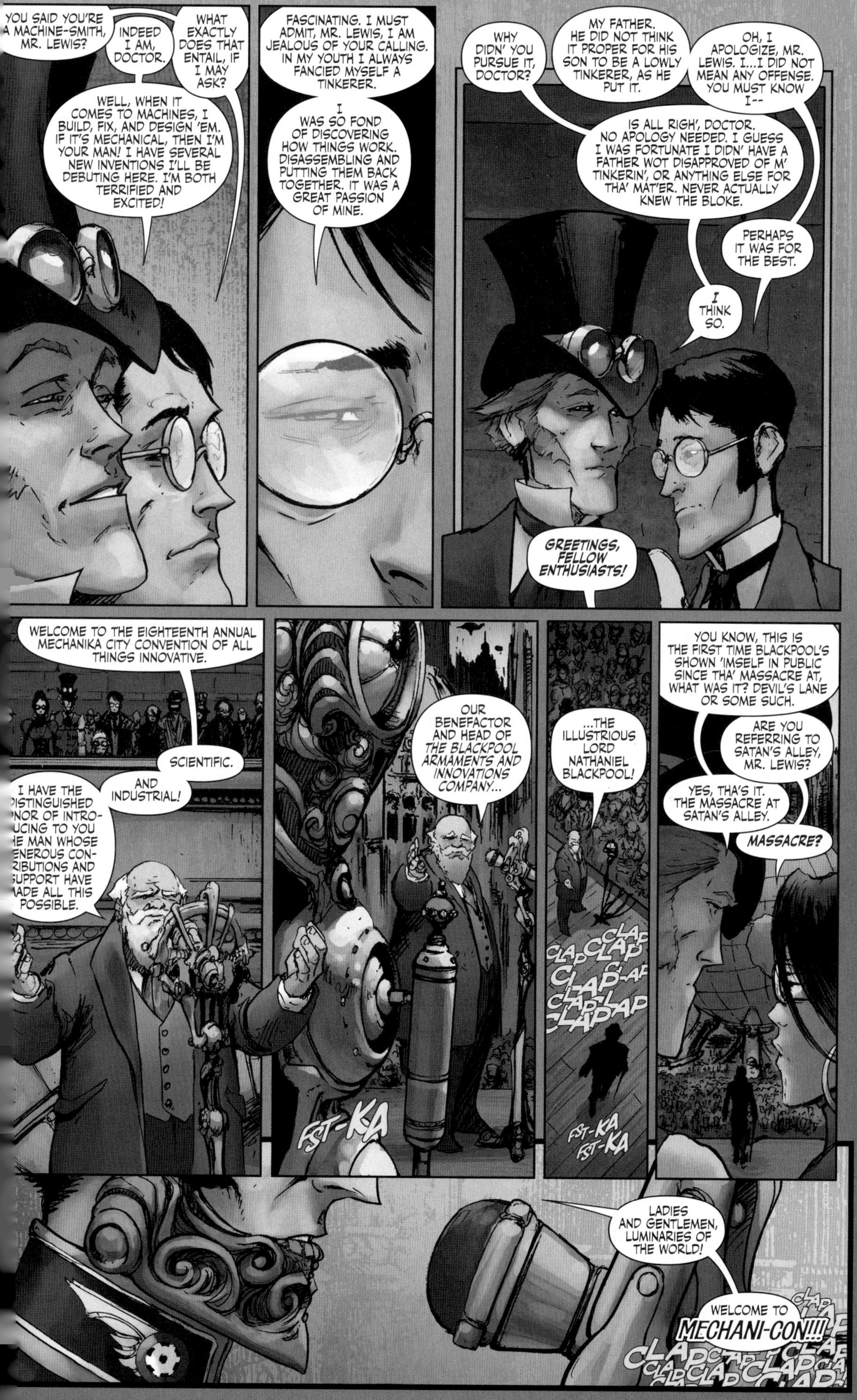
YOU SAID YOU'RE A MACHINE-SMITH, MR. LEWIS?
INDEED I AM, DOCTOR.
WHAT EXACTLY DOES THAT ENTAIL, IF I MAY ASK?
WELL, WHEN IT COMES TO MACHINES, I BUILD, FIX, AND DESIGN 'EM. IF IT'S MECHANICAL, THEN I'M YOUR MAN! I HAVE SEVERAL NEW INVENTIONS I'LL BE DEBUTING HERE. I'M BOTH TERRIFIED AND EXCITED!
FASCINATING. I MUST ADMIT, MR. LEWIS, I AM JEALOUS OF YOUR CALLING. IN MY YOUTH I ALWAYS FANCIED MYSELF A TINKERER.
I WAS SO FOND OF DISCOVERING HOW THINGS WORK. DISASSEMBLING AND PUTTING THEM BACK TOGETHER. IT WAS A GREAT PASSION OF MINE.
WHY DIDN' YOU PURSUE IT, DOCTOR?
MY FATHER. HE DID NOT THINK IT PROPER FOR HIS SON TO BE A LOWLY TINKERER, AS HE PUT IT.
OH, I APOLOGIZE, MR. LEWIS. I...I DID NOT MEAN ANY OFFENSE. YOU MUST KNOW I--
IS ALL RIGH', DOCTOR. NO APOLOGY NEEDED. I GUESS I WAS FORTUNATE I DIDN' HAVE A FATHER WOT DISAPPROVED OF M' TINKERIN', OR ANYTHING ELSE FOR THA' MAT'ER. NEVER ACTUALLY KNEW THE BLOKE.
PERHAPS IT WAS FOR THE BEST.
I THINK SO.
GREETINGS, FELLOW ENTHUSIASTS!
WELCOME TO THE EIGHTEENTH ANNUAL MECHANIKA CITY CONVENTION OF ALL THINGS INNOVATIVE.
SCIENTIFIC.
AND INDUSTRIAL!
I HAVE THE DISTINGUISHED ...NOR OF INTRO-UCING TO YOU ...HE MAN WHOSE ...ENEROUS CON-...RIBUTIONS AND ...UPPORT HAVE ...ADE ALL THIS POSSIBLE.
OUR BENEFACTOR AND HEAD OF THE BLACKPOOL ARMAMENTS AND INNOVATIONS COMPANY...
FST-KA
...THE ILLUSTRIOUS LORD NATHANIEL BLACKPOOL!
CLAP CLAP CLAP CLAP CLAP CLAP
FST-KA FST-KA
YOU KNOW, THIS IS THE FIRST TIME BLACKPOOL'S SHOWN 'IMSELF IN PUBLIC SINCE THA' MASSACRE AT, WHAT WAS IT? DEVIL'S LANE OR SOME SUCH.
ARE YOU REFERRING TO SATAN'S ALLEY, MR. LEWIS?
YES, THA'S IT. THE MASSACRE AT SATAN'S ALLEY.
MASSACRE?
LADIES AND GENTLEMEN, LUMINARIES OF THE WORLD!
WELCOME TO MECHANI-CON!!!
CLAP CLAP CLAP CLAP CLAP CLAP

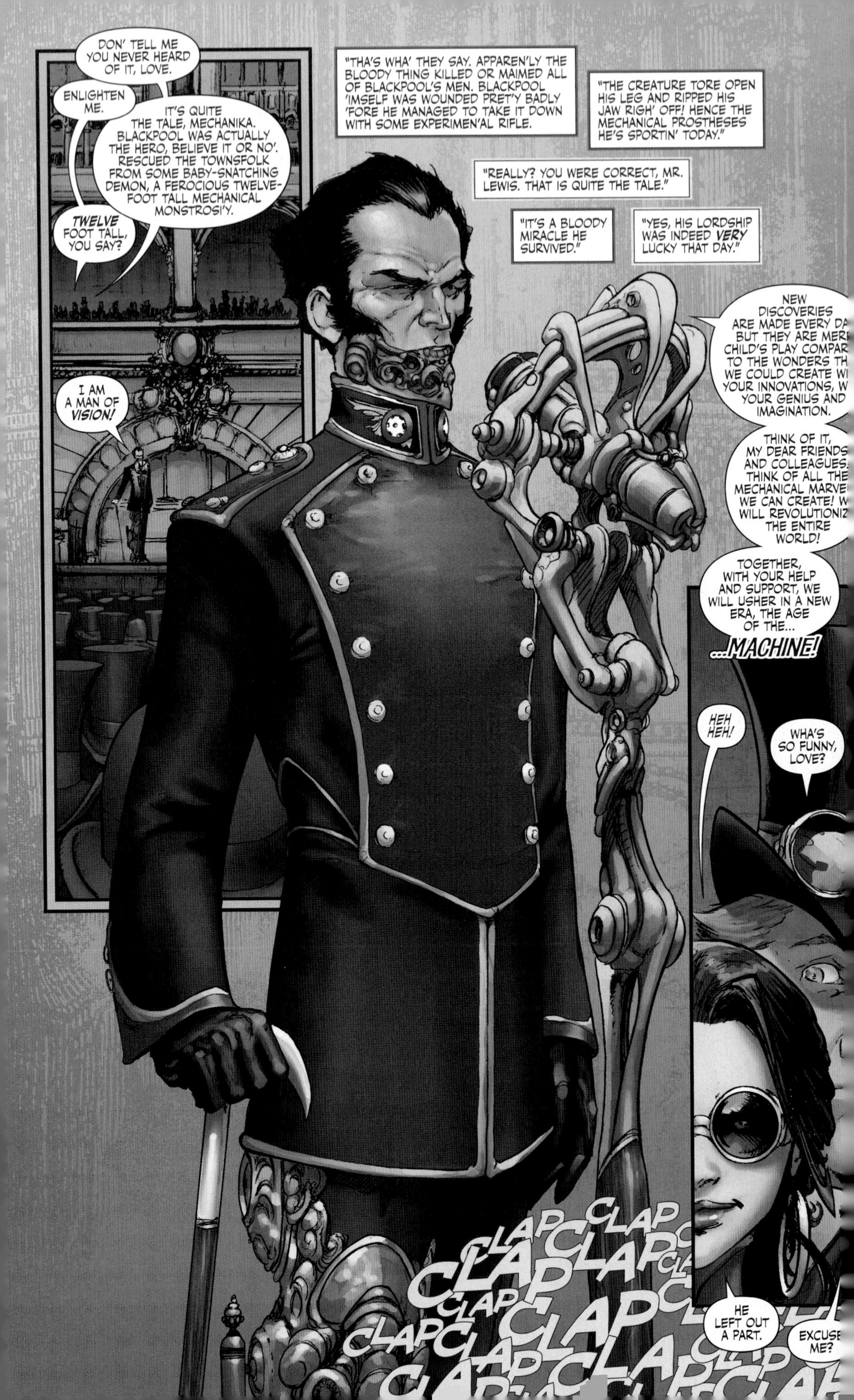
DON' TELL ME YOU NEVER HEARD OF IT, LOVE.
ENLIGHTEN ME.
IT'S QUITE THE TALE, MECHANIKA. BLACKPOOL WAS ACTUALLY THE HERO, BELIEVE IT OR NO'. RESCUED THE TOWNSFOLK FROM SOME BABY-SNATCHING DEMON, A FEROCIOUS TWELVE-FOOT TALL MECHANICAL MONSTROSI'Y.
TWELVE FOOT TALL, YOU SAY?
"THA'S WHA' THEY SAY. APPAREN'LY THE BLOODY THING KILLED OR MAIMED ALL OF BLACKPOOL'S MEN. BLACKPOOL 'IMSELF WAS WOUNDED PRET'Y BADLY 'FORE HE MANAGED TO TAKE IT DOWN WITH SOME EXPERIMEN'AL RIFLE.
"THE CREATURE TORE OPEN HIS LEG AND RIPPED HIS JAW RIGH' OFF! HENCE THE MECHANICAL PROSTHESES HE'S SPORTIN' TODAY."
"REALLY? YOU WERE CORRECT, MR. LEWIS. THAT IS QUITE THE TALE."
"IT'S A BLOODY MIRACLE HE SURVIVED."
"YES, HIS LORDSHIP WAS INDEED VERY LUCKY THAT DAY."
I AM A MAN OF VISION!
NEW DISCOVERIES ARE MADE EVERY DA BUT THEY ARE MER CHILD'S PLAY COMPAR TO THE WONDERS TH WE COULD CREATE WI YOUR INNOVATIONS, W YOUR GENIUS AND IMAGINATION.
THINK OF IT, MY DEAR FRIENDS AND COLLEAGUES. THINK OF ALL THE MECHANICAL MARVE WE CAN CREATE! W WILL REVOLUTIONIZ THE ENTIRE WORLD!
TOGETHER, WITH YOUR HELP AND SUPPORT, WE WILL USHER IN A NEW ERA, THE AGE OF THE...
...MACHINE!
HEH HEH!
WHA'S SO FUNNY, LOVE?
CLAP CLAP CLAP CLAP CLAP CLAP CLAP CLAP CLAP CLAP CLAP
HE LEFT OUT A PART.
EXCUSE ME?

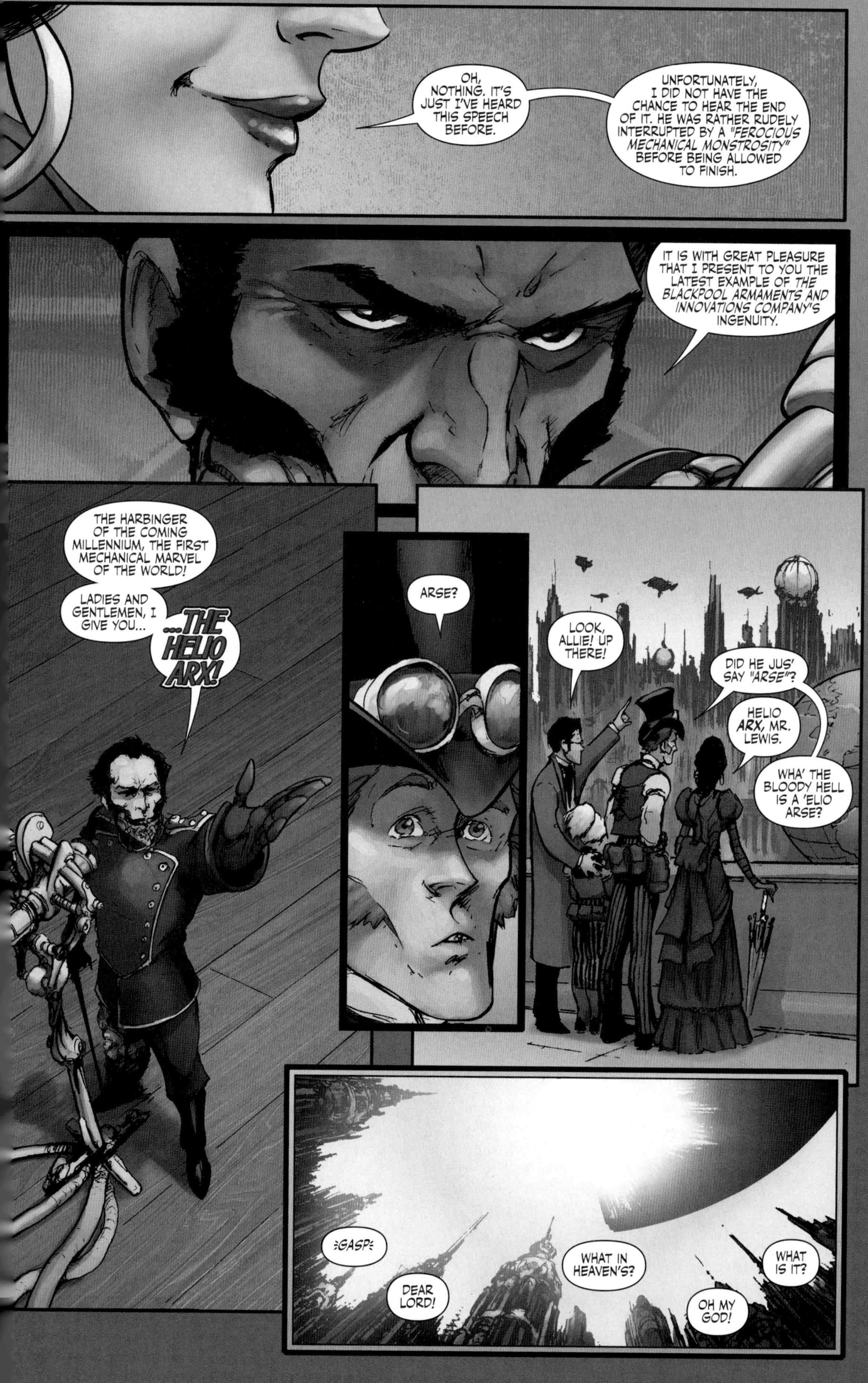
OH, NOTHING. IT'S JUST I'VE HEARD THIS SPEECH BEFORE.
UNFORTUNATELY, I DID NOT HAVE THE CHANCE TO HEAR THE END OF IT. HE WAS RATHER RUDELY INTERRUPTED BY A "FEROCIOUS MECHANICAL MONSTROSITY" BEFORE BEING ALLOWED TO FINISH.
IT IS WITH GREAT PLEASURE THAT I PRESENT TO YOU THE LATEST EXAMPLE OF THE BLACKPOOL ARMAMENTS AND INNOVATIONS COMPANY'S INGENUITY.
THE HARBINGER OF THE COMING MILLENNIUM, THE FIRST MECHANICAL MARVEL OF THE WORLD!
LADIES AND GENTLEMEN, I GIVE YOU...
...THE HELIO ARX!
ARSE?
LOOK, ALLIE! UP THERE!
DID HE JUS' SAY "ARSE"?
HELIO ARX, MR. LEWIS.
WHA' THE BLOODY HELL IS A 'ELIO ARSE?
GASP
DEAR LORD!
WHAT IN HEAVEN'S?
OH MY GOD!
WHAT IS IT?

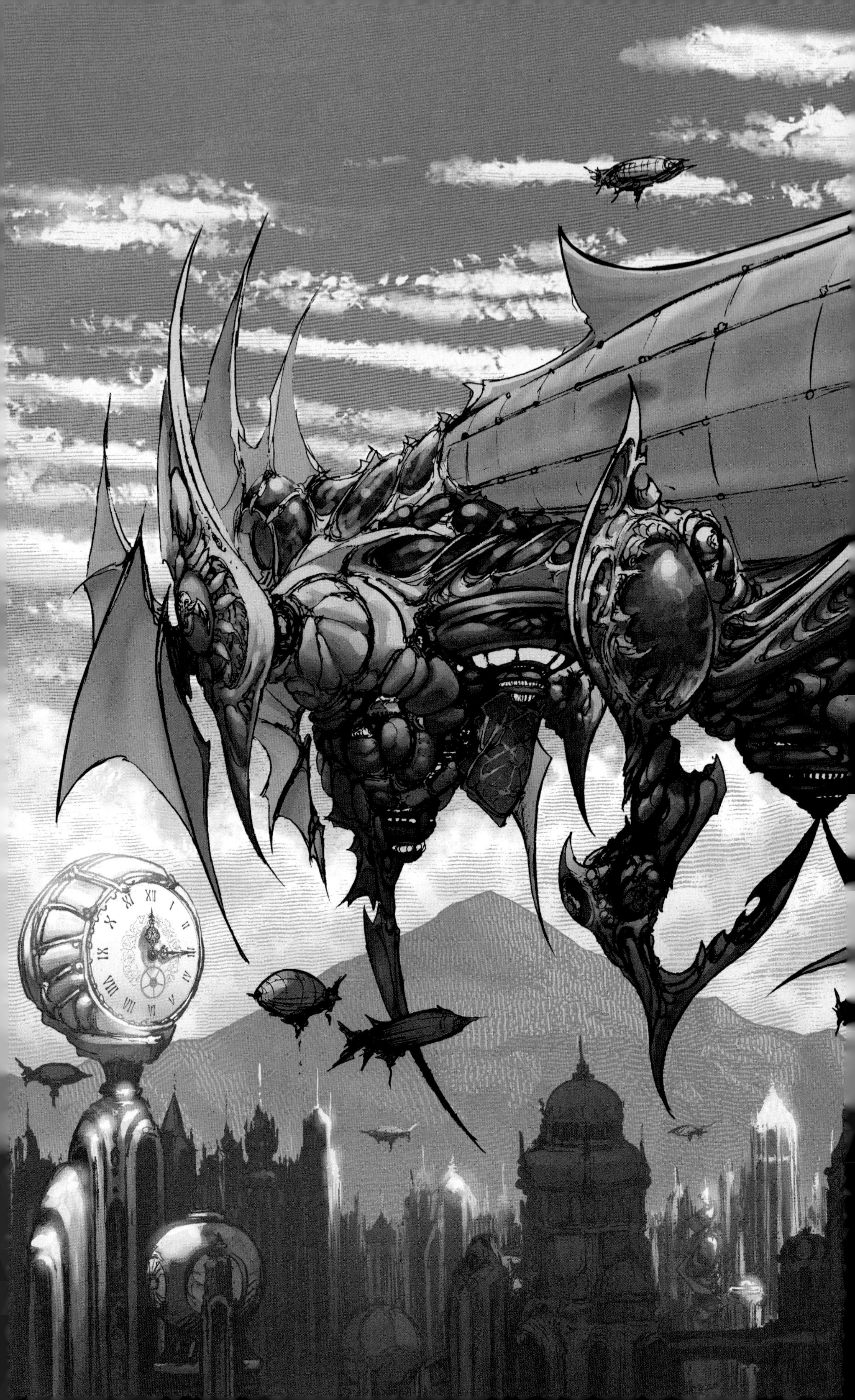

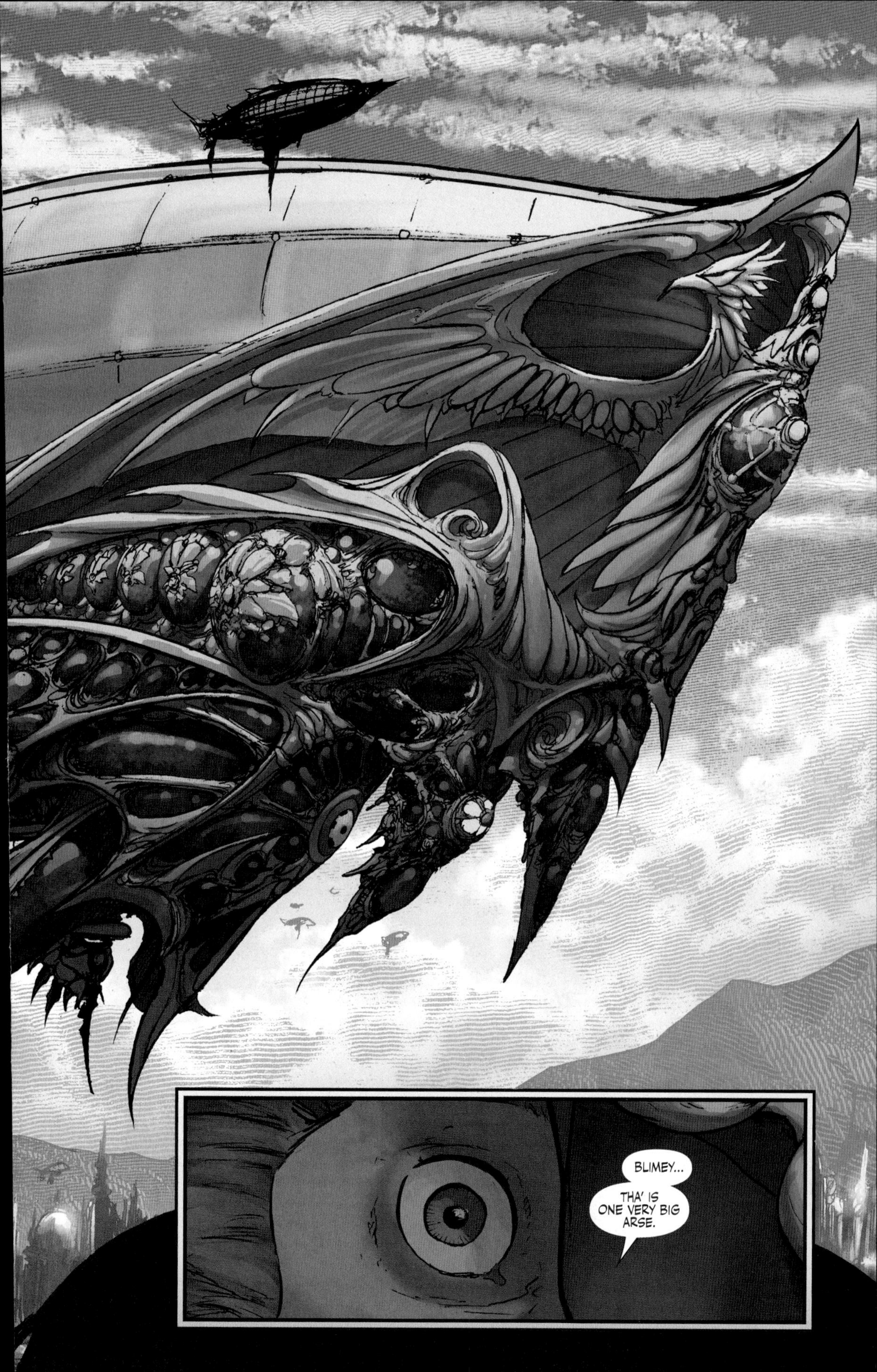
BLIMEY...
THA' IS ONE VERY BIG ARSE.

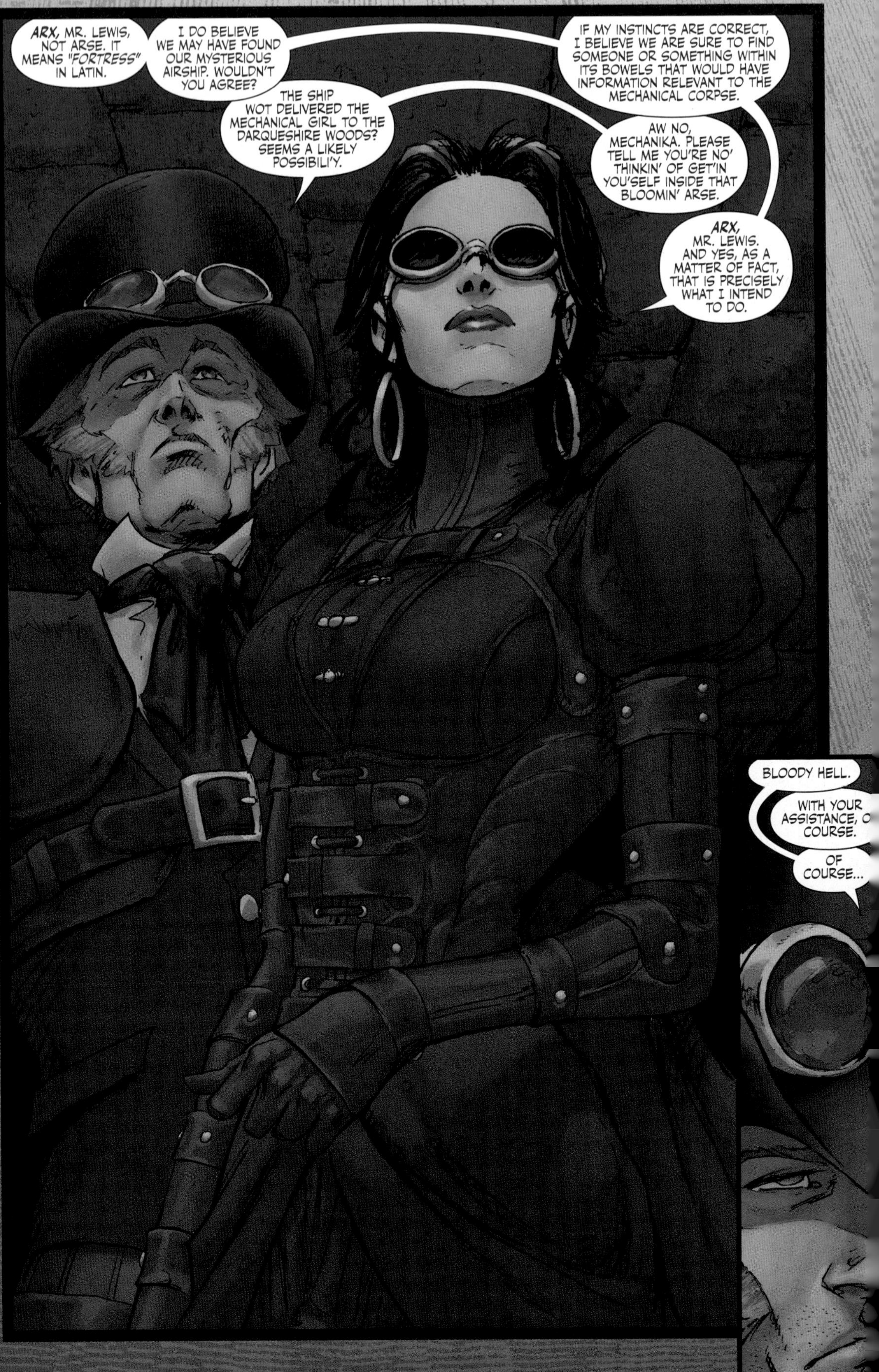
ARX, MR. LEWIS, NOT ARSE. IT MEANS "FORTRESS" IN LATIN.
I DO BELIEVE WE MAY HAVE FOUND OUR MYSTERIOUS AIRSHIP. WOULDN'T YOU AGREE?
THE SHIP WOT DELIVERED THE MECHANICAL GIRL TO THE DARQUESHIRE WOODS? SEEMS A LIKELY POSSIBILI'Y.
IF MY INSTINCTS ARE CORRECT, I BELIEVE WE ARE SURE TO FIND SOMEONE OR SOMETHING WITHIN ITS BOWELS THAT WOULD HAVE INFORMATION RELEVANT TO THE MECHANICAL CORPSE.
AW NO, MECHANIKA. PLEASE TELL ME YOU'RE NO' THINKIN' OF GET'IN YOU'SELF INSIDE THAT BLOOMIN' ARSE.
ARX, MR. LEWIS. AND YES, AS A MATTER OF FACT, THAT IS PRECISELY WHAT I INTEND TO DO.
BLOODY HELL.
WITH YOUR ASSISTANCE, O COURSE.
OF COURSE...

# Chapter Four

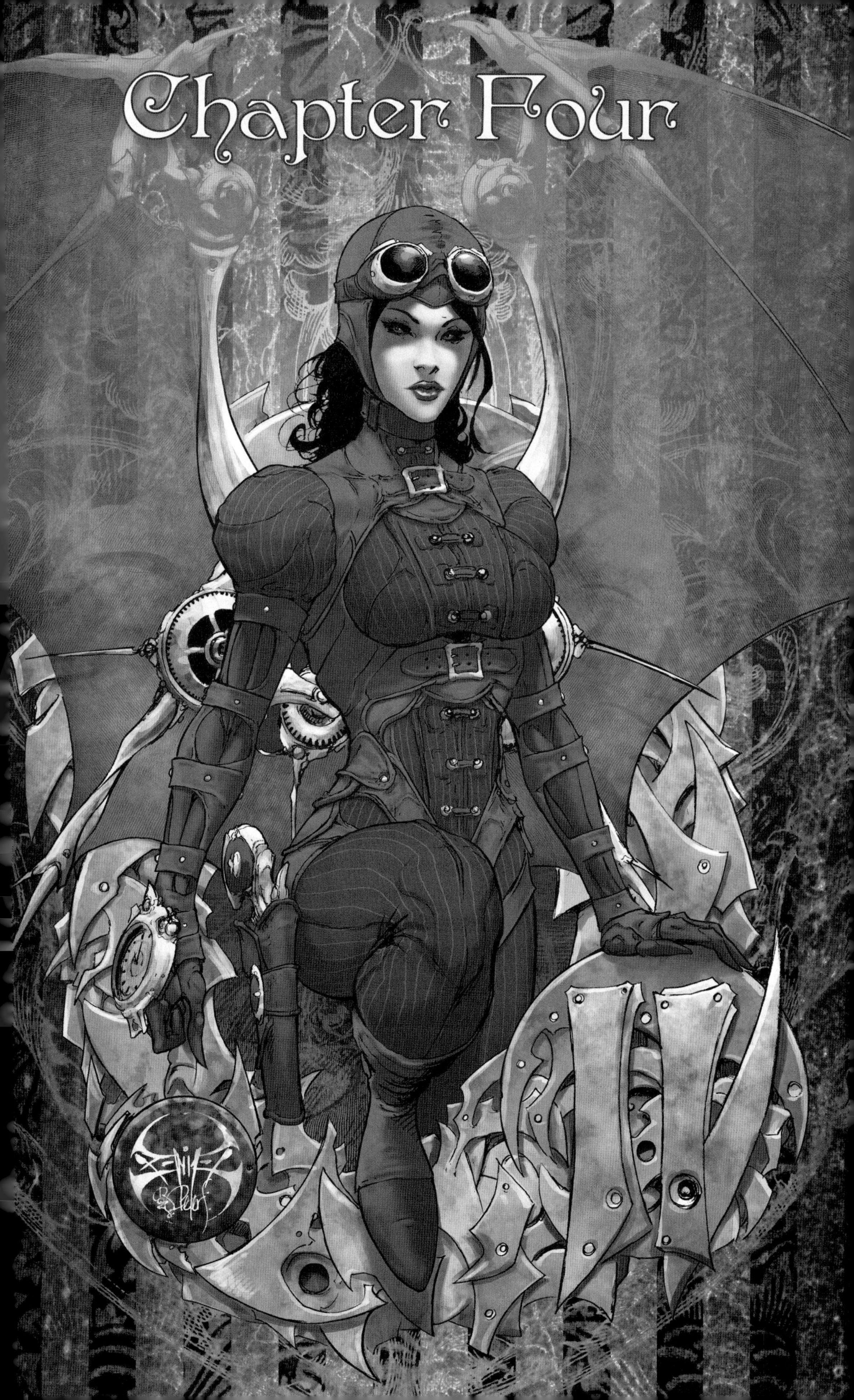

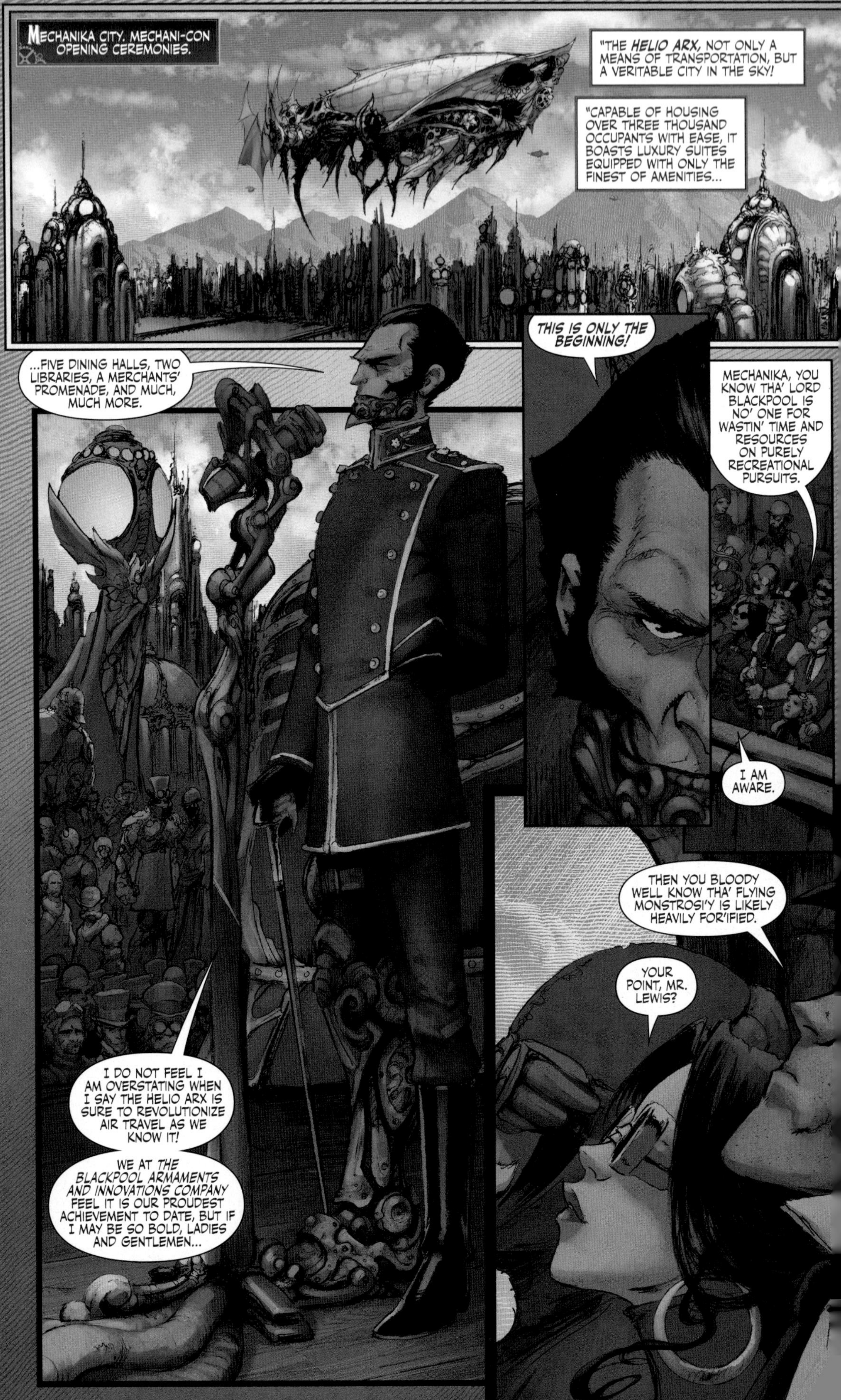
MECHANIKA CITY. MECHANI-CON OPENING CEREMONIES.
"THE HELIO ARX, NOT ONLY A MEANS OF TRANSPORTATION, BUT A VERITABLE CITY IN THE SKY!
"CAPABLE OF HOUSING OVER THREE THOUSAND OCCUPANTS WITH EASE, IT BOASTS LUXURY SUITES EQUIPPED WITH ONLY THE FINEST OF AMENITIES...
...FIVE DINING HALLS, TWO LIBRARIES, A MERCHANTS' PROMENADE, AND MUCH, MUCH MORE.
I DO NOT FEEL I AM OVERSTATING WHEN I SAY THE HELIO ARX IS SURE TO REVOLUTIONIZE AIR TRAVEL AS WE KNOW IT!
WE AT THE BLACKPOOL ARMAMENTS AND INNOVATIONS COMPANY FEEL IT IS OUR PROUDEST ACHIEVEMENT TO DATE, BUT IF I MAY BE SO BOLD, LADIES AND GENTLEMEN...
THIS IS ONLY THE BEGINNING!
MECHANIKA, YOU KNOW THA' LORD BLACKPOOL IS NO' ONE FOR WASTIN' TIME AND RESOURCES ON PURELY RECREATIONAL PURSUITS.
I AM AWARE.
THEN YOU BLOODY WELL KNOW THA' FLYING MONSTROSI'Y IS LIKELY HEAVILY FOR'IFIED.
YOUR POINT, MR. LEWIS?

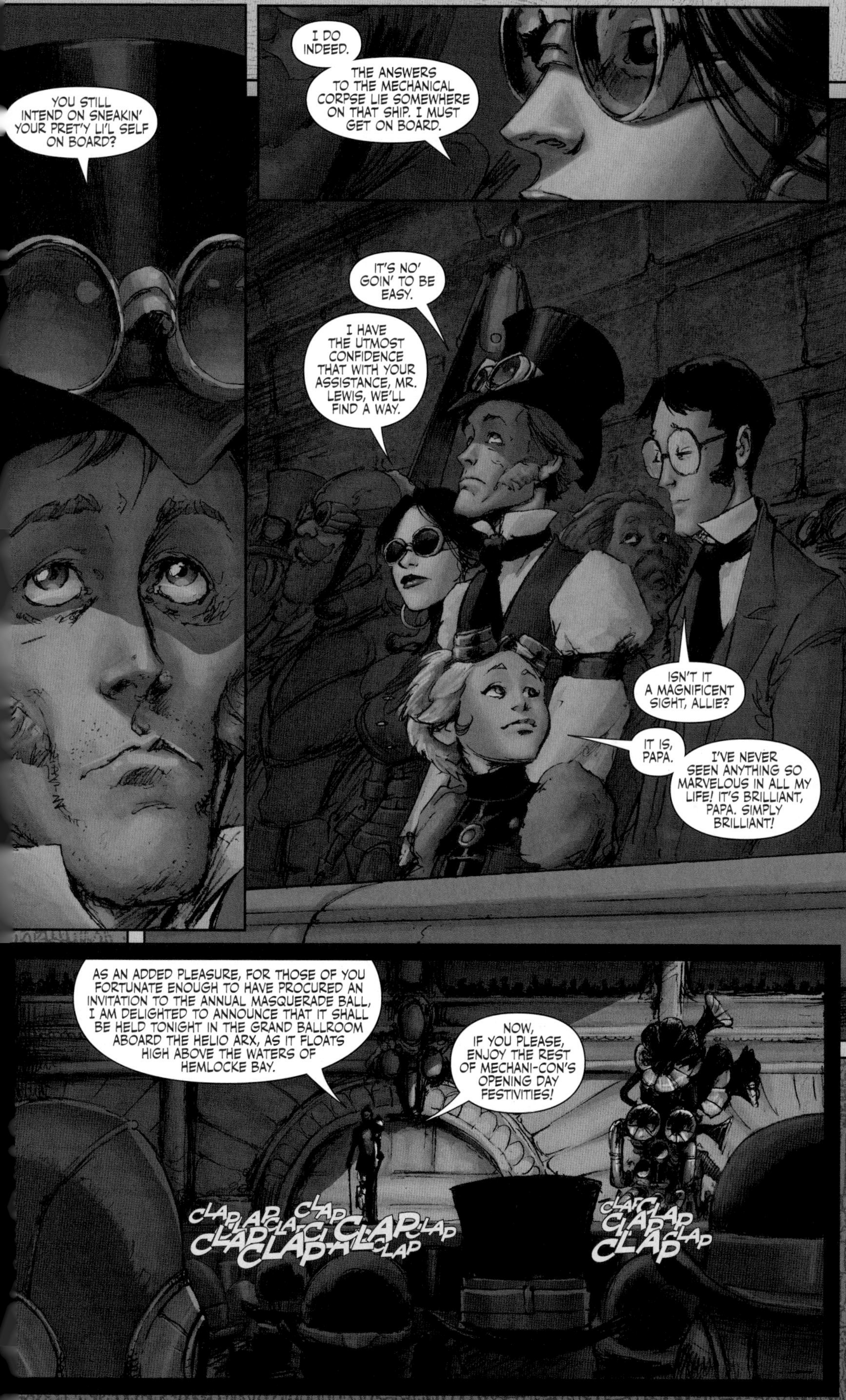
YOU STILL INTEND ON SNEAKIN' YOUR PRET'Y LI'L SELF ON BOARD?
I DO INDEED.
THE ANSWERS TO THE MECHANICAL CORPSE LIE SOMEWHERE ON THAT SHIP. I MUST GET ON BOARD.
IT'S NO' GOIN' TO BE EASY.
I HAVE THE UTMOST CONFIDENCE THAT WITH YOUR ASSISTANCE, MR. LEWIS, WE'LL FIND A WAY.
ISN'T IT A MAGNIFICENT SIGHT, ALLIE?
IT IS, PAPA.
I'VE NEVER SEEN ANYTHING SO MARVELOUS IN ALL MY LIFE! IT'S BRILLIANT, PAPA. SIMPLY BRILLIANT!
AS AN ADDED PLEASURE, FOR THOSE OF YOU FORTUNATE ENOUGH TO HAVE PROCURED AN INVITATION TO THE ANNUAL MASQUERADE BALL, I AM DELIGHTED TO ANNOUNCE THAT IT SHALL BE HELD TONIGHT IN THE GRAND BALLROOM ABOARD THE HELIO ARX, AS IT FLOATS HIGH ABOVE THE WATERS OF HEMLOCKE BAY.
NOW, IF YOU PLEASE, ENJOY THE REST OF MECHANI-CON'S OPENING DAY FESTIVITIES!
CLAP CLAP CLAP CLAP CLAP CLAP CLAP CLAP CLAP CLAP
CLAP CLAP CLAP CLAP CLAP

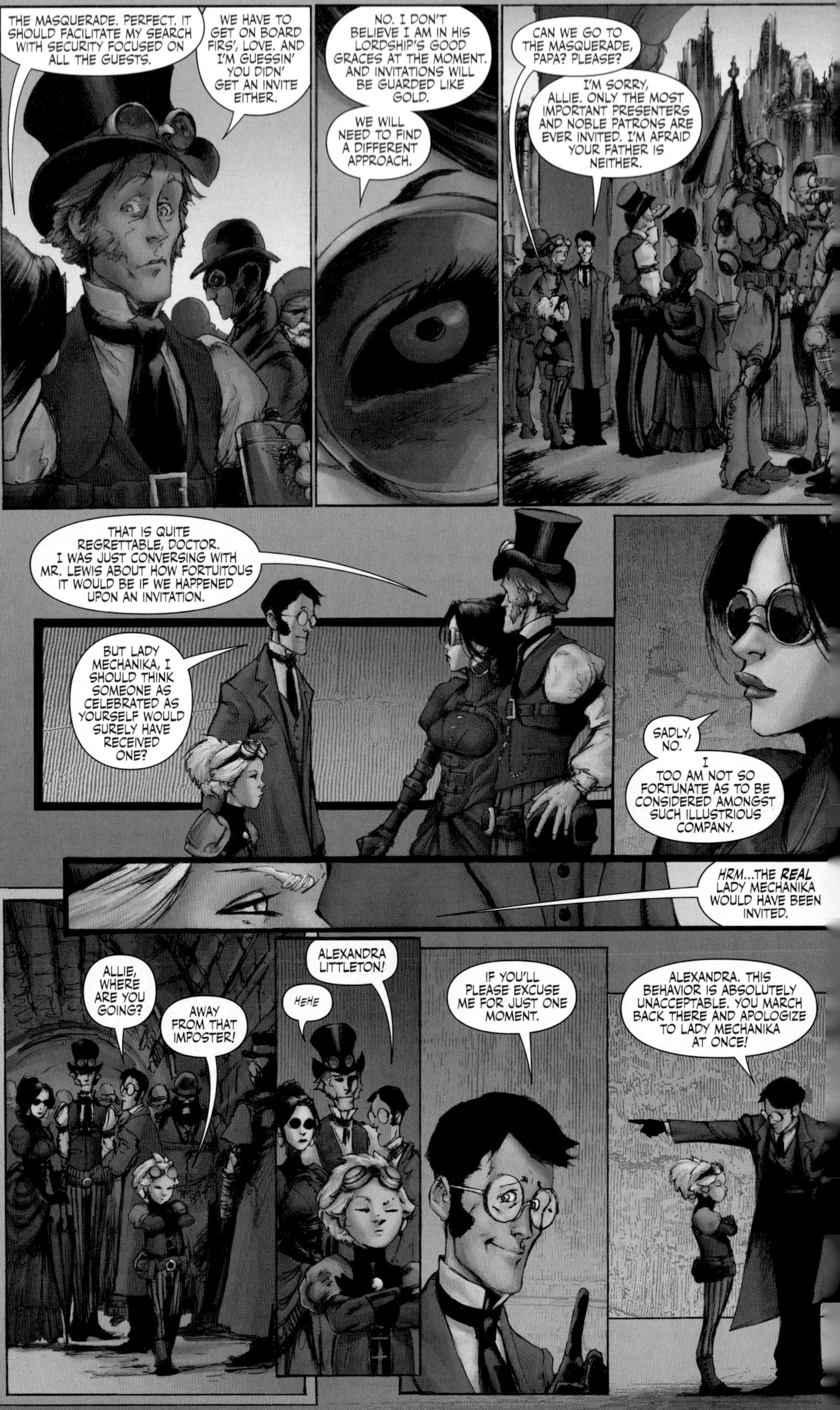

THE MASQUERADE. PERFECT. IT SHOULD FACILITATE MY SEARCH WITH SECURITY FOCUSED ON ALL THE GUESTS.
WE HAVE TO GET ON BOARD FIRS', LOVE. AND I'M GUESSIN' YOU DIDN' GET AN INVITE EITHER.
NO. I DON'T BELIEVE I AM IN HIS LORDSHIP'S GOOD GRACES AT THE MOMENT. AND INVITATIONS WILL BE GUARDED LIKE GOLD.
WE WILL NEED TO FIND A DIFFERENT APPROACH.
CAN WE GO TO THE MASQUERADE, PAPA? PLEASE?
I'M SORRY, ALLIE. ONLY THE MOST IMPORTANT PRESENTERS AND NOBLE PATRONS ARE EVER INVITED. I'M AFRAID YOUR FATHER IS NEITHER.
THAT IS QUITE REGRETTABLE, DOCTOR. I WAS JUST CONVERSING WITH MR. LEWIS ABOUT HOW FORTUITOUS IT WOULD BE IF WE HAPPENED UPON AN INVITATION.
BUT LADY MECHANIKA, I SHOULD THINK SOMEONE AS CELEBRATED AS YOURSELF WOULD SURELY HAVE RECEIVED ONE?
SADLY, NO.
I TOO AM NOT SO FORTUNATE AS TO BE CONSIDERED AMONGST SUCH ILLUSTRIOUS COMPANY.
HRM...THE REAL LADY MECHANIKA WOULD HAVE BEEN INVITED.
ALLIE, WHERE ARE YOU GOING?
AWAY FROM THAT IMPOSTER!
ALEXANDRA LITTLETON!
HEHE
IF YOU'LL PLEASE EXCUSE ME FOR JUST ONE MOMENT.
ALEXANDRA. THIS BEHAVIOR IS ABSOLUTELY UNACCEPTABLE. YOU MARCH BACK THERE AND APOLOGIZE TO LADY MECHANIKA AT ONCE!

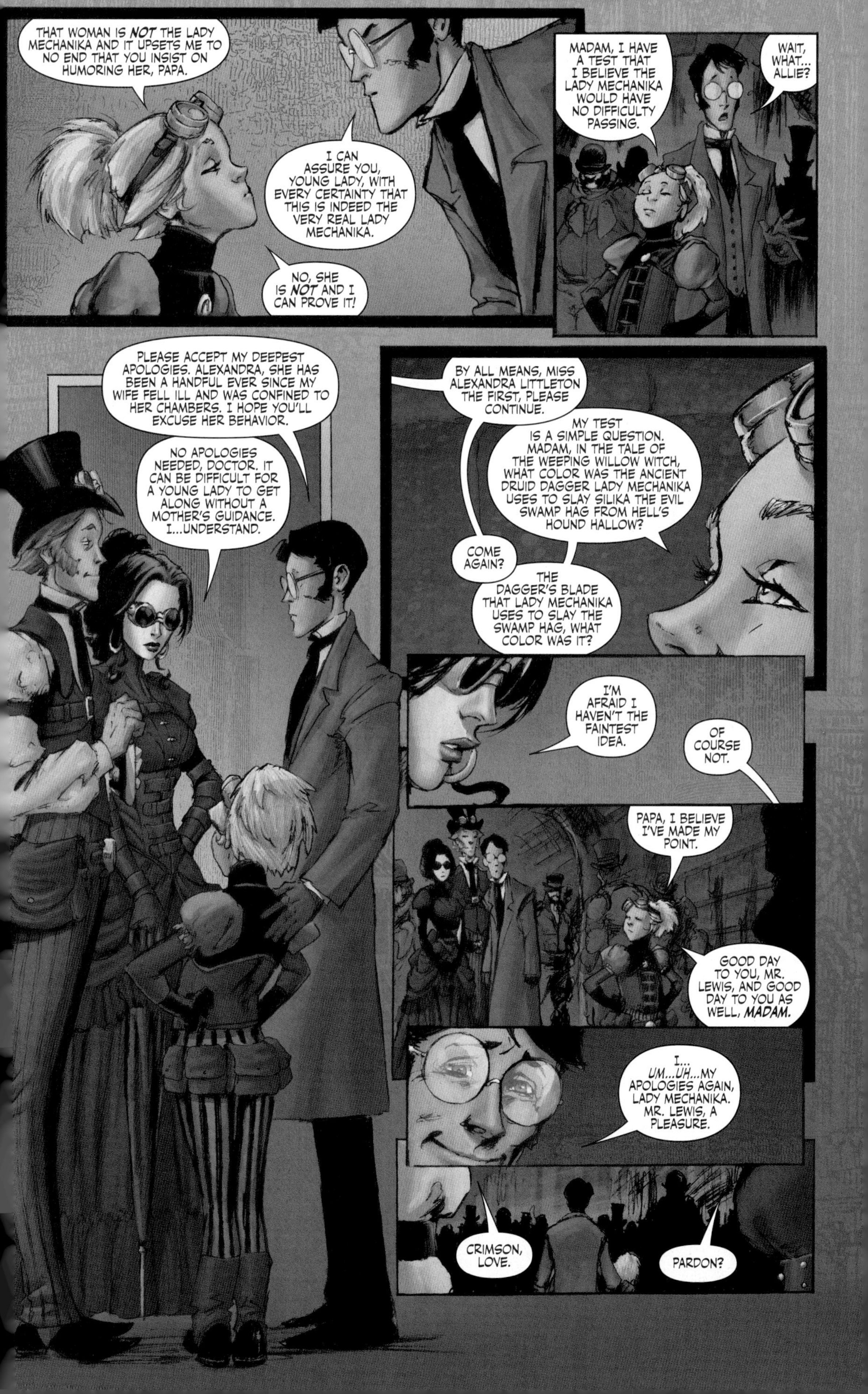
THAT WOMAN IS NOT THE LADY MECHANIKA AND IT UPSETS ME TO NO END THAT YOU INSIST ON HUMORING HER, PAPA.
I CAN ASSURE YOU, YOUNG LADY, WITH EVERY CERTAINTY THAT THIS IS INDEED THE VERY REAL LADY MECHANIKA.
NO, SHE IS NOT AND I CAN PROVE IT!
MADAM, I HAVE A TEST THAT I BELIEVE THE LADY MECHANIKA WOULD HAVE NO DIFFICULTY PASSING.
WAIT, WHAT... ALLIE?
PLEASE ACCEPT MY DEEPEST APOLOGIES. ALEXANDRA, SHE HAS BEEN A HANDFUL EVER SINCE MY WIFE FELL ILL AND WAS CONFINED TO HER CHAMBERS. I HOPE YOU'LL EXCUSE HER BEHAVIOR.
NO APOLOGIES NEEDED, DOCTOR. IT CAN BE DIFFICULT FOR A YOUNG LADY TO GET ALONG WITHOUT A MOTHER'S GUIDANCE. I...UNDERSTAND.
BY ALL MEANS, MISS ALEXANDRA LITTLETON THE FIRST, PLEASE CONTINUE.
MY TEST IS A SIMPLE QUESTION. MADAM, IN THE TALE OF THE WEEPING WILLOW WITCH, WHAT COLOR WAS THE ANCIENT DRUID DAGGER LADY MECHANIKA USES TO SLAY SILIKA THE EVIL SWAMP HAG FROM HELL'S HOUND HALLOW?
COME AGAIN?
THE DAGGER'S BLADE THAT LADY MECHANIKA USES TO SLAY THE SWAMP HAG, WHAT COLOR WAS IT?
I'M AFRAID I HAVEN'T THE FAINTEST IDEA.
OF COURSE NOT.
PAPA, I BELIEVE I'VE MADE MY POINT.
GOOD DAY TO YOU, MR. LEWIS, AND GOOD DAY TO YOU AS WELL, MADAM.
I... UM...UH...MY APOLOGIES AGAIN, LADY MECHANIKA. MR. LEWIS, A PLEASURE.
CRIMSON, LOVE.
PARDON?

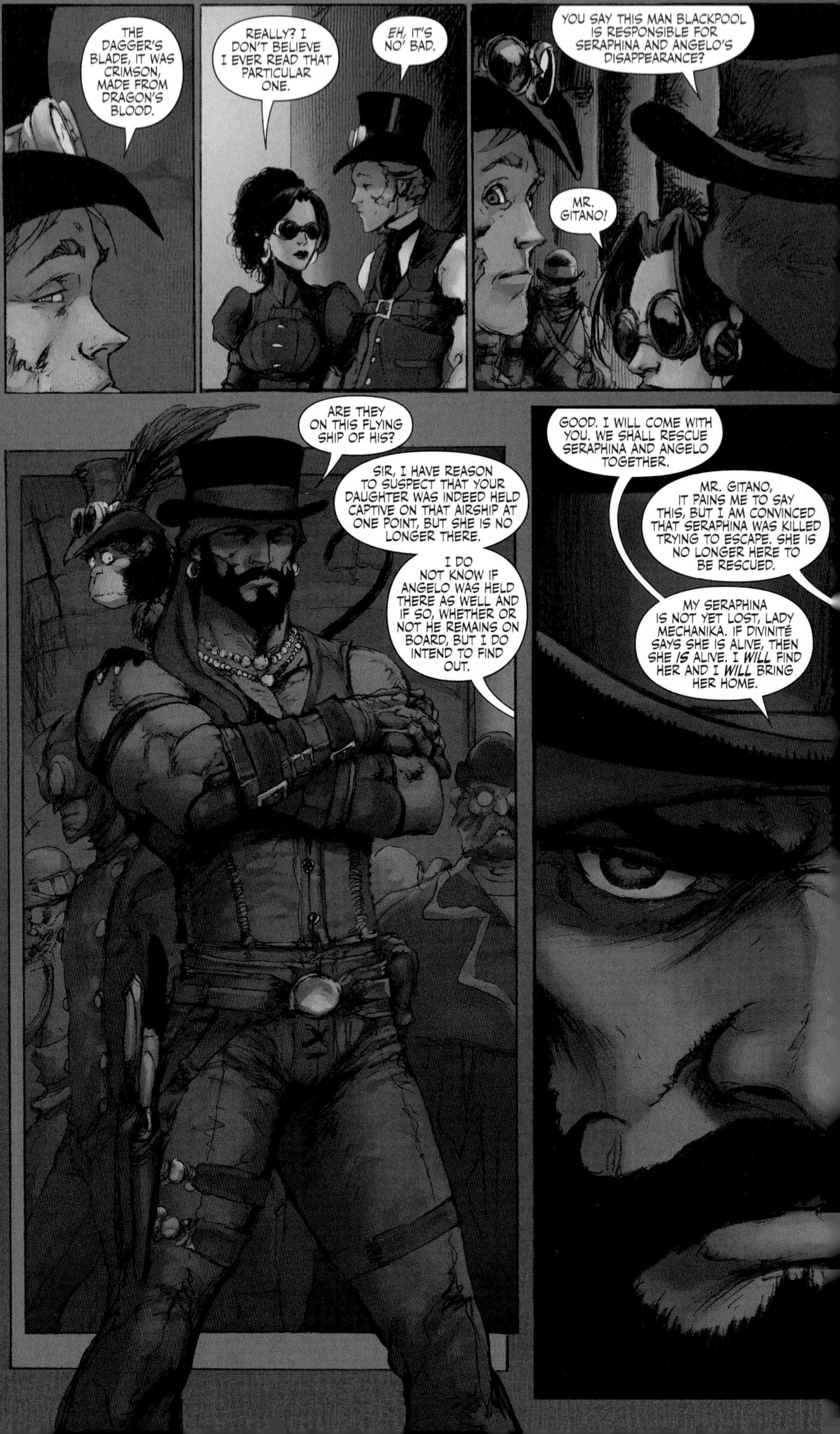
THE DAGGER'S BLADE, IT WAS CRIMSON, MADE FROM DRAGON'S BLOOD.
REALLY? I DON'T BELIEVE I EVER READ THAT PARTICULAR ONE.
EH, IT'S NO' BAD.
YOU SAY THIS MAN BLACKPOOL IS RESPONSIBLE FOR SERAPHINA AND ANGELO'S DISAPPEARANCE?
MR. GITANO!
ARE THEY ON THIS FLYING SHIP OF HIS?
SIR, I HAVE REASON TO SUSPECT THAT YOUR DAUGHTER WAS INDEED HELD CAPTIVE ON THAT AIRSHIP AT ONE POINT, BUT SHE IS NO LONGER THERE.
I DO NOT KNOW IF ANGELO WAS HELD THERE AS WELL AND IF SO, WHETHER OR NOT HE REMAINS ON BOARD, BUT I DO INTEND TO FIND OUT.
GOOD. I WILL COME WITH YOU. WE SHALL RESCUE SERAPHINA AND ANGELO TOGETHER.
MR. GITANO, IT PAINS ME TO SAY THIS, BUT I AM CONVINCED THAT SERAPHINA WAS KILLED TRYING TO ESCAPE. SHE IS NO LONGER HERE TO BE RESCUED.
MY SERAPHINA IS NOT YET LOST, LADY MECHANIKA. IF DIVINITÉ SAYS SHE IS ALIVE, THEN SHE IS ALIVE. I WILL FIND HER AND I WILL BRING HER HOME.

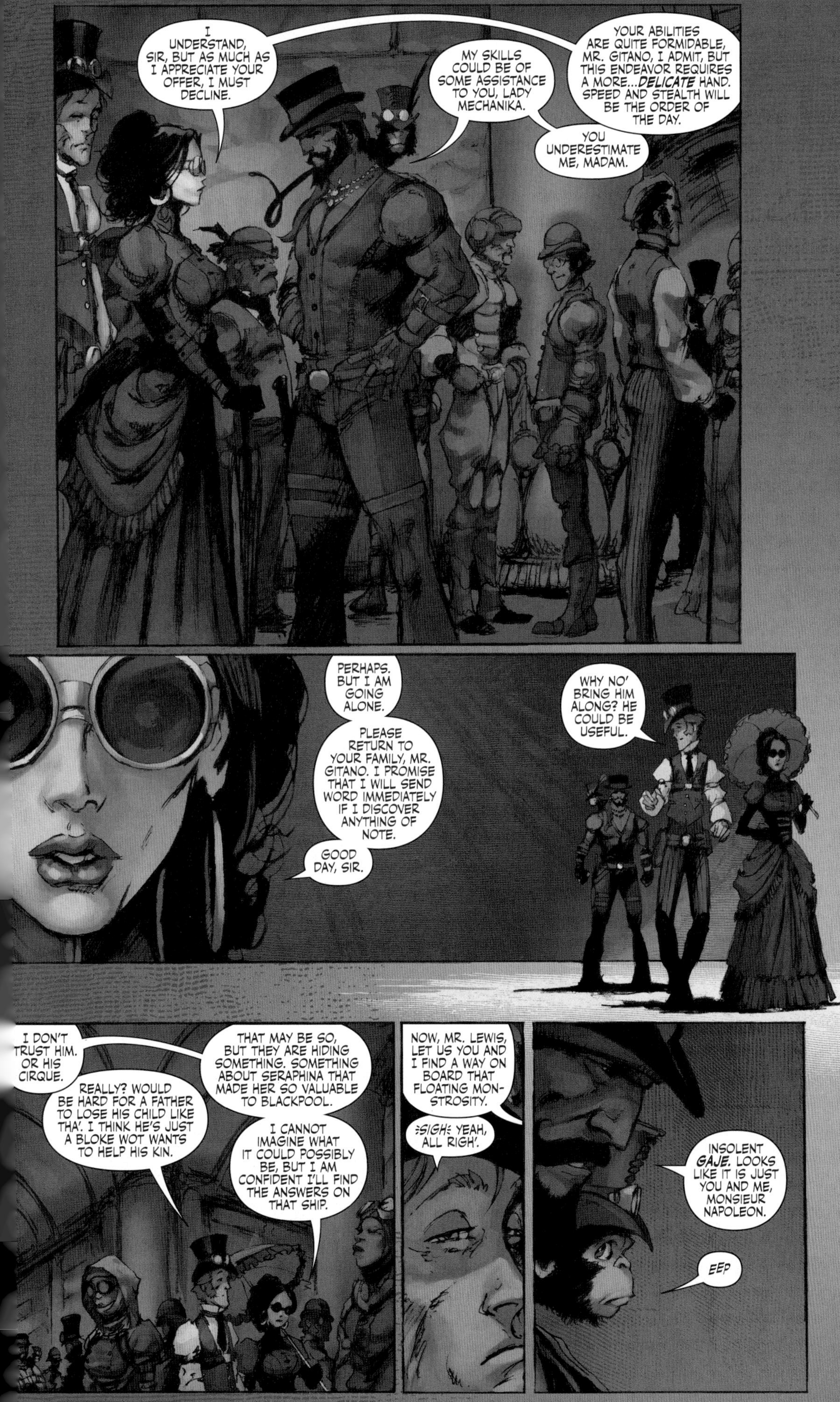

MY SKILLS COULD BE OF SOME ASSISTANCE TO YOU, LADY MECHANIKA.
YOUR ABILITIES ARE QUITE FORMIDABLE, MR. GITANO, I ADMIT, BUT THIS ENDEAVOR REQUIRES A MORE...DELICATE HAND. SPEED AND STEALTH WILL BE THE ORDER OF THE DAY.
YOU UNDERESTIMATE ME, MADAM.
I UNDERSTAND, SIR, BUT AS MUCH AS I APPRECIATE YOUR OFFER, I MUST DECLINE.
PERHAPS. BUT I AM GOING ALONE.
PLEASE RETURN TO YOUR FAMILY, MR. GITANO. I PROMISE THAT I WILL SEND WORD IMMEDIATELY IF I DISCOVER ANYTHING OF NOTE.
GOOD DAY, SIR.
WHY NO' BRING HIM ALONG? HE COULD BE USEFUL.
I DON'T TRUST HIM. OR HIS CIRQUE.
REALLY? WOULD BE HARD FOR A FATHER TO LOSE HIS CHILD LIKE THA'. I THINK HE'S JUST A BLOKE WOT WANTS TO HELP HIS KIN.
THAT MAY BE SO, BUT THEY ARE HIDING SOMETHING. SOMETHING ABOUT SERAPHINA THAT MADE HER SO VALUABLE TO BLACKPOOL.
I CANNOT IMAGINE WHAT IT COULD POSSIBLY BE, BUT I AM CONFIDENT I'LL FIND THE ANSWERS ON THAT SHIP.
NOW, MR. LEWIS, LET US YOU AND I FIND A WAY ON BOARD THAT FLOATING MONSTROSITY.
SIGH YEAH, ALL RIGH'.
INSOLENT GAJE. LOOKS LIKE IT IS JUST YOU AND ME, MONSIEUR NAPOLEON.
EEP

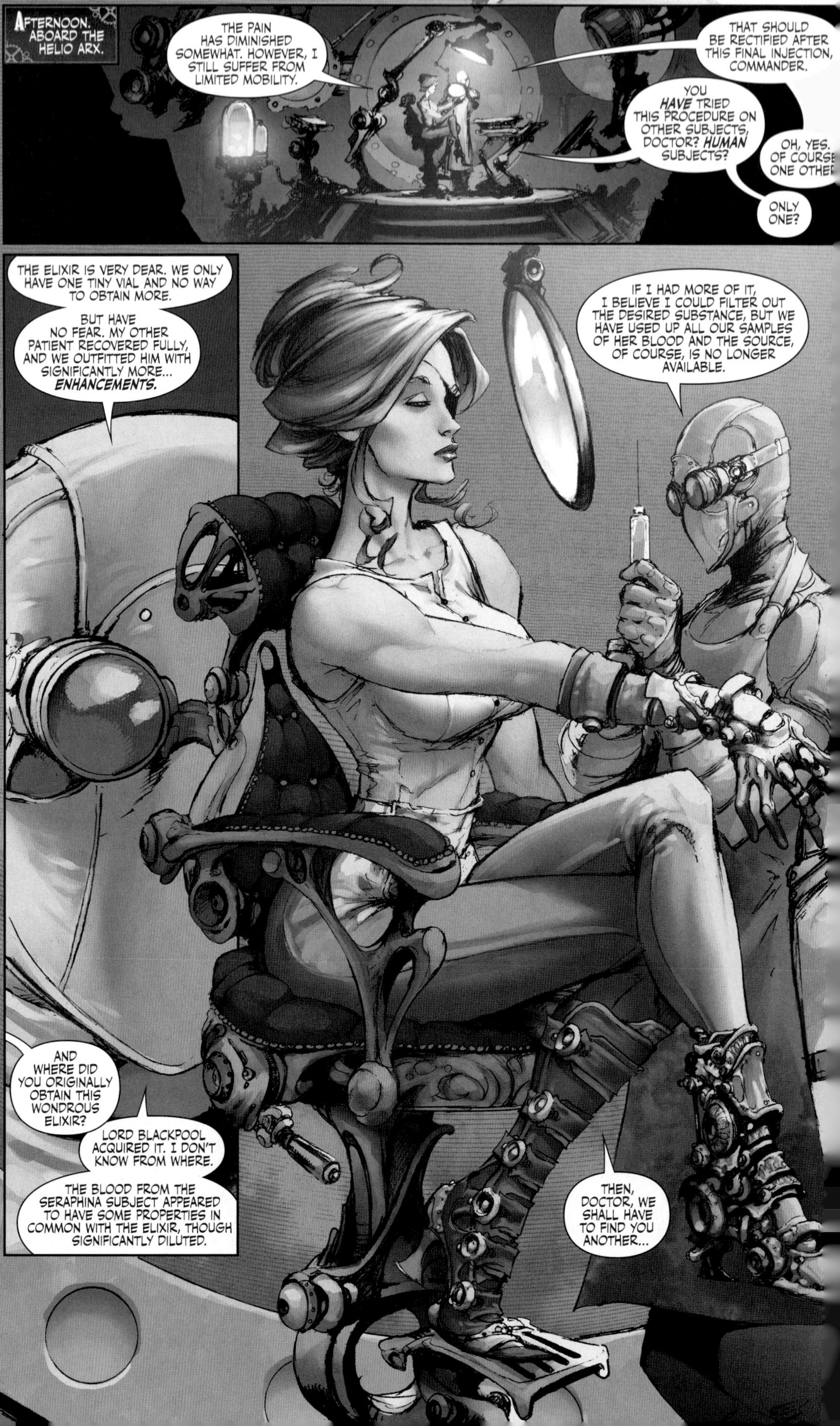
AFTERNOON. ABOARD THE HELIO ARX.
THE PAIN HAS DIMINISHED SOMEWHAT. HOWEVER, I STILL SUFFER FROM LIMITED MOBILITY.
THAT SHOULD BE RECTIFIED AFTER THIS FINAL INJECTION, COMMANDER.
YOU HAVE TRIED THIS PROCEDURE ON OTHER SUBJECTS, DOCTOR? HUMAN SUBJECTS?
OH, YES. OF COURSE ONE OTHER
ONLY ONE?
THE ELIXIR IS VERY DEAR. WE ONLY HAVE ONE TINY VIAL AND NO WAY TO OBTAIN MORE.
BUT HAVE NO FEAR. MY OTHER PATIENT RECOVERED FULLY, AND WE OUTFITTED HIM WITH SIGNIFICANTLY MORE... ENHANCEMENTS.
IF I HAD MORE OF IT, I BELIEVE I COULD FILTER OUT THE DESIRED SUBSTANCE, BUT WE HAVE USED UP ALL OUR SAMPLES OF HER BLOOD AND THE SOURCE, OF COURSE, IS NO LONGER AVAILABLE.
AND WHERE DID YOU ORIGINALLY OBTAIN THIS WONDROUS ELIXIR?
LORD BLACKPOOL ACQUIRED IT. I DON'T KNOW FROM WHERE.
THE BLOOD FROM THE SERAPHINA SUBJECT APPEARED TO HAVE SOME PROPERTIES IN COMMON WITH THE ELIXIR, THOUGH SIGNIFICANTLY DILUTED.
THEN, DOCTOR, WE SHALL HAVE TO FIND YOU ANOTHER...

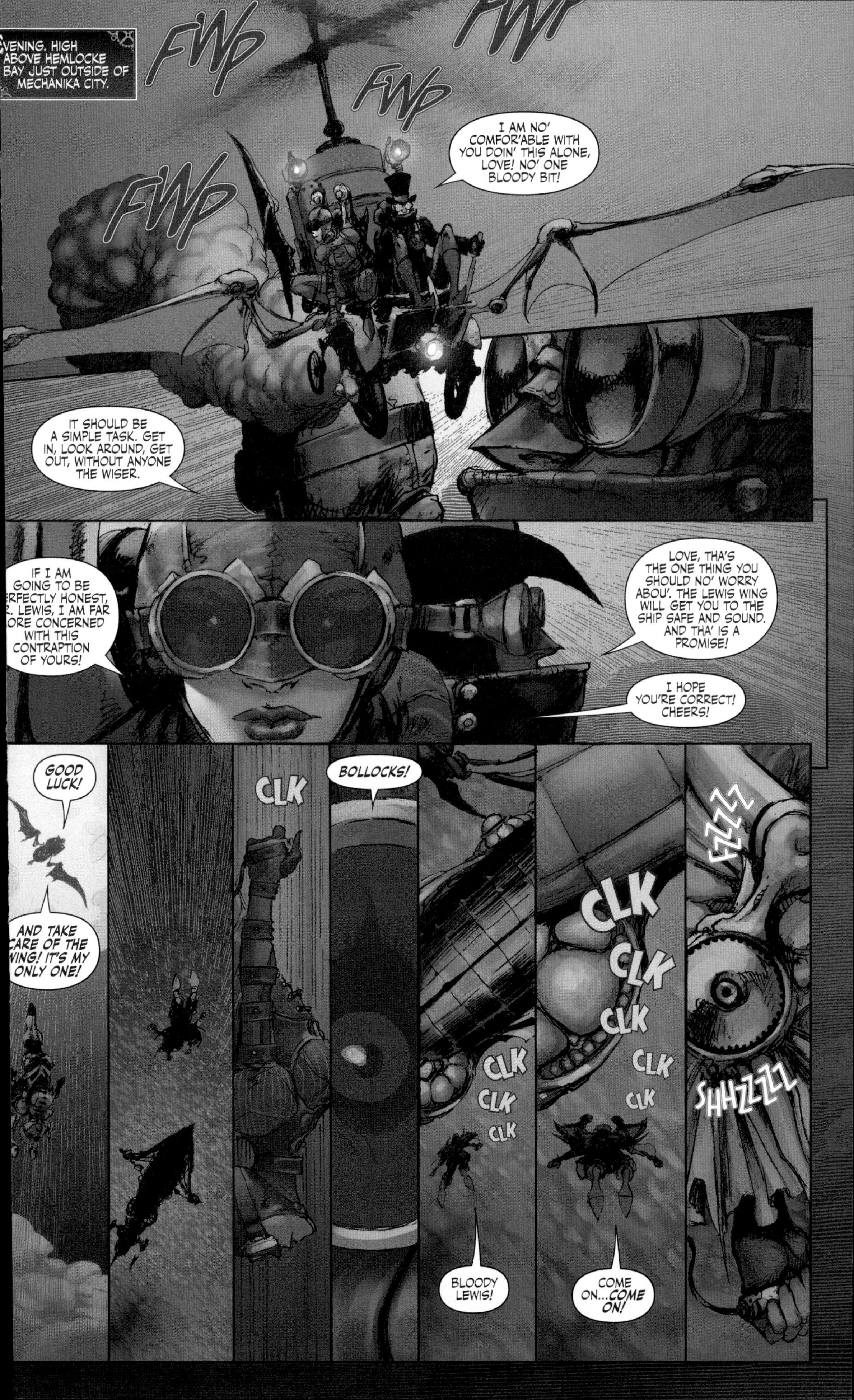

EVENING. HIGH ABOVE HEMLOCKE BAY JUST OUTSIDE OF MECHANIKA CITY.
FWP
FWP
FWP
FWP
I AM NO' COMFOR'ABLE WITH YOU DOIN' THIS ALONE, LOVE! NO' ONE BLOODY BIT!
IT SHOULD BE A SIMPLE TASK. GET IN, LOOK AROUND, GET OUT, WITHOUT ANYONE THE WISER.
IF I AM GOING TO BE PERFECTLY HONEST, MR. LEWIS, I AM FAR MORE CONCERNED WITH THIS CONTRAPTION OF YOURS!
LOVE, THA'S THE ONE THING YOU SHOULD NO' WORRY ABOU'. THE LEWIS WING WILL GET YOU TO THE SHIP SAFE AND SOUND. AND THA' IS A PROMISE!
I HOPE YOU'RE CORRECT! CHEERS!
GOOD LUCK!
AND TAKE CARE OF THE WING! IT'S MY ONLY ONE!
CLK
BOLLOCKS!
CLK CLK CLK
BLOODY LEWIS!
CLK CLK CLK CLK CLK
COME ON...COME ON!
FZZZZZ
SHHZZZZZ

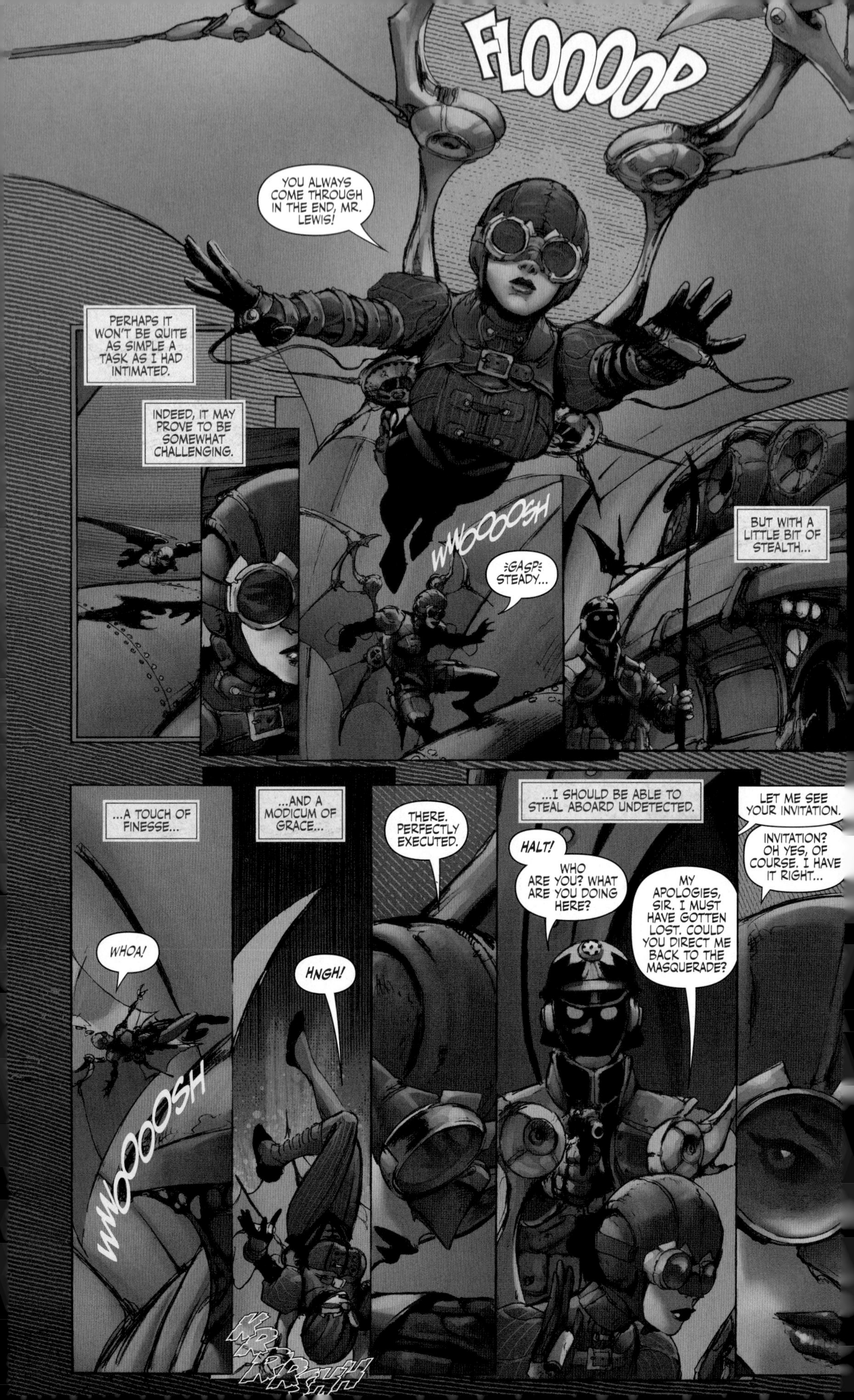
FLOOOOP
YOU ALWAYS COME THROUGH IN THE END, MR. LEWIS!
PERHAPS IT WON'T BE QUITE AS SIMPLE A TASK AS I HAD INTIMATED.
INDEED, IT MAY PROVE TO BE SOMEWHAT CHALLENGING.
WWOOOOSH
GASP STEADY...
BUT WITH A LITTLE BIT OF STEALTH...
...A TOUCH OF FINESSE...
WHOA!
WWOOOOSH
...AND A MODICUM OF GRACE...
HNGH!
KRRRSHH
THERE. PERFECTLY EXECUTED.
...I SHOULD BE ABLE TO STEAL ABOARD UNDETECTED.
HALT!
WHO ARE YOU? WHAT ARE YOU DOING HERE?
MY APOLOGIES, SIR. I MUST HAVE GOTTEN LOST. COULD YOU DIRECT ME BACK TO THE MASQUERADE?
LET ME SEE YOUR INVITATION.
INVITATION? OH YES, OF COURSE. I HAVE IT RIGHT...

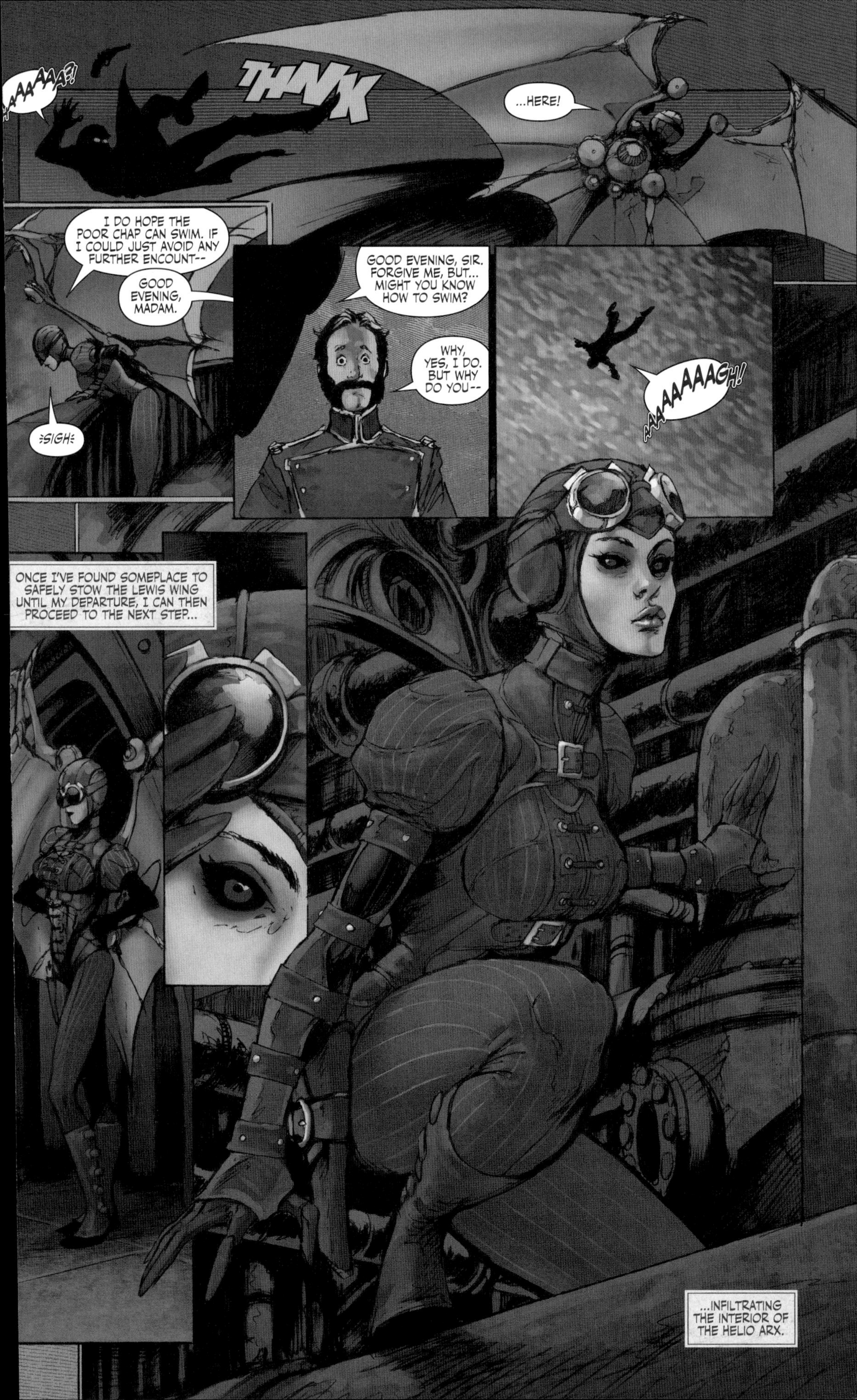

AAAAAA?!
THNK
...HERE!
I DO HOPE THE POOR CHAP CAN SWIM. IF I COULD JUST AVOID ANY FURTHER ENCOUNT--
GOOD EVENING, MADAM.
SIGH
GOOD EVENING, SIR. FORGIVE ME, BUT... MIGHT YOU KNOW HOW TO SWIM?
WHY, YES, I DO. BUT WHY DO YOU--
AAAAAAAAGH!
ONCE I'VE FOUND SOMEPLACE TO SAFELY STOW THE LEWIS WING UNTIL MY DEPARTURE, I CAN THEN PROCEED TO THE NEXT STEP...
...INFILTRATING THE INTERIOR OF THE HELIO ARX.

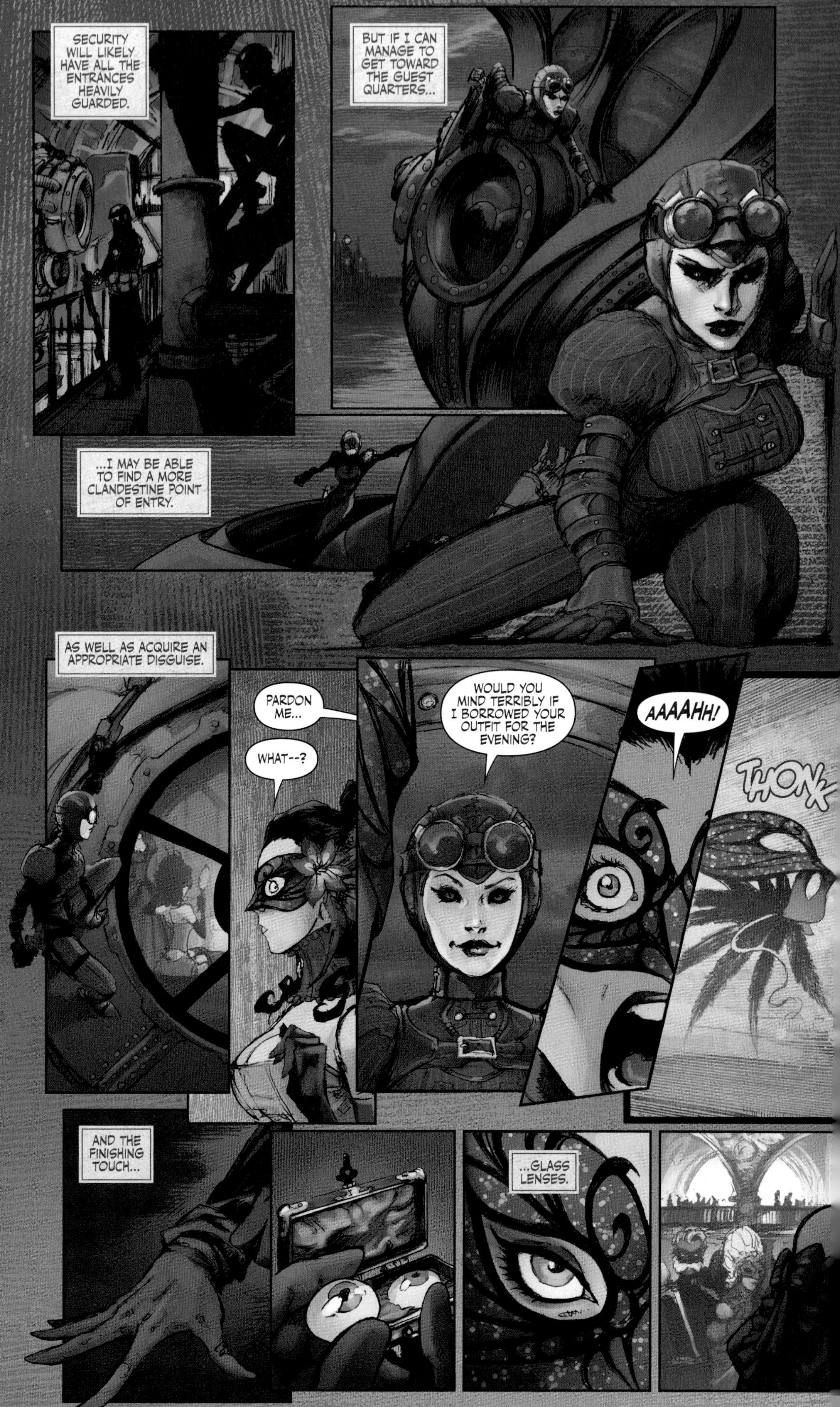
SECURITY WILL LIKELY HAVE ALL THE ENTRANCES HEAVILY GUARDED.
BUT IF I CAN MANAGE TO GET TOWARD THE GUEST QUARTERS...
...I MAY BE ABLE TO FIND A MORE CLANDESTINE POINT OF ENTRY.
AS WELL AS ACQUIRE AN APPROPRIATE DISGUISE.
PARDON ME...
WHAT--?
WOULD YOU MIND TERRIBLY IF I BORROWED YOUR OUTFIT FOR THE EVENING?
AAAAHH!
THONK
AND THE FINISHING TOUCH...
...GLASS LENSES.

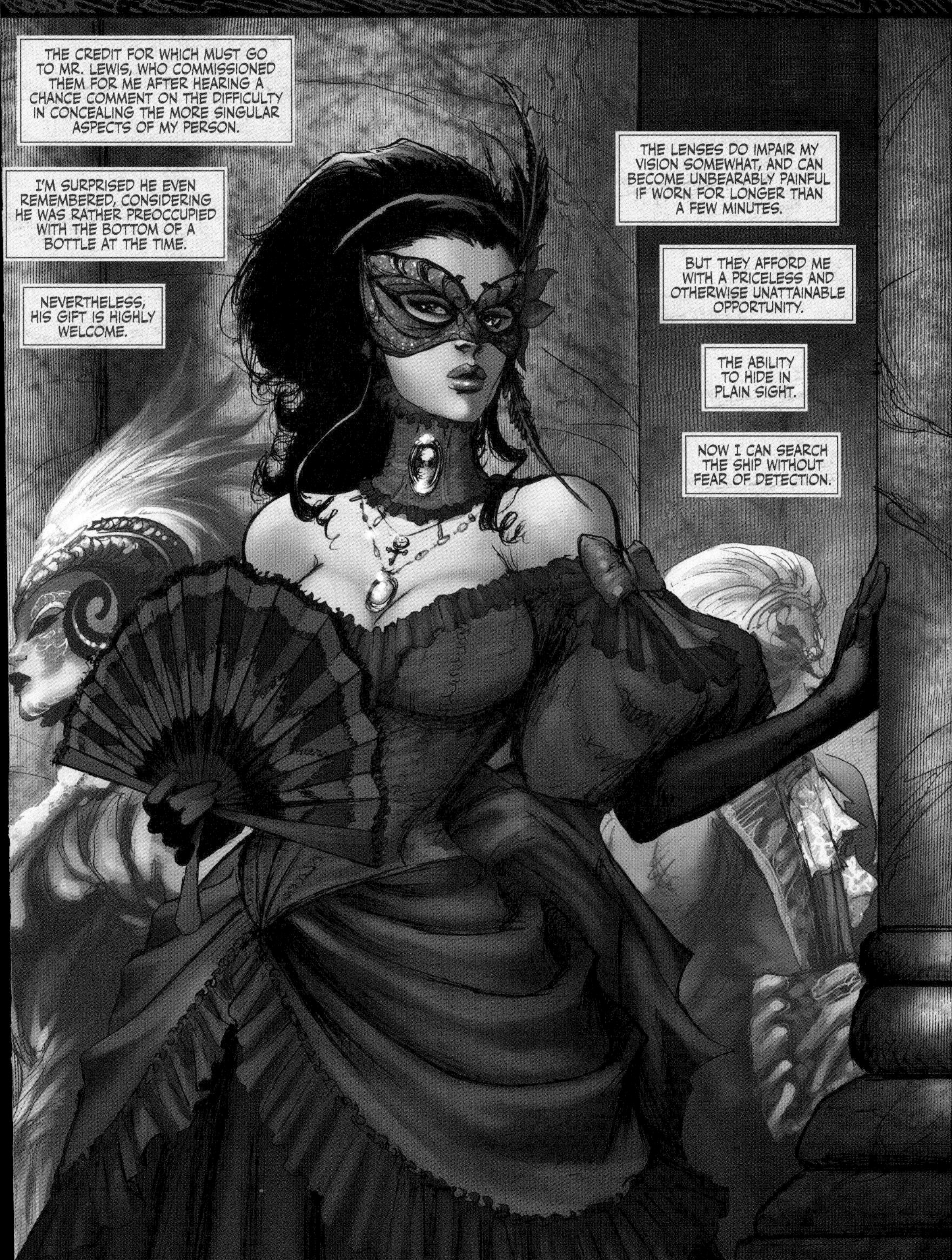
THE CREDIT FOR WHICH MUST GO TO MR. LEWIS, WHO COMMISSIONED THEM FOR ME AFTER HEARING A CHANCE COMMENT ON THE DIFFICULTY IN CONCEALING THE MORE SINGULAR ASPECTS OF MY PERSON.
I'M SURPRISED HE EVEN REMEMBERED, CONSIDERING HE WAS RATHER PREOCCUPIED WITH THE BOTTOM OF A BOTTLE AT THE TIME.
NEVERTHELESS, HIS GIFT IS HIGHLY WELCOME.
THE LENSES DO IMPAIR MY VISION SOMEWHAT, AND CAN BECOME UNBEARABLY PAINFUL IF WORN FOR LONGER THAN A FEW MINUTES.
BUT THEY AFFORD ME WITH A PRICELESS AND OTHERWISE UNATTAINABLE OPPORTUNITY.
THE ABILITY TO HIDE IN PLAIN SIGHT.
NOW I CAN SEARCH THE SHIP WITHOUT FEAR OF DETECTION.

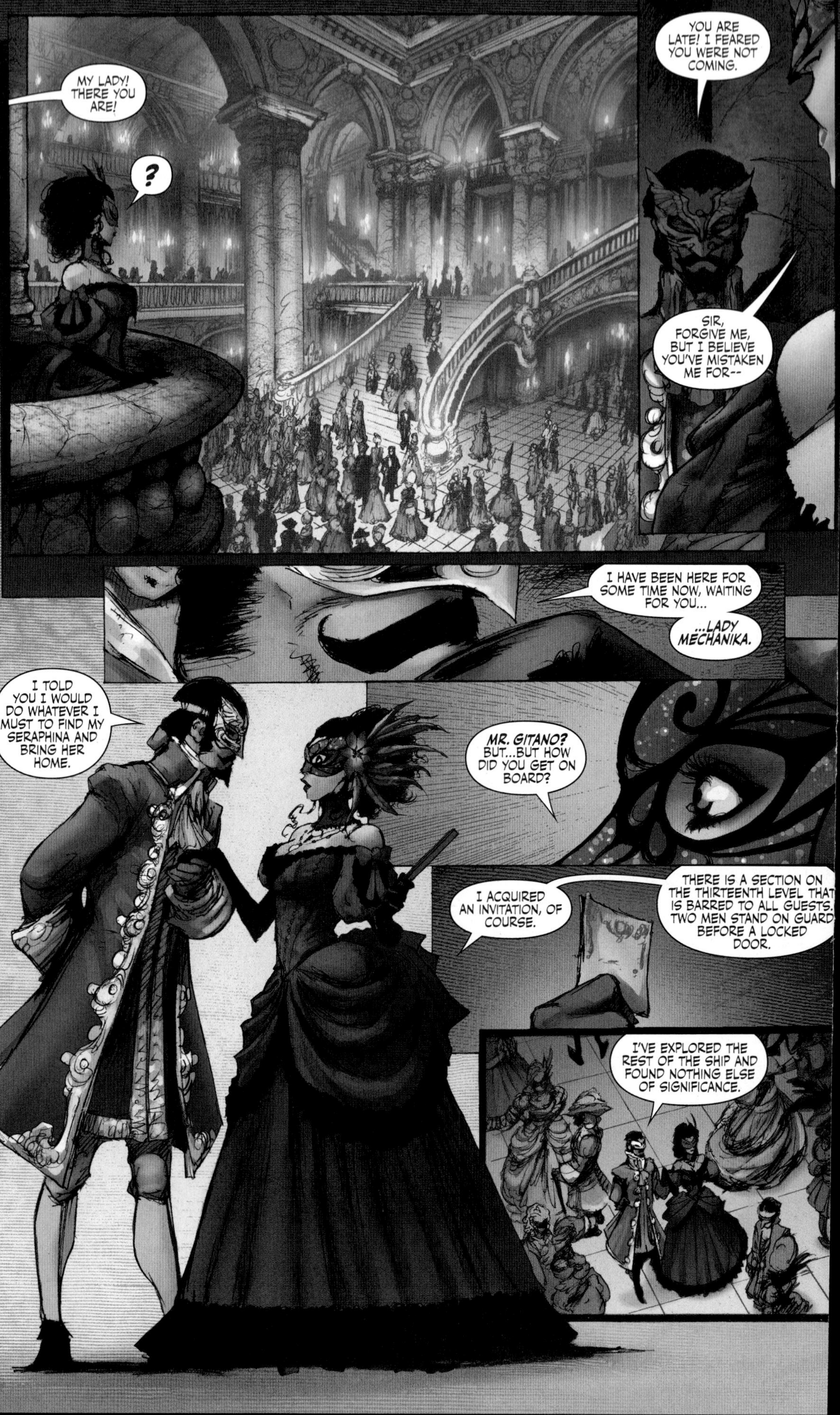
MY LADY! THERE YOU ARE!
?
YOU ARE LATE! I FEARED YOU WERE NOT COMING.
SIR, FORGIVE ME, BUT I BELIEVE YOU'VE MISTAKEN ME FOR--
I HAVE BEEN HERE FOR SOME TIME NOW, WAITING FOR YOU...
...LADY MECHANIKA.
MR. GITANO? BUT...BUT HOW DID YOU GET ON BOARD?
I TOLD YOU I WOULD DO WHATEVER I MUST TO FIND MY SERAPHINA AND BRING HER HOME.
I ACQUIRED AN INVITATION, OF COURSE.
THERE IS A SECTION ON THE THIRTEENTH LEVEL THAT IS BARRED TO ALL GUESTS. TWO MEN STAND ON GUARD BEFORE A LOCKED DOOR.
I'VE EXPLORED THE REST OF THE SHIP AND FOUND NOTHING ELSE OF SIGNIFICANCE.

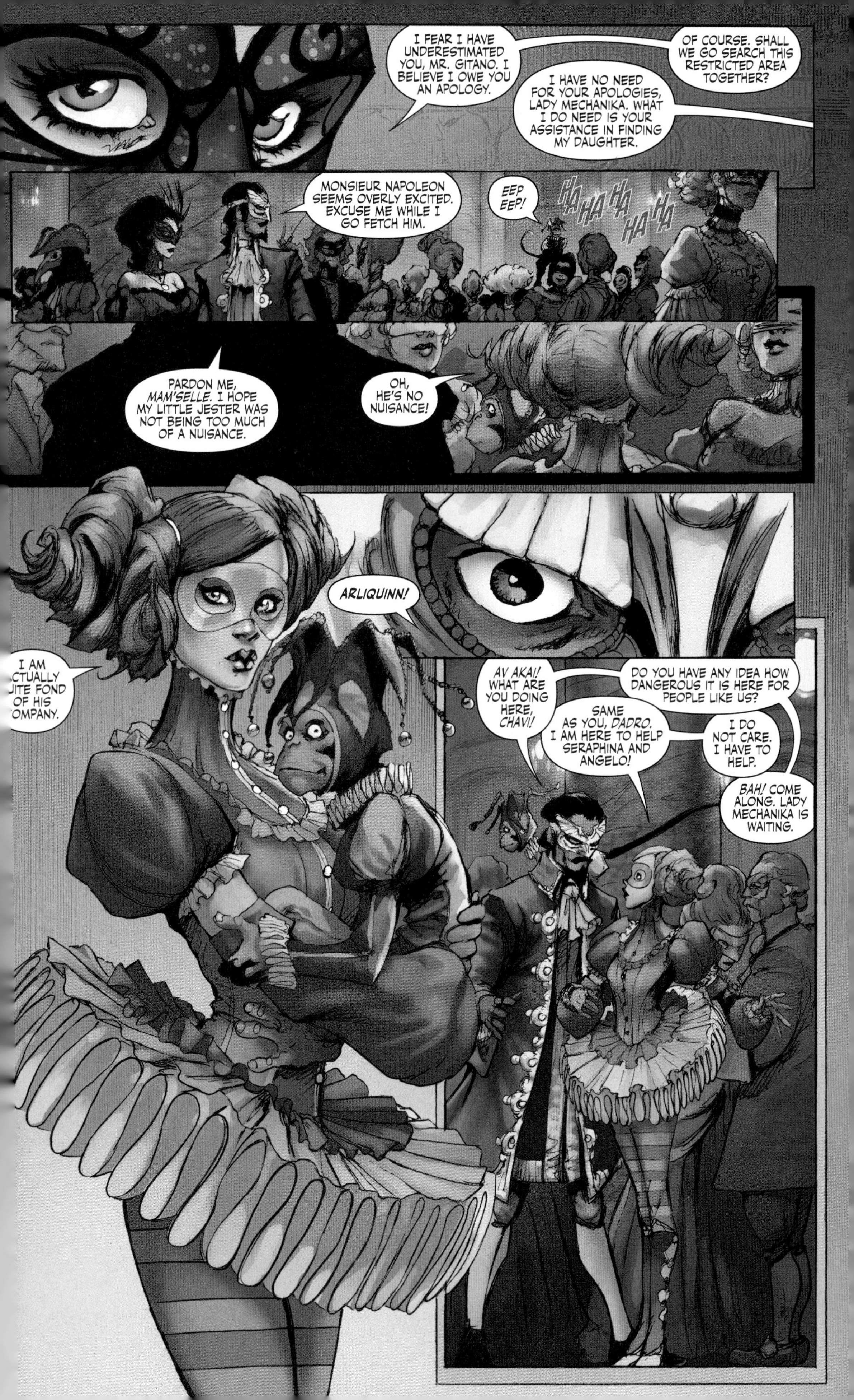
I FEAR I HAVE UNDERESTIMATED YOU, MR. GITANO. I BELIEVE I OWE YOU AN APOLOGY.
I HAVE NO NEED FOR YOUR APOLOGIES, LADY MECHANIKA. WHAT I DO NEED IS YOUR ASSISTANCE IN FINDING MY DAUGHTER.
OF COURSE. SHALL WE GO SEARCH THIS RESTRICTED AREA TOGETHER?
MONSIEUR NAPOLEON SEEMS OVERLY EXCITED. EXCUSE ME WHILE I GO FETCH HIM.
EEP EEP!
HA HA HA HA HA HA
PARDON ME, MAM'SELLE. I HOPE MY LITTLE JESTER WAS NOT BEING TOO MUCH OF A NUISANCE.
OH, HE'S NO NUISANCE!
I AM CTUALLY UITE FOND OF HIS OMPANY.
ARLIQUINN!
AV AKAI! WHAT ARE YOU DOING HERE, CHAVI!
SAME AS YOU, DADRO. I AM HERE TO HELP SERAPHINA AND ANGELO!
DO YOU HAVE ANY IDEA HOW DANGEROUS IT IS HERE FOR PEOPLE LIKE US?
I DO NOT CARE. I HAVE TO HELP.
BAH! COME ALONG. LADY MECHANIKA IS WAITING.

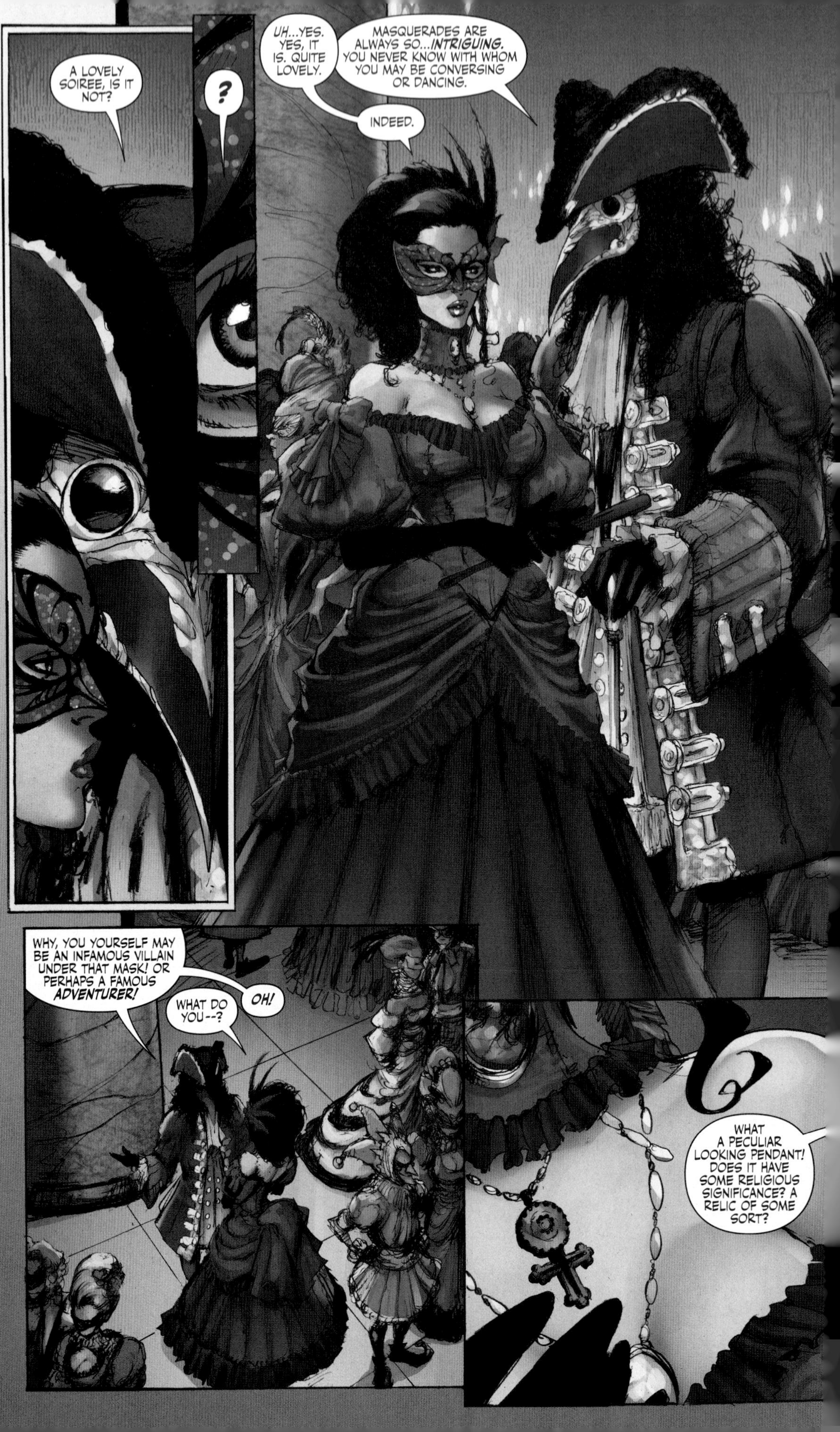
A LOVELY SOIREE, IS IT NOT?
?
UH...YES. YES, IT IS. QUITE LOVELY.
MASQUERADES ARE ALWAYS SO...INTRIGUING. YOU NEVER KNOW WITH WHOM YOU MAY BE CONVERSING OR DANCING.
INDEED.
WHY, YOU YOURSELF MAY BE AN INFAMOUS VILLAIN UNDER THAT MASK! OR PERHAPS A FAMOUS ADVENTURER!
WHAT DO YOU--?
OH!
WHAT A PECULIAR LOOKING PENDANT! DOES IT HAVE SOME RELIGIOUS SIGNIFICANCE? A RELIC OF SOME SORT?

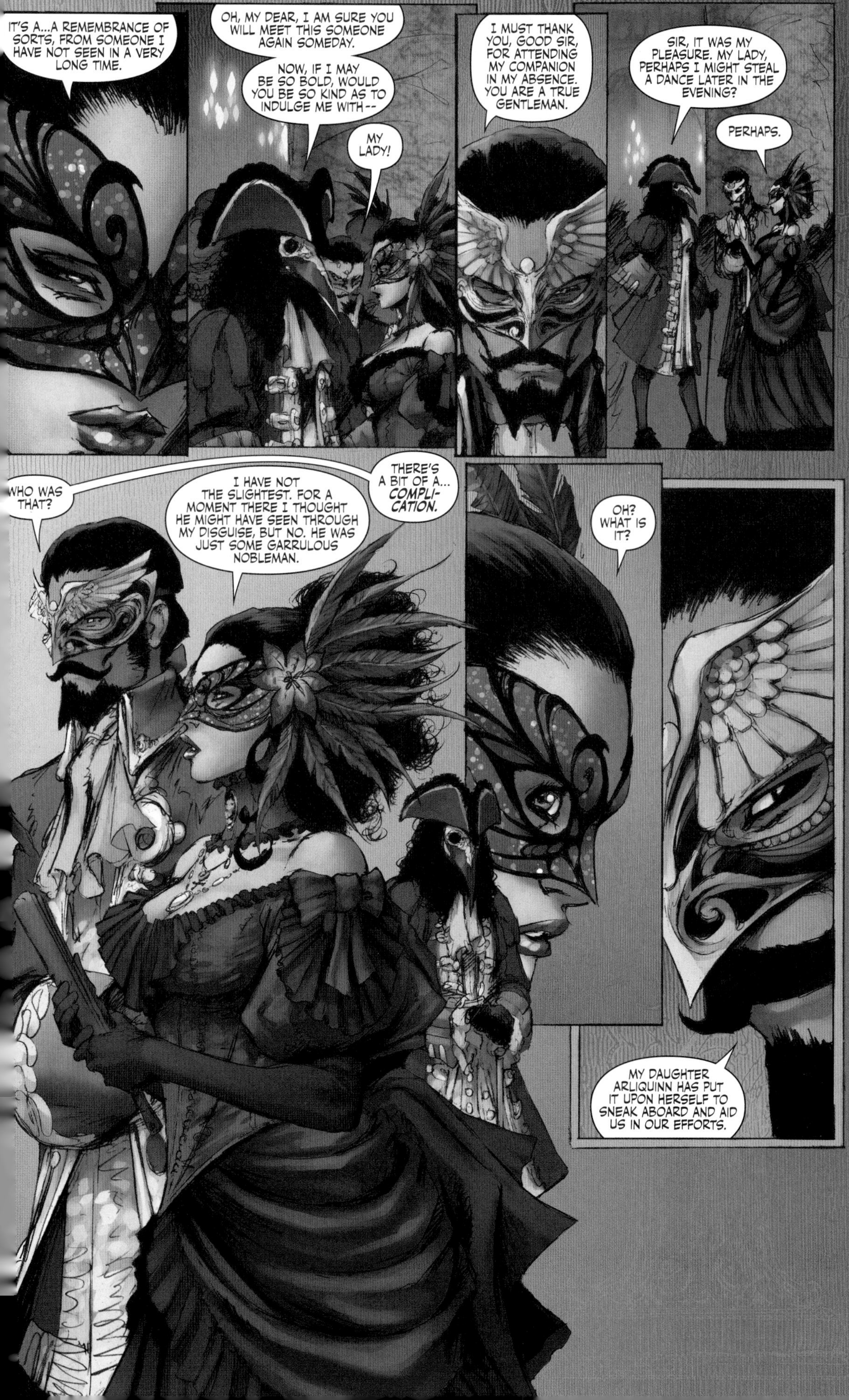
IT'S A...A REMEMBRANCE OF SORTS, FROM SOMEONE I HAVE NOT SEEN IN A VERY LONG TIME.
OH, MY DEAR, I AM SURE YOU WILL MEET THIS SOMEONE AGAIN SOMEDAY.
NOW, IF I MAY BE SO BOLD, WOULD YOU BE SO KIND AS TO INDULGE ME WITH--
MY LADY!
I MUST THANK YOU, GOOD SIR, FOR ATTENDING MY COMPANION IN MY ABSENCE. YOU ARE A TRUE GENTLEMAN.
SIR, IT WAS MY PLEASURE. MY LADY, PERHAPS I MIGHT STEAL A DANCE LATER IN THE EVENING?
PERHAPS.
WHO WAS THAT?
I HAVE NOT THE SLIGHTEST. FOR A MOMENT THERE I THOUGHT HE MIGHT HAVE SEEN THROUGH MY DISGUISE, BUT NO. HE WAS JUST SOME GARRULOUS NOBLEMAN.
THERE'S A BIT OF A... COMPLICATION.
OH? WHAT IS IT?
MY DAUGHTER ARLIQUINN HAS PUT IT UPON HERSELF TO SNEAK ABOARD AND AID US IN OUR EFFORTS.

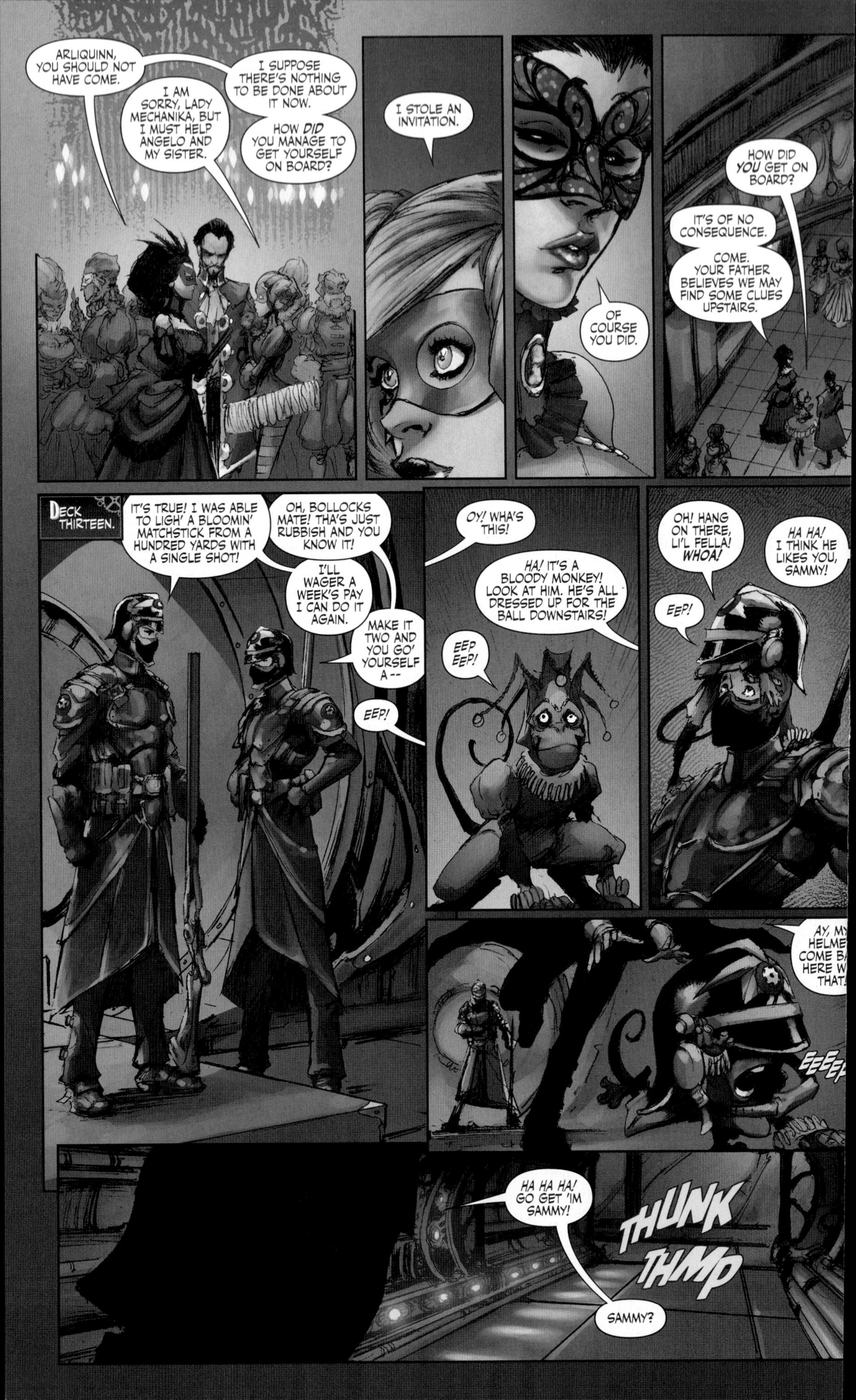
ARLIQUINN, YOU SHOULD NOT HAVE COME.
I AM SORRY, LADY MECHANIKA, BUT I MUST HELP ANGELO AND MY SISTER.
I SUPPOSE THERE'S NOTHING TO BE DONE ABOUT IT NOW.
HOW DID YOU MANAGE TO GET YOURSELF ON BOARD?
I STOLE AN INVITATION.
OF COURSE YOU DID.
HOW DID YOU GET ON BOARD?
IT'S OF NO CONSEQUENCE.
COME. YOUR FATHER BELIEVES WE MAY FIND SOME CLUES UPSTAIRS.
DECK THIRTEEN.
IT'S TRUE! I WAS ABLE TO LIGH' A BLOOMIN' MATCHSTICK FROM A HUNDRED YARDS WITH A SINGLE SHOT!
OH, BOLLOCKS MATE! THA'S JUST RUBBISH AND YOU KNOW IT!
I'LL WAGER A WEEK'S PAY I CAN DO IT AGAIN.
MAKE IT TWO AND YOU GO' YOURSELF A --
EEP!
OY! WHA'S THIS!
HA! IT'S A BLOODY MONKEY! LOOK AT HIM. HE'S ALL DRESSED UP FOR THE BALL DOWNSTAIRS!
EEP EEP!
OH! HANG ON THERE, LI'L FELLA! WHOA!
EEP!
HA HA! I THINK HE LIKES YOU, SAMMY!
AY, MY HELME COME BA HERE W THAT!
EEEEP
HA HA HA! GO GET 'IM SAMMY!
THUNK
THMP
SAMMY?

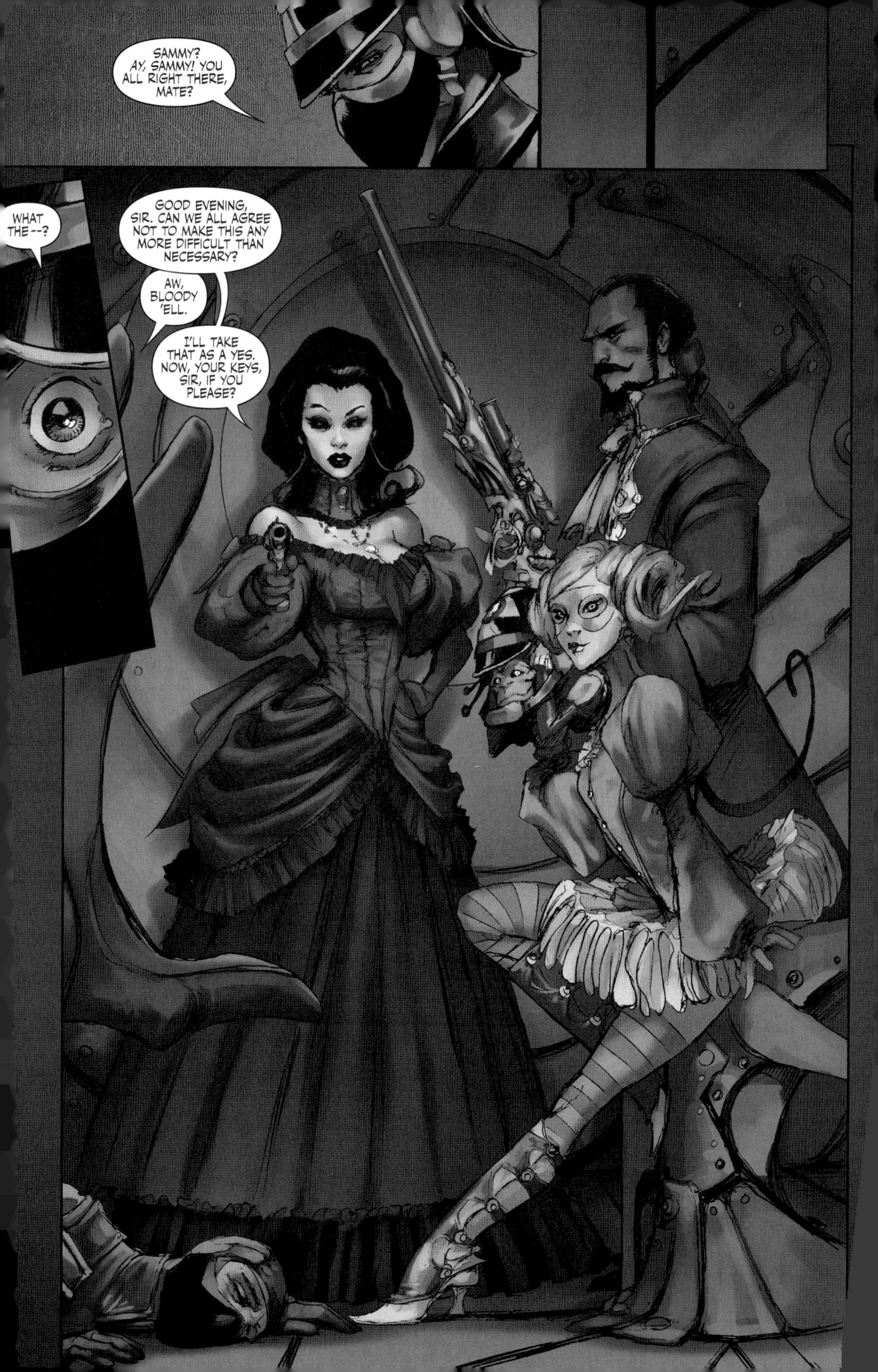
SAMMY? AY, SAMMY! YOU ALL RIGHT THERE, MATE?
WHAT THE--?
GOOD EVENING, SIR. CAN WE ALL AGREE NOT TO MAKE THIS ANY MORE DIFFICULT THAN NECESSARY?
AW, BLOODY 'ELL.
I'LL TAKE THAT AS A YES. NOW, YOUR KEYS, SIR, IF YOU PLEASE?

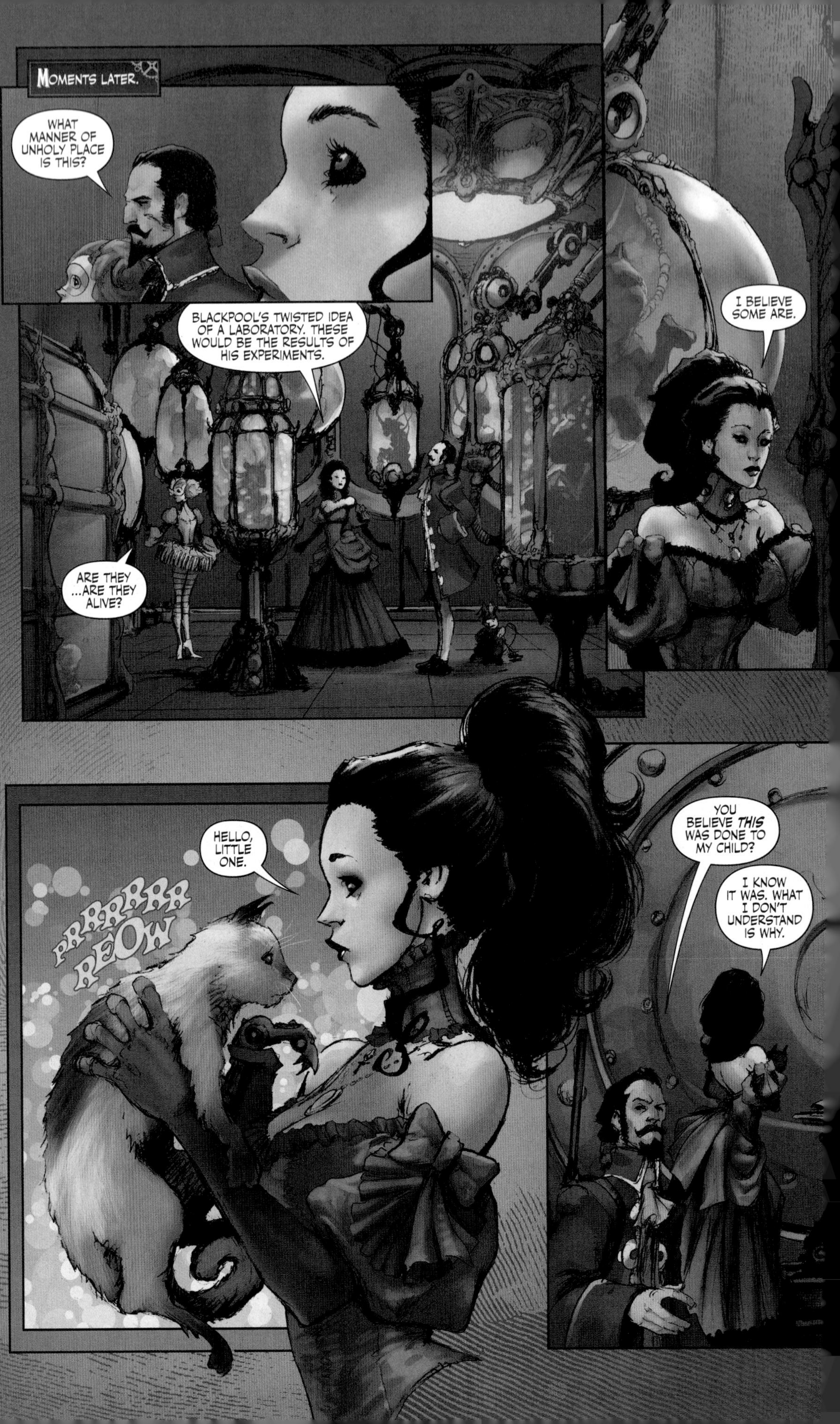
MOMENTS LATER.
WHAT MANNER OF UNHOLY PLACE IS THIS?
BLACKPOOL'S TWISTED IDEA OF A LABORATORY. THESE WOULD BE THE RESULTS OF HIS EXPERIMENTS.
ARE THEY ...ARE THEY ALIVE?
I BELIEVE SOME ARE.
HELLO, LITTLE ONE.
PRRRRRR REOW
YOU BELIEVE *THIS* WAS DONE TO MY CHILD?
I KNOW IT WAS. WHAT I DON'T UNDERSTAND IS WHY.

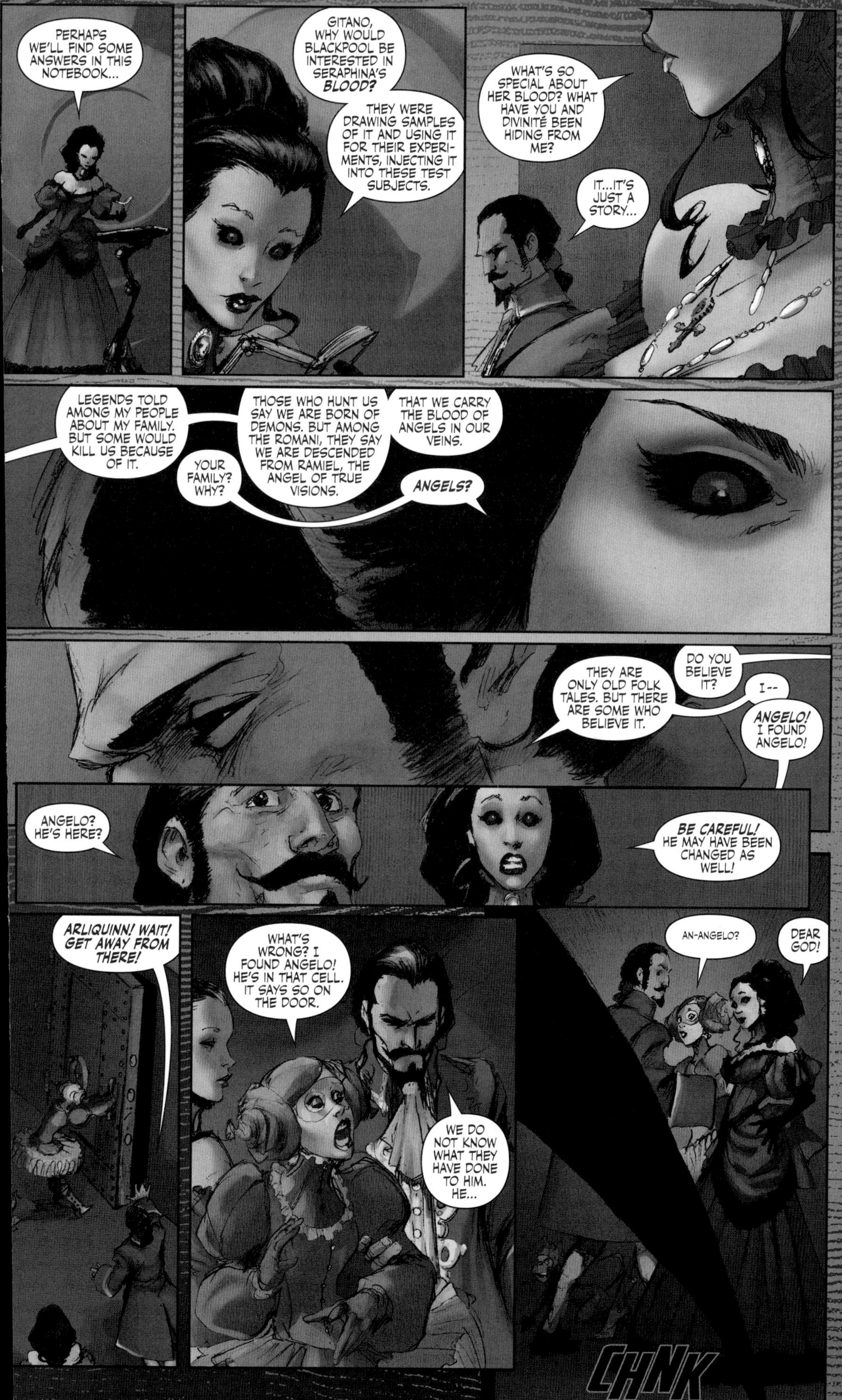
PERHAPS WE'LL FIND SOME ANSWERS IN THIS NOTEBOOK...
GITANO, WHY WOULD BLACKPOOL BE INTERESTED IN SERAPHINA'S BLOOD?
THEY WERE DRAWING SAMPLES OF IT AND USING IT FOR THEIR EXPERI-MENTS, INJECTING IT INTO THESE TEST SUBJECTS.
WHAT'S SO SPECIAL ABOUT HER BLOOD? WHAT HAVE YOU AND DIVINITÉ BEEN HIDING FROM ME?
IT...IT'S JUST A STORY...
LEGENDS TOLD AMONG MY PEOPLE ABOUT MY FAMILY. BUT SOME WOULD KILL US BECAUSE OF IT.
YOUR FAMILY? WHY?
THOSE WHO HUNT US SAY WE ARE BORN OF DEMONS. BUT AMONG THE ROMANI, THEY SAY WE ARE DESCENDED FROM RAMIEL, THE ANGEL OF TRUE VISIONS.
THAT WE CARRY THE BLOOD OF ANGELS IN OUR VEINS.
ANGELS?
THEY ARE ONLY OLD FOLK TALES. BUT THERE ARE SOME WHO BELIEVE IT.
DO YOU BELIEVE IT?
I--
ANGELO! I FOUND ANGELO!
ANGELO? HE'S HERE?
BE CAREFUL! HE MAY HAVE BEEN CHANGED AS WELL!
ARLIQUINN! WAIT! GET AWAY FROM THERE!
WHAT'S WRONG? I FOUND ANGELO! HE'S IN THAT CELL. IT SAYS SO ON THE DOOR.
WE DO NOT KNOW WHAT THEY HAVE DONE TO HIM. HE...
AN-ANGELO?
DEAR GOD!
CHNK

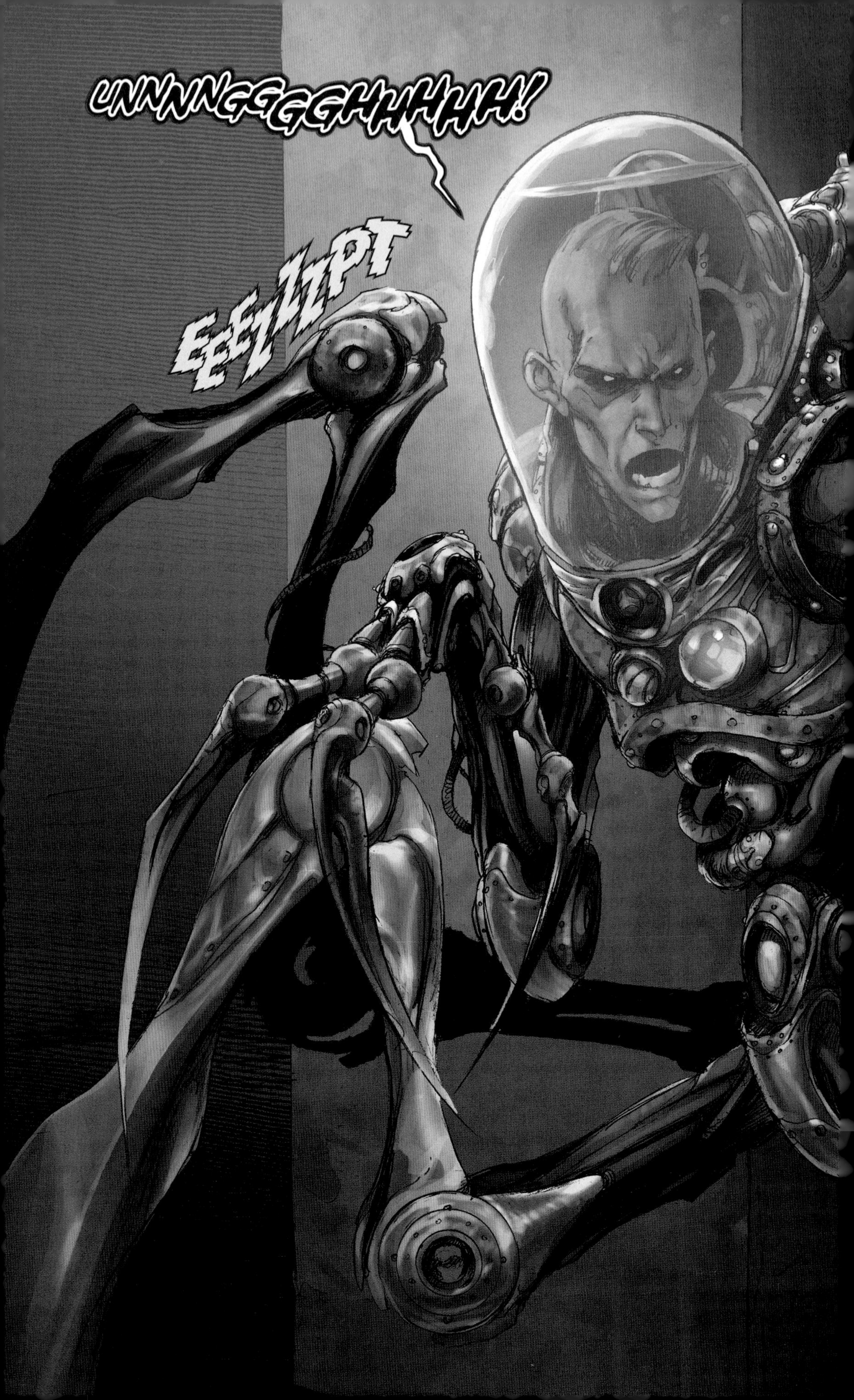
UNNNNGGGGHHHHH!
EEEZZZZPT

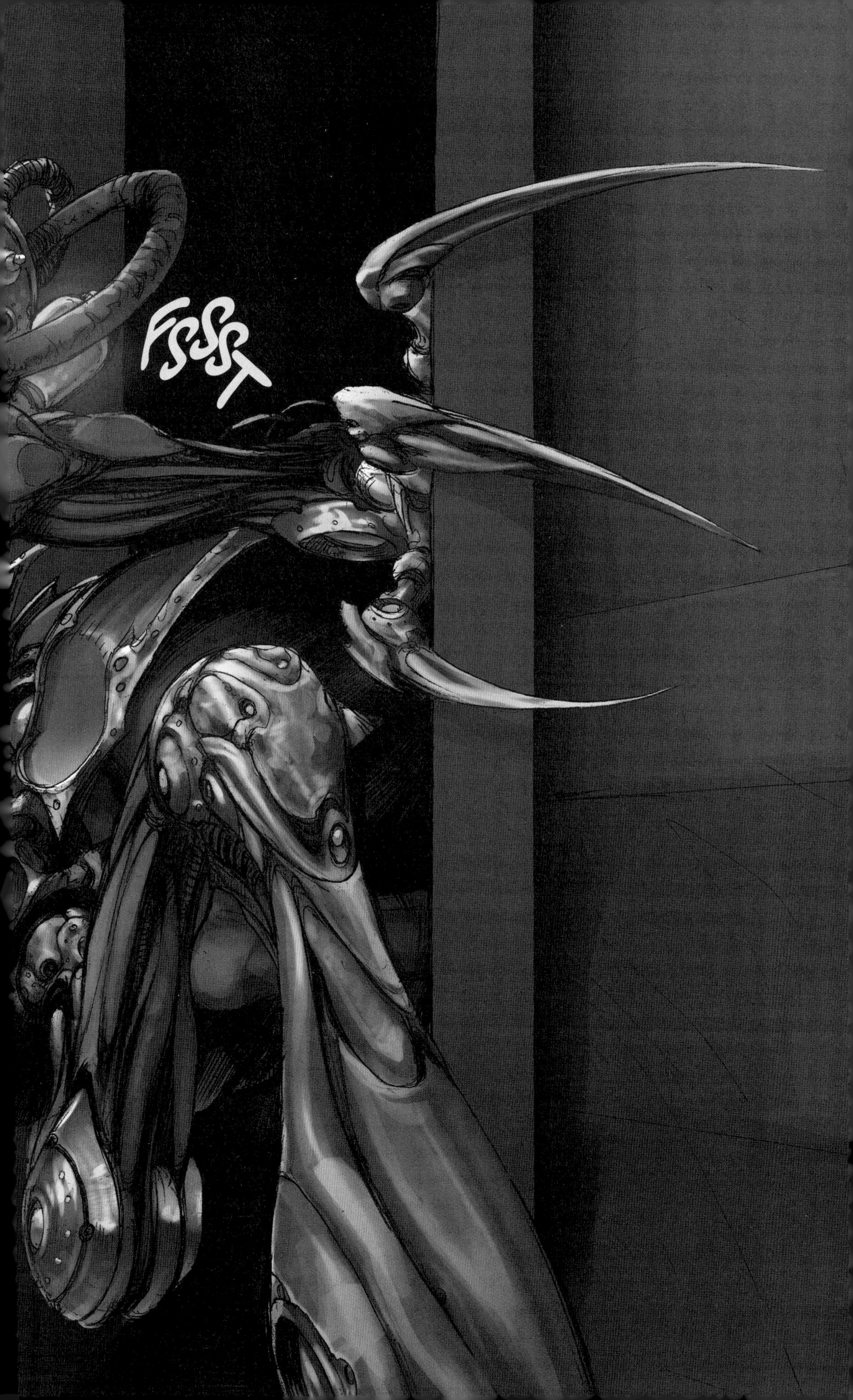
FSSST

# Chapter Five

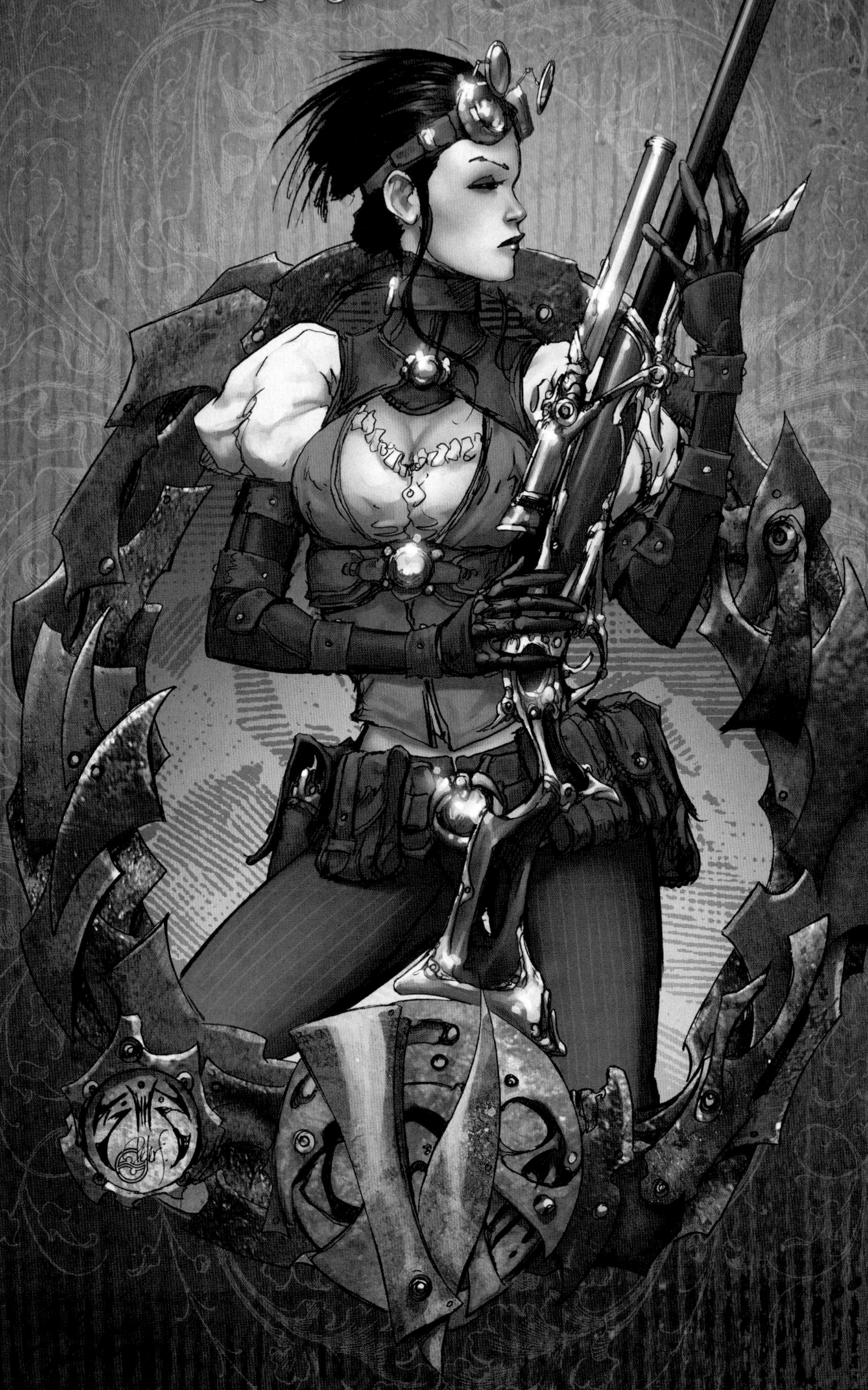

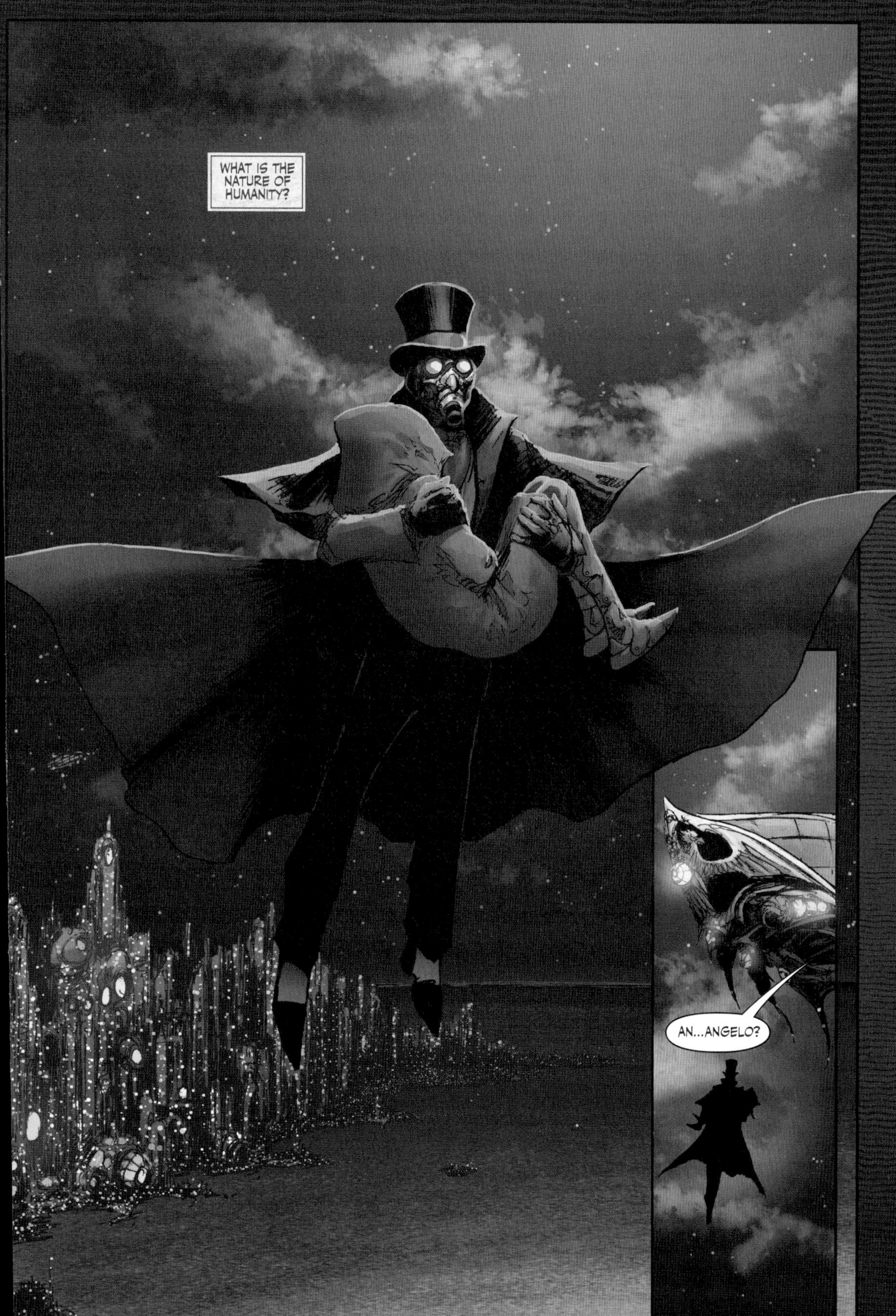
WHAT IS THE NATURE OF HUMANITY?
AN...ANGELO?

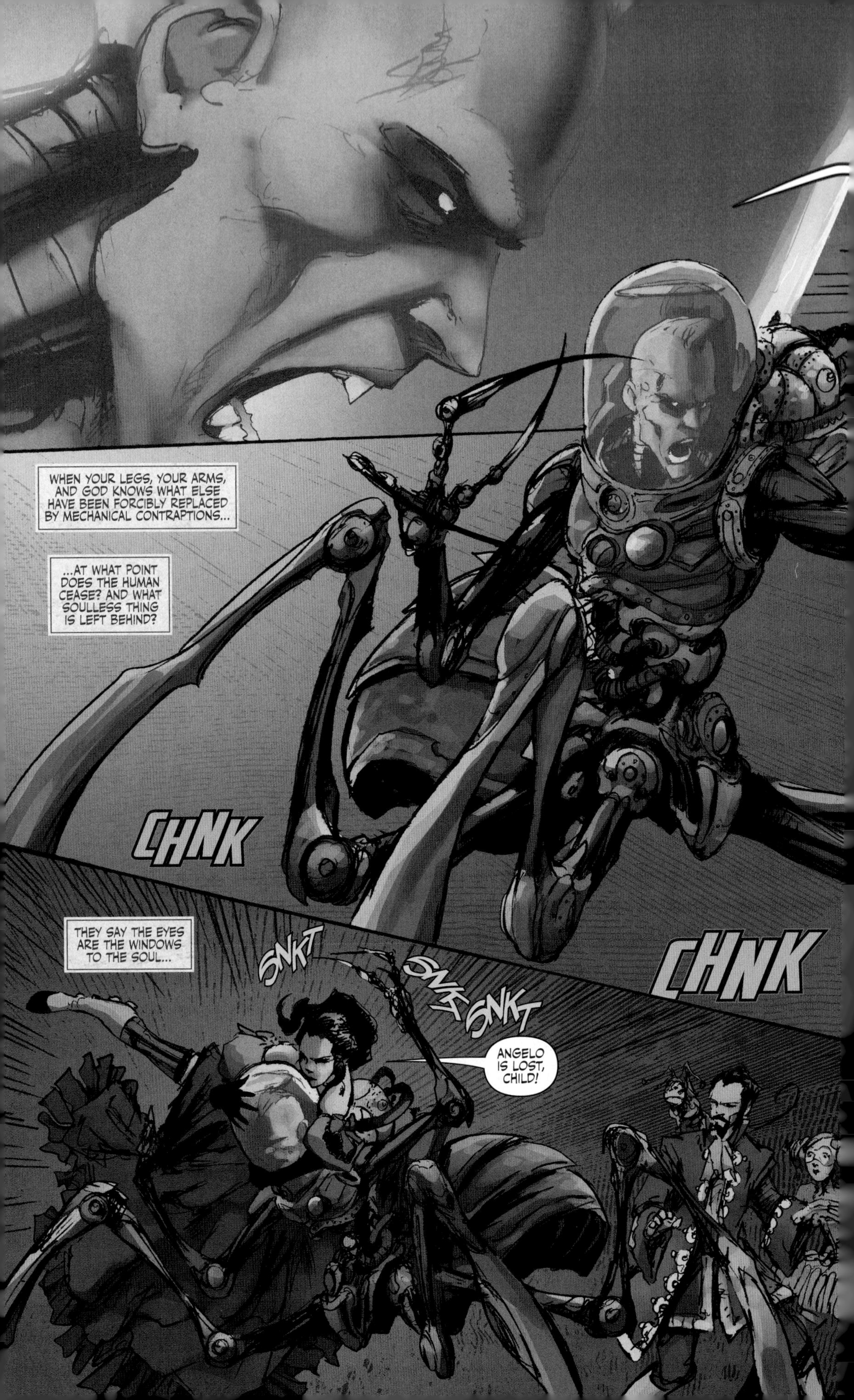
WHEN YOUR LEGS, YOUR ARMS, AND GOD KNOWS WHAT ELSE HAVE BEEN FORCIBLY REPLACED BY MECHANICAL CONTRAPTIONS...
...AT WHAT POINT DOES THE HUMAN CEASE? AND WHAT SOULLESS THING IS LEFT BEHIND?
CHNK
CHNK
THEY SAY THE EYES ARE THE WINDOWS TO THE SOUL...
SNKT
SNKT
SNKT
ANGELO IS LOST, CHILD!

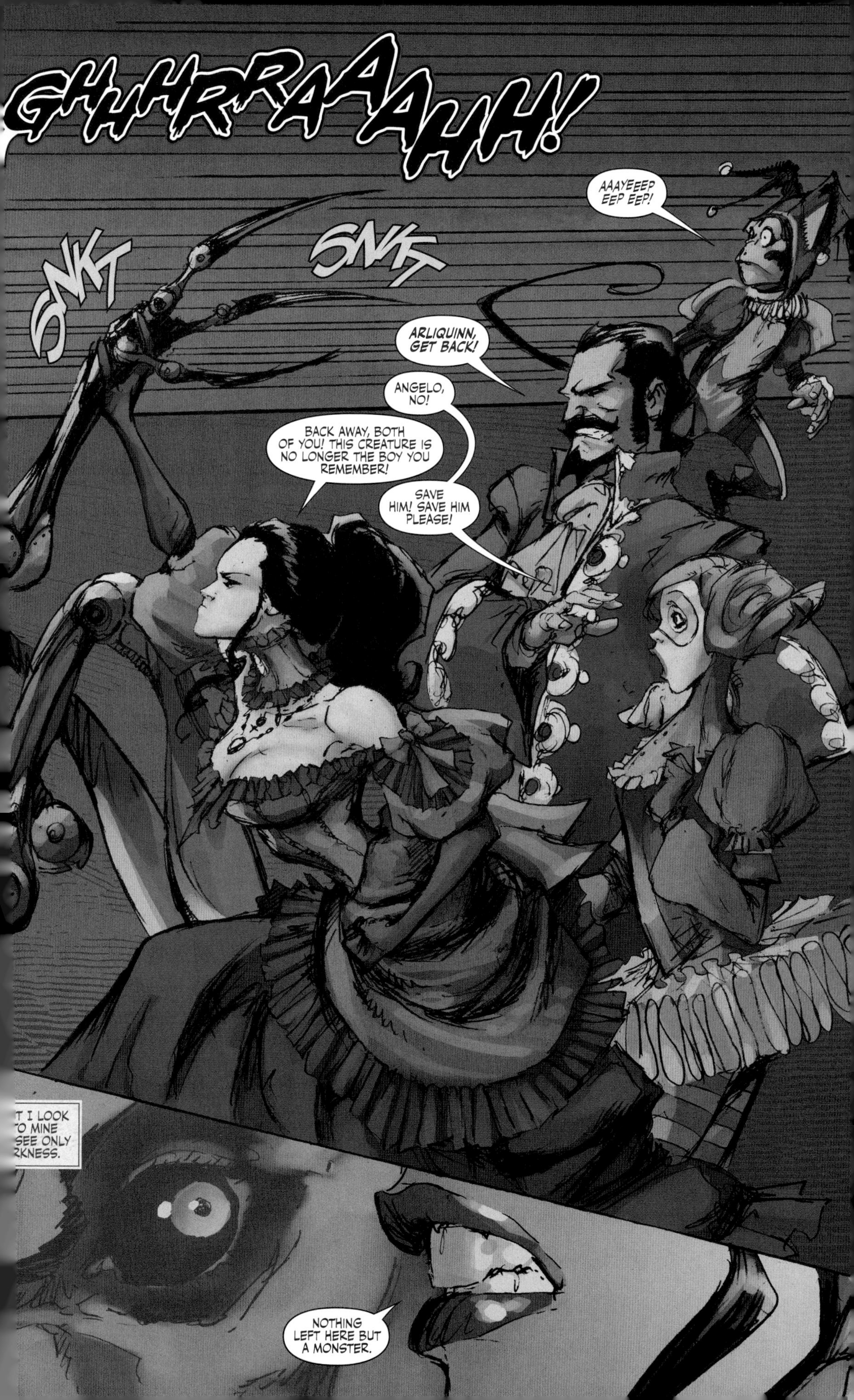

GHHRRAAAHH!
AAAYEEEP EEP EEP!
SNKT
SNKT
ARLIQUINN, GET BACK!
ANGELO, NO!
BACK AWAY, BOTH OF YOU! THIS CREATURE IS NO LONGER THE BOY YOU REMEMBER!
SAVE HIM! SAVE HIM PLEASE!
T I LOOK
O MINE
SEE ONLY
RKNESS.
NOTHING LEFT HERE BUT A MONSTER.

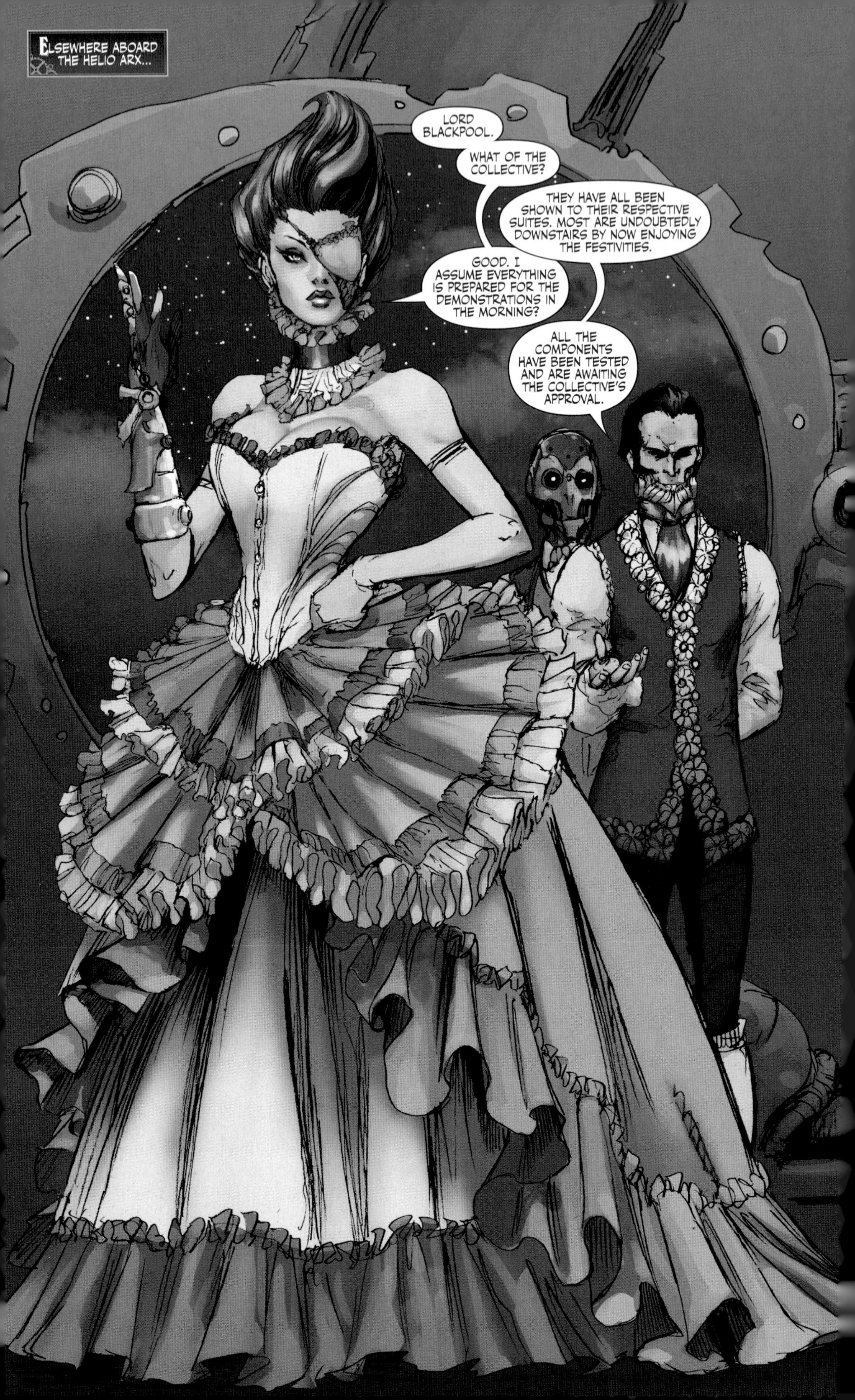
ELSEWHERE ABOARD THE HELIO ARX...
LORD BLACKPOOL.
WHAT OF THE COLLECTIVE?
THEY HAVE ALL BEEN SHOWN TO THEIR RESPECTIVE SUITES. MOST ARE UNDOUBTEDLY DOWNSTAIRS BY NOW ENJOYING THE FESTIVITIES.
GOOD. I ASSUME EVERYTHING IS PREPARED FOR THE DEMONSTRATIONS IN THE MORNING?
ALL THE COMPONENTS HAVE BEEN TESTED AND ARE AWAITING THE COLLECTIVE'S APPROVAL.

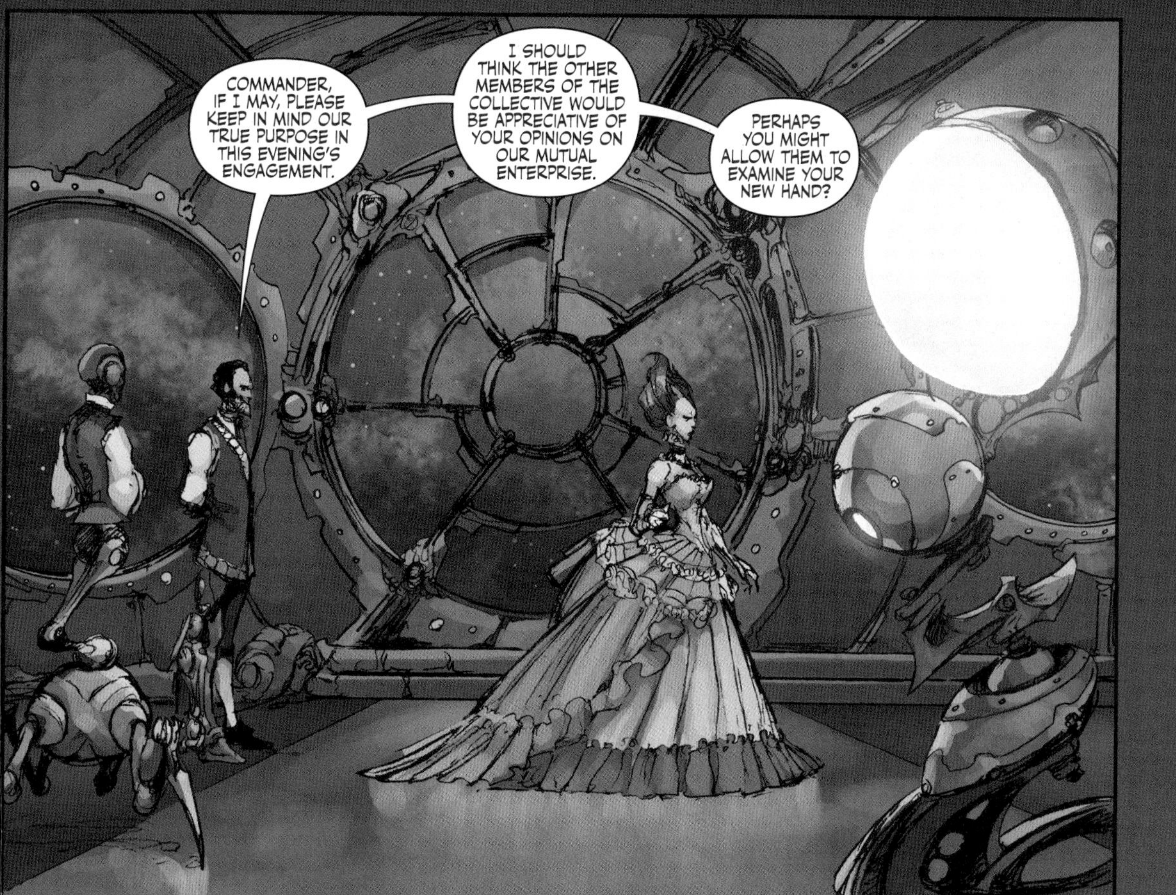
COMMANDER, IF I MAY, PLEASE KEEP IN MIND OUR TRUE PURPOSE IN THIS EVENING'S ENGAGEMENT.
I SHOULD THINK THE OTHER MEMBERS OF THE COLLECTIVE WOULD BE APPRECIATIVE OF YOUR OPINIONS ON OUR MUTUAL ENTERPRISE.
PERHAPS YOU MIGHT ALLOW THEM TO EXAMINE YOUR NEW HAND?
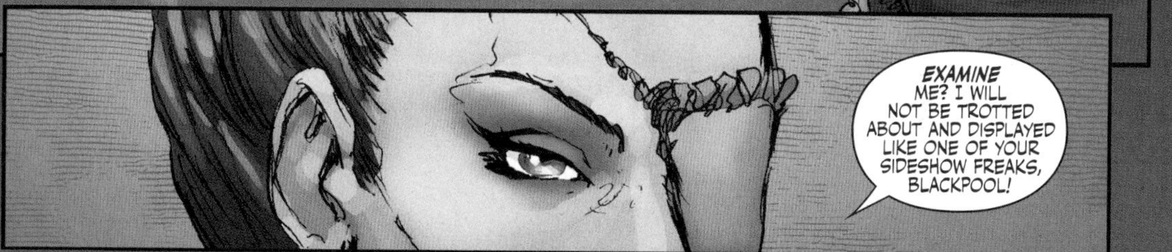
*EXAMINE* ME? I WILL NOT BE TROTTED ABOUT AND DISPLAYED LIKE ONE OF YOUR SIDESHOW FREAKS, BLACKPOOL!
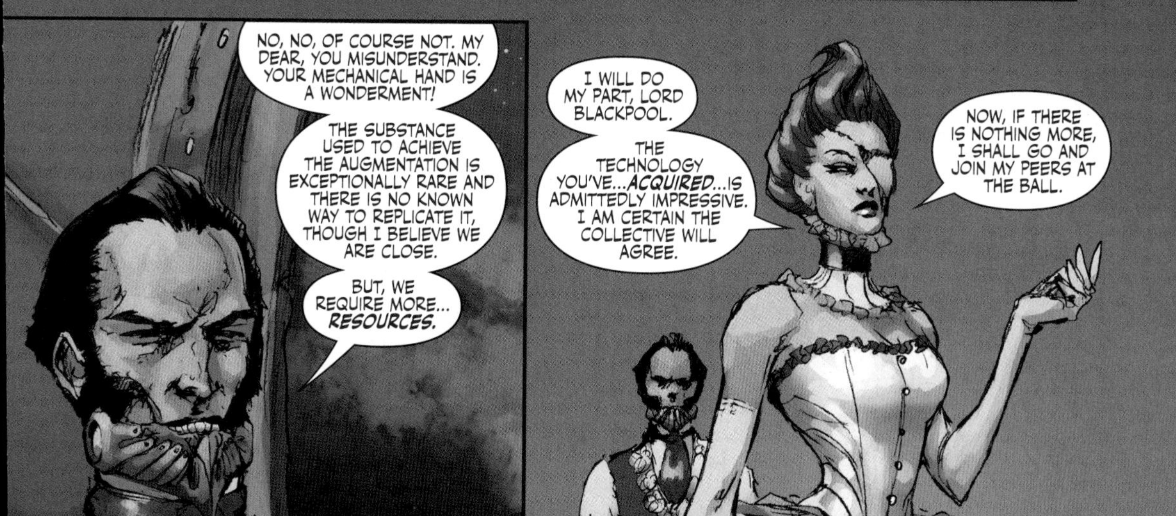
NO, NO, OF COURSE NOT. MY DEAR, YOU MISUNDERSTAND. YOUR MECHANICAL HAND IS A WONDERMENT!
THE SUBSTANCE USED TO ACHIEVE THE AUGMENTATION IS EXCEPTIONALLY RARE AND THERE IS NO KNOWN WAY TO REPLICATE IT, THOUGH I BELIEVE WE ARE CLOSE.
BUT, WE REQUIRE MORE... *RESOURCES.*
I WILL DO MY PART, LORD BLACKPOOL.
THE TECHNOLOGY YOU'VE... *ACQUIRED*... IS ADMITTEDLY IMPRESSIVE. I AM CERTAIN THE COLLECTIVE WILL AGREE.
NOW, IF THERE IS NOTHING MORE, I SHALL GO AND JOIN MY PEERS AT THE BALL.

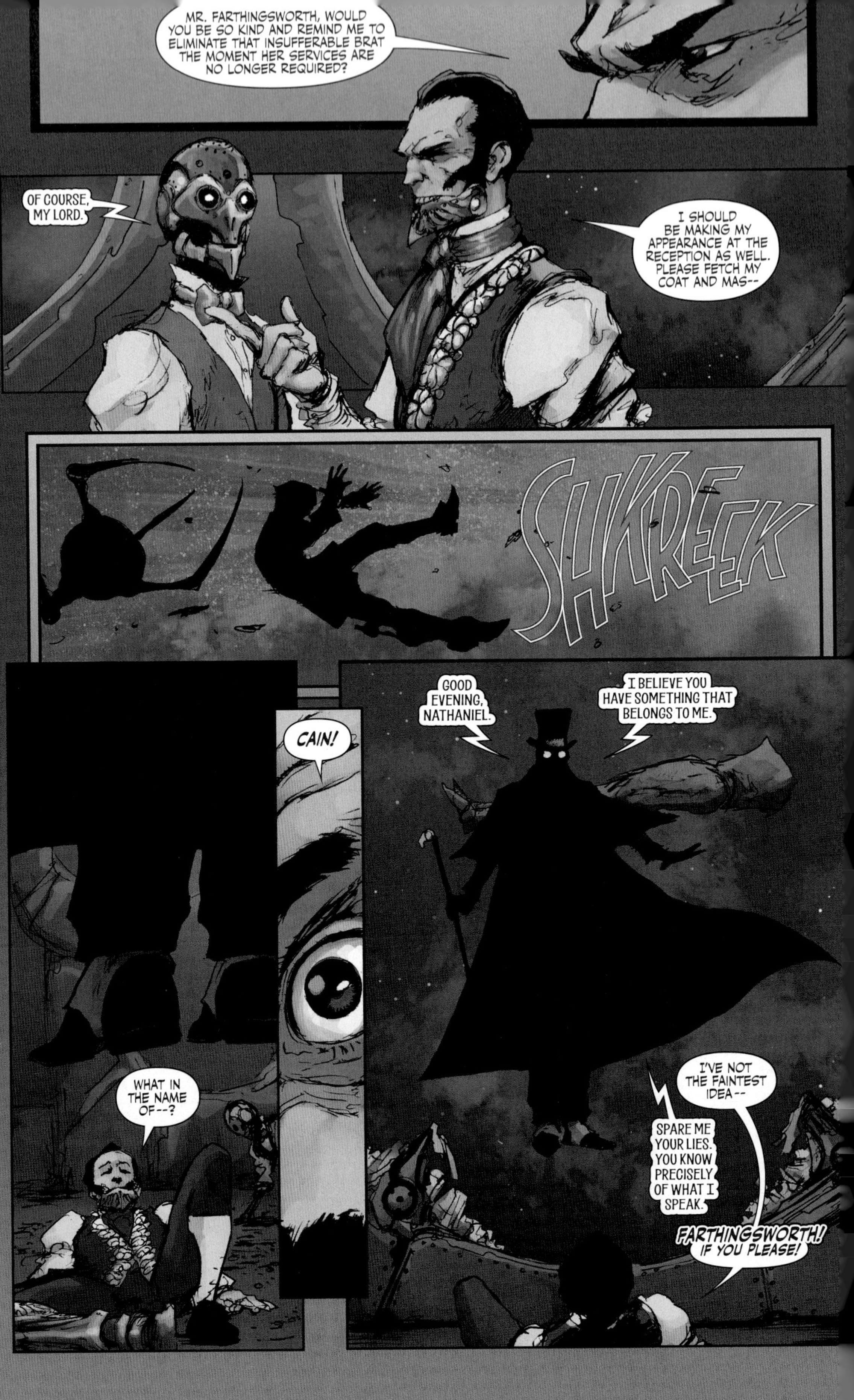
MR. FARTHINGSWORTH, WOULD YOU BE SO KIND AND REMIND ME TO ELIMINATE THAT INSUFFERABLE BRAT THE MOMENT HER SERVICES ARE NO LONGER REQUIRED?
OF COURSE, MY LORD.
I SHOULD BE MAKING MY APPEARANCE AT THE RECEPTION AS WELL. PLEASE FETCH MY COAT AND MAS--
SHKREEK
CAIN!
GOOD EVENING, NATHANIEL.
I BELIEVE YOU HAVE SOMETHING THAT BELONGS TO ME.
WHAT IN THE NAME OF--?
I'VE NOT THE FAINTEST IDEA--
SPARE ME YOUR LIES. YOU KNOW PRECISELY OF WHAT I SPEAK.
FARTHINGSWORTH! IF YOU PLEASE!

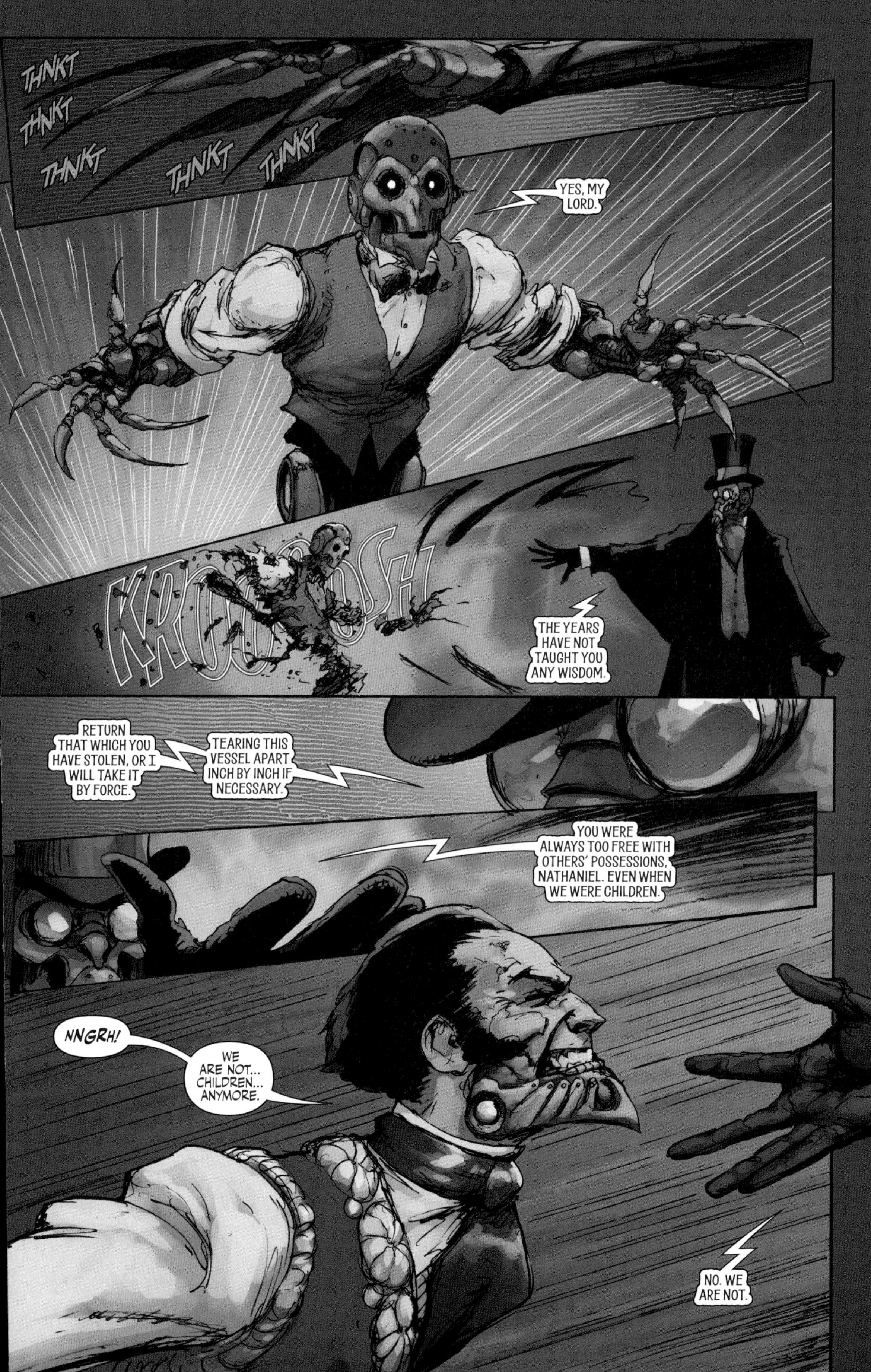
THNKT
THNKT
THNKT
THNKT
THNKT
YES, MY LORD.
KROOOOSH
THE YEARS HAVE NOT TAUGHT YOU ANY WISDOM.
RETURN THAT WHICH YOU HAVE STOLEN, OR I WILL TAKE IT BY FORCE.
TEARING THIS VESSEL APART INCH BY INCH IF NECESSARY.
YOU WERE ALWAYS TOO FREE WITH OTHERS' POSSESSIONS, NATHANIEL. EVEN WHEN WE WERE CHILDREN.
NNGRH!
WE ARE NOT... CHILDREN... ANYMORE.
NO. WE ARE NOT.

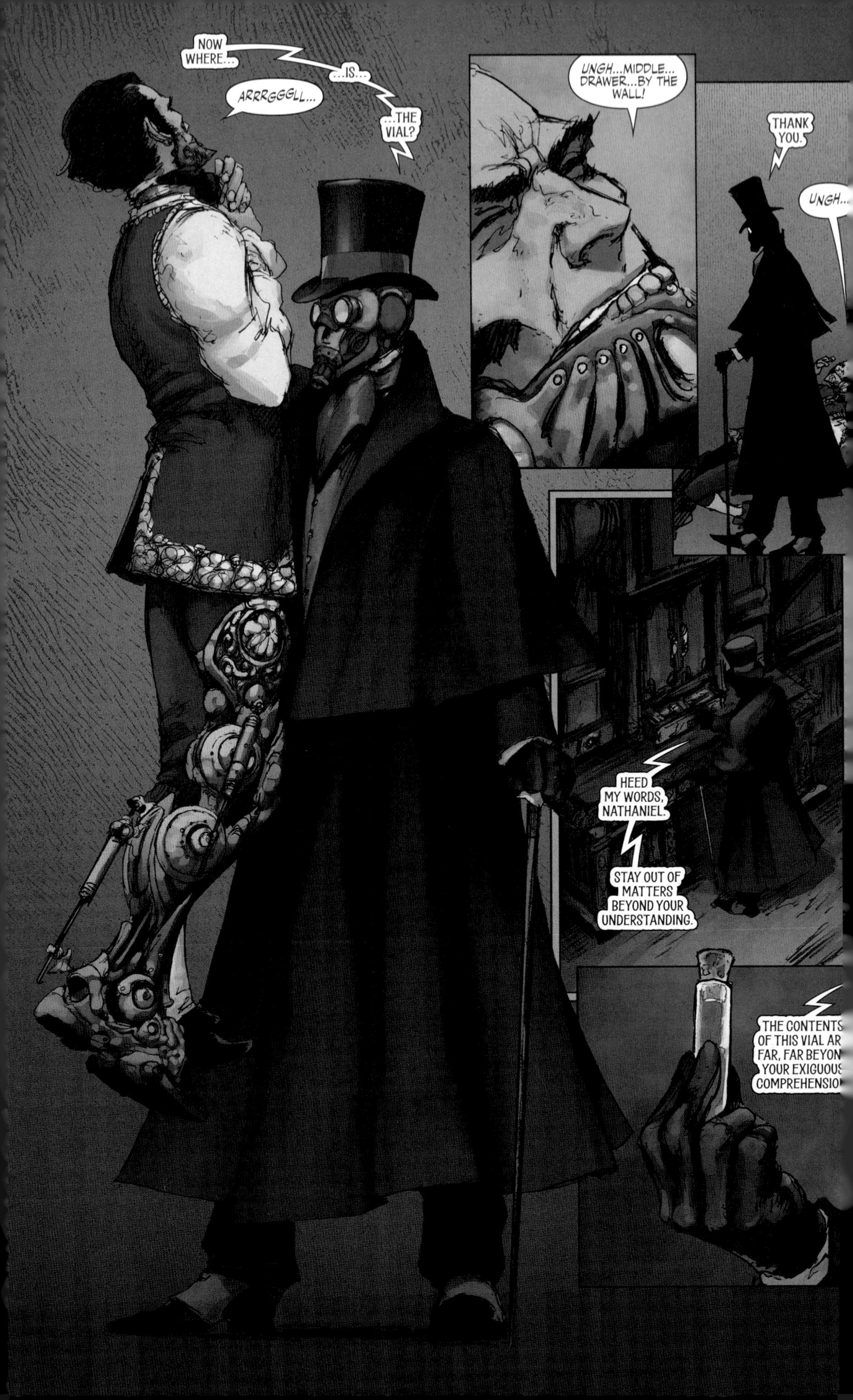
NOW WHERE...
...IS...
ARRRGGGLL...
...THE VIAL?
UNGH...MIDDLE... DRAWER...BY THE WALL!
THANK YOU.
UNGH...
HEED MY WORDS, NATHANIEL.
STAY OUT OF MATTERS BEYOND YOUR UNDERSTANDING.
THE CONTENTS OF THIS VIAL AR FAR, FAR BEYON YOUR EXIGUOUS COMPREHENSIO

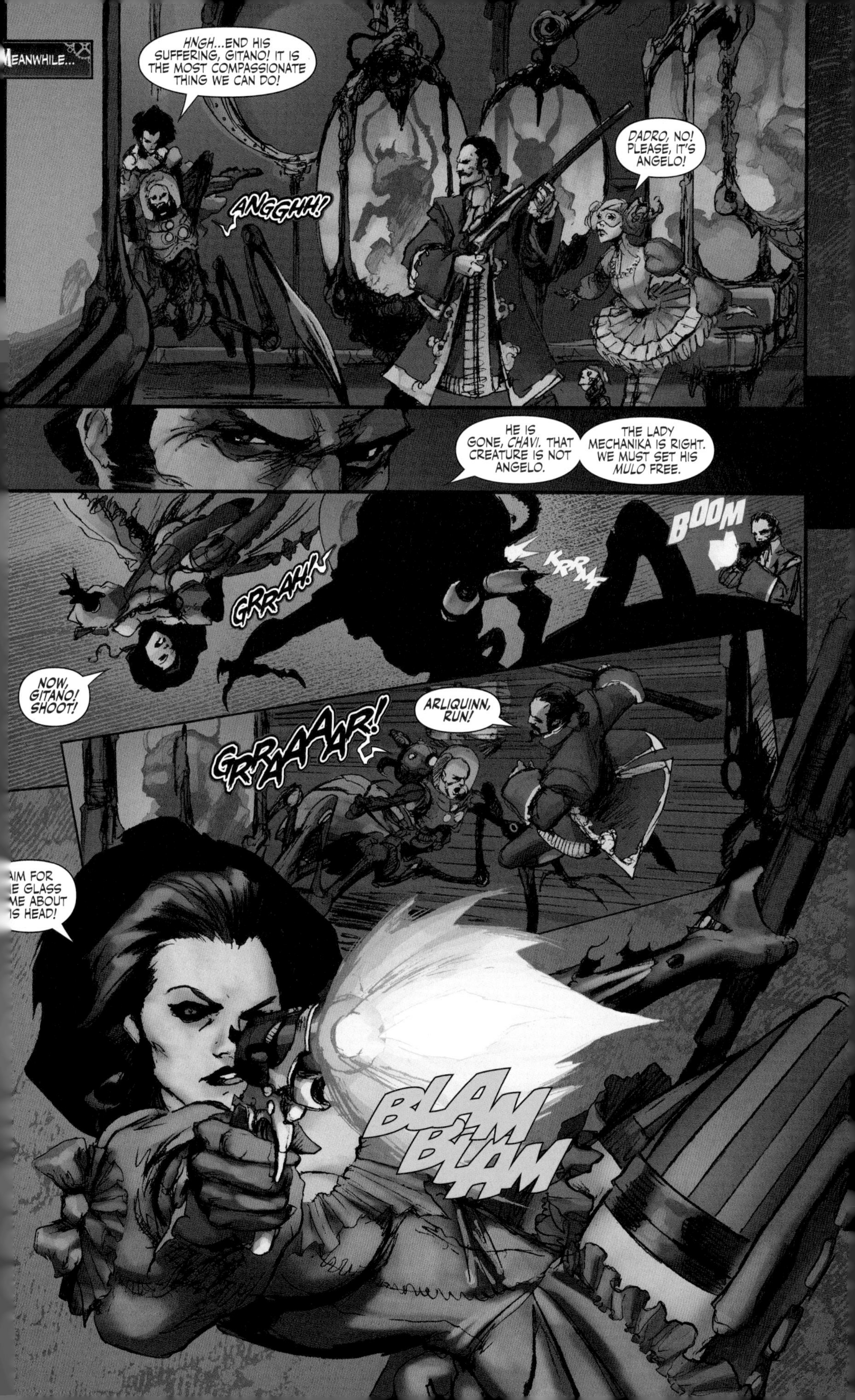
MEANWHILE...
HNGH...END HIS SUFFERING, GITANO! IT IS THE MOST COMPASSIONATE THING WE CAN DO!
ANGGHH!
DADRO, NO! PLEASE, IT'S ANGELO!
HE IS GONE, CHAVI. THAT CREATURE IS NOT ANGELO.
THE LADY MECHANIKA IS RIGHT. WE MUST SET HIS MULO FREE.
BOOM
KRRAK
GRRAH!
NOW, GITANO! SHOOT!
ARLIQUINN, RUN!
GRRAAAAR!
AIM FOR
E GLASS
ME ABOUT
IS HEAD!
BLAM BLAM BLAM

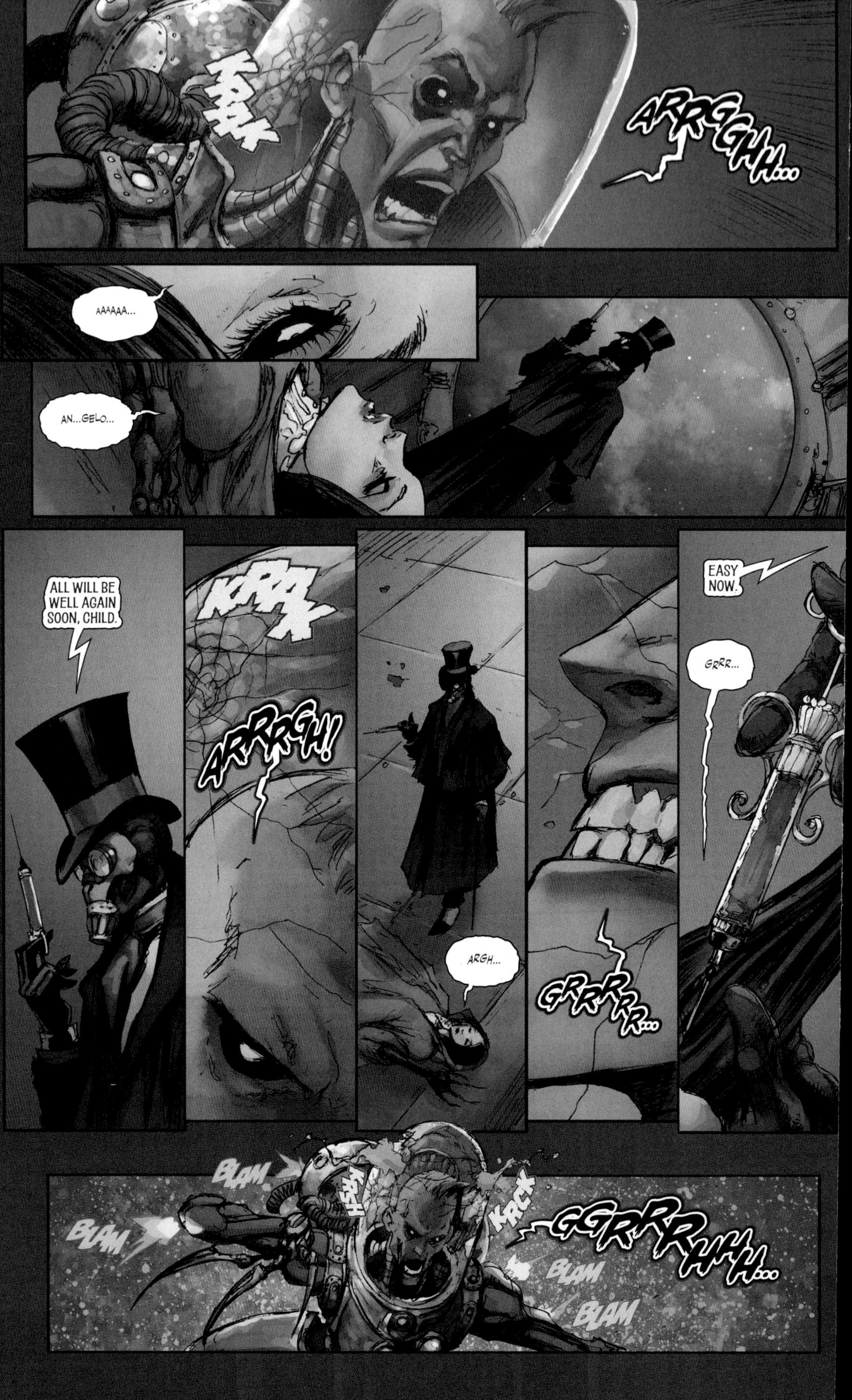
KRAK
ARRGGHH...
AAAAAA...
AN...GELO...
ALL WILL BE WELL AGAIN SOON, CHILD.
KRAK
ARRRGH!
ARGH...
GRRRRR...
EASY NOW.
GRRR...
BLAM
BLAM
KRASH
KRACK
GGRRRRHHH...
BLAM
BLAM

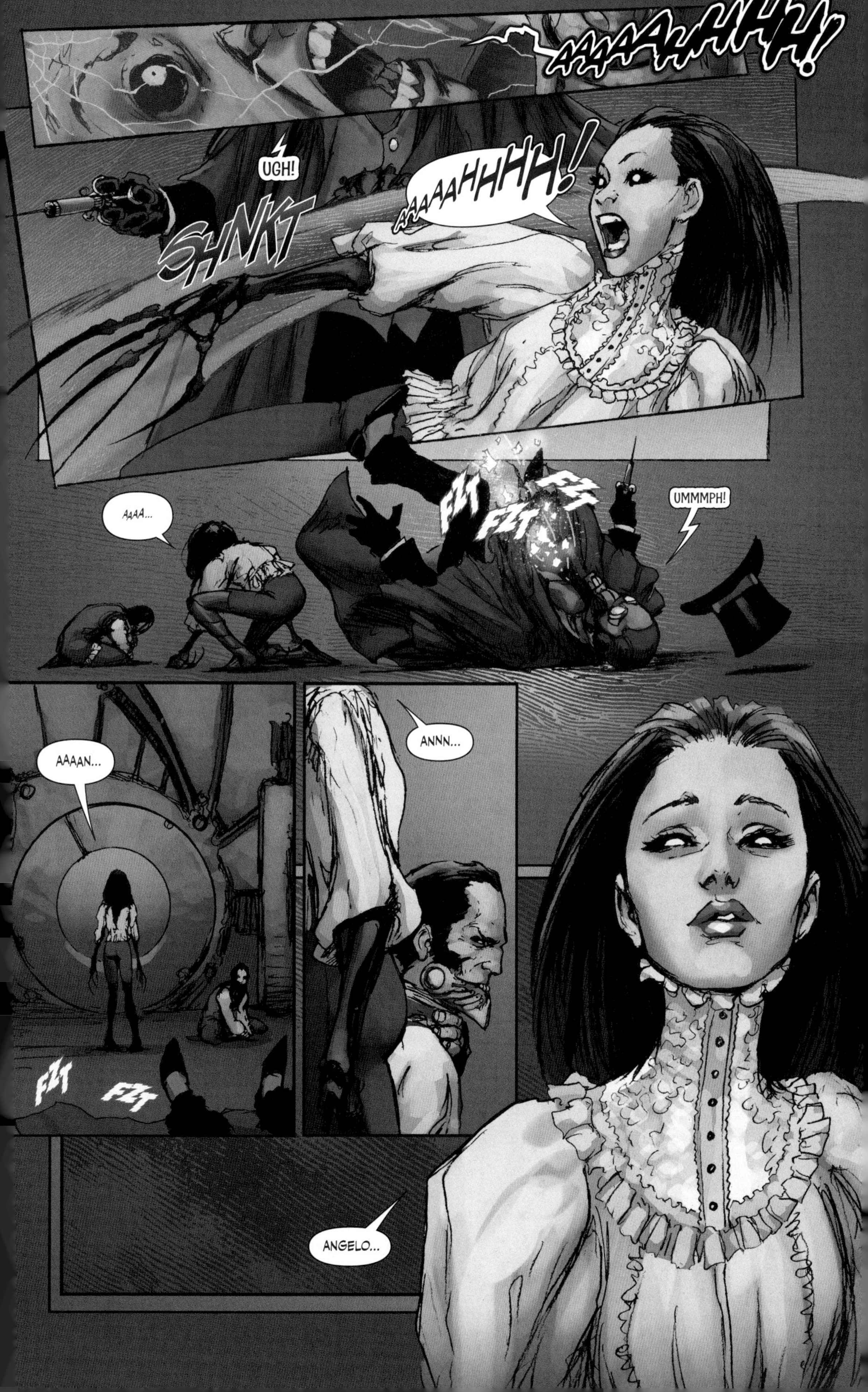
AAAAAHHHH!
UGH!
SHNKT
AAAAAHHHHH!
AAAA...
FZT
FZT
FZT
UMMMPH!
AAAAN...
FZT
FZT
ANNN...
ANGELO...

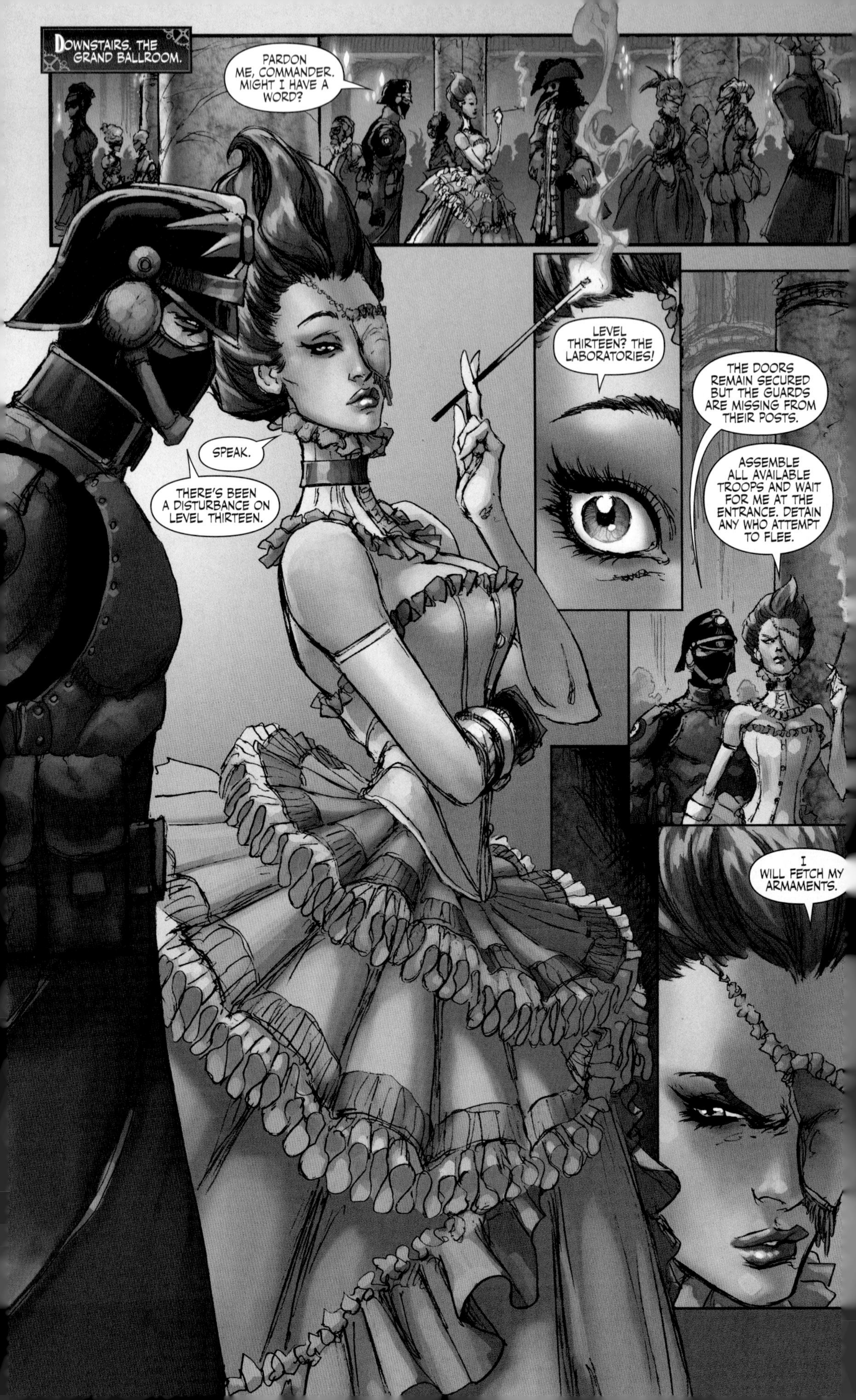
DOWNSTAIRS, THE GRAND BALLROOM.
PARDON ME, COMMANDER. MIGHT I HAVE A WORD?
SPEAK.
THERE'S BEEN A DISTURBANCE ON LEVEL THIRTEEN.
LEVEL THIRTEEN? THE LABORATORIES!
THE DOORS REMAIN SECURED BUT THE GUARDS ARE MISSING FROM THEIR POSTS.
ASSEMBLE ALL AVAILABLE TROOPS AND WAIT FOR ME AT THE ENTRANCE. DETAIN ANY WHO ATTEMPT TO FLEE.
I WILL FETCH MY ARMAMENTS.

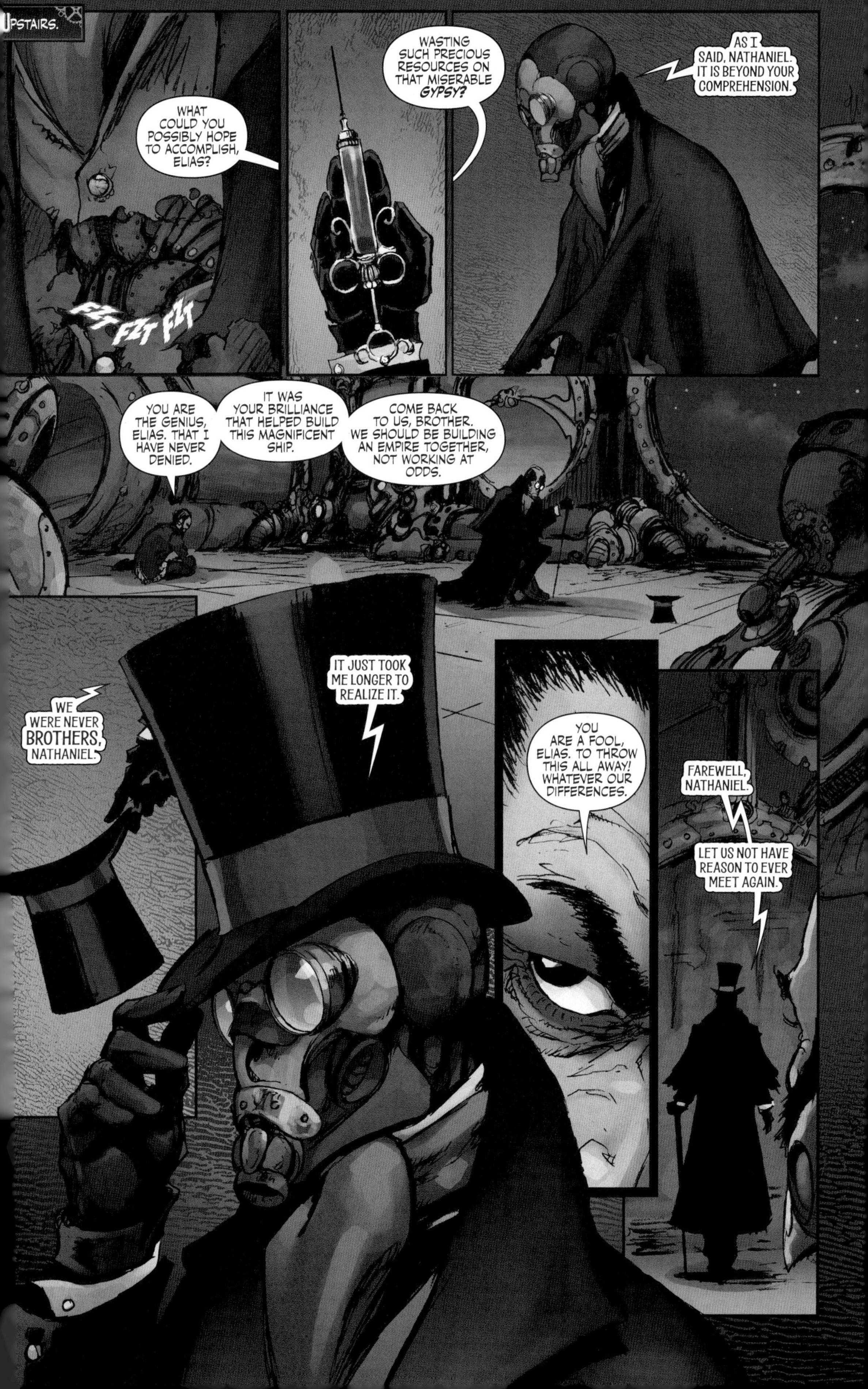
UPSTAIRS.
WHAT COULD YOU POSSIBLY HOPE TO ACCOMPLISH, ELIAS?
FZT FZT FZT
WASTING SUCH PRECIOUS RESOURCES ON THAT MISERABLE GYPSY?
AS I SAID, NATHANIEL. IT IS BEYOND YOUR COMPREHENSION.
YOU ARE THE GENIUS, ELIAS. THAT I HAVE NEVER DENIED.
IT WAS YOUR BRILLIANCE THAT HELPED BUILD THIS MAGNIFICENT SHIP.
COME BACK TO US, BROTHER. WE SHOULD BE BUILDING AN EMPIRE TOGETHER, NOT WORKING AT ODDS.
WE WERE NEVER BROTHERS, NATHANIEL.
IT JUST TOOK ME LONGER TO REALIZE IT.
YOU ARE A FOOL, ELIAS. TO THROW THIS ALL AWAY! WHATEVER OUR DIFFERENCES.
FAREWELL, NATHANIEL.
LET US NOT HAVE REASON TO EVER MEET AGAIN.

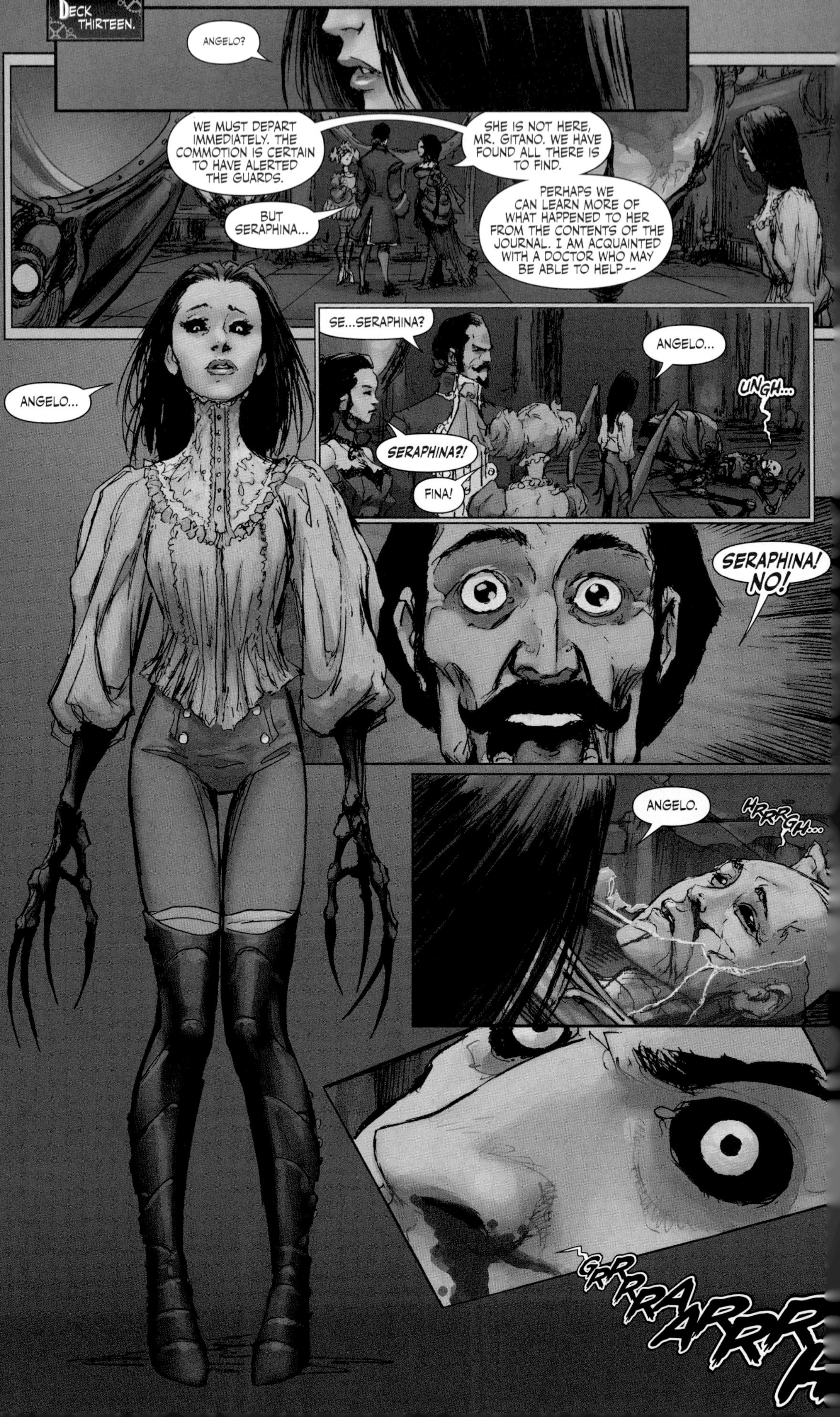
DECK THIRTEEN.
ANGELO?
WE MUST DEPART IMMEDIATELY. THE COMMOTION IS CERTAIN TO HAVE ALERTED THE GUARDS.
SHE IS NOT HERE, MR. GITANO. WE HAVE FOUND ALL THERE IS TO FIND.
BUT SERAPHINA...
PERHAPS WE CAN LEARN MORE OF WHAT HAPPENED TO HER FROM THE CONTENTS OF THE JOURNAL. I AM ACQUAINTED WITH A DOCTOR WHO MAY BE ABLE TO HELP--
ANGELO...
SE...SERAPHINA?
ANGELO...
UNGH...
SERAPHINA?!
FINA!
SERAPHINA! NO!
ANGELO.
HRRRGH...
GRRRRAARRR

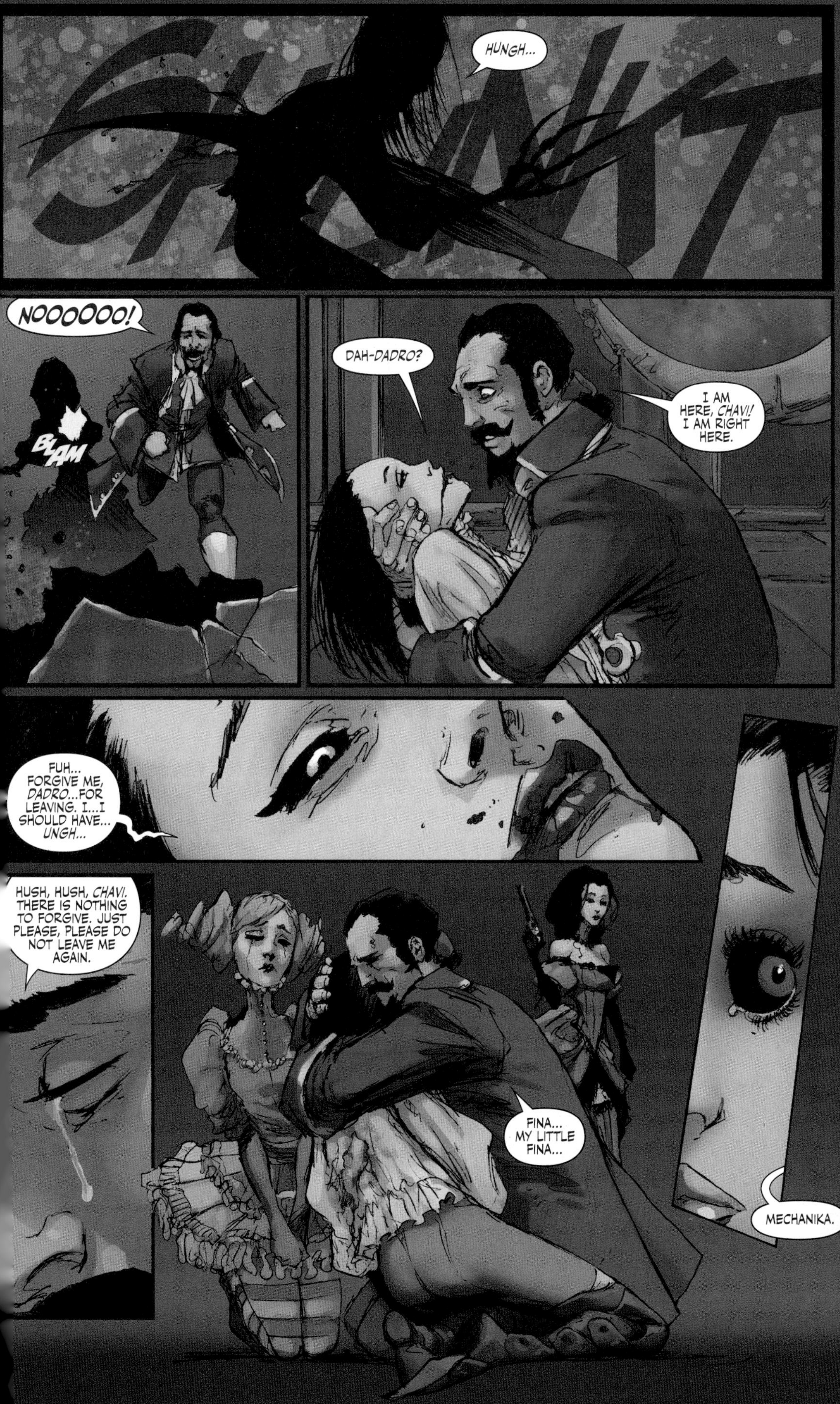
HUNGH...
NOOOOOO!
BLAM
DAH-DADRO?
I AM HERE, CHAVI! I AM RIGHT HERE.
FUH... FORGIVE ME, DADRO...FOR LEAVING. I...I SHOULD HAVE... UNGH...
HUSH, HUSH, CHAVI. THERE IS NOTHING TO FORGIVE. JUST PLEASE, PLEASE DO NOT LEAVE ME AGAIN.
FINA... MY LITTLE FINA...
MECHANIKA.

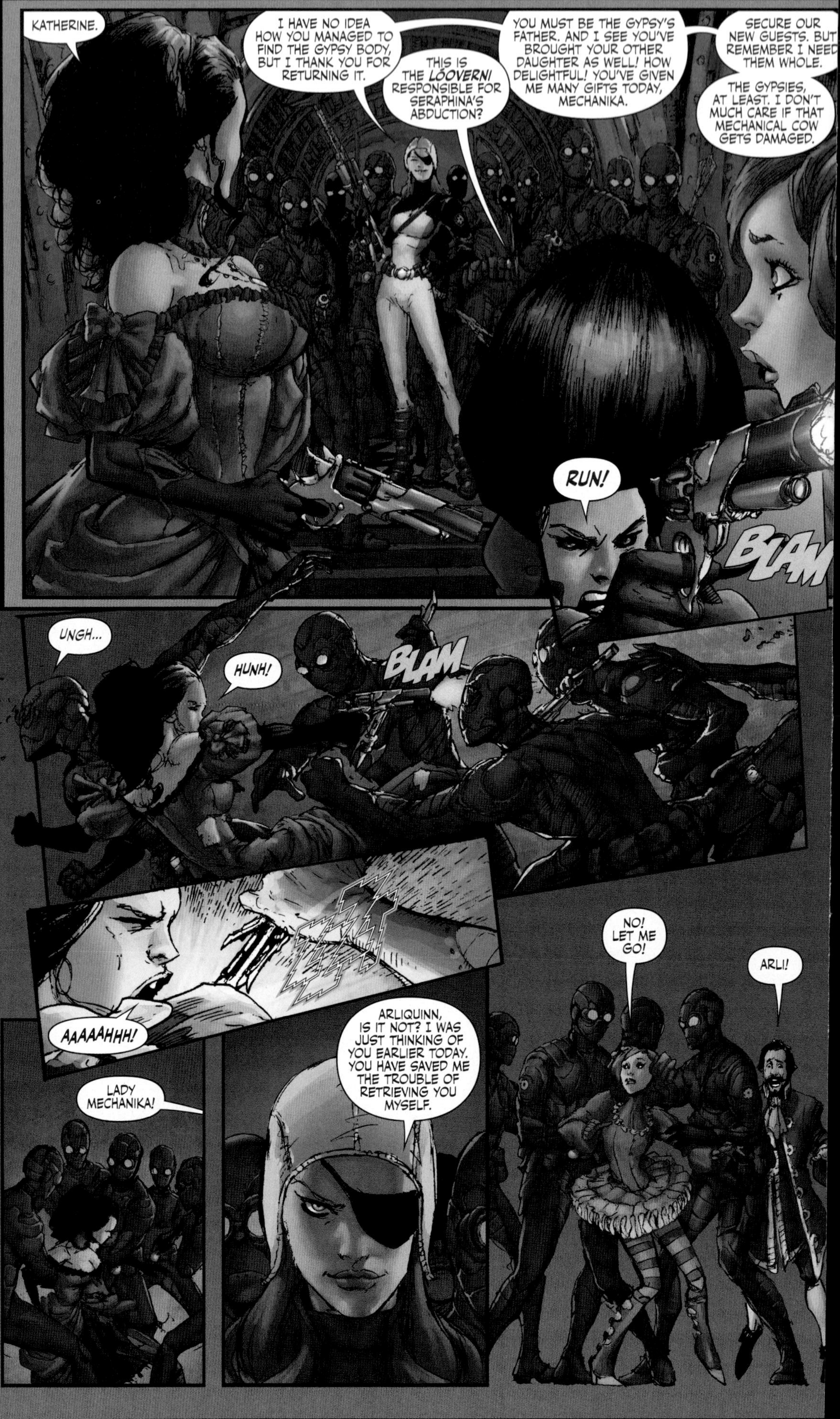
KATHERINE.
I HAVE NO IDEA HOW YOU MANAGED TO FIND THE GYPSY BODY, BUT I THANK YOU FOR RETURNING IT.
THIS IS THE LÓOVERNI RESPONSIBLE FOR SERAPHINA'S ABDUCTION?
YOU MUST BE THE GYPSY'S FATHER. AND I SEE YOU'VE BROUGHT YOUR OTHER DAUGHTER AS WELL! HOW DELIGHTFUL! YOU'VE GIVEN ME MANY GIFTS TODAY, MECHANIKA.
SECURE OUR NEW GUESTS. BUT REMEMBER I NEED THEM WHOLE.
THE GYPSIES, AT LEAST. I DON'T MUCH CARE IF THAT MECHANICAL COW GETS DAMAGED.
RUN!
BLAM
UNGH...
HUNH!
BLAM
AAAAAHHH!
LADY MECHANIKA!
ARLIQUINN, IS IT NOT? I WAS JUST THINKING OF YOU EARLIER TODAY. YOU HAVE SAVED ME THE TROUBLE OF RETRIEVING YOU MYSELF.
NO! LET ME GO!
ARLI!

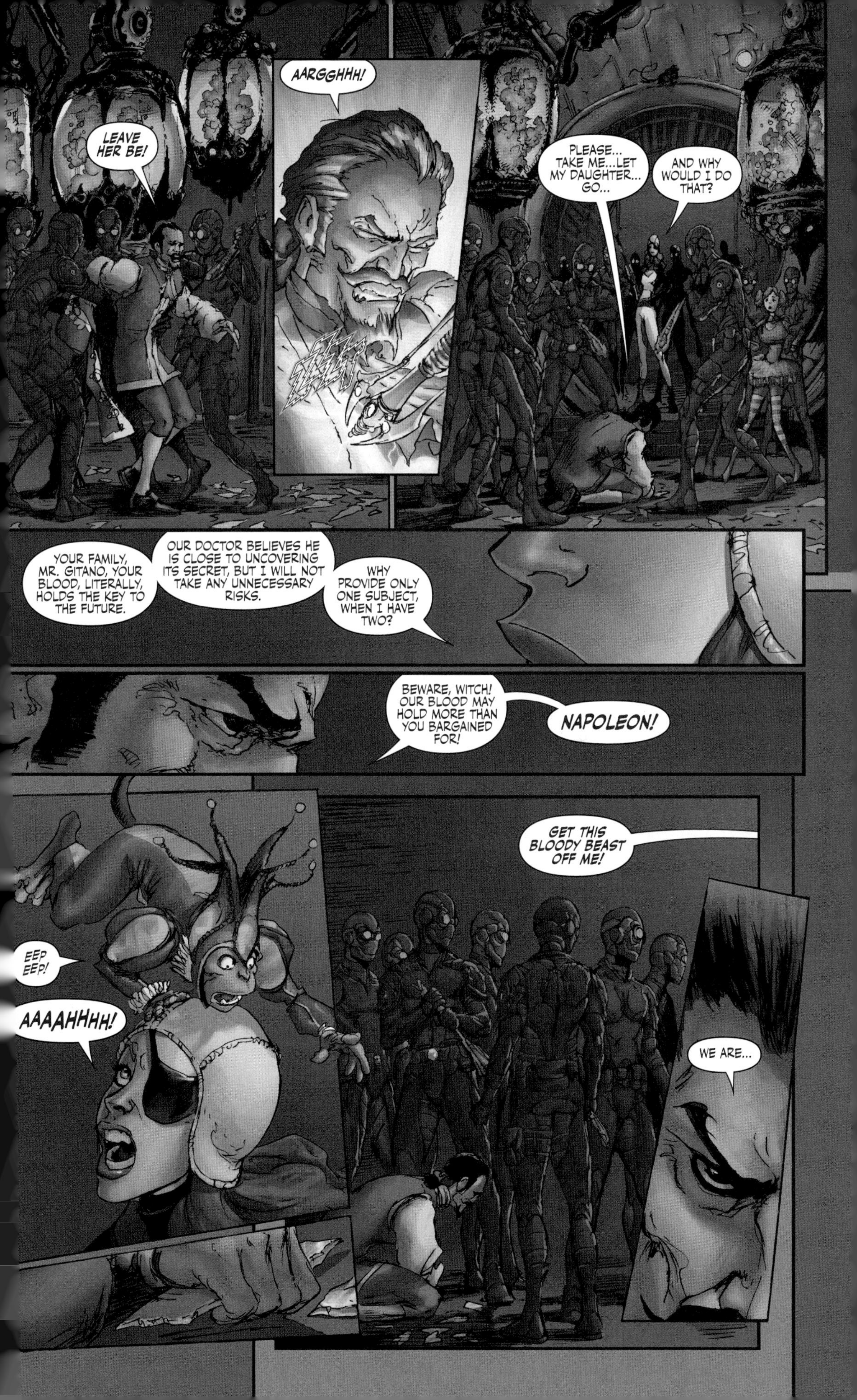
LEAVE HER BE!
AARGGHHH!
PLEASE... TAKE ME...LET MY DAUGHTER... GO...
AND WHY WOULD I DO THAT?
YOUR FAMILY, MR. GITANO, YOUR BLOOD, LITERALLY, HOLDS THE KEY TO THE FUTURE.
OUR DOCTOR BELIEVES HE IS CLOSE TO UNCOVERING ITS SECRET, BUT I WILL NOT TAKE ANY UNNECESSARY RISKS.
WHY PROVIDE ONLY ONE SUBJECT, WHEN I HAVE TWO?
BEWARE, WITCH! OUR BLOOD MAY HOLD MORE THAN YOU BARGAINED FOR!
NAPOLEON!
GET THIS BLOODY BEAST OFF ME!
EEP EEP!
AAAAHHHH!
WE ARE...

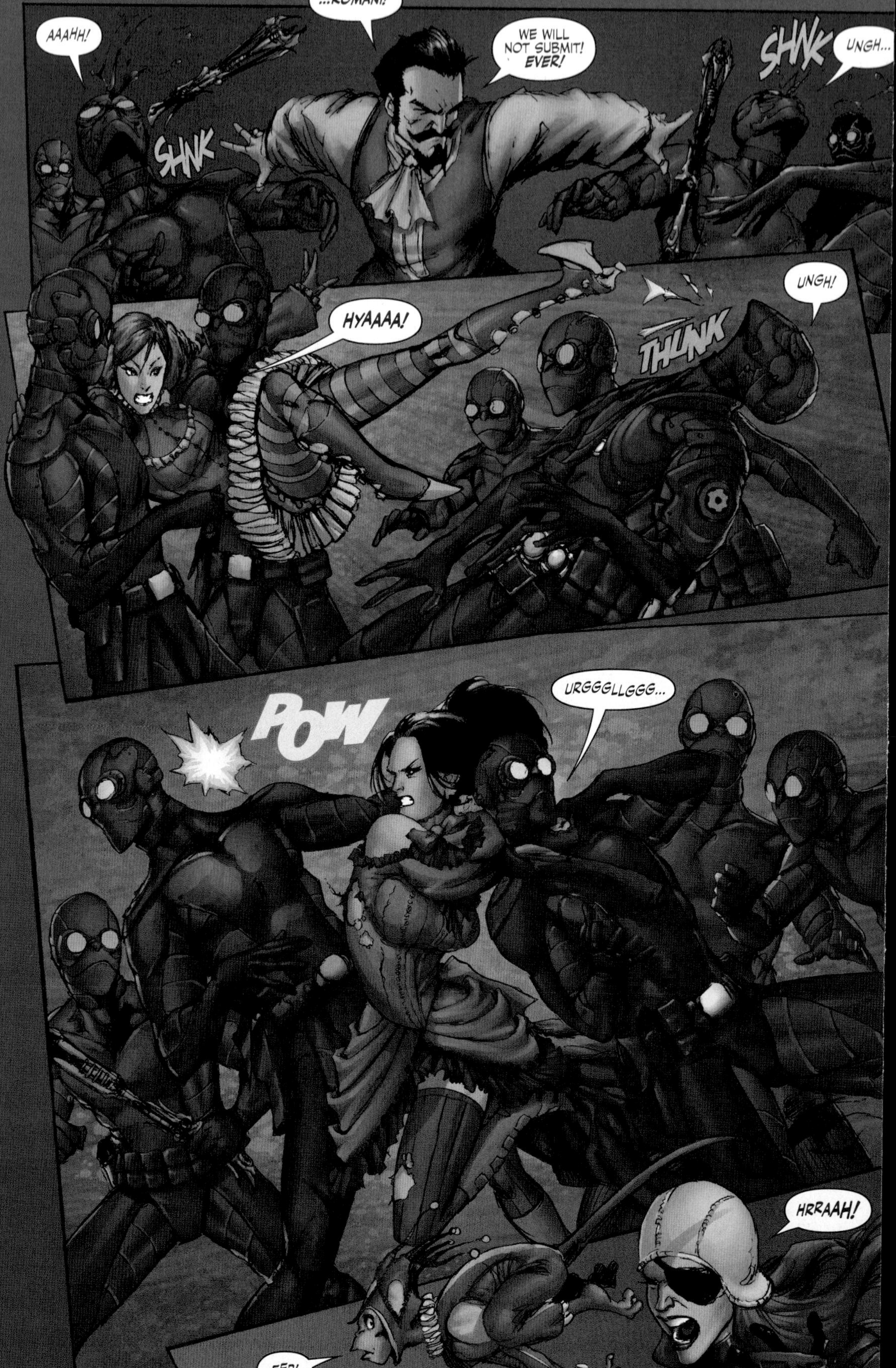
AAAHH!
...ROMANI!
WE WILL NOT SUBMIT! EVER!
SHNK
SHNK
UNGH...
HYAAAA!
THUNK
UNGH!
POW
URGGGLLGGG...
HRRAAH!
EEP!

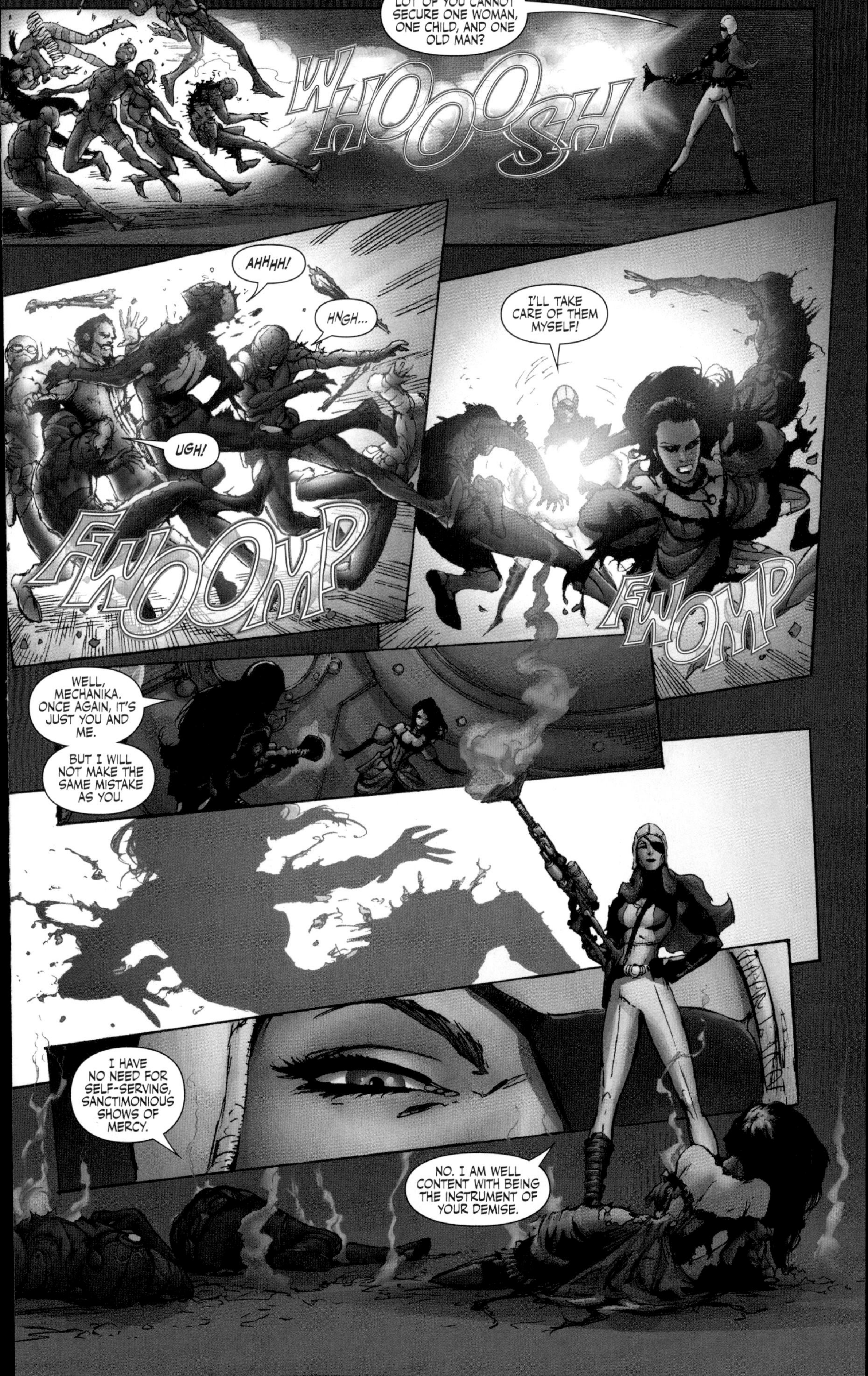
THE BLOODY LOT OF YOU CANNOT SECURE ONE WOMAN, ONE CHILD, AND ONE OLD MAN?
WHOOOOSH
AHHHH!
HNGH...
UGH!
FWOOOMP
I'LL TAKE CARE OF THEM MYSELF!
FWOMP
WELL, MECHANIKA. ONCE AGAIN, IT'S JUST YOU AND ME.
BUT I WILL NOT MAKE THE SAME MISTAKE AS YOU.
I HAVE NO NEED FOR SELF-SERVING, SANCTIMONIOUS SHOWS OF MERCY.
NO. I AM WELL CONTENT WITH BEING THE INSTRUMENT OF YOUR DEMISE.

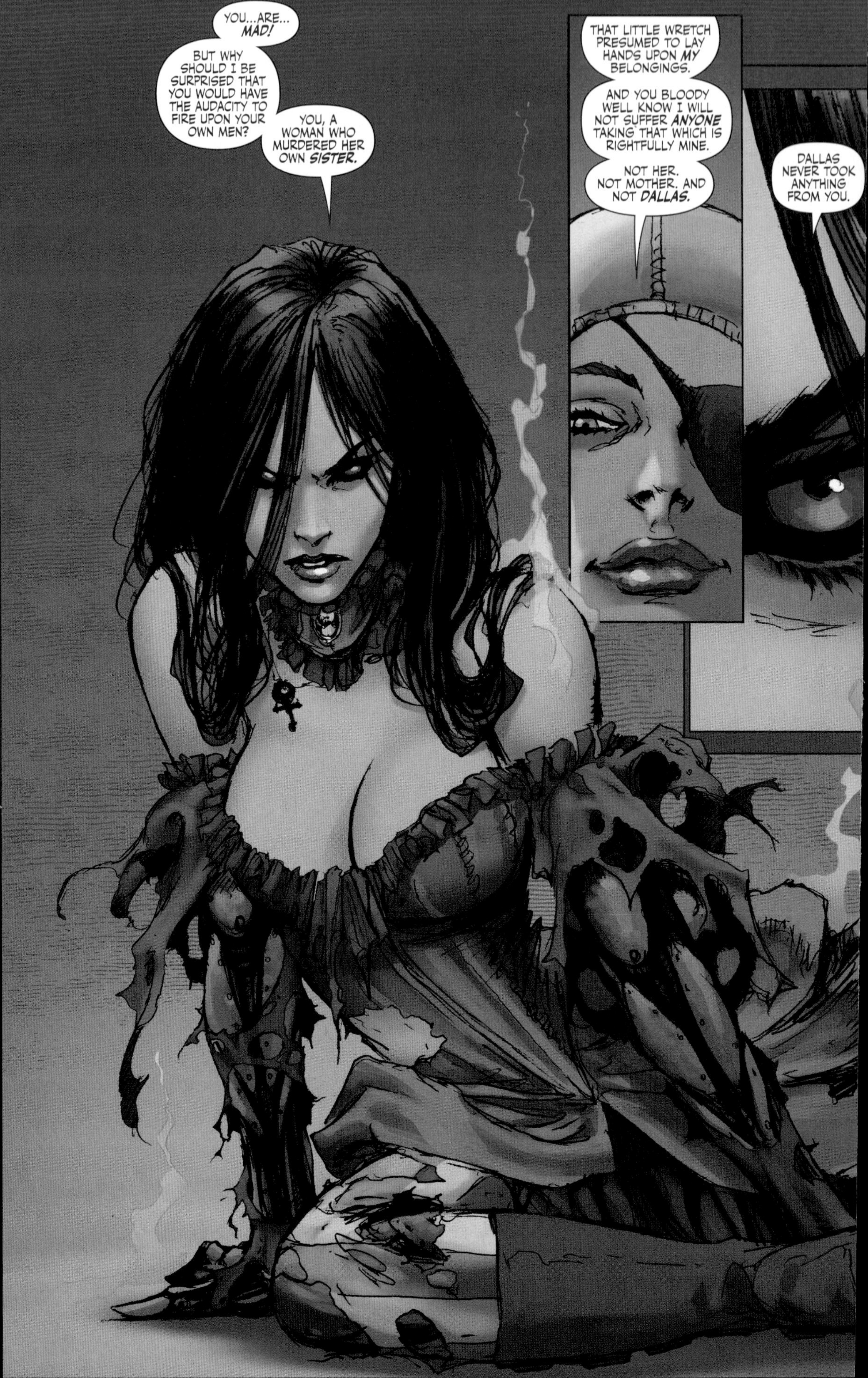
YOU...ARE... MAD!
BUT WHY SHOULD I BE SURPRISED THAT YOU WOULD HAVE THE AUDACITY TO FIRE UPON YOUR OWN MEN?
YOU, A WOMAN WHO MURDERED HER OWN SISTER.
THAT LITTLE WRETCH PRESUMED TO LAY HANDS UPON MY BELONGINGS.
AND YOU BLOODY WELL KNOW I WILL NOT SUFFER ANYONE TAKING THAT WHICH IS RIGHTFULLY MINE.
NOT HER. NOT MOTHER. AND NOT DALLAS.
DALLAS NEVER TOOK ANYTHING FROM YOU.

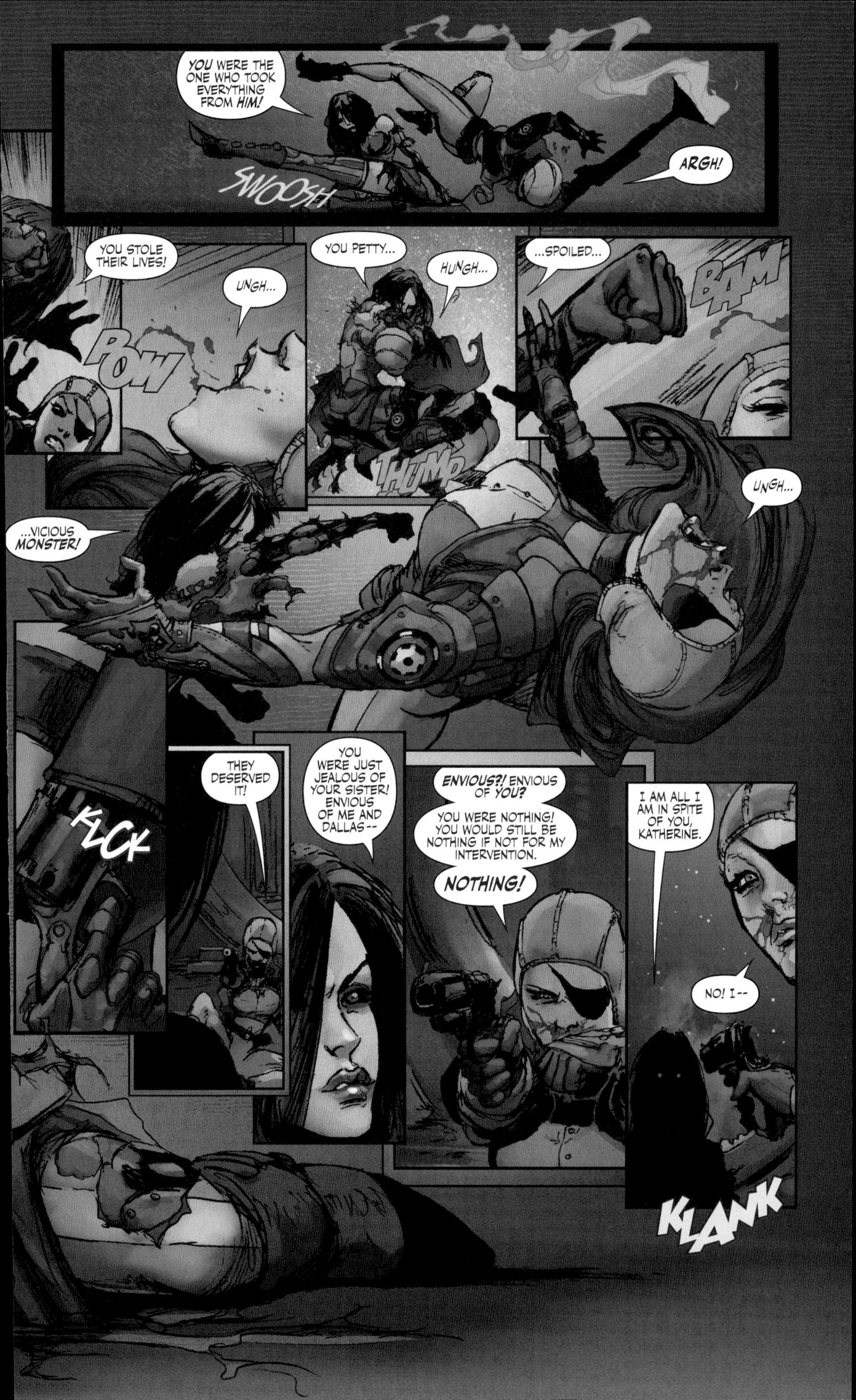

YOU WERE THE ONE WHO TOOK EVERYTHING FROM HIM!
SWOOSH
ARGH!
YOU STOLE THEIR LIVES!
UNGH...
POW
YOU PETTY...
HUNGH...
THUMP
...SPOILED...
BAM
...VICIOUS MONSTER!
UNGH...
KLCK
THEY DESERVED IT!
YOU WERE JUST JEALOUS OF YOUR SISTER! ENVIOUS OF ME AND DALLAS--
ENVIOUS?! ENVIOUS OF YOU?
YOU WERE NOTHING! YOU WOULD STILL BE NOTHING IF NOT FOR MY INTERVENTION.
NOTHING!
I AM ALL I AM IN SPITE OF YOU, KATHERINE.
NO! I--
KLANK

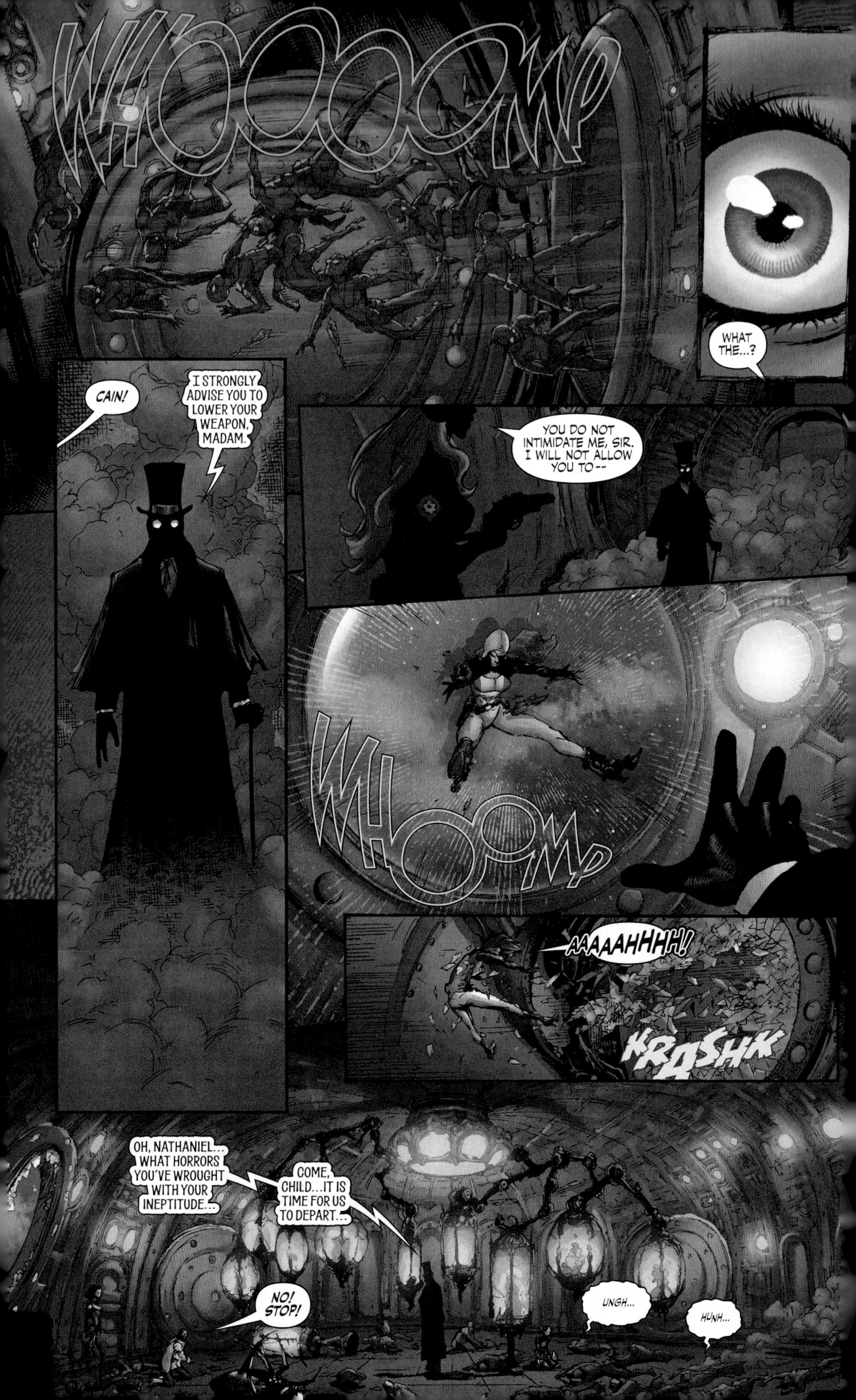
WHOOOOOMP
WHAT THE...?
CAIN!
I STRONGLY ADVISE YOU TO LOWER YOUR WEAPON, MADAM.
YOU DO NOT INTIMIDATE ME, SIR. I WILL NOT ALLOW YOU TO--
WHOOOMP
AAAAAHHHH!
KRASHK
OH, NATHANIEL... WHAT HORRORS YOU'VE WROUGHT WITH YOUR INEPTITUDE...
COME, CHILD...IT IS TIME FOR US TO DEPART...
NO! STOP!
UNGH...
HUNH...

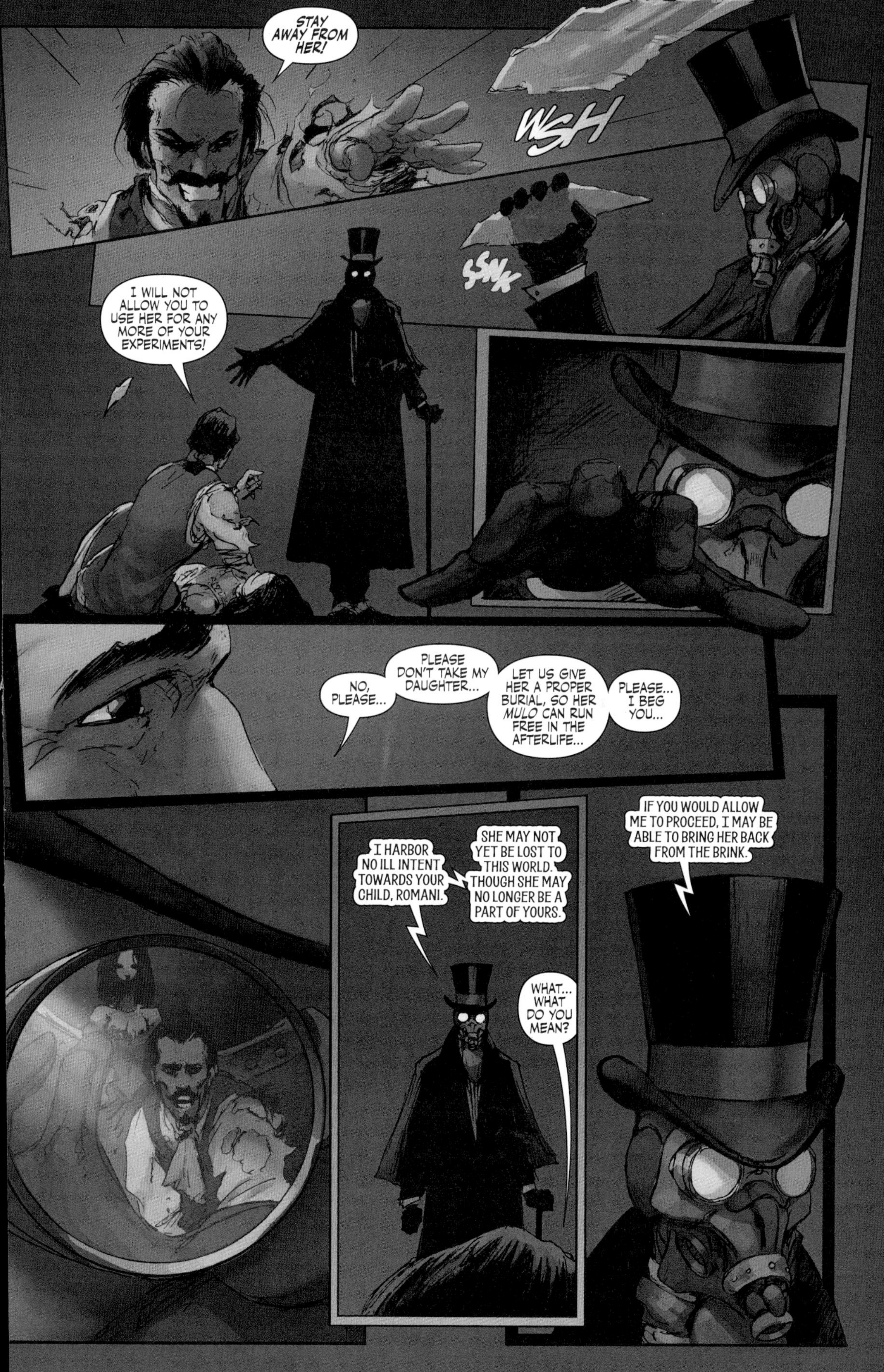
STAY AWAY FROM HER!
WSH
SSNK
I WILL NOT ALLOW YOU TO USE HER FOR ANY MORE OF YOUR EXPERIMENTS!
NO, PLEASE...
PLEASE DON'T TAKE MY DAUGHTER...
LET US GIVE HER A PROPER BURIAL, SO HER MULO CAN RUN FREE IN THE AFTERLIFE...
PLEASE... I BEG YOU...
I HARBOR NO ILL INTENT TOWARDS YOUR CHILD, ROMANI.
SHE MAY NOT YET BE LOST TO THIS WORLD. THOUGH SHE MAY NO LONGER BE A PART OF YOURS.
WHAT... WHAT DO YOU MEAN?
IF YOU WOULD ALLOW ME TO PROCEED, I MAY BE ABLE TO BRING HER BACK FROM THE BRINK.

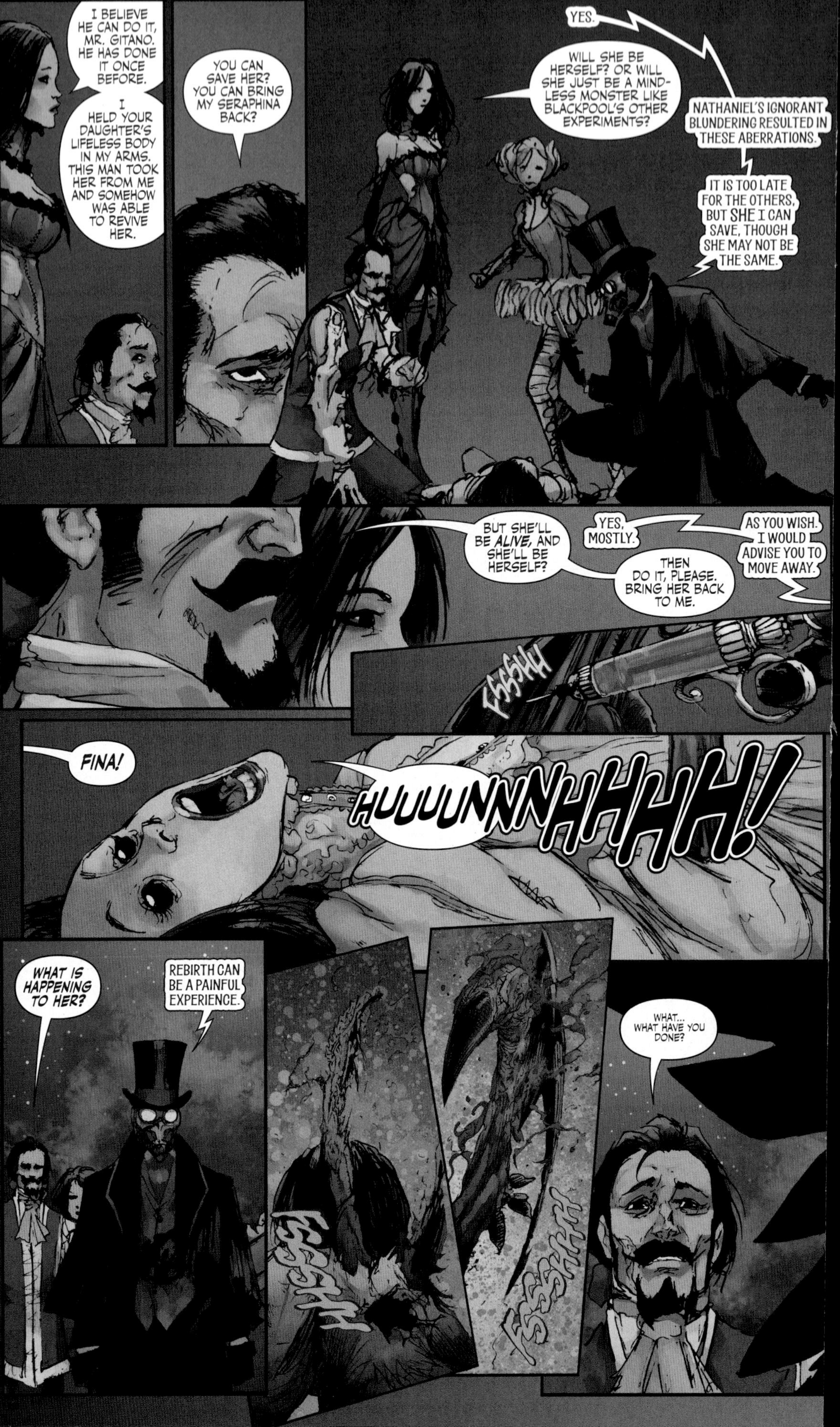

I BELIEVE HE CAN DO IT, MR. GITANO. HE HAS DONE IT ONCE BEFORE.
I HELD YOUR DAUGHTER'S LIFELESS BODY IN MY ARMS. THIS MAN TOOK HER FROM ME AND SOMEHOW WAS ABLE TO REVIVE HER.
YOU CAN SAVE HER? YOU CAN BRING MY SERAPHINA BACK?
YES.
WILL SHE BE HERSELF? OR WILL SHE JUST BE A MINDLESS MONSTER LIKE BLACKPOOL'S OTHER EXPERIMENTS?
NATHANIEL'S IGNORANT BLUNDERING RESULTED IN THESE ABERRATIONS.
IT IS TOO LATE FOR THE OTHERS, BUT SHE I CAN SAVE, THOUGH SHE MAY NOT BE THE SAME.
BUT SHE'LL BE ALIVE, AND SHE'LL BE HERSELF?
YES, MOSTLY.
THEN DO IT, PLEASE. BRING HER BACK TO ME.
AS YOU WISH. I WOULD ADVISE YOU TO MOVE AWAY.
FINA!
HUUUUNNNHHHHH!
WHAT IS HAPPENING TO HER?
REBIRTH CAN BE A PAINFUL EXPERIENCE.
WHAT... WHAT HAVE YOU DONE?

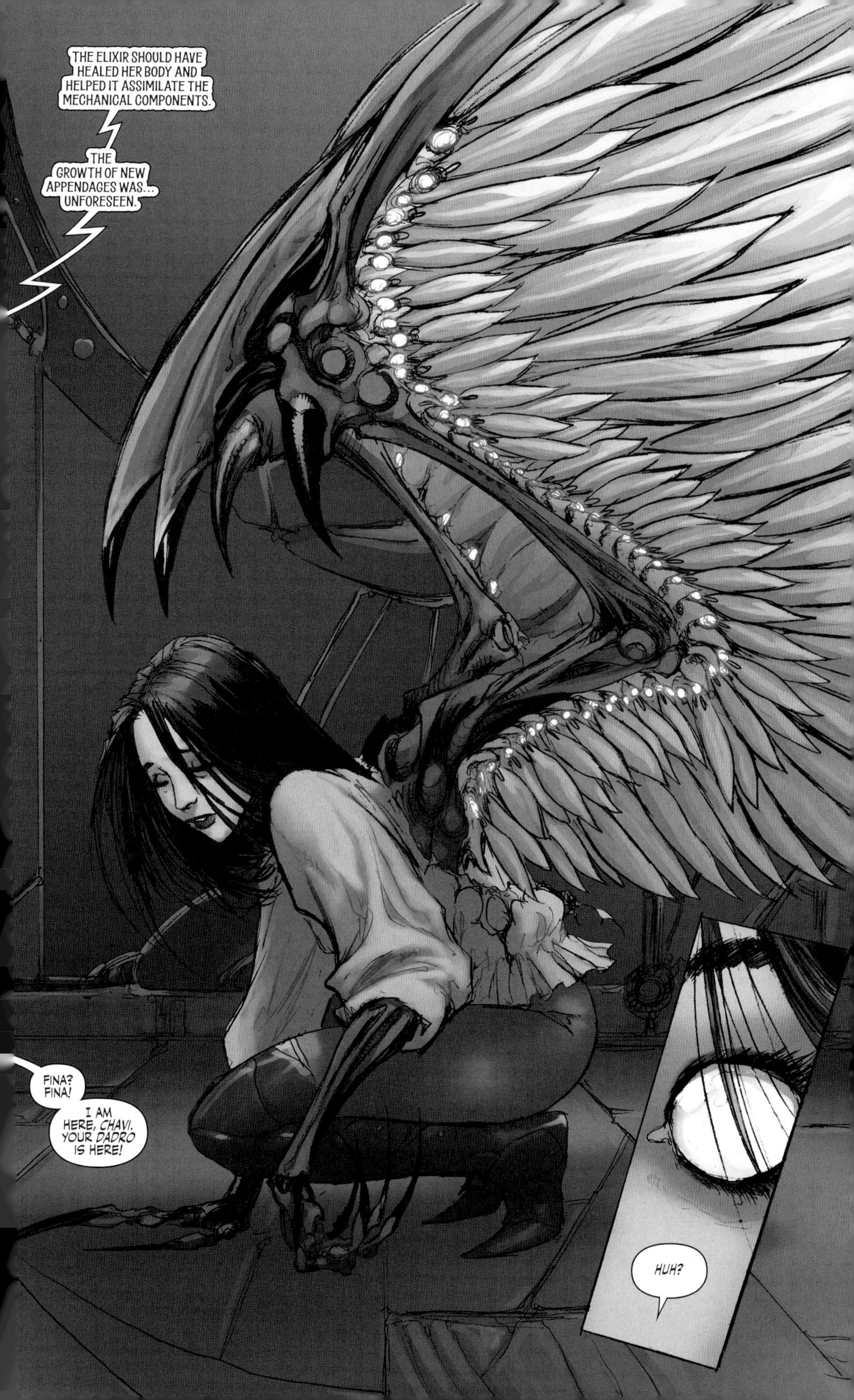
THE ELIXIR SHOULD HAVE HEALED HER BODY AND HELPED IT ASSIMILATE THE MECHANICAL COMPONENTS.
THE GROWTH OF NEW APPENDAGES WAS... UNFORESEEN.
FINA? FINA!
I AM HERE, CHAVI. YOUR DADRO IS HERE!
HUH?

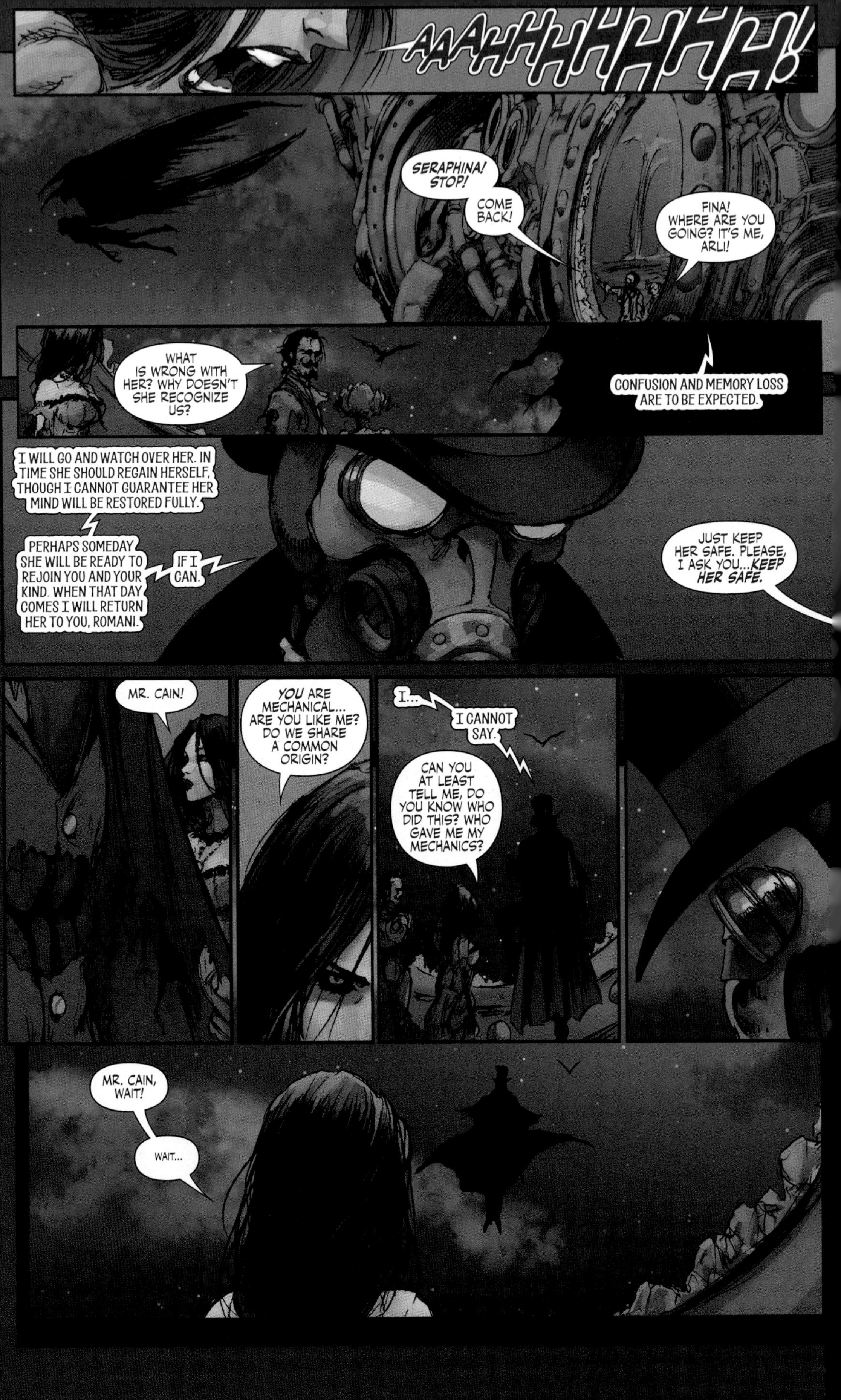
AAAHHHHHHHH!
SERAPHINA! STOP!
COME BACK!
FINA! WHERE ARE YOU GOING? IT'S ME, ARLI!
WHAT IS WRONG WITH HER? WHY DOESN'T SHE RECOGNIZE US?
CONFUSION AND MEMORY LOSS ARE TO BE EXPECTED.
I WILL GO AND WATCH OVER HER. IN TIME SHE SHOULD REGAIN HERSELF, THOUGH I CANNOT GUARANTEE HER MIND WILL BE RESTORED FULLY.
PERHAPS SOMEDAY SHE WILL BE READY TO REJOIN YOU AND YOUR KIND. WHEN THAT DAY COMES I WILL RETURN HER TO YOU, ROMANI.
IF I CAN.
JUST KEEP HER SAFE. PLEASE, I ASK YOU...KEEP HER SAFE.
MR. CAIN!
YOU ARE MECHANICAL... ARE YOU LIKE ME? DO WE SHARE A COMMON ORIGIN?
I...
I CANNOT SAY.
CAN YOU AT LEAST TELL ME, DO YOU KNOW WHO DID THIS? WHO GAVE ME MY MECHANICS?
MR. CAIN, WAIT!
WAIT...

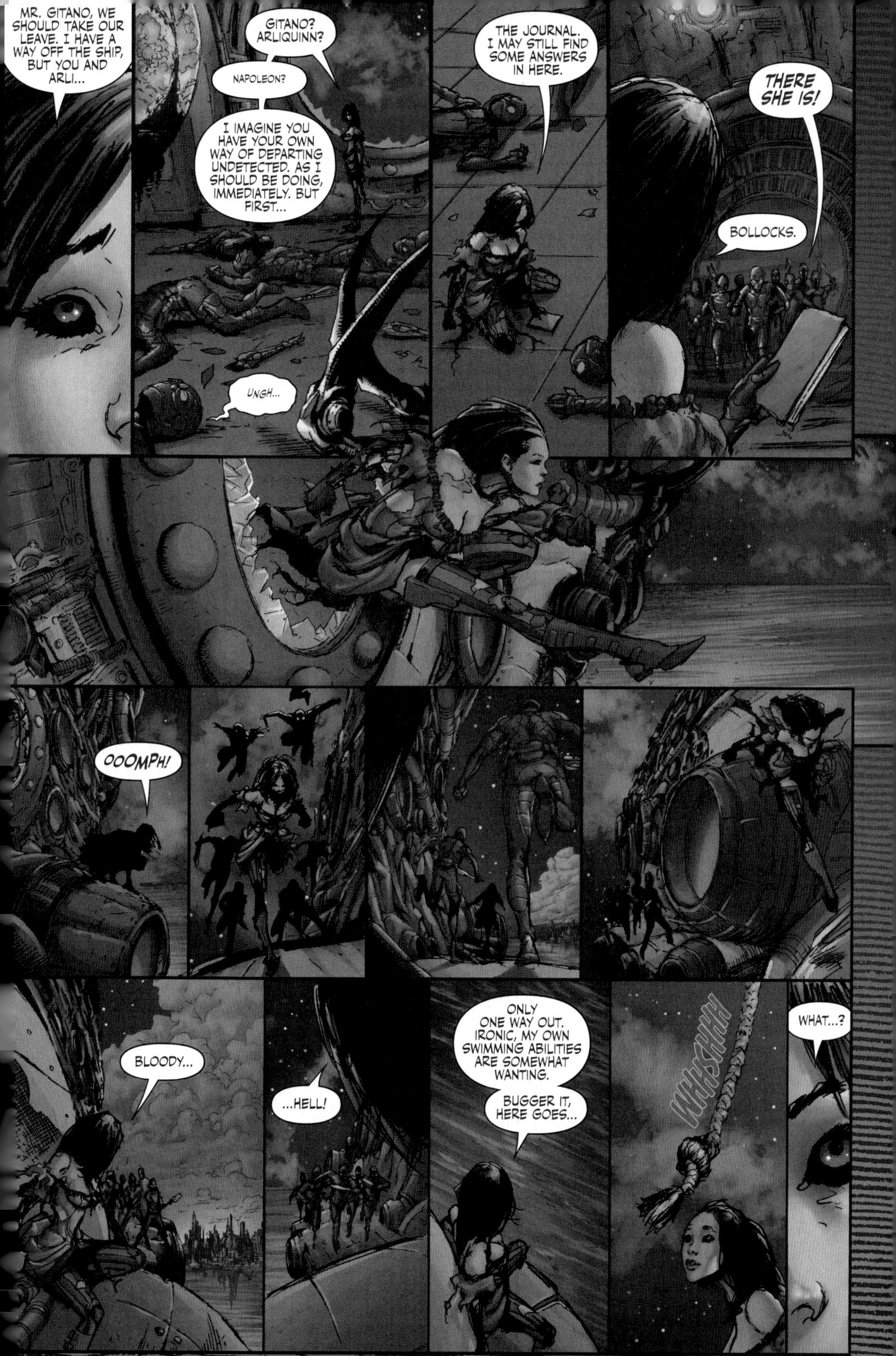
MR. GITANO, WE SHOULD TAKE OUR LEAVE. I HAVE A WAY OFF THE SHIP, BUT YOU AND ARLI...
GITANO? ARLIQUINN?
NAPOLEON?
I IMAGINE YOU HAVE YOUR OWN WAY OF DEPARTING UNDETECTED. AS I SHOULD BE DOING, IMMEDIATELY. BUT FIRST...
UNGH...
THE JOURNAL. I MAY STILL FIND SOME ANSWERS IN HERE.
THERE SHE IS!
BOLLOCKS.
OOOMPH!
BLOODY...
...HELL!
ONLY ONE WAY OUT. IRONIC, MY OWN SWIMMING ABILITIES ARE SOMEWHAT WANTING.
BUGGER IT, HERE GOES...
WHHSHHH
WHAT...?

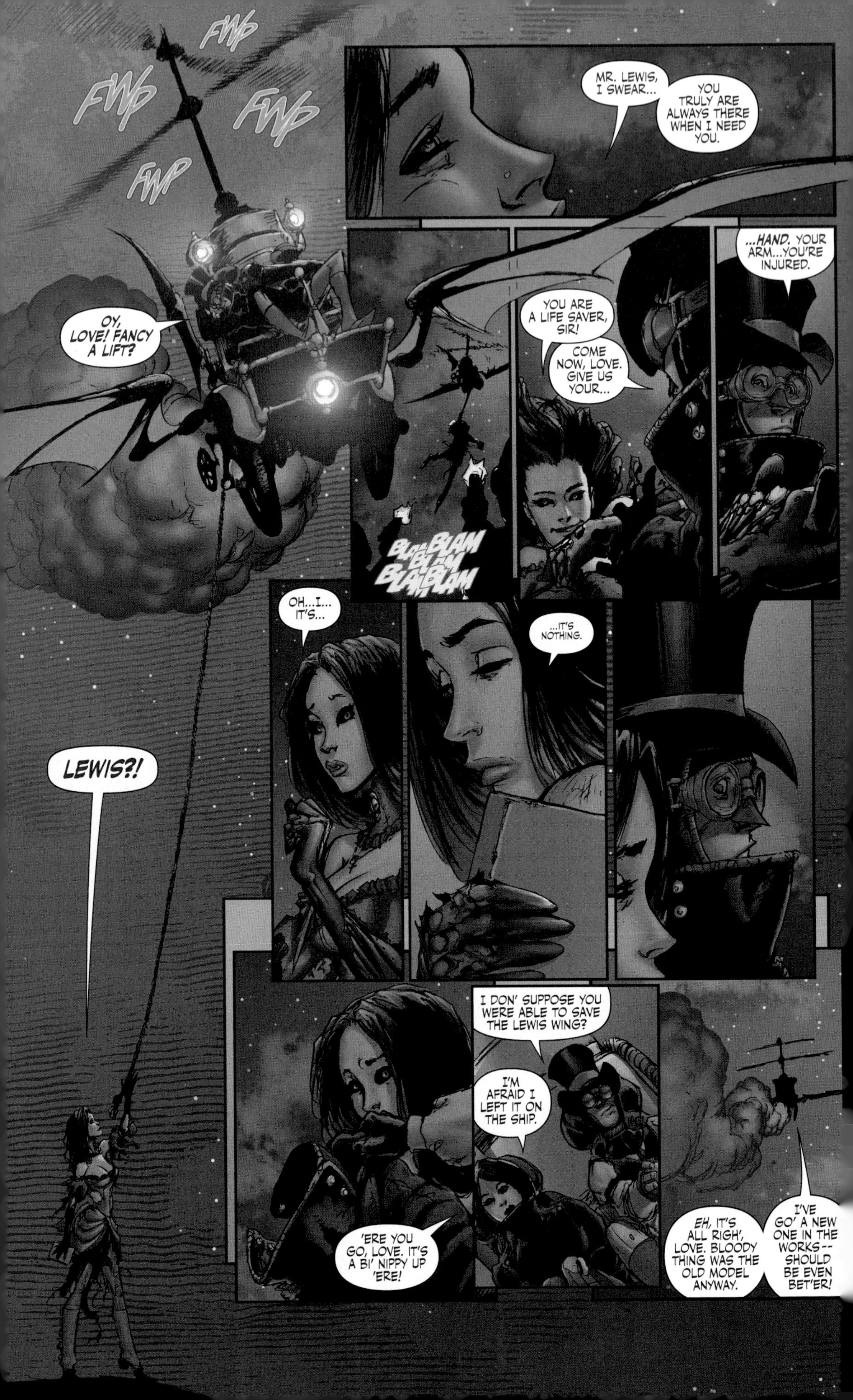
FWP
FWP
FWP
FWP
OY, LOVE! FANCY A LIFT?
MR. LEWIS, I SWEAR...
YOU TRULY ARE ALWAYS THERE WHEN I NEED YOU.
BLAM BLAM BLAM BLAM BLAM
YOU ARE A LIFE SAVER, SIR!
COME NOW, LOVE. GIVE US YOUR...
...HAND. YOUR ARM...YOU'RE INJURED.
LEWIS?!
OH...I... IT'S...
...IT'S NOTHING.
'ERE YOU GO, LOVE. IT'S A BI' NIPPY UP 'ERE!
I DON' SUPPOSE YOU WERE ABLE TO SAVE THE LEWIS WING?
I'M AFRAID I LEFT IT ON THE SHIP.
EH, IT'S ALL RIGH', LOVE. BLOODY THING WAS THE OLD MODEL ANYWAY.
I'VE GO' A NEW ONE IN THE WORKS--SHOULD BE EVEN BET'ER!

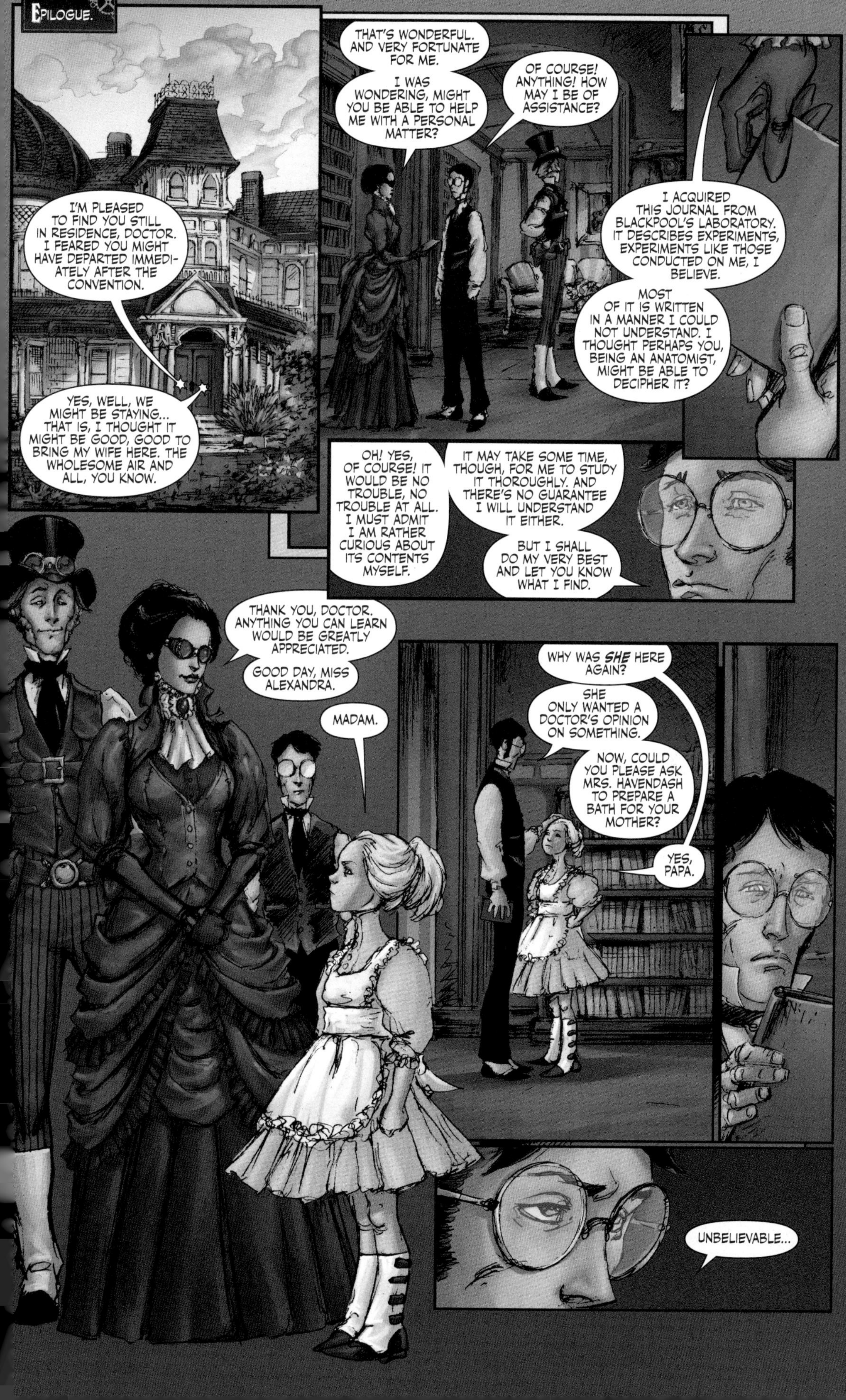
EPILOGUE.
I'M PLEASED TO FIND YOU STILL IN RESIDENCE, DOCTOR. I FEARED YOU MIGHT HAVE DEPARTED IMMEDIATELY AFTER THE CONVENTION.
YES, WELL, WE MIGHT BE STAYING... THAT IS, I THOUGHT IT MIGHT BE GOOD, GOOD TO BRING MY WIFE HERE. THE WHOLESOME AIR AND ALL, YOU KNOW.
THAT'S WONDERFUL. AND VERY FORTUNATE FOR ME.
I WAS WONDERING, MIGHT YOU BE ABLE TO HELP ME WITH A PERSONAL MATTER?
OF COURSE! ANYTHING! HOW MAY I BE OF ASSISTANCE?
I ACQUIRED THIS JOURNAL FROM BLACKPOOL'S LABORATORY. IT DESCRIBES EXPERIMENTS, EXPERIMENTS LIKE THOSE CONDUCTED ON ME, I BELIEVE.
MOST OF IT IS WRITTEN IN A MANNER I COULD NOT UNDERSTAND. I THOUGHT PERHAPS YOU, BEING AN ANATOMIST, MIGHT BE ABLE TO DECIPHER IT?
OH! YES, OF COURSE! IT WOULD BE NO TROUBLE, NO TROUBLE AT ALL. I MUST ADMIT I AM RATHER CURIOUS ABOUT ITS CONTENTS MYSELF.
IT MAY TAKE SOME TIME, THOUGH, FOR ME TO STUDY IT THOROUGHLY. AND THERE'S NO GUARANTEE I WILL UNDERSTAND IT EITHER.
BUT I SHALL DO MY VERY BEST AND LET YOU KNOW WHAT I FIND.
THANK YOU, DOCTOR. ANYTHING YOU CAN LEARN WOULD BE GREATLY APPRECIATED.
GOOD DAY, MISS ALEXANDRA.
MADAM.
WHY WAS SHE HERE AGAIN?
SHE ONLY WANTED A DOCTOR'S OPINION ON SOMETHING.
NOW, COULD YOU PLEASE ASK MRS. HAVENDASH TO PREPARE A BATH FOR YOUR MOTHER?
YES, PAPA.
UNBELIEVABLE...

I NOTICED THA' THE GYPSY CIRCUS IS GONE.

THEY HAVE SUFFERED A GREAT LOSS. I'M NOT SURPRISED THEY WOULD WANT TO GET FAR AWAY FROM HERE.

AT LEAST THE GIRL IS ALIVE.

BUT WHAT KIND OF LIFE WILL SHE HAVE NOW?

ANYTHING IS BET'ER THAN DEATH, TO THEM WOT'S LEFT BEHIND...

WELL, MR. LEWIS! UP FOR ANOTHER ADVENTURE?

I HAVE A JOB COMING UP. IN THE ALPS, HUNTING A SNOW BEAST OF SORTS, IF YOU CAN BELIEVE THAT.

WHAT DO YOU SAY?

EH? I DON' KNOW. SOUNDS TOO BLOODY COLD...

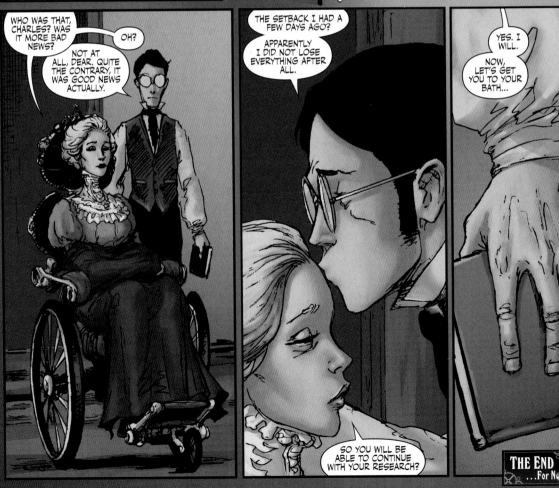

WHO WAS THAT, CHARLES? WAS IT MORE BAD NEWS?

OH?

NOT AT ALL, DEAR. QUITE THE CONTRARY, IT WAS GOOD NEWS ACTUALLY.

THE SETBACK I HAD A FEW DAYS AGO?

APPARENTLY I DID NOT LOSE EVERYTHING AFTER ALL.

SO YOU WILL BE ABLE TO CONTINUE WITH YOUR RESEARCH?

YES. I WILL.

NOW, LET'S GET YOU TO YOUR BATH...

THE END
...For No

# Cover Gallery

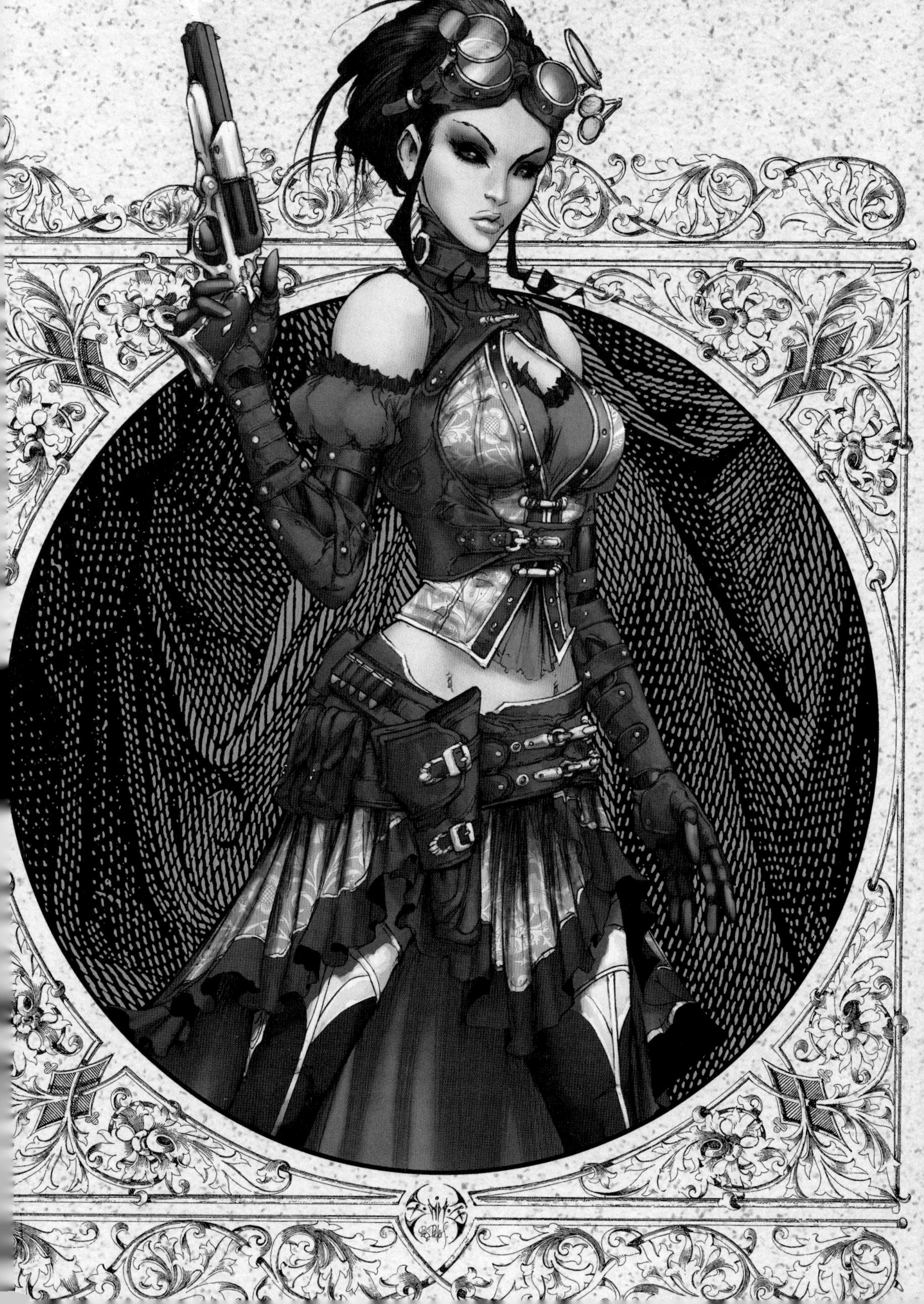

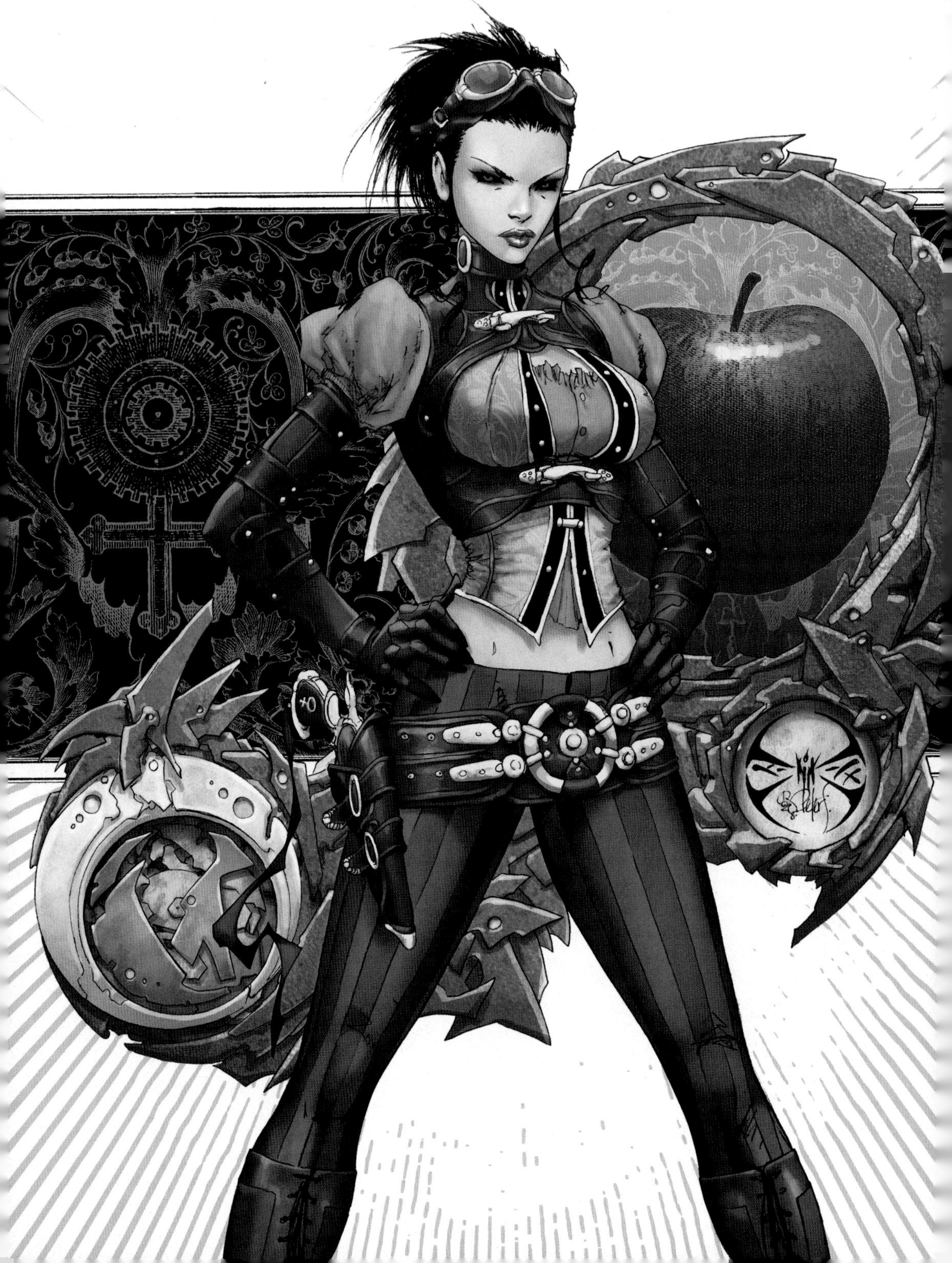

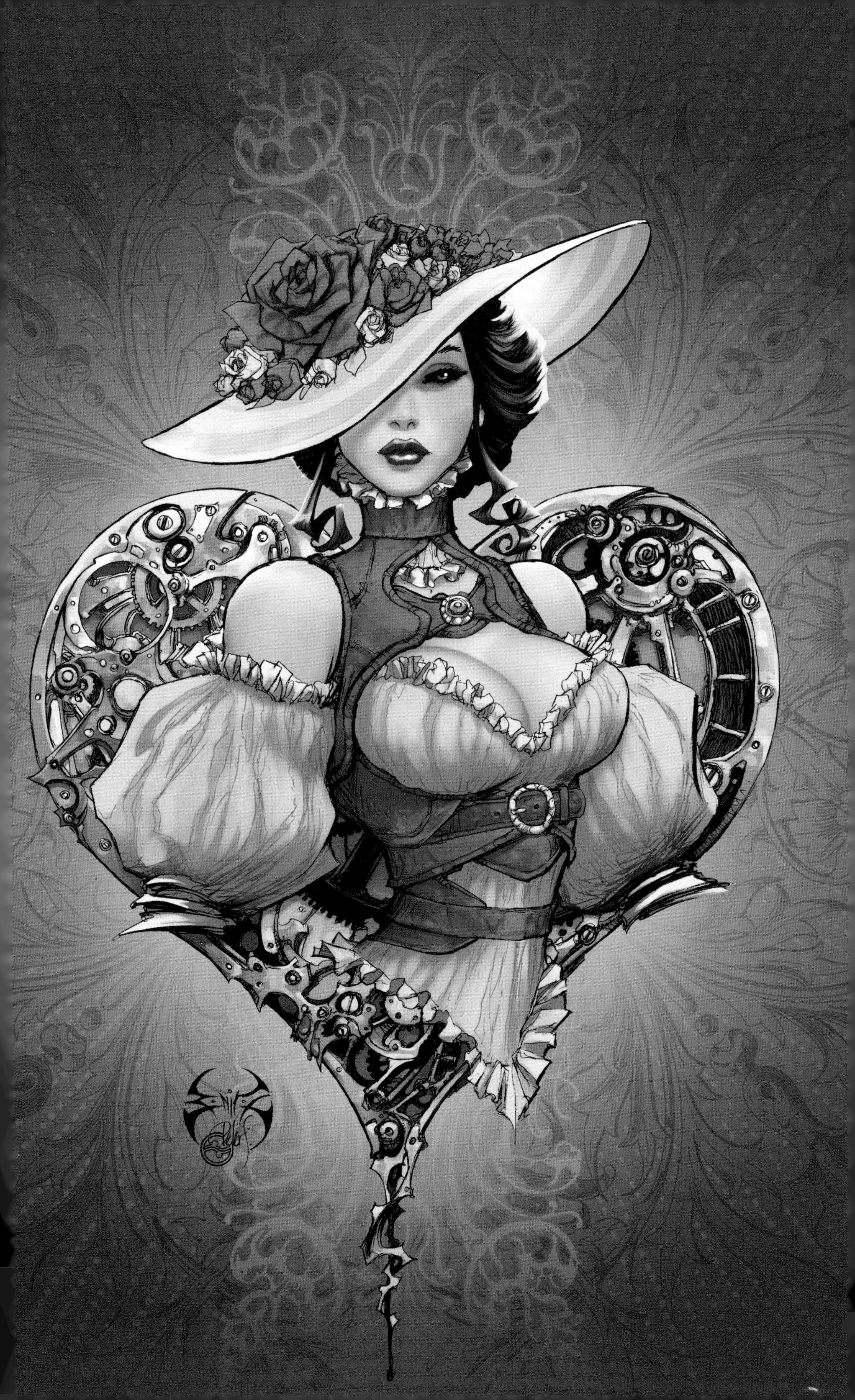

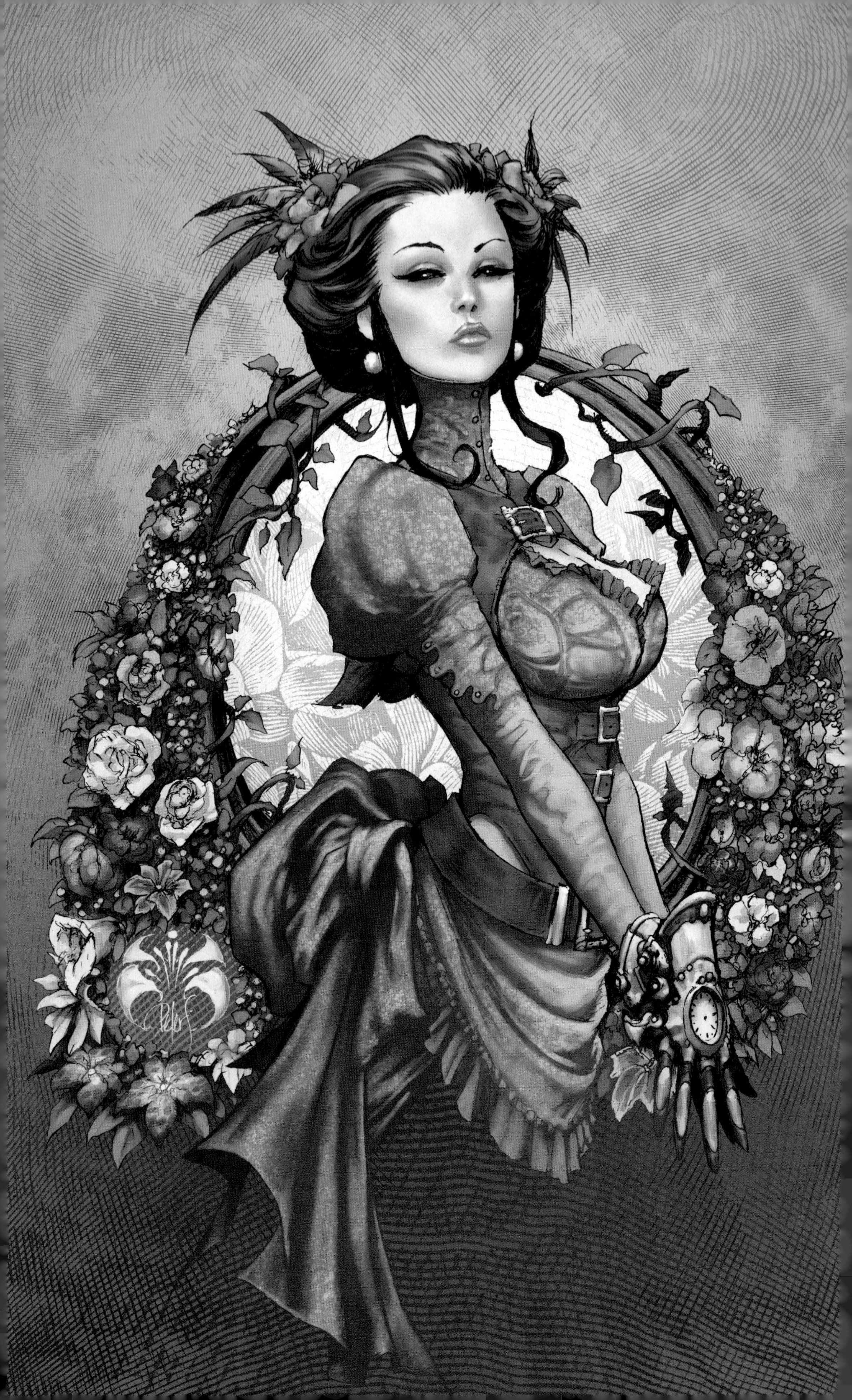

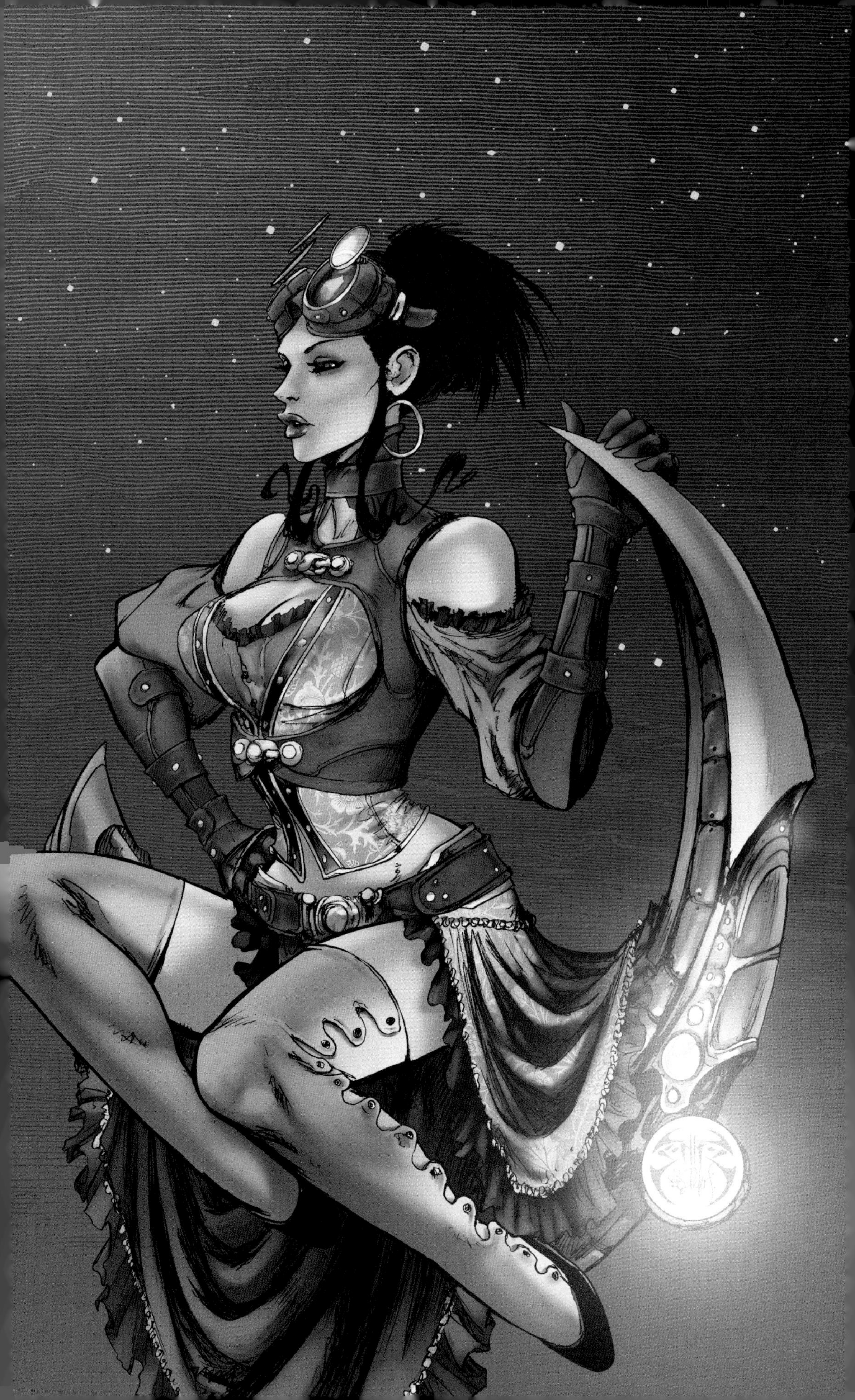

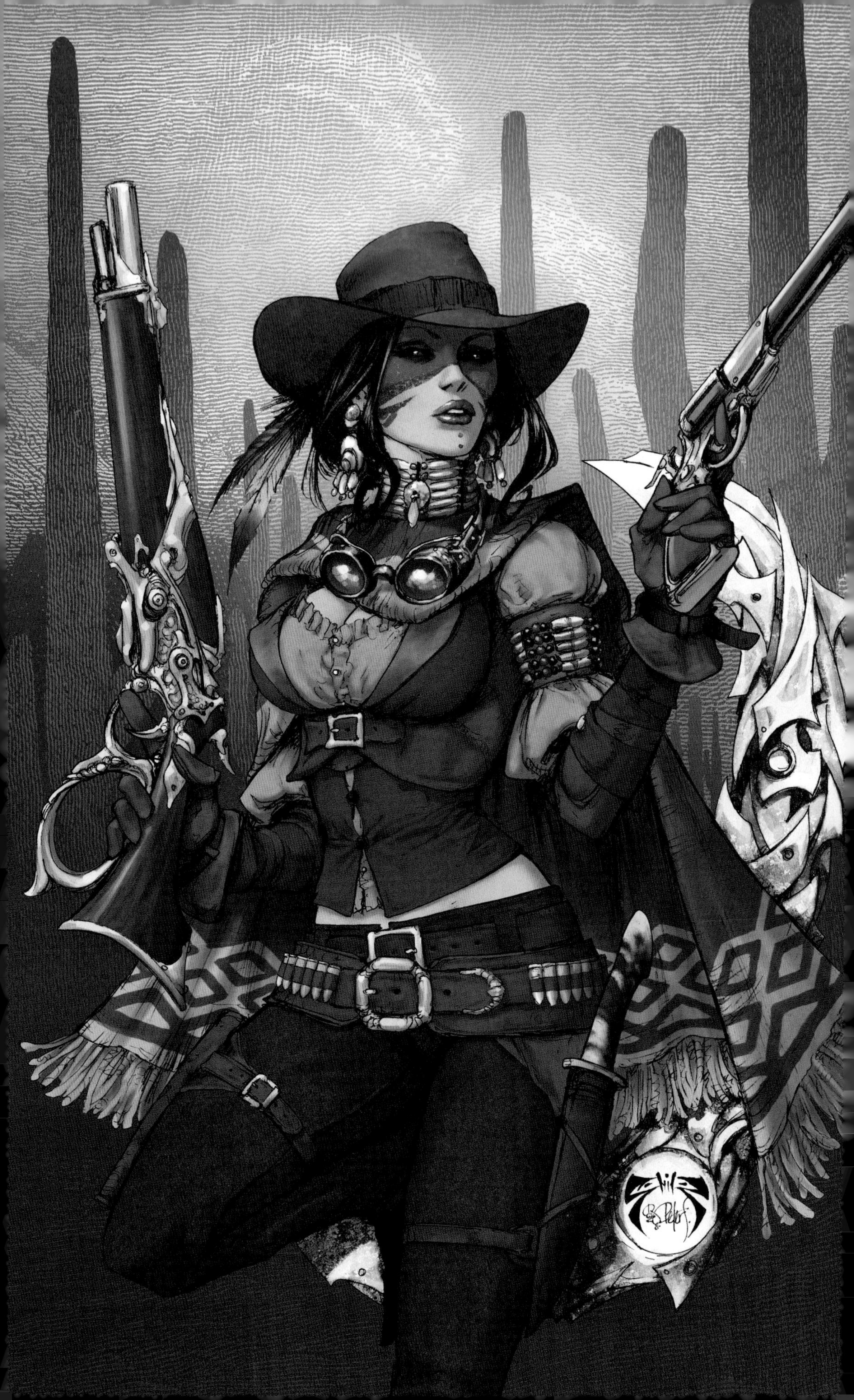

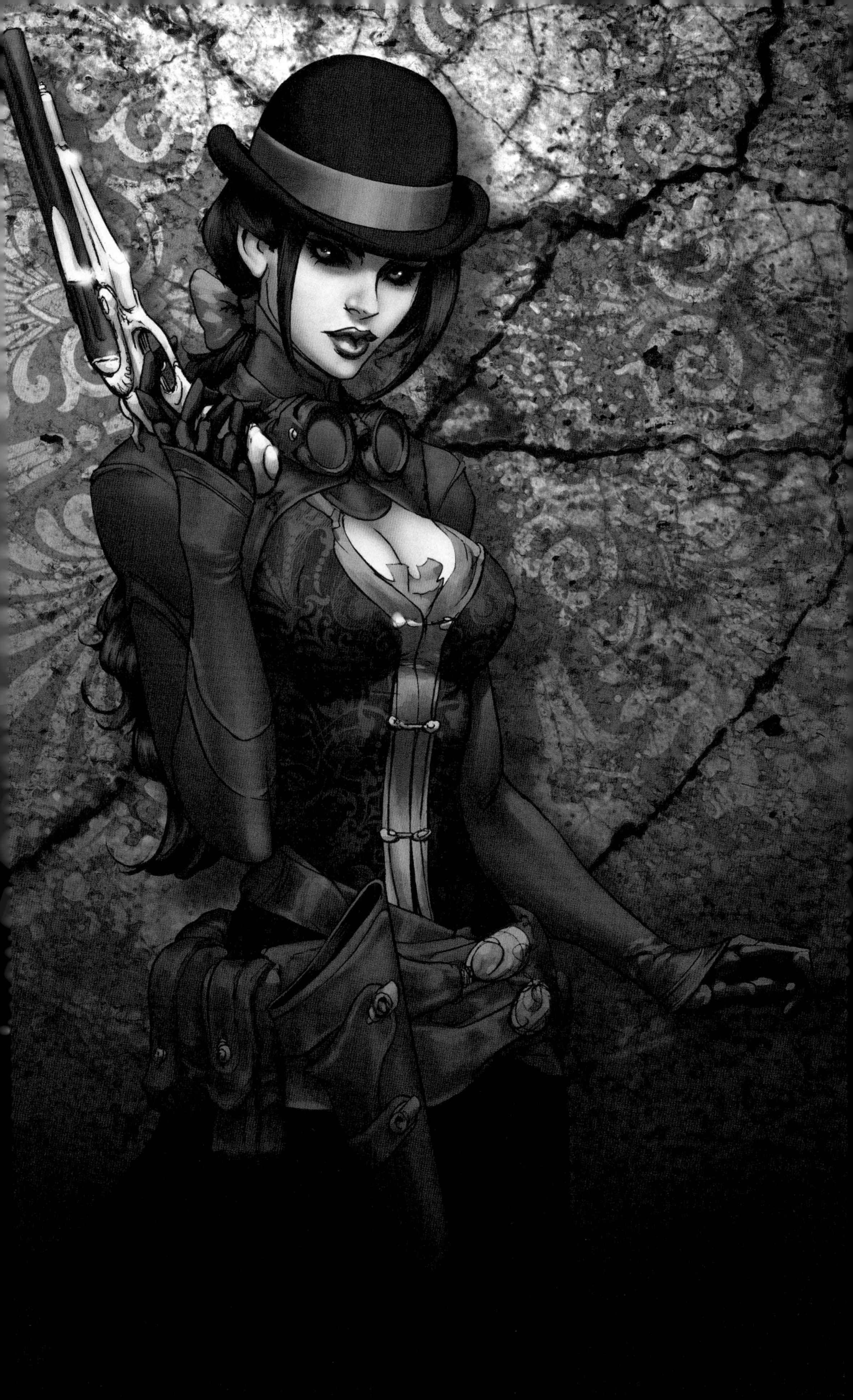

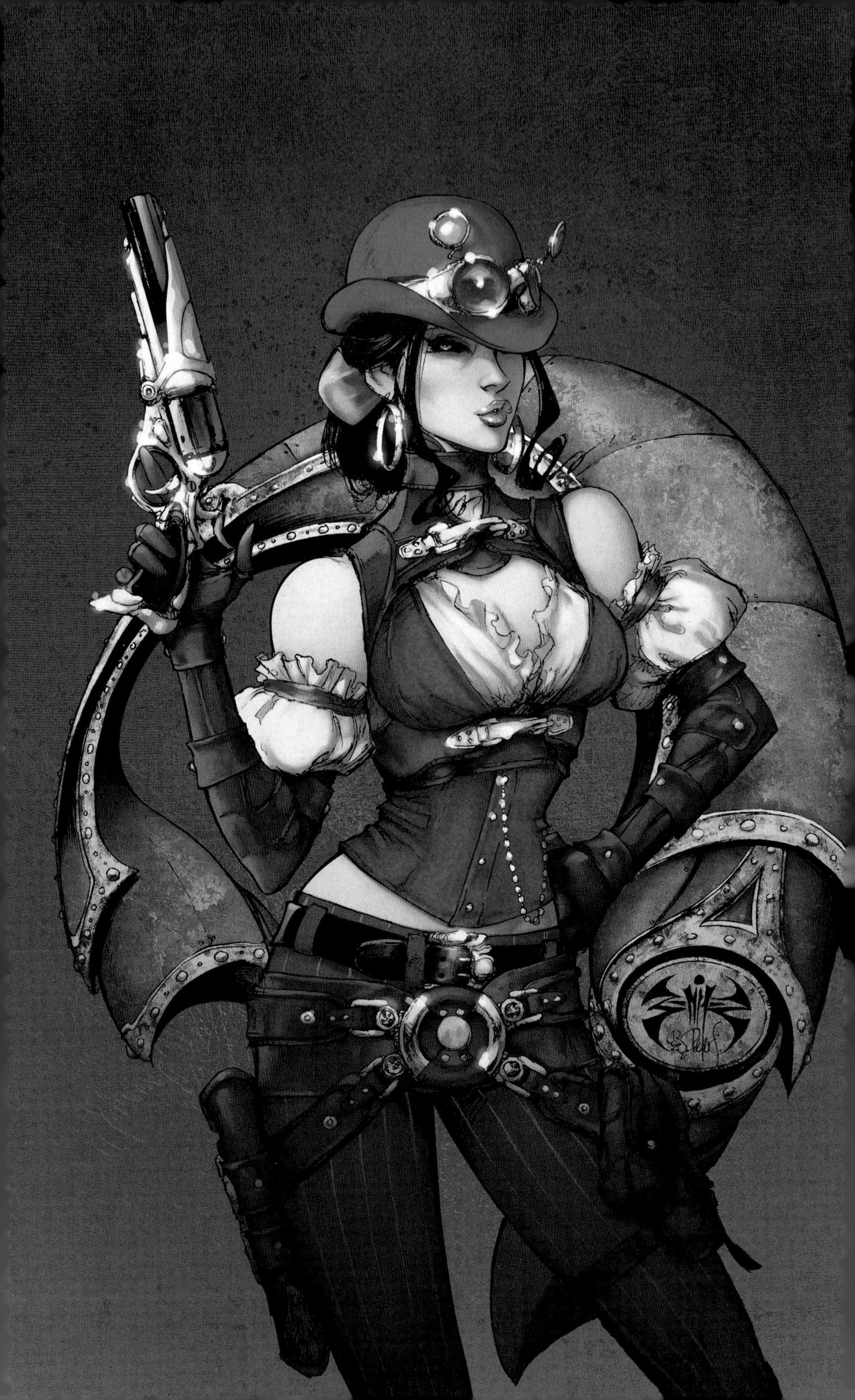

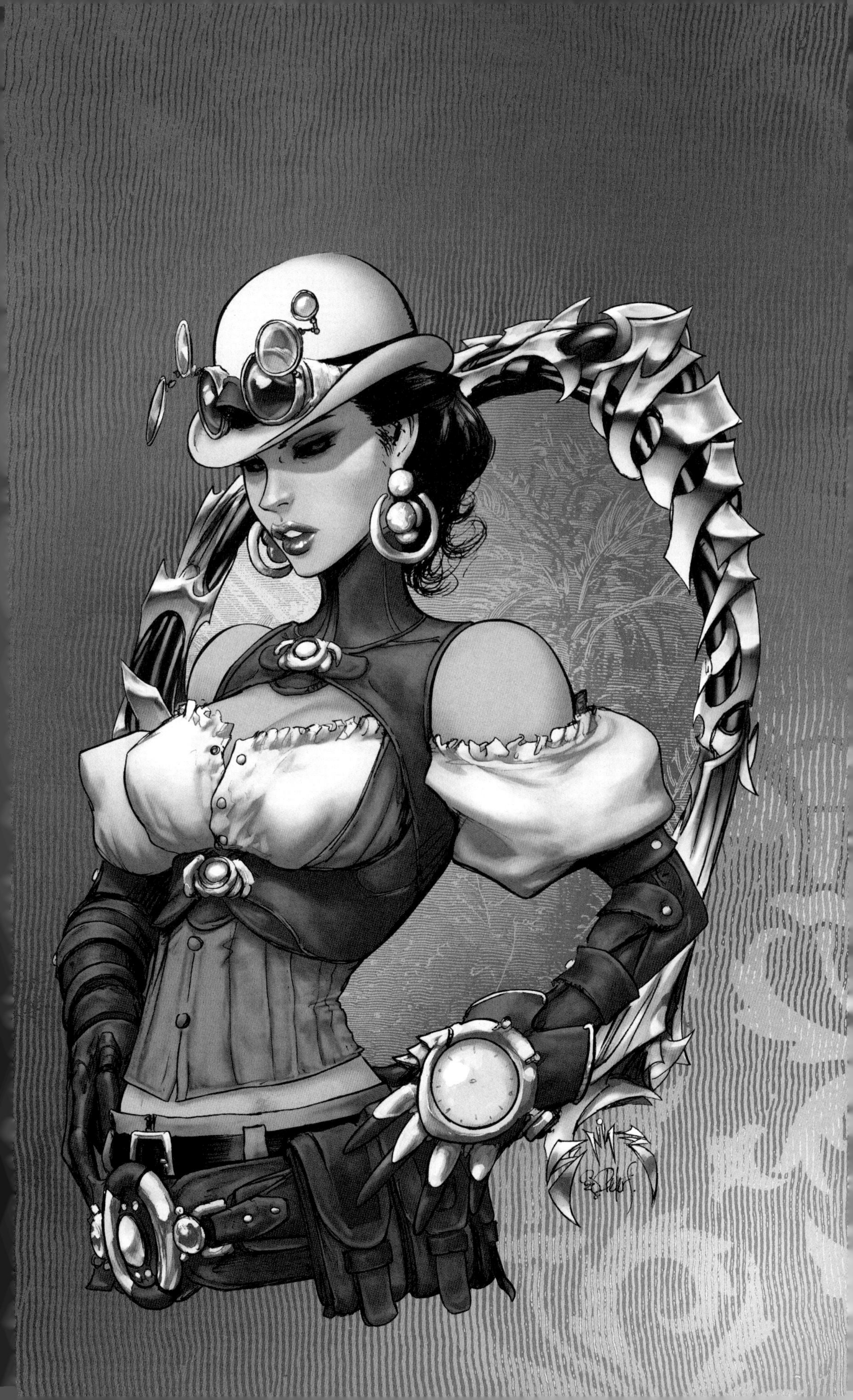

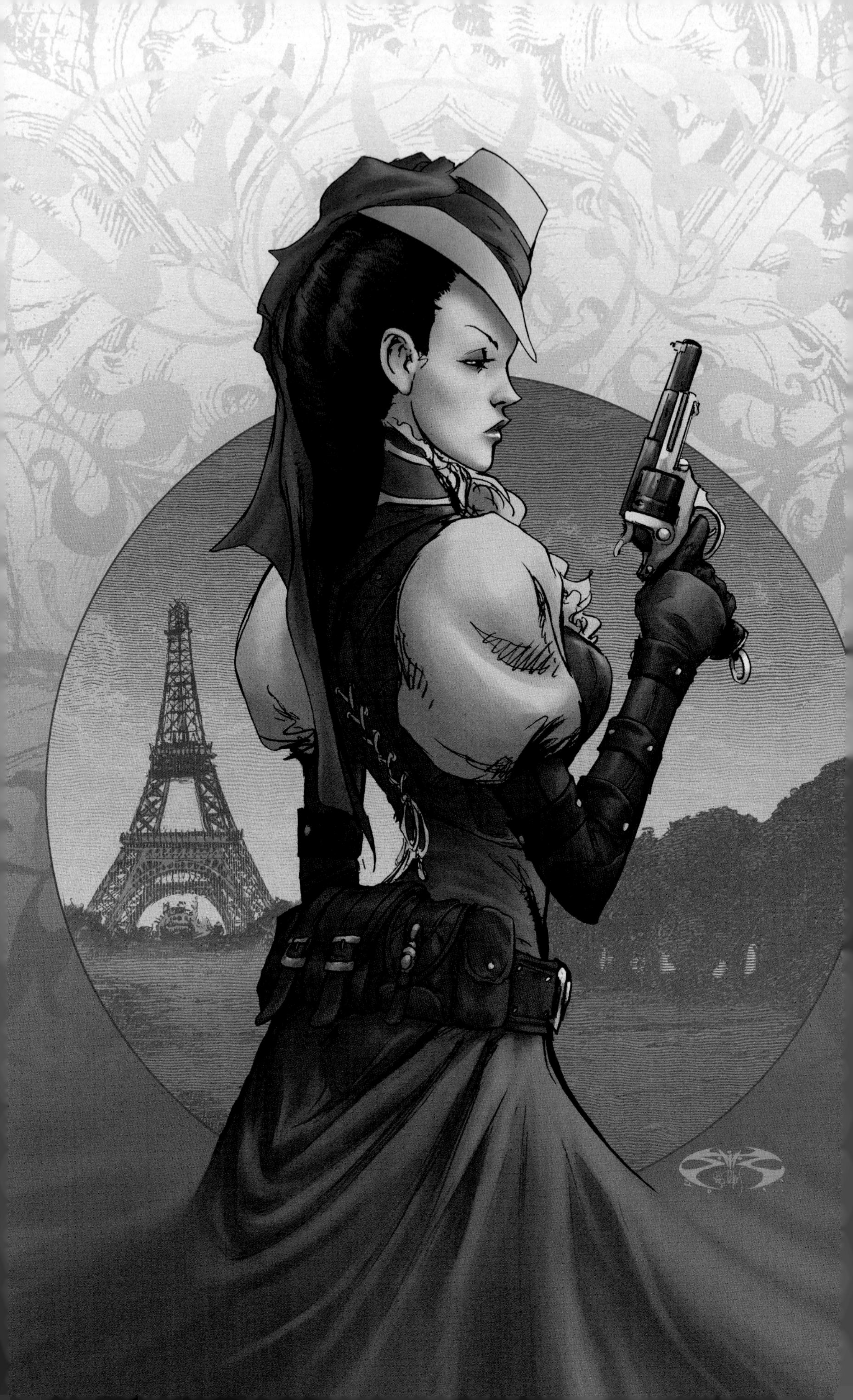

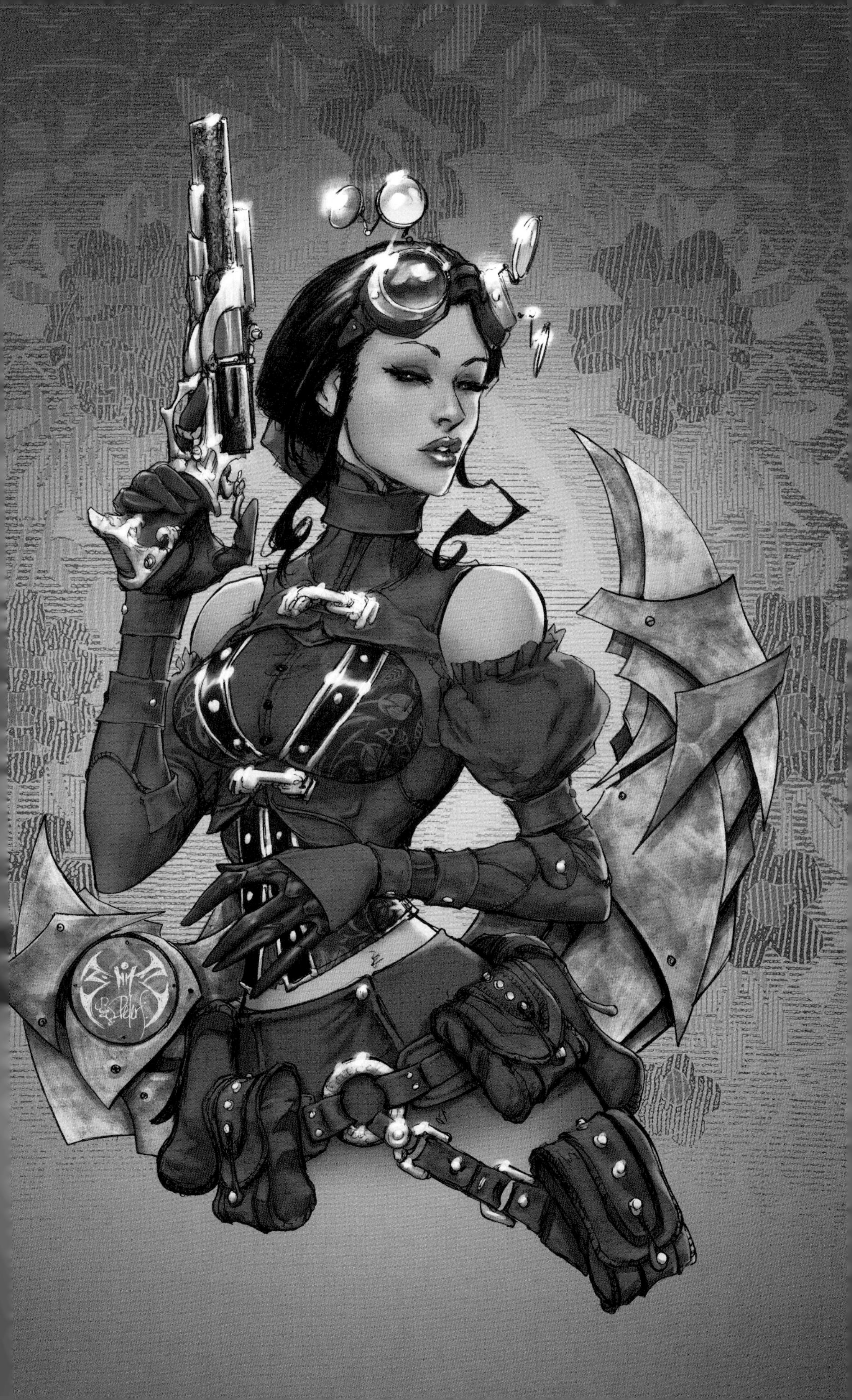

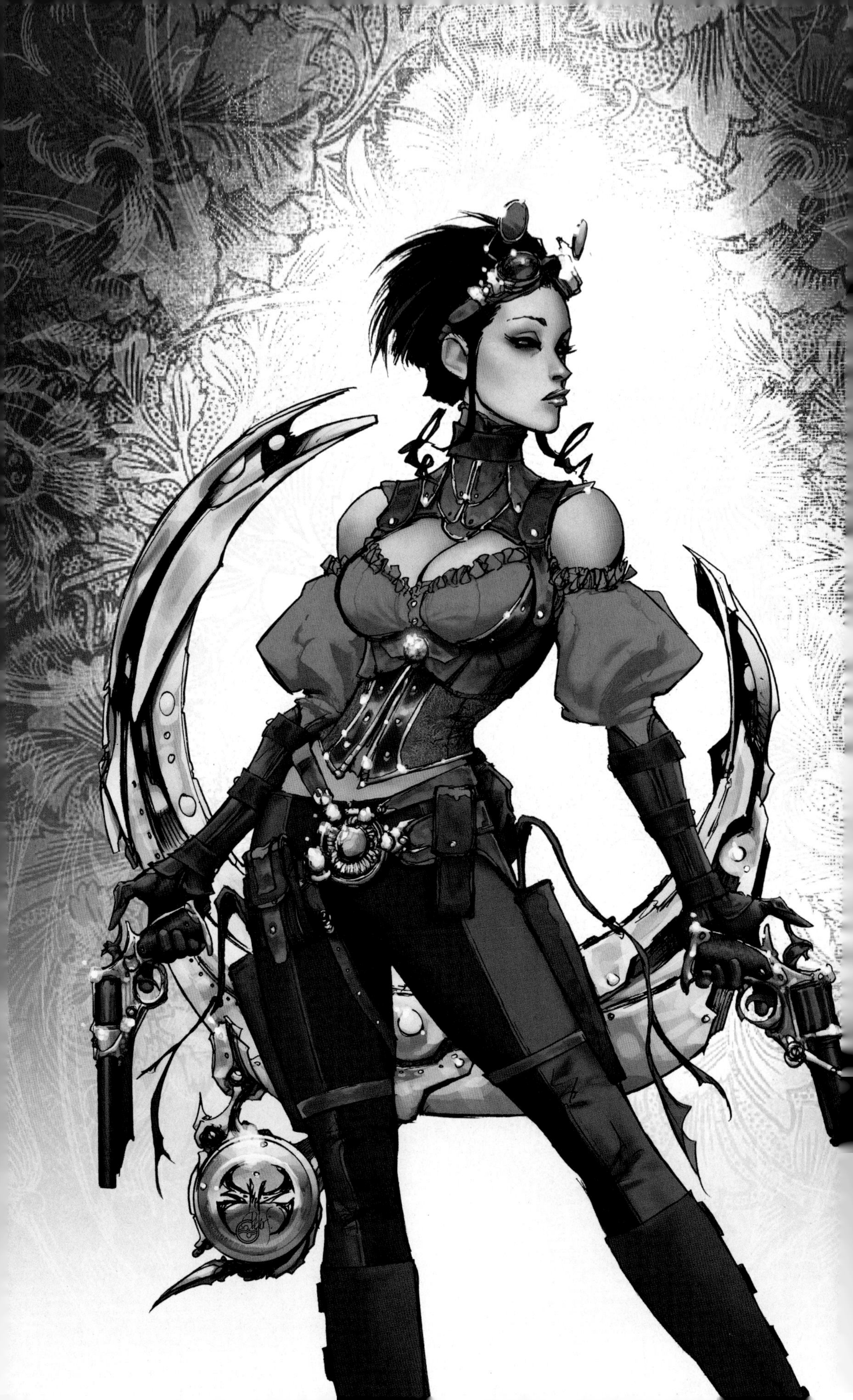

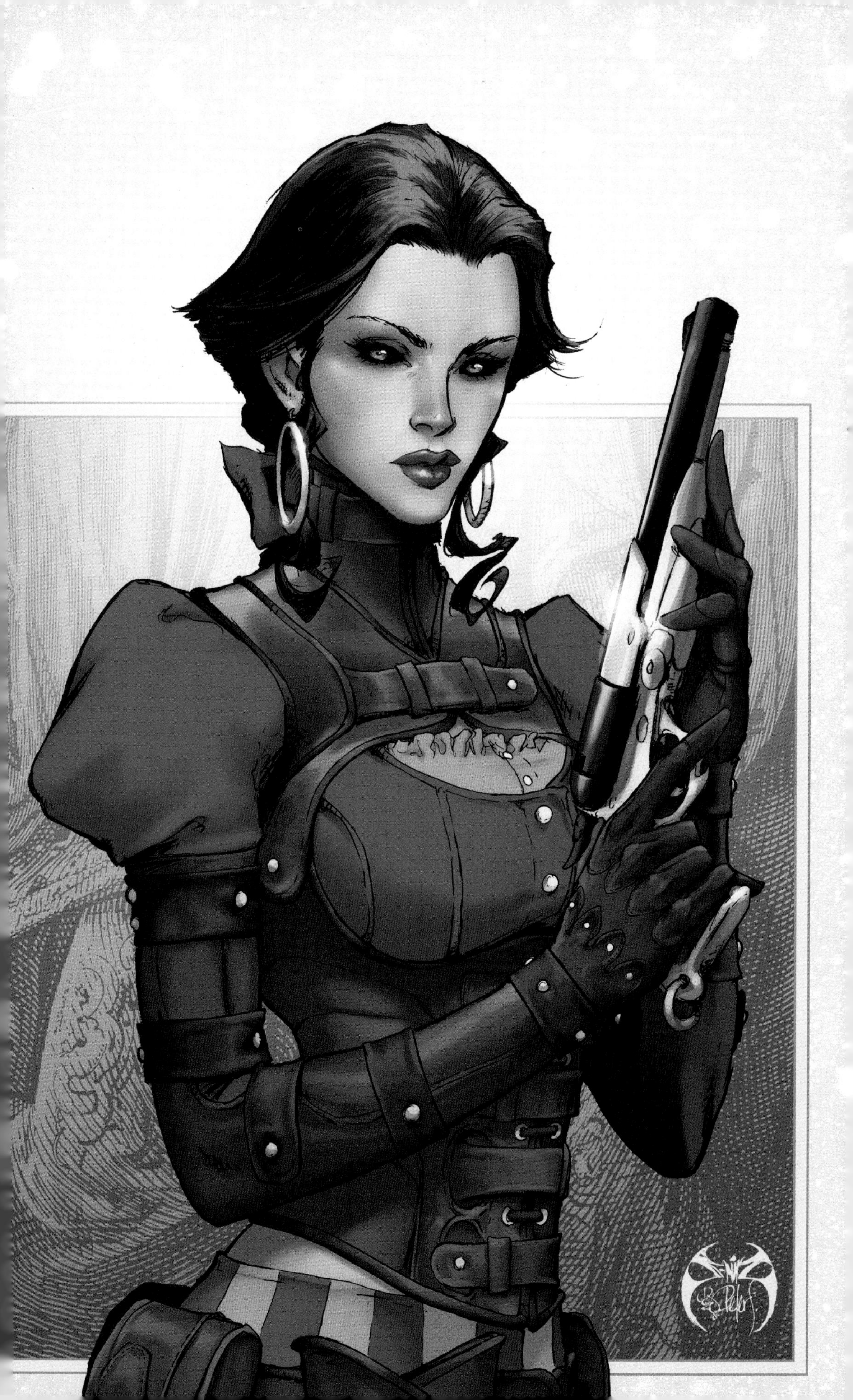

# Gues

Cover B to **LADY MECHANIKA #1**
by J. Scott **CAMPBELL** & Peter **STEIGERWALD**

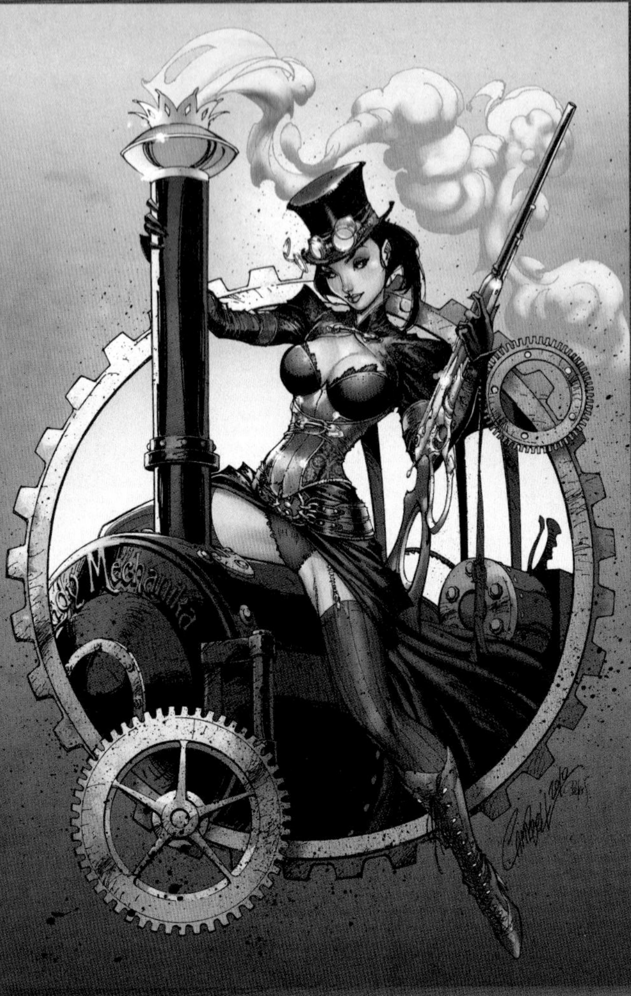

Cover B to **LADY MECHANIKA #2**
by Alé **GARZA** & Peter **STEIGERWALD**

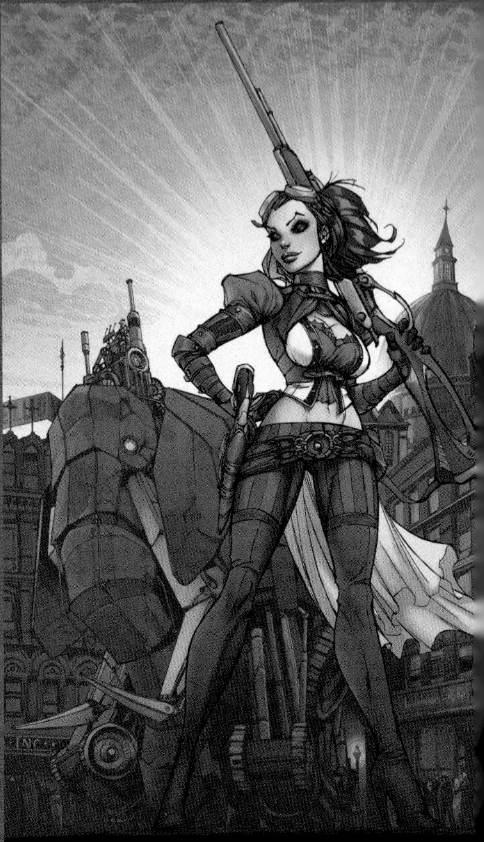

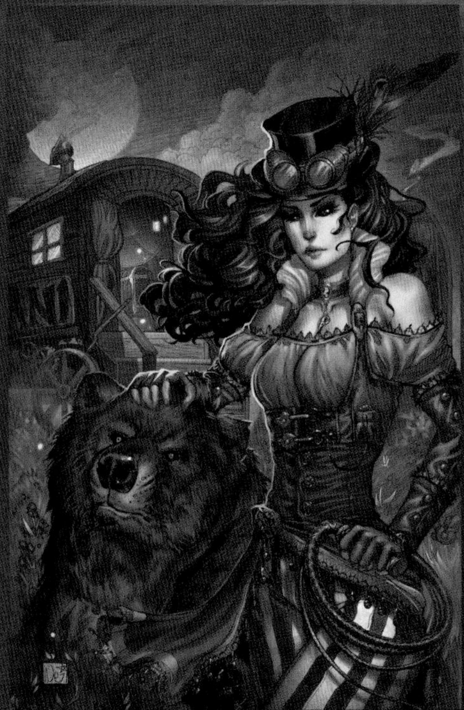

Cover H to **LADY MECHANIKA #2**
by Nei **RUFFINO**

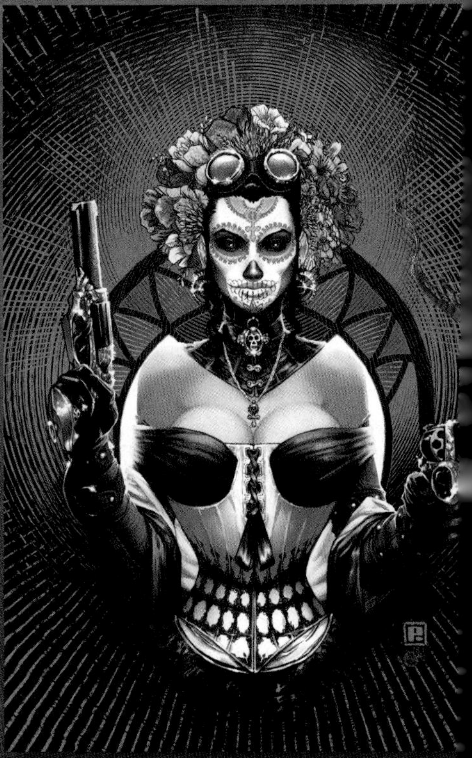

Cover E to **LADY MECHANIKA #**
by Peter **STEIGERWALD**

# Cover Artists

Cover B to **LADY MECHANIKA #3**
by Billy **TAN** & Peter **STEIGERWALD**

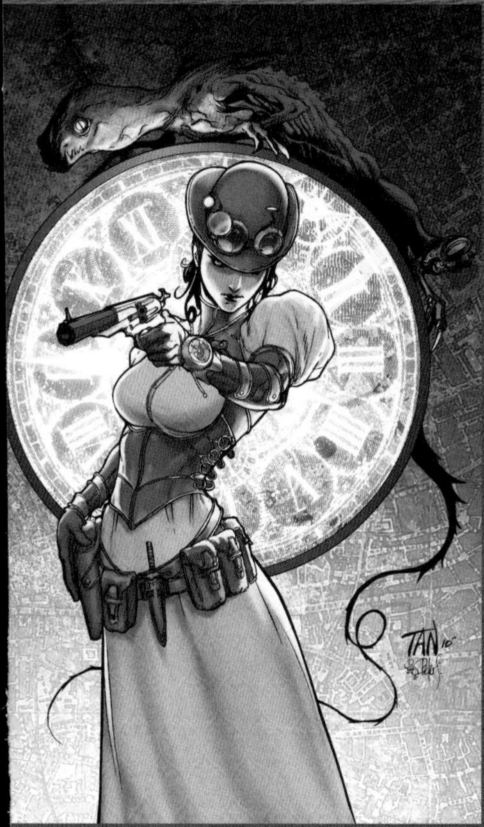

Cover B to **LADY MECHANIKA #4**
by Kenneth **ROCAFORT**

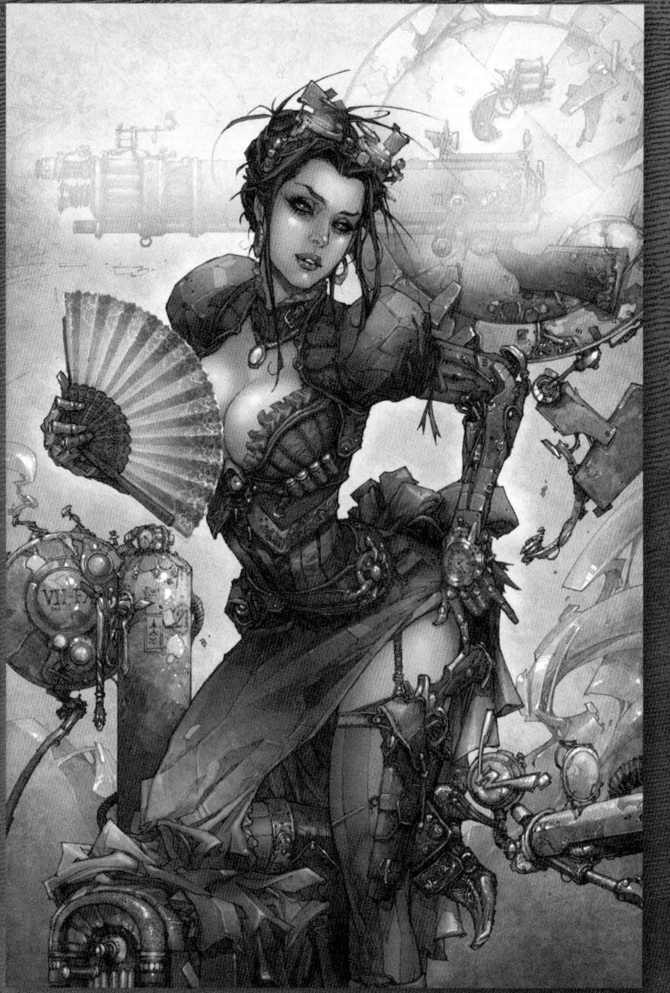

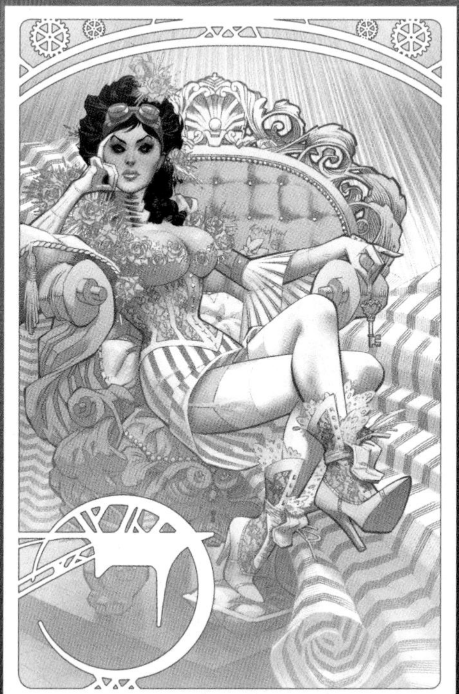

Cover B to **LADY MECHANIKA #5**
by **FRANCHESCO** & Peter **STEIGERWALD**

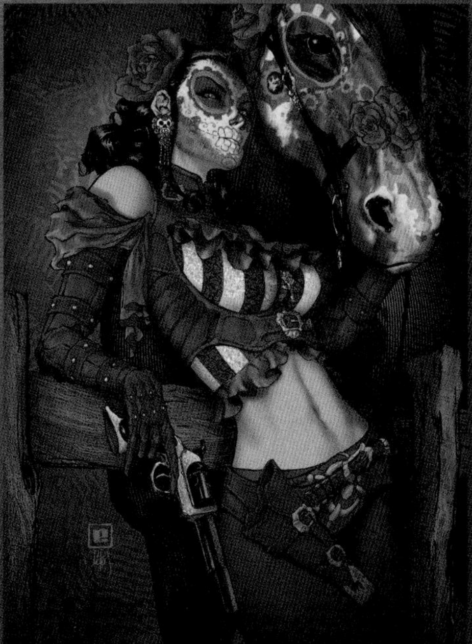

Cover F to **LADY MECHANIKA #5**
by Peter **STEIGERWALD**

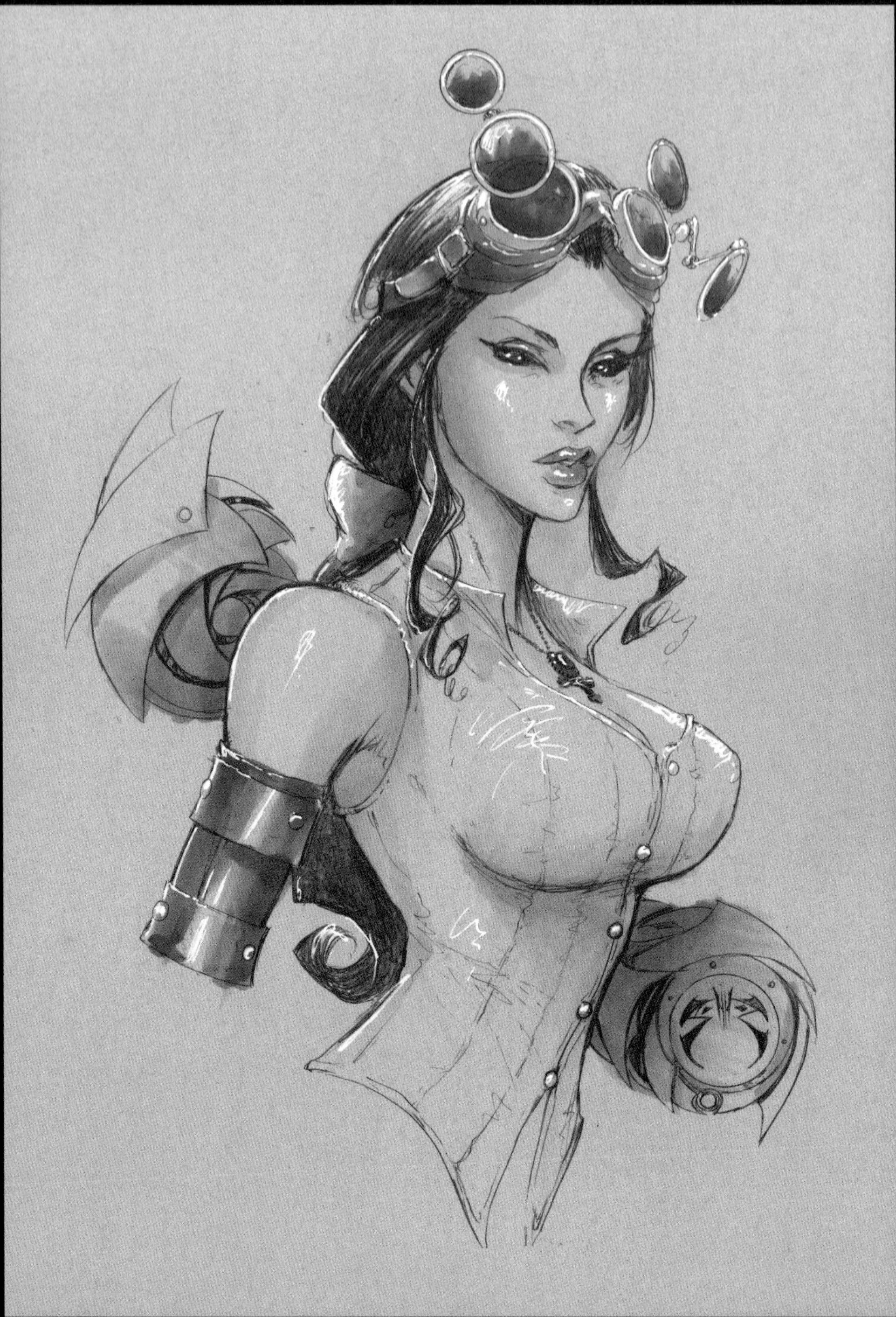

Cover D to LADY MECHANIKA #4 by Joe Benitez

**Lady Mechanika Titles:**

Lady Mechanika (*The Mystery of the Mechanical Corpse*)

The Tablet of Destinies

The Lost Boys of West Abbey

La Dama de la Muerte

The Clockwork Assassin

La Belle Dame Sans Merci

Sangre

**BENITEZ PRODUCTIONS, INC.** • **Joe Benitez**: Creative Director / Chief Executive Office **Marcia Chen**: Editor-in-Chief / Chief Financial Officer • **Michael Heisler**: Production Directo **Tabitha Martin**: Convention Director • **BENITEZPRODUCTIONS.COM**

**IMAGE COMICS, INC.** • **Todd McFarlane**: President • **Jim Valentino**: Vice President • M Silvestri: Chief Executive Officer • **Erik Larsen**: Chief Financial Officer • **Robert Kirkman**: C Operating Officer • **Eric Stephenson**: Publisher / Chief Creative Officer • **Nicole Lapal** Controller • **Leanna Caunter**: Accounting Analyst • **Sue Korpela**: Accounting & HR Manag **Marla Eizik**: Talent Liaison • **Jeff Boison**: Director of Sales & Publishing Planning • **Dirk Wo** Director of International Sales & Licensing • **Alex Cox**: Director of Direct Market Sales • **Ch** **Ramos**: Book Market & Library Sales Manager • **Emilio Bautista**: Digital Sales Coordinator • **Schlaffman**: Specialty Sales Coordinator • **Kat Salazar**: Director of PR & Marketing • **D** **Fitzgerald**: Marketing Content Associate • **Heather Doornink**: Production Director • **Drew** Art Director • **Hilary DiLoreto**: Print Manager • **Tricia Ramos**: Traffic Manager • **Melissa Giff** Content Manager • **Erika Schnatz**: Senior Production Artist • **Ryan Brewer**: Production Art **Deanna Phelps**: Production Artist • **IMAGECOMICS.COM**